Sign up for our newsletter to hear
about new and upcoming releases.

www.ylva-publishing.com

Other Books by Cheyenne Blue

The Number 94 Project
All at Sea
A Heart This Big
Code of Conduct
Party Wall

Girl Meets Girl Series:
Never-Tied Nora
Not-So-Straight Sue
Fenced-In Felix
The Girl Meets Girl Collection (box set)

For the Long Run

CHEYENNE BLUE

Chapter 1

Follow That Ponytail

SHAN GLANCED TO HER LEFT. Her training partner, Celia, ran steadily, crinkly ponytail bobbing against her black shoulders as she picked up her pace. Shan increased her speed to match, remaining half a stride behind Celia as she rounded the curve and entered the final hundred-metre straight. Celia would kick now, as agreed. Shan focussed on the finish line.

Sure enough, Celia surged, pulling away to a full pace in front. *Ha! I got you.*

The air moved faster in and out of Shan's lungs as she, too, increased her pace, matching Celia then pulling ahead. One stride. Two. She caught Celia's annoyed frown as she passed, but the adrenaline spike pushed her on for the final sprint and she crossed the line a metre ahead of Celia.

Breathing deeply, Shan rested her hands on her knees and bent forward, sucking air into her lungs, her spiky blonde hair plastered flat to her forehead.

"What the hell was that all about?" Pieter's voice came from somewhere over her head. "This is *training*, Shan, not the bloody Olympics. The race is next week, not today. This was supposed to be an easy, final sharpening, workout. At least Celia can follow instructions."

She raised her head to see her coach's annoyed face. "Runner's instinct. She was slightly ahead of me. I couldn't let that happen."

"Well, don't do it again." Pieter's mouth twitched as he nearly cracked a smile. "It was a strong finish, though. You ran those four hundred metres in sixty-five seconds. Too bloody fast for training."

"Thanks." Shan straightened, went over to Celia, and clapped a hand on her friend's sweaty shoulders. "Sorry. I felt good and couldn't resist."

Celia's annoyed frown melted. "I should be used to it from you by now. You just have to be that bit ahead, even on the slowest of recovery runs. But don't expect me to hold back in the race. Big stakes for that one."

"I know, and I won't. Maybe we'll come first and second and both make the trials."

Celia turned and started walking to cool down. "Or maybe Jamila will thrash both of us—again."

"Well, she is the number one female distance runner in Australia. We're just a lowly six and seven." Shan nudged Celia's arm as they walked across the grass. "But not for much longer if we have any say about it."

"Yeah." Celia stopped in the middle of the grass and started her stretches. "I'm hoping for a top three finish. Even though it's a road race, the course is flat, and I should get a good time."

"Me too." She shot Celia a cheeky grin. "I'll wait for you at the finish line."

"I'll be finished, cooled down, stretched, and waiting for you with coffee while you're still trundling along the final kilometre." Celia switched to stretching her hamstring. "Do you want a ride to the race?"

Shan shot her a glance, but Celia's dark eyes were wide and free of guile. Maybe it was just a lift to the race. Even so... "Thanks, but I should be fine. I'll take the tram and chill."

"No worries. We can catch up after." Celia's gaze switched to the other side of the track. "Pieter's beckoning us over."

Their coach was making big, elaborate sweeps of his arms that might have meant, "Get your arses over here!" or "Clear the field, the rescue chopper's about to land."

Together, they broke into a jog and returned to the group.

Pieter sat on the bench while the runners gathered around him. "Right, everyone, you've all got your plan for Sunday. As of this morning, Jamila has pulled out. Shan, Celia, Hanuni, you're aiming for a top five finish. Don't hold back. For all that this is a road race with the usual shambolic public fun run starting behind the elites"—his sour expression showed what he thought of that—"it's possible to get a good time. Trina and Sunita, you won't place but should finish in the top group. Use the race to fine tune your strategies. Jessie, you're just running for the experience. Questions?" He glanced around.

Shan shifted from foot to foot trying to keep her muscles warm and shook her head.

"No? Well, I'll see you all afterwards for the usual post-race briefing." Pieter gave a short nod, stood, and walked off.

Shan and Celia went back to their sports bags and pulled on tracksuits, then ambled once around the track as was their custom.

"Got plans for the week?" Celia asked. "I've postponed a couple of my clients, but I can't put them all off. I'm going to couch-potato as much as I can, and then call the cute tradie I met a couple of weeks ago, see if she's up for some more fun. You should see her tool belt." Celia winked. "Unless of course, you've changed your mind?"

"It's still a no, Celia." Shan grinned to soften the sting. "I've got to work tomorrow and Thursday, but after that no real plans. Just a couple of light, slow runs. Keep to my routine."

"Mm. You're great at that."

"If it works, why break it? I couldn't do it your way."

"My way's more fun." Celia wrinkled her nose.

Shan laughed. "I'm sure it is." She stopped and turned to face her friend. "This could be it. Our big break. I don't think I've ever had a race with such high stakes." The buzz in her stomach was like a hive of bees. If she felt like this now, she'd be bursting out of her skin by Sunday.

"Me neither." Celia did a jiggy dance step. "Last time this came up, I was injured. Time before, I wasn't half the runner I am now. This is the first time I've got an actual chance."

"I just missed out last time. I don't mean to mess up now." Shan gripped Celia's forearms. "I'm aiming to win on Sunday. Sorry about that. But you can come second."

They resumed walking.

"Do you remember when we first ran together?" Celia asked. "I do. Cross country in primary school. I beat you."

"We were eight. You had bad hair and great teeth. I had the opposite."

"The hair wasn't my fault. The foster mother of the time tried to plait it, and when it didn't work, she hacked most of it off." Celia shook back her thick hair, still in its ponytail.

"The teeth weren't my fault either, but orthodontists can do great things."

They reached the entrance to the sports field. "Want a lift?" Celia asked.

"Thanks, but no. I think I'll walk." She leaned in to peck Celia on the cheek. "See you Sunday at Fawkner Park."

"Don't be late."

"Of course not. Imagine how awful that would be!" Shan turned and shouldered her sports bag, turning for home.

It was a thirty-minute walk to her apartment. She took deep breaths, focussing on the clear autumn day, on the elm trees resplendent in orange and gold, the crisp smell of mown grass, and the warmth of the sun on the exposed back of her neck.

Sunday would come soon enough.

She couldn't wait.

Chapter 2

Endangered Species

THE KNOTS OF PEOPLE GREW thicker as Shan jogged toward Fawkner Park. She cut through a gaggle of women with strollers and cursed under her breath as they meandered out of her way. Increasing her pace, she took a shortcut over the grass toward the gathering of tents and stalls.

A group of people dressed in corporate colours unfurled a banner and arranged themselves behind it for a group photo. For a second, Shan considered running through it, arms upraised as if she'd won the Boston Marathon, but instead she cut a loop around them.

The pens of runners were now only a couple hundred metres ahead. Celia would be among them, no doubt wondering where Shan had got to. Maybe she wasn't too late after all.

Shan's anxiety spiked. If she could gain access to the elite pen before the starting pistol went, she would be okay. Nerves twanging, she shrugged off her tracksuit top and yanked at the pants, pulling them over her shoes. The material gave with a rip, and she tugged it free, then left it with a pile of similar clothing under a tree. In her running singlet and shorts, her race number already tied around her middle, the chip that would record her time affixed to her shoe, she ran toward the starting line.

Not for the first time, she cursed the driver who'd cut across in front of the tram she was on, causing the tram to clip the car's rear. A flash of anger spiked for the obstinate tram driver who'd refused to let passengers off simply because it wasn't a recognised stop. Eventually, he'd relented, and Shan had run the remaining four kilometres to the race start at a pace that would be the envy of most of the fun runners.

It was hardly the greatest way to warm up for a race—her final race ahead of the all-important trials in four weeks' time.

The crack of a starting pistol split the air.

Shit! Shan pressed her lips together as her heart rate bumped up a notch. The mass of penned runners shuffled toward the line. Already, the elite athletes at the head of the field streamed out, limbs moving like quicksilver along the course.

Shit, shit, shit. By the time she reached the starting line, the elite start was long gone, and the runners jogging toward the start were the casual runners. Two middle-aged men high-fived each other as they approached the start.

"Here's to finishing in under an hour," one said.

Shan dodged around a marshal and started to duck under the rope.

"Hey, you can't do that," the marshal said. "Wait your turn like everyone else."

Shan straightened. "I missed my start." She pointed to her number, the red signifying her elite status.

The official shrugged. "Sorry, mate, I can't let you in now. Health and safety. You'll have to go to the back."

Yeah, yeah. Shan flashed him a closed-lip grimace and walked back along the pens. Finding a gap in the ropes, she glanced left and right, then slipped in. With muttered apologies, she pushed her way forward, slipping into gaps in the crowd, past strollers, toddlers, and charity runners dressed in costume. The constant high-pitched beep as each runner crossed the starting line grew louder, until finally—*finally*—she crossed the line herself.

Shan dodged around the groups of friends walking arm-in-arm five or six people across. Her mind pounded an urgent refrain: *Go forward, go faster, get ahead of these people.* It wasn't anyone's fault except her own that she'd missed the elite start. She should have left her apartment earlier, screamed and beat the doors of the stationary tram until the driver let her out.

If only she'd taken Celia's offer of a ride.

The brown fur and bouncing tail of someone dressed in a kangaroo suit caught her eye. How could anyone even walk five kilometres dressed like that?

A gap opened up ahead, and Shan put on a spurt. Out of the corner of her eye, she saw the elite field stream past in the opposite direction along the looping course. She refused to let herself look for Celia, but saw her anyway, black ponytail tied high on her head, legs and arms pumping as she matched another runner stride for stride. She would get the perfect race, while Shan was wasting energy and forward motion weaving around people dressed as Aussie wildlife.

She passed someone in a platypus costume, the duckbill on the head waving from side to side as they jogged at a tortuously slow pace. Next to them, someone dressed as a wombat shuffled along. It must be a group from a conservation charity. In other races, she had cheered such groups as they crossed the line, a long time after her own finish.

The joggers on the gravel path in front of her momentarily parted. Shan pushed her legs to a faster pace, her stomach unknotting a little. She fixed her gaze on the line she'd take as her arms settled into their racing swing. She accelerated toward someone in a koala suit jogging next to a woman holding tightly to a small child.

As she approached them, the child slipped from the woman's grasp and ran ahead. A burble of laughter drifted back to Shan.

"Reece, come back!"

The child stopped dead to listen.

All at once, the koala stepped into Shan's path and crouched down to the child. "Reece, you have to listen—" The cartoon-like eyes stared at Shan, and with a gasp the koala pushed the child out of the way.

Panic pulsed in Shan's throat, and she swerved left, feet scrabbling as her running shoes failed to get grip on the gravel path. Her foot slipped from underneath her, and she lurched, twisting to try to remain upright. She fell forward, her heart rate pounding a mile a minute as her arms flailed for balance. Her hamstring twinged but she ignored it.

The koala was less than a pace in front. *Shit!* Desperately, she tried to avoid the furry lump. *No! Too close!* Her foot caught the koala's body and her knee twisted with a pop that echoed through her bones to her brain. Shards of fire and red-hot agony lanced through the joint. She fell heavily, her shoulder taking the brunt, her palms skidding along the gravel.

She rolled over and sat up. Her left knee pulsed pain, sharp and abrupt, and for a second her vision blurred. Sound washed over her: running feet, the child screaming, and somewhere a woman's voice, high-pitched with concern: "Oh my God, are you okay? I'm so sorry. It was my fault. Are you all right? Your leg…"

Shan's knee shot bullets of pain into her thigh, and she cupped the knee as if she could knit it back together with her hands. Surely, if she didn't, it would disintegrate into a thousand fragments. She swallowed against the nausea. Either she would throw up or pass out; she wasn't sure which.

She stared into the furry face of the koala, at its big, black nose and ridiculous wide eyes. Another wave of pain, and she screwed up her eyes, trying to stop her vision swimming, to merge the two koala faces back into one. "I'm…" The pain bloomed to a white-hot agony, and she slumped to the ground.

Chapter 3

Karma of the Universe

LIZZIE CROUCHED NEXT TO THE runner on the ground. The woman was whiter than bleached bone, the angles of her face standing out like knife cuts.

Next to her, Dee scooped up her son, rubbing his back and telling him in soothing tones that he was okay.

Lizzie's mind whirled in panicky circles. First aid. What should she do? The runner seemed to have passed out. *Think, Lizzie.* What was the point of slogging through first aid refreshers every year if she couldn't remember the first thing about it? Was the woman breathing? That was it. She placed a hand on her abdomen. It was moving steadily up and down. Now what?

"Dee, can you help me get her into the recovery position?"

The runner moved, groaned, and her eyelids flickered open. Hazel eyes, golden brown and flecked with green, stared up at her. A frown creased the woman's forehead and then her eyes screwed up tight.

With a lurch, the runner sat up and gripped her left knee with shaking hands. "Fuck. Oh fuck it. Oh fucking fuck it."

Beside her, Dee tutted at the language, her pale face pinched with disapproval.

"Are you okay?" Lizzie heaved a breath. It was possibly the most banal and stupid thing to say. Obviously, the woman wasn't okay. Her chest moved in shallow pants, and her striking eyes stared out of skin so white it was almost translucent. She shivered in the cool morning. Shock, maybe. And even now, Lizzie could see the knee swelling underneath her hands.

"My knee." She glanced around, as if only now realising where she was.

"I'm so sorry," Lizzie said again. Guilt welled in her throat. It *was* her fault. Of course there would be runners on the course—it was a freakin' fun run, for crying out loud. She should have been more careful.

Dee nudged her with her toe. "It was an accident." Her blue eyes flashed a warning to Lizzie. "Could have happened to anyone. Just like when I ran up the arse of that Bentley on Toorak Road. The light wasn't supposed to turn red. And this runner here shouldn't have been going so fast."

The runner rolled her eyes at Dee. "You must have crashed out of law school very early. Can you help me off the path?"

Lizzie stood. "I'll get the first aiders. They'll have a stretcher. Ice."

"No." The runner's teeth chattered. "I need to go to the hospital, get a scan."

"You can't drive," Lizzie said. Quite apart from her knee, the woman was trembling, her face tight with pain.

"I don't have a car." She clenched her hand over her knee. "I'll get a taxi."

Lizzie stood. "I'll drive you. My car's over there." She pointed to the row of cars that lined St Kilda Road, only a hundred or so metres from where they were.

"If you drive the same way you run, I'll be safer in a taxi." The runner loosened her grip on her knee and peered at the swelling. "This isn't good. Please help me up so I can get medical attention."

"I'm a safe driver. Let me take you." Lizzie heaved a breath. "It was my fault you fell, after all."

"No argument there."

Lizzie turned to Dee. "You're continuing the race?" At Dee's nod, she added, "Then I'll see you at work tomorrow."

Dee hesitated. "Sure you'll be okay? I mean, she doesn't look like a psychopath, but you can't be too careful. Remember Great-Aunt Esme?"

"I can't forget," Lizzie said. "I've never eaten fruitcake since you told me that story. It's fine, Dee."

"I haven't stabbed anyone this week," the runner said. "But if you don't help me up, that might change."

"Okay." Dee set Reece down. "One each side." She hooked her arm under the runner's right shoulder as Lizzie went to the left.

They waited until the woman manoeuvred her uninjured leg closer to her body and gave a tight nod.

"Three, two, one, and away she goes," Dee chanted.

The runner surged upright and stood balanced on her good leg as she leaned heavily on Lizzie's shoulder. If anything, she had now blanched a whiter shade of pale.

Lizzie stood solidly, letting her stabilise herself.

"Do you need me to help you to the car?" Dee asked.

The runner shook her head. "No. Thanks. I think." She put her injured leg to the ground and shifted a little weight onto it. "I'll manage. You're wrong about the Bentley, by the way. I'd pay up if I were you."

Dee narrowed her eyes. "It wasn't my fault."

"Whatever." The runner shrugged, her face tight with pain. "You better get your kid before he brings down the government."

Dee turned to where Reece was legging it as fast as he could after the stragglers in the race. "Shit!" She took off at a sprint after him. "Text me when you get home," she yelled over her shoulder.

Lizzie nodded. She pushed back the head of the koala suit so that her face was visible and summoned a smile. "I'm Lizzie, by the way, and Australia's greatest parent who might catch her child eventually is Destiny. But don't call her that; she goes by Dee."

"I'm Shan."

"Can you walk?"

Sweat beaded Shan's face and she took a tentative half step. "I think so, if we go slow. Which car is yours?"

"The blue hatchback."

"Okay." Shan rested more of her weight on Lizzie's shoulder. "Let's do this."

By the time they reached the car, Shan's arm was damp with sweat against Lizzie's neck and her short blonde hair was plastered to her forehead. Lizzie opened the passenger door and leaned in to shovel the assorted junk from the passenger seat and throw it into the back.

Shan lowered herself into the car, lifting her injured leg in with both hands.

Lizzie stripped off the koala suit and threw it in the boot. Dressed in shorts and a T-shirt, she slipped into the driver's seat.

Shan studied her. "So there's an actual person inside the marsupial. You must have been boiling alive."

"It is better for winter fun runs," Lizzie agreed. She touched the back of her hand to Shan's arm. "You're icy cold." She pulled a blanket off the rear seat. "Wrap yourself in this. Sorry, it stinks of dog—I foster rescue dogs and they're sometimes in the car."

Shan pulled it around her shoulders. "Thanks."

"You'll smell like a German shepherd. You won't thank me when every dog in the neighbourhood wants to hump your leg."

Shan's expression didn't change. "I've had worse."

"Like now." Lizzie touched the back of Shan's hand. She told herself it was to check her skin temperature. Which it was. Of course it was. It had nothing to do with her touchable pale skin.

"Yeah, I've had better days." Shan closed her eyes and rested her head back against the seat.

Lizzie glanced at her sharp, narrow face rising out of the dog blanket like a thin-skinned greyhound on a winter's night. That knee didn't look good. And Shan hadn't looked like a casual runner; more likely, her usual place was at the head of the field, striding out for the win, not shuffling along with the fun runners like her. She started the engine and turned the radio down when it blared.

"Which hospital? The Alfred is closest."

Shan opened her eyes and treated Lizzie to a piercing hazel stare. "Not there. Epworth."

Lizzie pulled out into the road.

The prestigious Epworth hospital often treated acute sports injuries. Every Saturday night newscast had the obligatory shot of a reporter outside the Epworth as they reported on the latest footy player to get carted off the field groaning in agony.

Worry pushed into her throat. *How serious is Shan's injury?* She concentrated on driving smoothly, and in only a few minutes, they arrived at the Epworth and pulled up outside Emergency.

A porter approached with a wheelchair and assisted Shan into it.

Lizzie dithered. Should she accompany Shan in? After all, she'd have to wait, and then unless they admitted her, she'd need to get home. The knife of guilt gave another twist in her gut.

"I'll park the car and come and wait with you."

"There's no need. Thanks for driving me here." Shan handed back the blanket. "Your doggo pal will need this." She faced the emergency room doors as the porter wheeled her away.

Dismissed. Lizzie shook her head. Well, she'd offered.

A polite beep made her turn. The driver of a shiny four-wheel drive gestured to her car, which was blocking the drive.

Lizzie mouthed an apology, got into her car, and started the engine. It still didn't feel right to simply abandon Shan like that. She was dressed only in the briefest of shorts and a singlet. No phone, unless she'd stuck it in her sports bra. Maybe no money.

Lizzie drove off and turned into a side street. The last time she'd been to Emergency was a few years ago when she'd had appendicitis. Even that had meant a three-hour wait. And a knee injury, however painful, wasn't life-threatening—Shan's wait could be longer. She clenched the steering wheel, guilt and duty rising in her chest.

A car in front of her pulled out from a parking space. If Dee was here, she'd smile smugly and say she'd willed the space into existence.

Karma of the universe. Whatever it was, that space had her name on it. She reversed into it first try. Maybe Dee had a point about karma.

She grabbed her bag and jogged back to the hospital. Emergency was half-full, and she spotted Shan sitting in a wheelchair near the desk.

"The triage nurse will be with you shortly," the receptionist was saying. "Are you alone?"

"Yes," said Shan.

"No," said Lizzie at the same time. "I'm with her. It took me a few minutes to find a park."

The receptionist nodded. "If you could wheel your friend to the first cubicle on the left, the nurse will be along in a few minutes."

"Thanks." Ignoring Shan's frosty stare, Lizzie grabbed the wheelchair handles and pushed Shan in the direction of the cubicles.

The Emergency Department walls were so white they hurt her eyes, and the area had an air of hurried calm. It was very different from the rather tired-looking Emergency in the large public hospital she'd been to.

She parked Shan so that she was facing out of the cubicle and took the seat next to her.

"You didn't need to return." Shan stared fixedly ahead, as if the bank of monitors and trays of medical equipment were the most fascinating things she'd seen all day. "I could be here a while."

"That's why I came back," Lizzie said. "It would be pretty dull being here alone. Also, I didn't know if you had anything with you. Money, phone, keys, that sort of thing. You seemed to be travelling rather light."

"I don't race with a wheelie case trundling behind me, if that's what you mean. But I have what I need." Shan unzipped an inner pocket in her shorts and pulled out a ring with two keys, a credit card, a Myki public transport pass, and some glucose sweets. "See? I'm fine."

"And you'll call a taxi how?"

"I'm sure the receptionist will organise one."

"Okay." Lizzie settled back into the chair. "Then I'll just wait until you're seen, and the nurse clears you to leave by yourself. What if they won't discharge you unless there's someone with you?"

"I'll phone a friend."

"And wait for them to arrive? Most people are still crashed out on a Sunday morning or wrangling their kids at the park. I'm not trying to impose, but it's got to be easier to have me wait with you and then drive you home, if that's what the doctors allow, rather than bothering someone else. And yes, I do feel responsible, before you throw that at me."

Shan's eyes crinkled in what Lizzie thought was her first genuine smile, although it may have been a grimace of pain.

"That's the pleasantries out of the way. Can I get you anything? Are you warm enough?" Emergency seemed overly warm to her, but at least Shan wasn't shivering anymore.

"I'd kill for some painkillers and a litre of water, but there's no way you'll be able to get those."

"No way at all. Nil by mouth until we're finished here." A nurse dressed in scrubs hustled into the cubicle and swept the curtain closed behind her. "I'm Linh, the triage nurse. Can you tell me your full name, age, date of birth?"

Shan hesitated, eyes boring holes in Lizzie's face.

Of course! Heat rushed up her neck into her cheeks, and she stood. Keeping Shan company was one thing, but being privy to her personal and medical information was another. "I'll wait outside."

"Okay." Linh gave a short nod. "Waiting area is around to the right. I'll let you know when I'm done so you can return. Now"—she switched her attention back to Shan—"those details, please."

"Thanks." Lizzie edged around Linh and out into the corridor. As she moved away, she heard Shan say, "Shannon Majella Metz, I'm twenty-eight..."

Most of the cubicles seemed occupied, and medical personnel wearing scrubs or white coats moved swiftly around or conferred with their colleagues. Lizzie hitched her bag higher on her shoulder and returned to the waiting area. She spied a coffee machine in the corner and headed in that direction.

The outside doors burst open, and paramedics pushed someone in on a trolley. For a second, Lizzie caught the patient's panicked expression as they were wheeled straight through to the treatment area.

Life or death? Maybe. Coffee forgotten, Lizzie slumped in a chair. Shan's emergency was nothing compared to heart attacks and strokes, and probably a thousand other things she'd never heard of.

They could be here a while.

"Hey," Lizzie said as she re-entered Shan's cubicle. "How did you go?"

Shan shrugged. "The triage nurse can't tell me what's wrong. I have to see an orthopaedic specialist. They'll probably do scans." She swallowed down the knot of anxiety that pushed into her throat. Linh had been carefully non-committal in her comments, simply saying that Shan would need further tests before they could discharge her.

"So, we wait." Lizzie's voice held a bright optimism. "Did they say how long?"

"Maybe a couple of hours. I'm not a priority case."

Lizzie's gaze fixed on the tablets and tiny cup of water on the trolley. "Are they for you? Painkillers?"

"Yeah." She should take them. The pain in her knee was now a dull, pulsing ache, but the boulder of worry lodged in her chest was growing bigger by the minute. What if her knee was totally stuffed? Would she need surgery?

When can I run again?

Lizzie picked up the tablets. "Hold out your hand." When Shan did so, she placed the tablets on her palm and curled her fingers around them. "They don't work if you don't take them."

Obediently, Shan swallowed the two tablets. *Now what?* She closed her eyes and the fall replayed itself behind her eyelids. The child stopping dead. Lizzie in the ridiculous furry suit pushing him out of the way. And Shan herself, going too fast to stop, her foot catching on Lizzie's body.

The popping sound as her knee twisted.

And then regaining consciousness on the ground with that bloody koala peering down at her.

Shan's eyes shot open. She needed a distraction to stop the scene replaying over and over. She glanced around. No TV, no three-year-old copy of *Women's Weekly* with its recipes and child-rearing articles.

She focussed on Lizzie. Long, black hair was woven into a thick plait which hung down her back. Her skin was an even gold tone. A dark metal infinity symbol hung on a leather cord around her neck.

"So why did your idiot friend run up the back of a Bentley? More to the point, how could she think it wasn't her fault?"

Lizzie's lips twitched. Rather gorgeous lips, Shan noted absently, with a thin bow at the top, but a full lower lip that even now was curving up into a beautiful smile.

"Dee believes she can alter the universe in small ways to make life easier for herself. At work, her desk is opposite mine. She thinks she can make it so that calls from our difficult clients come through on my line rather than hers."

"And do they?"

Lizzie's lips completed the smile. "Not all the time. But I do seem to get more of the awkward ones. We work at an agency matching jobseekers with employers and there are nightmare clients on both sides. Anyway, Dee thinks she can will a parking space into existence when she needs it most, or traffic lights to turn green as she approaches, or the supermarket to mark the chicken down to half-price thirty seconds before she arrives."

Shan snorted. "Right." Dee was obviously delusional. "What's her record with the lottery? I bet it's not good."

"You're right. She claims she can only alter the universe on small things that don't impact others. If a lottery win went to her rather than an elderly widow with sixteen cats who was in danger of being thrown out of her home for non-payment of rates, then that seriously messes with the universe. According to Dee, anyway."

"Very convenient."

"Anyway, a couple of weeks ago, Dee was driving along Toorak Road. There was a sleek silver Bentley in front of her. The traffic lights were green. Dee willed them to stay that way, so she accelerated knowing the lights would remain in her favour. You can probably guess the rest."

"They went red; the Bentley stopped, and Dee didn't."

"Pretty much. She claimed the light was yellow and the Bentley should have kept going. The driver and the Melbourne police disagreed. Apparently, having the universe on your side isn't a good enough defence."

"I'm siding with the police." A wave of pain washed through her knee, and she bit down so hard on her lip she tasted blood. "Pity she didn't get the universe to control her son this morning."

"Reece is hyperactive. That's why we were both keeping an eye on him."

"Not well enough, it seems." She waited a couple of breaths for the knot of anger to subside. "What would you be doing this morning if you weren't in Emergency with me?"

"Not much. I'd have gone for coffee with Dee, then home and cleaned house, maybe called a friend to see a pub band or something. You know, usual urban millennial activities. What about you?"

Shan pressed her lips together. What had she expected? That Lizzie would be doing something meaningful and important? "Debrief the race with my training partner, Celia, and others from our running club. Coffee. Rest up this afternoon, then a short walk and stretches this evening. And food of course."

"You're serious about running, aren't you?"

"Yes." Shan looked away, out to the corridor. She didn't want to talk about how serious she was right now. Not until she knew how bad her knee was. Maybe she could attempt Dee's trick and will a doctor into seeing her sooner. She closed her eyes and visualised someone in a white coat sweeping in.

Medical personnel scurried to and fro, but none entered Shan's cubicle. Of course.

Lizzie shuffled in her chair. "Do you live nearby?"

"Parkville. I have a small apartment there." A small *cheap* apartment, one that she could afford on her limited income, but was still near the large parks and running tracks. "What about you?" For a second, she wondered why she cared enough to even ask—but at least it was a slight distraction from the drumbeat of worry in her head.

"Abbotsford. I rent a terrace house. It's just me at the moment. Actually, it's been just me for a while, ever since my girlfriend moved out almost a year ago. I should find a roommate, but I haven't got around to it." Lizzie lifted one shoulder.

Maybe Lizzie had somehow sabotaged her girlfriend as she had Shan. She bit back the uncharitable thought and said, "That's tough."

Lizzie shrugged. "We weren't meant to be, and it was an amicable split. No dramatics. We're still casual friends." She fished her phone out of her pocket and held it out to Shan. "Do you need to call anyone? Say where you are?"

Did she? Shan considered. It was a loose arrangement with her club, people either turned up or they didn't, but she should let Celia and Pieter know. She took the phone. "Thanks."

"Do you need privacy?"

"No, it's okay. This will only take a couple of minutes." Luckily, she had Celia's number memorised.

Celia answered on the fourth ring. "Hello."

"Hi, Celia, it's me."

"Shan? I didn't recognise the number. Has your phone broken?"

"No. It's someone else's phone. I'm just letting you know I won't be at the debrief. I'm at Emergency waiting to have my knee scanned. Can you let Pieter know?"

"That's a bugger," Celia said. "I wondered what had happened to you. Hopefully it's nothing much. I'll tell Pieter. I'm meeting friends this afternoon, but I can put them off if you need a ride home from the hospital."

"I'll get a taxi. How..." She swallowed hard against the lump in her throat. "How did you go?"

"Second." Celia's voice hummed with satisfaction.

"Congratulations." She hoped her voice radiated some enthusiasm and didn't sound as flat as she felt. "That's great. You'll be a shoo-in for the trial now."

"Thanks. If your knee's okay, you could still be in with a chance. Look, I have to go. I'll see you next week."

Shan ended the call and closed her eyes for a second. That was great for Celia, fantastic. But... *I could have finished second. Or even first.* Her fist clenched on the arm of the wheelchair and she gave in to the white-hot moment of anger. It was all Lizzie's fault. Lizzie in her stupid koala suit, that idiot friend and her uncontrollable son. Shan clenched her jaw so hard her back teeth ground together.

"Shan? Are you okay?"

Lizzie's voice came from somewhere above her head, just as when she'd passed out on the path.

"Of course I'm not bloody okay." Her voice sounded harsh in her own ears, and she opened her eyes.

Lizzie took a step back. "Shall I call the nurse?"

"No." She closed her eyes again, but this time an image of Lizzie danced behind her eyelids.

Lizzie, with her T-shirt dipped down to reveal a wedge of skin the colour of warm teak on her chest. Toned, lightly muscled arms and legs. Lizzie didn't have a professional runner's build—she was too solid for that—but she obviously took care of herself. Clear skin, white teeth, and a nice amount of padding.

Shan pulled her thoughts up sharply. Lizzie was irrelevant to her life. She shook her head to shake those thoughts loose. The painkillers Linh had given her must be strong to make her think like that.

Lizzie slumped back in her chair. "I could murder a chocolate-dipped raspberry jam doughnut right about now. Maybe even two. I haven't eaten much today because of the fun run." She eyed Shan. "I'm sure you haven't either."

Right. There in one sentence was everything that set Shan apart from Lizzie. *Doughnut* wasn't a word in Shan's vocabulary. Neither was *fun run*. Running was serious; running was what life was for. Doughnuts didn't make the cut.

"What would you eat right now in normal circumstances?" Lizzie continued.

"High GI carbs and protein," Shan said. "Maybe a smoothie with yoghurt, and something like a chicken sandwich. Not doughnuts." She managed to keep the horror from her voice.

"Friday doughnuts are one of the reasons I run," Lizzie said. "And wine." She closed her eyes and sighed as a small smile curved her lips.

Such a different motivation. There wouldn't be a pastry in sight at the running club debrief, and the talk would be of personal bests and splits, not merlot or cab sauv. Lizzie's motivations seemed so... unambitious. Sure, not everyone could be at the elite level, but sport was as much about personal challenge. It wasn't about eating junk food.

"I yearn for something sweet and sticky," Lizzie said, "but tonight, I'll go home and eat a salad. Everything in balance." Her eyes opened again, and for a second, her gaze pinned Shan.

Shan forgot to breathe.

And then Lizzie broke the connection and leaned down to scratch her ankle. "I wonder how long you'll have to wait. Surely they can let you have some water?"

"They have to do the scan first," Shan said. "To make sure my blood vessels and nerves are all where they should be. Then, if I don't need immediate surgery, I can guzzle half the Yarra River if I want."

"Dee used to swim in that as a kid. She doubtlessly peed in it a time or three."

"I don't doubt it. I've had coffee that wasn't as brown as the Yarra."

Lizzie rose and stretched, then peered out into the corridor. "I'd get a coffee, but I don't want you to rip it out of my hand in desperation."

"Go ahead. No point both of us suffering."

Lizzie took a step toward the corridor. A white-coated man with iron-grey hair picked up the clipboard from outside and entered the cubicle. Lizzie moved aside to let him pass.

"Shannon Metz? I'm Dr Simon Gupta. I hear you've messed up your knee. Let's take a look." He eased up the blanket covering her leg.

"I'll be outside," Lizzie said.

"We need to arrange scans," Dr Gupta said as Lizzie left. He fired off a series of questions which Shan answered. Then his warm hands pressed and manipulated her knee.

"I'm very sure you've ruptured your ACL—anterior cruciate ligament. There's a lot of swelling, but we'll still do some preliminary scans to make sure there's no further damage. If I'm correct in that preliminary diagnosis, we can discuss surgery at an outpatient appointment." He set down the clipboard. "Let's take you over to radiology." He gestured to an attendant who entered, removed the wheelchair's brake, and guided Shan out of the cubicle.

It was as if she was being wheeled to her doom.

Chapter 4

6 x 18 = 108

SHAN CLOSED HER EYES AND let the anger wash through her. It was unfair, so fucking unfair. The additional painkillers Linh had given her were clenched in her fist, and a paper cup holding a couple of mouthfuls of water rested on the trolley. But what was the point of dulling her pain? The ache in her knee was nothing to the agony in her chest right now.

One smash on the chair's arm for the career goal now out of reach.

Another pound for the surgery she needed.

And a third, fourth, and fifth thump for the coming months of rehab, the loss of fitness, and the lack of running that would be her life for the next few months. *Life? What life?* Staring at the bland walls of her apartment? She might as well be in a cell watching her muscles waste away. A final pound on the arm of the chair made her fist hurt.

"Hey," Lizzie said somewhere above her head. "No point hurting your hand as well as your leg." Soft hands cradled Shan's, stilling them. "What did the scans show?"

Shan opened her eyes.

Lizzie stood in front of her, dark eyes radiating concern.

"There's a lot of swelling, but they were able to see the ACL's ruptured."

"Oh," Lizzie said softly. "That's not good. But they can do amazing things these days. You might be up and running soon."

"Unlikely." Shan stared at Lizzie's face. Her dark eyes were nearly the same shade as the strands of black hair escaping her messy plait. Her olive skin spoke of southern European heritage. Shan pulled her attention away from Lizzie's sympathetic expression. "My life for the next few months is totally stuffed. Do you know what I'm supposed to be doing next month? No, of course you don't. How could you?" She huffed a laugh. "A good finish this morning would have secured me some decent prize money and confidence going into the Commonwealth Games trials. Even if I didn't make that, sponsors would take note. I'd be eligible for more funding. I wasn't running for fun this morning; it was my last race before the trials." She stopped as misery swelled in her chest.

"You're a pro athlete?" Lizzie whispered. "I...I had no idea."

"How could you know? I missed the elite start; I shouldn't have been near the back with people in koala suits."

"Won't the selectors know what you can do?" Lizzie asked. "Won't they hold a place for you?"

"It doesn't work like that. If an athlete drops out, there are a dozen others desperate to take their place."

"I'm so sorry." Lizzie dropped heavily into the chair opposite, leaned forward, and put her hand on Shan's good knee. The other hand hovered for a moment over the injured knee, then withdrew. "I feel this is my fault. Mostly."

Shan closed her eyes against the concern and guilt that flashed across Lizzie's face like twin demons. "I feel you're right. Mostly." Her voice was harsher than she intended, but somehow it made it easier to blame someone else. She opened her eyes again and stared at Lizzie.

She winced. "You don't mince words, do you? What happens next?"

"Why do you care?" Shan shot back. "You can drive away and meet your friend for lunch and guzzle a bucket of wine with your doughnuts, or whatever you were going to do."

"That's unfair." Lizzie squeezed Shan's good knee then released. She sat back. "I accept some blame, but not all. No one expects an elite runner to be trundling along with the charity runners. That's why they have graded starts. If you hadn't missed your start time, this wouldn't have happened. And you could have seriously hurt Reece if you'd tripped over him instead of me."

"And it's reasonable to expect an unruly kid to be under control."

"Reece isn't a dog to be kept on a leash." Lizzie's eyes shot sparks.

Shan dropped her head and focussed on her hands twisting in her lap. "You're right. I'm being an arse, but this is hard for me to take right now."

Lizzie stared at her for a moment, as if assessing Shan's sincerity. She gave a short nod. "So are you free to go now? Do you need to make an appointment? Pick up meds?"

"I can leave." Her lips twisted. "I've been given painkillers, and I need to call tomorrow to make an appointment with the ortho. I've got crutches and a knee brace." She nodded to where they leaned against the wall.

"Then let's go." Lizzie moved around to the wheelchair handles. "Might as well use the chariot while we can. Maybe there's someone we can have a wheelchair race with down the corridor."

"You don't have to take me home," Shan said. Her stiff lips could barely form the words. "I can get a taxi."

"I've met some wonderful taxi drivers, but not all of them are able to help you and your crutches move in and out of the cab. Or manoeuvre into your apartment. I can take you. Please don't be stubborn. I think you've figured by now I'm not a serial killer."

Despite herself, Shan's lips twitched. "No, that would be Dee's great-aunt."

"That's right. I can tell you that story on the way to your place if you want."

It *would* be easier to accept the offer of a ride. "Thanks. I'd like the lift."

"I'll leave you at the door and come around with my car."

Lizzie flicked a glance at Shan under the guise of checking the side mirror. Her face was drawn tight, pale skin taut over her prominent cheekbones. Lizzie tapped a finger on her own face; she'd kill for cheekbones like Shan's.

Was she in pain? Her left leg stretched awkwardly in front of her, and she clutched the door handle with white knuckles. Lizzie knew she wasn't *that* bad a driver, so she'd assume it was pain. "Do you want me to stop for anything?"

Shan gestured to the south. "The Melbourne Cricket Ground is down there. We've time for a couple of quick overs with the women's team. You didn't go past Rod Laver Arena, so I'm guessing tennis is out."

"Ha ha, funny girl," Lizzie said, ignoring the biting sarcasm. "I'll take you up on the tennis when your knee is recovered—if you're still talking to me then. But I actually meant do you want to go to a friend's place rather than your own, or stop for groceries?"

"I'd rather go home."

"I get that. Nothing beats your own mattress and snuggly doona." Lizzie accelerated away from the lights as the traffic moved up Victoria Parade. "Do you want to hear about Dee's Great-Aunt Esme?"

"Sure."

Shan's voice was as flat as the Nullarbor Plain, and she radiated disinterest, but telling the story would be better than her stony silence. "In the nineties, Great-Aunt Esme worked as the personal assistant to one of Australia's richest and luckiest property barons. He seduced her, strung her along with promises of marriage, then up and married a socialite half his age. Great-Aunt Esme got her revenge by mixing a solution of strychnine and brandy and pouring it over her fruitcakes. You can guess the rest."

"She got caught?"

"After he died, yes. Great-Aunt Esme was paroled in 2010. She disappeared from public view. Dee's convinced she's got a little bakery business somewhere—her fruitcake was that good. But I never eat fruitcake now, just in case it's a Great-Aunt Esme special." Lizzie caught Shan's half-smile out of the corner of her eye. Good. The distraction was working. "Have you any kooky relatives?"

"No. I come from a very ordinary family. My mother and her partner own a carpet warehouse." Shan shifted her position and stretched her leg another couple of centimetres.

Lizzie looked quickly away from the length of thigh the movement revealed. "Guess there's no polished floorboards in their house." Lizzie swung right and moved steadily toward Parkville. "Can you direct me once we get to Royal Park?"

"Sure."

It only took a few minutes before Shan said, "This is it."

Lizzie dived into a lucky parking spot and turned off the engine. "Which one? The red brick or the one that's all glass?" She peered upward. "Ooh, look. The people on the second floor are kissing. If you live in the glass block, I hope you've got blinds."

"I'm in the red brick."

Lizzie swung out of the car and opened the passenger door, then hauled the crutches and knee brace from the boot. "Do you want me to help, or will I make it worse?"

"I'll try by myself. After all, I'll have to get used to it."

Lizzie angled the crutches toward Shan and watched as she executed a perfect one-leg raise. Her bad leg remained off the ground as she settled her crutches and made her way slowly to the door.

Lizzie walked a pace behind carrying the knee brace. Shan had amazing legs—better than amazing, actually. Lean with defined muscles. The strength shone out of them. No wonder she'd been able to lift herself from a seated position on one leg. Lizzie looked down at her own legs, which she'd always thought were pretty good. Nope. Not a patch on Shan's.

They reached the front door. Shan rested one crutch against the wall and fumbled with her free hand at her shorts.

"Let me." Lizzie moved closer. "Or at least step away from that drain. If you drop your keys down that, you're on your own."

Shan dropped her hand to her side. "Be my guest. I'm not up for sewer diving today."

Lizzie moved her hands to the waist of Shan's shorts. She ran her finger around the back side of the waistband, searching for the hidden zip pocket. The backs of her fingers brushed Shan's waist. *Holy freaking moly. Forget steel. Her abs are titanium.* Lizzie's fingers twitched. The urge to turn her hand around and feel that fine skin with her fingertips, and absorb the sensation, consumed her.

"Sorry," she said in a voice she hoped was something like normal. Heat crawled up her cheeks. "I can't find the zip."

"It's the other side."

Was that amusement in Shan's voice? Lizzie risked a glance at her face. There was a half-smile on Shan's rather aristocratic lips. Yes, she was definitely enjoying Lizzie's lost-in-space moment. She found the pouch and pulled out the ring with two keys. The first one opened the door into a small, tiled lobby area. Two doors led off on each side, and a narrow flight of stairs led up. No lift. "Please tell me you live on the ground floor."

Shan sighed. "For the first time in my life, I'm wishing I did. I'm on the fourth floor."

"This isn't going to be easy. Is there a chair I can put on the next landing for you to have a rest?"

Shan shook her head. "I'll be fine. It might be the only workout I get for the next while; maybe I'll time myself."

"I'll race you." Lizzie spoke flippantly, but her stomach churned with worry. How was Shan going to manage those stairs for the next week or so? And after her operation, what then? Athlete or not, it was a dangerous manoeuvre to do on crutches. What if she fell? Shan was slender, but Lizzie wasn't sure she could catch her if it came to it.

One of the overhead lights flickered and went out with a pop, casting the upper part of the stairwell in shadow. Shan positioned herself close to the bottom step, steadied her crutches, and swung her legs up to balance on her good leg. Then she brought the crutches up to the step.

"See? Easy."

"One down, how many to go?" Lizzie moved to stand behind Shan on the hurt side.

"Six flights of stairs. Eighteen steps in a flight, a hundred-and-eight steps in all," Shan said. "I normally run up them."

"Lucky you have strong legs. Sorry...leg."

Shan swung up the remaining steps to the first landing. "Nothing to it." She flicked a closed-lipped half-smile at Lizzie.

The heat that had taken residence in Lizzie's chest since her inadvertent touch of Shan's skin turned up to a slow simmer. Shan's smile was doing strange things to her insides. She rolled her eyes behind Shan's back. No point going there. Shan seemed as prickly as the arse end of an echidna—and who could blame her.

By the time they reached the third floor, the tendrils of Shan's hair stuck to the back of her neck. Lizzie eyed them. It wasn't hot, but the film of sweat on Shan's shoulders and neck showed her effort—and possibly her pain levels.

"Shall we take five?" Lizzie pointed at a chair by the door of one of the units. "I'm sure those people won't mind if you sit."

"No." Shan's shoulder muscles bunched as she gripped the crutches more firmly. "It's only two more flights."

Lizzie hovered as Shan made her slow way to the fourth floor. A tiny sigh of relief escaped her as Shan mounted the final stair. One obstacle down. God knew how many to go. She moved past Shan and fumbled the key into the lock.

The door swung open straight into an open plan area with polished floorboards decorated by a couple of bright rugs. A small kitchen took up one corner, a café-style table with two chairs sat by a side window, and a comfy-looking couch was angled so a person could look at the TV in the corner or out of the front window. The apartment was neat and sparse, with none of the clutter Lizzie had in her house. Lizzie moved over to look at the view. The taller apartment next door obscured most of it, but there was a view of the park across the road.

"Nice." She swung back to look at Shan, who leaned heavily on her crutches in the doorway, staring around at her apartment with a bemused expression.

"What's the matter?" Lizzie tilted her head. "Have we broken into the next-door apartment?"

"No, it's mine." Shan moved slowly across to the breakfast bar and perched her bum on one of the stools. "I was thinking it's probably all I'm going to see for the next few weeks. No runs, no social life. No work." Her lips twisted. "I'm a part-time barista. There's no way I can work."

Lizzie's breath huffed in jerky exhales. Could it get any worse? Could she feel any more guilty? "What do you need right now? Do you want me to prepare some food for you? Is there anyone you want me to call? Help you to the shower?" *Oh no, not that.*

"Honestly?" Shan's sigh equalled Lizzie's. "Please just go. I'll be fine. There's food in the fridge. I'll manage a shower. I have everything I need." A brief nod. "Thank you."

"You've got someone to call to help you?"

"I do have friends!"

"Of course." Lizzie bit her lip. Without overthinking it, she walked over to the fridge. *Chicken thighs, pasta, broccoli, energy bars* was written on a whiteboard on the front. Lizzie uncapped the marker hanging next to it and wrote her mobile number underneath *energy bars*.

"I'm not far away. If your friends are busy and you need anything, that's my number. Now, I'll leave you be." She returned to the door and opened it, hesitated, then turned. "I'm so very sorry this happened to you."

At Shan's jerky nod, Lizzie left, taking the stairs two at a time down to the street.

She had to forget about Shan. Wallowing around in guilt for what, when it came down to it, was an unfortunate accident, wasn't the way to go.

The thing was, Lizzie was a pro at guilt.

Chapter 5

Nellie-No-Friends

SHAN MADE HER SLOW WAY to the sink and refilled her water bottle. She clipped it to one of her crutches and hopped back to the couch, choosing the end that allowed her to look out the window. The leaves on next door's elm were starting to turn brown. She stared at the gravel track that ran around the perimeter of the park. The three-kilometre loop was one reason she'd rented this apartment. That, and the fact the place was cheap, as it had no lift, no air conditioning, and no balcony.

She would love a balcony right now, to be able to sit outside her apartment that already had the closed-in claustrophobia of a prison. Even to feel the breeze, and watch people pass without the barrier of glass and brick between them would be magic. The noisy hum of traffic would be preferable to slumping on the cushions like the worst sort of couch potato.

At least she could watch TV. Get up to speed on all the daytime soaps and shouty talk shows she never normally had time for. A flick of the channels told her there was nothing worth watching. She settled for a match in the Women's Super League and stared mindlessly at the women chasing the ball.

Mentally she reviewed the rest of her Sunday. She needed a shower. Warmer clothes. Food. She was an idiot. She should have taken Lizzie up on her offer to prepare something. Even putting together a sandwich was going to be an endurance feat, let alone anything more complicated. Hopefully, she had food in the fridge as she'd told Lizzie. Sunday was usually her day for grocery shopping and housework. The layer of dust on the coffee table was an irritant in her usually tidy apartment and seemed to mock her helplessness. Even the garbage needed taking out.

Maybe she could talk Celia into coming around and bringing some takeaway with her. Celia wouldn't do housework, but she'd at least help her into the shower. There was nothing she hadn't seen before. She picked up her phone and pressed Celia's number.

It rang for most of a minute before Celia picked up. "You must be home if you've got your phone back."

"Yes, about an hour ago. Where are you?" The background buzz of conversation meant she was most likely in a café. If she was close by, maybe she'd come around after.

"St Kilda. About to see a zydeco band at the Espy with Jules and Franco. Pity you're not here too. How's your knee?"

"Fucked." There was no other word that would cover it.

"That's succinct. Do you need surgery?"

"Almost certainly, if I want to keep running. But they have to let the swelling go down first. In the meantime, I'm trapped at home on crutches."

"That sucks." Celia's voice was brisk. "Lucky someone invented Uber Eats. You won't starve. You'll let me know if there's anything I can do, won't you?"

"I will." Shan twitched the toes on her bad leg. "Want to come around and hang out after the band?"

"You know I would normally, but I'll be too tired. I can come by after work in the week, if you'd like?"

"That would be great."

A discordant blare of guitar and accordion came over the line. "The band's starting. I have to go. I'll call you tomorrow. Bye."

The line clicked off, leaving Shan staring at the blank screen on her phone. There was no reason to feel so let down. Celia was usually busy—if not with her running, then with her part-time job as a disability support worker, or her very active social life.

She fiddled with her phone, reviewing the contacts list. Was there anyone else she could call to come and keep her company? Someone who wouldn't already be out on a gorgeous autumn day, or who cared enough to change plans and come over anyway? Most of her friends were runners, and they would be tied up in the full-time life that was the serious running world. Or taking time for their families.

She had to let Pieter know how she was, but her coach wasn't the up-close-and-personal kind. He'd tell her in a brisk voice to let him know once she had a definite diagnosis and timeframe for recovery.

Her finger hovered over her mother's number. But Mum and her partner, Connor, were travelling around Australia in their motorhome. They were currently in the Pilbara region in Western Australia, and phone reception was patchy. She tried the number anyway, but it went straight to voice-mail.

Shan threw the phone on the couch. Was she really so friendless that the kindness of a stranger was the best thing that had happened to her today? Even if that stranger was responsible for Shan's predicament in the first place. But anyone who wanted to get to the top in their chosen field had to be as one-eyed as she was. You couldn't succeed in athletics if you had a huge friendship group to fritter the time away.

As she was doing now, lying on the couch, feeling like Nellie-No-Friends.

Shan levered herself up and started the slow process of having a shower.

Lizzie tapped her pen on her notepad. "Are you currently employed, Merri?" She nodded as she wrote down the woman's answer. She could be a good match for the advertised position. And how great would it be to fill the position from the first call of the day? "When can you come in for an interview and testing?"

She booked an appointment for Merri and turned to Dee. "Coffee?"

"Hell, yeah," Dee said. "I didn't have time to stop this morning. Reece was stubborn and refused to wear shoes. I don't care if he goes barefoot, but the childcare won't allow him in without something on his feet."

Dee's phone rang and she glared at it before snatching it up. "Best Foot Forward, this is Dee."

"Guess the universe isn't on your side this morning," Lizzie said with a grin. "I'll go order."

Dee gave her a mock glare and a thumbs up.

By the time Dee arrived at the coffee shop in the foyer of their office block, Lizzie was already ensconced at the counter by the window, two coffees in front of her.

"That call was someone enquiring about the data entry job," Dee said. "But their speed is only five thousand keystrokes per hour." She picked up her flat white and took a gulp. "I so need this today."

"How did you go in the race yesterday?" Lizzie asked. "Did you finish?"

"Yeah. Eventually. Reece wouldn't get in the stroller and insisted on walking, so it took us nearly two hours. The marquees were packing up, and most of the officials had gone home by the time we crossed the line. They rolled up the timing mat behind us. I still got my finisher's medal, though. Well, they gave it to Reece, and he wore it to childcare, so I doubt I'll see it again."

"Reece will be beating us both hollow in a couple of years."

"That's not difficult. I'm a plodder, not a runner."

An image of Shan's lean thighs and slight, runner's body flashed into Lizzie's mind. Shan would float over the ground as effortlessly as the wind. That was running. Not what Lizzie and Dee did: doggedly putting one foot in front of the other, legs burning with effort, puffing like the steam train that ran through the Dandenong Ranges. What would it be like to run as Shan did?

Exhilarating. Euphoric. Glorious.

That was what she'd expected it to be like when she started running most of a year ago. So far, it hadn't come close.

"Did you get that person who fell over you to hospital?" Dee asked.

"Yeah. She might need a knee reconstruction." Lizzie worried her infinity pendant, taking comfort in the familiar shape of the iron. What sort of an idiot was she, not getting Shan's number? It wouldn't take much to call, see if she needed anything. But although she'd given Shan her number, Shan hadn't reciprocated. Really, that was the end of it. She sipped her coffee, enjoying the sweet, milky taste.

"Ouch. Knee surgery like that could ground her for a while," Dee said. "Still, worse things happen at sea, as my gran says."

"I'm not sure Shan would agree with you right now."

"You were good to help. Nothing more you can do now." Dee tipped her head back and drained the last drops of her coffee. "We better get back. Monday mornings, everyone wakes up, decides they can't face their job a moment longer, and calls us."

They walked out of the coffee shop and over to the lift.

"How can you drink your coffee so hot?" Lizzie asked. She took another sip of her own that she'd carried out.

"Asbestos mouth. When you've got a kid like Reece, you learn to drink quick or miss out. But no point whingeing about that. I wouldn't trade him in for all the leisurely coffee breaks in the world. Now, if only I could find a bloke who agreed."

"You'll find someone."

"That's what you said the last time I complained, and the time before."

"Well, you will."

"And you'll find the person of your dreams too. When was the last time you went on a date?"

Lizzie didn't have to think too hard about that. "Tyson. Seven months ago. The one who thought 'bisexual' meant that twenty minutes after I met him, I'd be up for a threesome with him and his girlfriend."

A harried businessman approached the lift, and Lizzie shut her mouth. She didn't need random strangers hearing about her non-existent sex life.

As she was making calls and setting up jobseekers with word processing tests, Shan hung in the back of her mind. Was she okay? Had someone come to help her? It would be hard enough doing the simple things like getting dinner and having a shower. Lizzie hadn't even thought to check if Shan had icepacks to put on her knee, or a pressure bandage.

Opposite, Dee banged down the phone and fell forward, her head on her keyboard. "The universe hates me this morning."

"It loves me," Lizzie said smugly. "Not one bad call. Must be the good karma from taking Shan to the hospital yesterday. What was that call?"

Dee hooked a strand of hair over her ear. "The usual. Someone who wants to apply for the executive assistant role with Maxalottel, but she wants to modify the hours, requires a car allowance, and asked if the free lunch provided uses organic ingredients. Oh, and she's got no experience, but can start tomorrow as long as her conditions are met."

"Their canteen is great," Lizzie said. "No idea if it's organic though."

"Remember that bloke who would only eat fresh fruit picked under a full moon?" Dee snorted. "I told him that meant it would only be fresh for about two days each month. He's either starved to death by now or modified his diet."

Diet.

Lizzie excused herself and went to the loo—her thinking place. Shan ate healthily if her digs about Lizzie's doughnut addiction were anything to go by. How would she lug bags of vegetables up to her apartment? Home delivery, she supposed, if a delivery person would take those six flights of stairs. She'd heard stories of deliveries being dumped outside of front doors. And how would Shan get to any medical appointments?

I'm being ridiculous.

This was the twenty-first century, when anything your heart desired could be delivered into your hands. There were taxis, Uber Eats, home delivery. And Shan had friends. She didn't need Lizzie.

But still. What if she did? And Shan's predicament was all her fault.

Lizzie hauled up her pants and flushed. There would be no harm in dropping past Shan's apartment on the way home. The worst that could happen was Shan would freeze her out, in which case, she would take the hint, go home, pour a glass of merlot, and forget all about Shan, her razor cheekbones, and intense eyes.

Lizzie tailgated her way into Shan's apartment block, swinging in behind an elderly lady who went into a first-floor apartment. She climbed the stairs to the fourth floor and went to Shan's door. No bell. Of course there wouldn't be. Most people doubtless buzzed from the entrance. She knocked on the door in the silly pattern her dad always used.

The slow thud of someone on crutches came from behind the door. Then it swung open.

"Celia, I'm glad you made it after all. I'm desperate to know how— Oh! You." Shan's voice plummeted from light-hearted to flat in two words.

Lizzie swallowed the impulse to turn and flee and summoned a smile. She should just leave. Shan was obviously expecting someone. "Hi. I was just passing and wondered how you were doing. I'm going for groceries if there's anything I can pick up for you." Her eyes flicked up and down Shan's body.

Blonde hair stuck up in spikes, as if she'd repeatedly combed her fingers through it. Her T-shirt had ridden up to expose a strip of toned belly, and a sarong wrapped around her waist, knotted at one side. Crutches were jammed into her armpits, the toe of her injured leg balanced on the ground. Something small and hot unfurled in Lizzie's stomach and she gripped her shoulder bag so she didn't do something stupid, like wrap a hand around Shan's waist under the guise of helping her…but really, just to see how her skin felt.

Shan gave a half-smile. "Come in. Celia's obviously blown me off in favour of the recovery session at the running club." She swung the door open. "Where do you work that you were 'just passing'?"

Lizzie walked in, and her gaze raked around the kitchen. Unlike the day before, the counter was now piled with plates and cutlery, and food scraps littered the surface. The couch cushions bore the imprint of Shan's body, and the coffee table held the TV remote, a phone, a vial of tablets, and a couple of physio resistance bands.

She swung around and put her hands on her hips. "Okay, you've caught me. I work in the city, and I detoured past here to see if you needed anything. It looks like you need a cleaning service, to be honest."

Shan manoeuvred her way back to the couch and sat heavily. She picked up one of the resistance bands and fiddled with it. "I'm normally very tidy. I can't exactly play Mrs Mop the cleaning lady on one leg. I don't like looking at this mess any more than you do."

"You didn't give me your number. Not that you had to," Lizzie added. "But I was thinking about you at work—wondering how you were coping—so I thought I'd drop around." She lifted a shoulder. "It's no big deal." No need to tell Shan that she'd been thinking about her in ways that were not just caring. "Do you get your groceries delivered?"

"Negative, Captain. The delivery guys won't walk up the stairs, so they leave them in the lobby. Normally that's fine, but now… At least I talked Uber Eats into coming up the stairs with the promise of a good tip."

"I really am going to the supermarket if you want anything." Lizzie tried a smile.

Shan cracked a grin in return, a genuine one that crinkled the skin around her eyes and made her face come alive. "If you're sure, that would be good."

"I'm sure." Lizzie's tension seeped out of her. Shan was gorgeous when she was all angles and focus, but this new, lighter, smiley Shan was doing strange things to her insides. She spied a notepad and pen on the counter and took it across to Shan. "Write a list."

Lizzie sat in the chair opposite while Shan wrote. It didn't take long.

Shan handed over the list. "Is this too much to manage? I'll give you my credit card." She pulled it from a bag by the couch. "You won't need a pin for this amount."

"You're very trusting." Lizzie scanned the list, which seemed to be a trip through the veggie and poultry aisles. "This is fine." Her gaze lit on the item at the end. "Chocolate? Not so healthy after all!"

"Everyone's allowed a guilty pleasure. Dark chocolate is mine."

Shan shifted and the sarong parted, revealing her knee.

Oh, that does not look good. Lizzie closed her eyes momentarily, but the vivid purple bruising and swelling that all but obliterated the kneecap remained behind her eyelids. She stood. "I'll be back in under an hour. Okay?"

"Thank you. There are keys on the hook by the front door. Grab them. It will save me having to buzz you in. I won't be going anywhere in the meantime." She twitched the sarong so it covered her injured knee once more.

Lizzie nodded, took the keys, and left.

Chapter 6

Rubber Chicken

WHEN LIZZIE FLED OUT THE door—there was no other way to describe it—Shan leaned back against the couch and blew out a breath. Lizzie had probably not expected Shan to take her up on her offer. Even now, she was probably driving too fast down Brunswick Road, cursing people who didn't recognise a polite, not-really-meant offer when they heard one. Except Shan heard plenty of those from Celia, and Lizzie's offer had sounded very genuine.

Lizzie in her work clothes had been a surprise too. The tailored pants and dark-purple blouse had set off her black hair and olive skin beautifully. No plait today; Lizzie's hair had been pulled up in some complicated pleat at the back of her head and held with a tortoiseshell clip. Her expressive dark eyes had been enhanced with subtle make-up. Make-up! Shan wasn't sure any of her friends even owned any of that. But Lizzie had said she worked in HR. She could hardly go to work in shorts and a T-shirt as Shan did to her barista job.

Work. Shan pursed her lips as another knot of worry bloomed in her stomach—this one labelled "Money". There was no way she could work the lunchtime shift tomorrow. She stared down at her knee. Still swollen, still dark with bruising, still hurting like hell. She should have called Daz before now, but she'd been hoping against all hope and rational thought that she'd wake up, her knee would be fine, and she'd be able to do her shift.

Dream on. She wasn't Superwoman. She picked up her phone, scrolled to Daz's number, and pressed the call button.

"Shan, mate, what's up?" Her boss's gruff tones came down the line.

"I'm sorry for the short notice, but I won't be able to work tomorrow. In fact"—she took a deep breath—"I'm not sure when I'll be able to return. I blew out my knee on the weekend. I'll probably need surgery." Saying the words out loud made it all seem so final. Her shoulders slumped and her knee throbbed in sympathy with her mood.

"Not good, mate, not good. Sorry to hear that. So you'll be out, what? A couple of weeks?"

"Longer." The word grated in her throat. "Maybe a couple of months. Depends on how it heals. I'm sorry, Daz."

"Not your fault. I'll have to hire someone to fill your shifts, you know that. I can't keep your job open for you that long. But when you're fit again, give me a bell. I'll take you back in a blink if I've got a position going. Stay in touch, okay? Best of luck with your surgery."

"Thanks. I'll let you know." She ended the call and put the phone back on the coffee table. There was no other way that conversation could have gone. Now her only income was the stipend she got from the professional body, and a couple of meagre sums for promoting running products on Instagram. She had some money put aside; hopefully it would see her through until she could work again.

Her stomach rumbled. To distract herself, she rose and made her slow way to the kitchen. There was no need to be a total slob. Especially as Lizzie would be back soon.

Lizzie reached Shan's floor and set down the three bags of shopping. Her breath came in short pants. Maybe she wasn't as fit as she thought. She knocked twice on Shan's door, then used the key.

"I'm back." Her lips twitched. "Honey, I'm home," was probably not appropriate in this situation, but they were the words that came to mind. It would be no hardship to come home to someone like Shan. Lizzie had returned to an empty house—apart from the occasional foster dog—since she and Sonia had agreed to split.

"You were quick." Shan was sitting on the couch, the TV remote in her hand.

"In and out. Zip, zip. That's me." Lizzie set the bags on the counter and looked around. "You've done a clean-up. Looks good."

"I couldn't stand looking at crumbs and wilted lettuce any longer."

"If you direct, I'll put this stuff away." Lizzie pulled out the chicken thighs and posed, one hand on her hip, the other balancing the chicken on her palm. "Succulent, free-range chicken. Fresh from the cold cabinet. Not even out of date. Where would you like it?"

"The answer's going to be the same for everything: fridge—top shelf or veggie drawer."

"What are you having for dinner?" Lizzie asked. "Going by your purchases, I'm guessing chicken and salad."

"Got it in one, but with some quinoa on the side."

"Want me to make it?"

Shan's lips pursed, and Lizzie wondered if she'd overstepped. "I don't mean to imply you can't do it. I'm probably barging too far into your space." She turned away and started placing the groceries into the fridge. It meant she didn't have to see Shan's expression: annoyance, irritation, or just a get-out-of-my-apartment scrunched forehead.

The thump of crutches sounded on the wooden floor. "I'm sorry. I didn't mean to put you off." Shan's sigh sounded from above her head as she crouched in front of the veggie drawer. "If you really don't mind making salad, then that'd be great."

Lizzie smiled into the salad crisper. A warmth in her chest started spreading until it seemed her heart was a ball of mush. Relief, she told herself. No one likes to overstep boundaries or outstay their welcome, and she hadn't done either. She pulled out the lettuce, tomatoes, and sweet potato she'd just placed in the drawer and stood. "Then there's no point me putting these away just yet."

Shan's smile flickered briefly. It did strange things to Lizzie's chest: a flip-flop as her heart realised she was standing close to a gorgeous woman who, while not looking like she was pleased to see her, at least wasn't staring as if she wished to pulverise Lizzie under her $200 running shoes.

Yeah, right, Lizzie. I bet she's just delighted she doesn't have to make dinner.

"How do you usually cook the chicken?"

Shan shrugged. "I just microwave it in a bowl of water."

Lizzie considered the fridge, and then raised an eyebrow in question. "May I?" She pointed at the pantry.

"Go for it." Shan hopped over to the far side of the breakfast bar and settled onto a stool.

Lizzie scanned the neat rows of alphabetised herbs, then pulled olive oil, lemon juice, and dried rosemary from the cupboard and set them on the counter. She ripped open the pack of chicken thighs, "How many will you eat? Do you want me to cook the rest to use in the next couple of days?"

"I'll have two." Shan cocked her head. "Are you rushing home for anything? Would you like to eat with me? After all, you're preparing it."

"You don't know how good a cook I am," Lizzie said. "I may be about to burn your salad, slap some raw chicken on a plate, and rush out the door before you can complain."

"That's possible," Shan said. "But I'm a good shot. That raw chicken would hit you on the back of the head before you'd left the kitchen. But if you don't want to, just say."

"No plans. I'd like to stay." She turned away to hide her pleased smile. "Where are your bowls?"

"To the right of the stove."

Lizzie found a bowl and whisked up a mix of olive oil and lemon juice. She seasoned it with salt and pepper and added some dried rosemary, sliced the chicken into strips and added it to the bowl, then found the quinoa in the pantry and set it to cook.

"You know your way around a kitchen." Shan took a sip from her ever-present water bottle.

"I'm the only girl in a traditional Greek family. The boys learned manly things like home repairs, and how to be the breadwinner. They're all older than me. Mumma was so relieved I was a girl. Cooking for five males, all of whom sat at the table promptly at six every evening expecting dinner to appear in front of them, was a lot of work. I was helping Mumma prepare food when I was four, cooking simple meals when I was seven."

"Who did the cleaning up?"

Lizzie rolled her eyes. "Who do you think? The kitchen fairy? Luckily, Mumma got a dishwasher for her birthday one year—you don't need to tell me how sexist that is—and she then had a little more time." She tore the lettuce and dumped it into the salad spinner. "I love my family, but I can't live with them. That's why they're in Sydney, and I'm in Melbourne."

"Do your brothers live at home still?"

"Two of them do. They're in their thirties and still sit down at six every night and wait to be fed. The other two are married—Yannis to a good Greek girl, and I'm sure he expects to be waited on, too. Theo married an Aussie from a mining town in Western Australia." She smiled. "I love Ruth—she takes no shit from anyone. Theo has to pull his weight around the house. My parents are horrified!" Lizzie rinsed the other salad ingredients and put them in front of Shan. "Can you chop these? You can do that sitting down."

Shan picked up the knife. "No comparisons to your brothers please."

"You're already doing more than they do. I love them, but seeing them a couple of times a year is enough." Lizzie put the sweet potato into the microwave, then found a frying pan, tipped the chicken into it, and put it on the stove.

"You have to pick your battles."

That was really it. Lizzie's hands stilled. She knew all about the expectations placed on the children of immigrants. The old familiar guilt rose in her throat. She shook her head and pushed it down. She'd made peace with her decision to leave Sydney nearly three years ago.

She'd drifted off for too long. Shan stared at her, a quizzical expression on her face.

"It's ancient history." Lizzie shook herself into a flurry of cooking action. The distraction worked. She took the salad ingredients Shan had sliced with impressive precision and tipped them into the bowl, turned the chicken, opened the microwave when it dinged, and stuck a knife into the sweet potato. "Doesn't every kid have battles with their parents?"

"I don't," Shan said. "But that's because they do their thing, and I do mine. I haven't seen them for nearly a year, although we call each other quite often."

"Lucky you. My parents and I have a truce, but I still get pressured to return to Sydney." And of course she had yet to come out to them. That was one battle she wasn't ready to face. Lizzie found plates and sliced the sweet potato onto them. "This is almost done. Once the quinoa's cooked, we're ready."

"I normally drink water, but I think I have a bottle of wine in the cupboard if you prefer," Shan said. "It's some sort of red."

Lizzie's lips twitched. "You've obviously got me pegged as the queen of unhealthy food choices, but actually, I'd prefer water." She found glasses and filled them from the tap.

Shan attacked her food as if she were an apex predator in the forest. When she was done, she wiped a finger over the plate and sucked it. "Great marinade on the chicken."

Lizzie lowered her gaze to her plate to hide her pleased smile. At least she could do something right. "Thanks." She finished her own meal and pushed her cutlery together neatly on the plate. "How was your knee today? If that's not a stupid question."

Shan heaved a sigh that could have blown the leaves from the trees. "I have a clinic appointment in two days. I guess I'll find out what will happen then. Surgery or no surgery." She picked up her water glass and turned it around and around in her hands.

"How will you get there?" The words popped out of Lizzie's mouth before she really considered them.

"Uber. It's the middle of the day."

"I can take you. If you want. If no one else can."

Nice one, Lizzie, implying she's got no friends.

Shan opened her mouth, and Lizzie rushed in again. "I'm sure you're set. Maybe you want to sit in an Uber and not talk to anyone."

"Nice thought," Shan said. "You'll be at work though."

"I have a lot of flexibility. I visit clients, work from home a couple of days a week. It's no problem."

Shan's face shut down to a blank mask. "Then I'll take you up on it. A small payback for messing up my life."

Ouch! So much for their brief accord. Lizzie quashed the pang of hurt that Shan's harsh words had caused. "What time will I need to pick you up?"

"Eleven-thirty work for you?"

"I can make it work." Lizzie stood and gathered the plates. "Now, let me clear up, and then I'll be out of your hair—at least until Wednesday."

Shan pushed a hand through her cropped hair. "I don't have much hair for you to get caught in."

Lizzie whirled around to the sink to hide her flushed cheeks. Shan didn't seem to have any idea of the effect she was having—when she wasn't sniping at Lizzie—and that was a very good thing. There was no point adding an inconvenient attraction to the layers between them.

Chapter 7

An Offer You Can't Refuse

A FEW MINUTES BEFORE LIZZIE was due to arrive, Shan rested her butt on the wall outside her apartment. She'd managed the stairs alone, although there'd been a moment when her crutch had slipped on the shiny tile. She'd lurched to one side, and her heart rate had smashed through the ceiling as she struggled to stop herself plummeting down the rest of the flight.

She'd paused a moment to heave a deep breath, then continued, slower and with a lot more care.

Lizzie's blue hatchback pulled over on the far side of the road then did an illegal U-turn and double-parked outside Shan's apartment block.

"Hi." Lizzie, wearing office clothes and the most enormous pair of sunglasses, bobbed out of her car. "I would have come up to get you."

"I'm good on the crutches now," Shan lied. No need to tell her about the near slip.

"Oh? So you're going to stump off to Coles and get your groceries, maybe take the tram to the beach for a spot of kite surfing?" Lizzie opened the car door.

"Not that good." Shan lowered herself carefully into the passenger seat and waited while Lizzie stowed the crutches in the back.

"The Epworth again?" Lizzie asked as she buckled in.

"Mm." Shan looked at the park as Lizzie drove away. People walked dogs, a couple of joggers moved sedately along, and a touch football match was happening on the oval in the centre. Normal life. After three days inside, it almost seemed strange. The sunlight was brighter, the traffic noise louder, life simply more vibrant. Her toes twitched to be out there, body humming with the joy of a run.

But that wouldn't happen any time soon. Not unless her knee had miraculously knit itself together again, unless it was all a mistake. The swelling was down somewhat already. The bruising doubtless looked worse than it was. Maybe Dr Gupta would say the previous scan was wrong, and a couple of weeks' rest and physio was all that was needed.

By the time they pulled up outside Epworth hospital, Shan had almost talked herself into believing her own sunny prognosis.

Dr Gupta turned the screen to face her and circled an area with a pointer. "There's your torn ACL."

The grey-and-white images could have been sonar of the seabed for all Shan knew. A cold knot of misery expanded in her chest. "How long for it to heal?"

Dr Gupta steepled his fingers. "If you were a sixty-year-old whose only sporting ambition was a meal at the bowls club on Fridays, I'd send you off for rest and physio to see how you went, with surgery as back up. But for you..." He picked up the desk phone. "Maria, do I still have surgery time on the twenty-fifth?" He nodded as Maria replied. "Please put Shannon Metz in there." Then to Shan, "Twenty-fifth March. Two weeks should be enough to have the swelling down sufficiently to operate. Ask Maria for the pre-surgical information and exercises to strengthen the surrounding muscles. You can go home the next day if there's someone to stay with you—if you live alone, you'll need to make arrangements. You'll be in a brace for at least a couple of weeks. Follow-up appointment two weeks after surgery. Okay?"

"Okay," she said through stiff lips.

Dr Gupta stood and waited politely as she rose to her good leg.

Lizzie set down the magazine she was leafing through and got to her feet when Shan entered the waiting room. The sunglasses rested on top of her head, and Shan caught the question in her eyes. Ignoring her, she went to the desk, where Maria handed her a folder.

"Read this carefully and call if you have any questions. We'll see you for surgery in two weeks."

"Thank you." Only then did she turn to Lizzie.

Her cream blouse and dark-green slim skirt set off her colouring beautifully—and her shape. Shan hadn't appreciated before now how Lizzie's waist tapered in before flaring to her hips. Despite the turmoil in her head, the sight gave her a jolt of appreciation.

"Are you ready?"

At Shan's nod, Lizzie moved to her side and accompanied her along the corridor.

Once they were in the car and chugging in first gear in the slow-moving traffic up Punt Road, Lizzie said, "So surgery in two weeks then?"

"Yeah." Shan expelled a sigh. "Then a knee brace. Then physio."

Lizzie drummed on the steering wheel as a car cut in front of her. "What are you going to do?"

"What do you mean? I don't have much choice here."

"About your apartment. How will you manage with all those stairs? I don't see hordes of people at your door ready to help you." She shot Shan an inscrutable glance.

"Yeah, well, Celia's been busy."

"Is Celia your only friend?" Curiosity, not censure, coloured Lizzie's question.

Shan opened her mouth to deny that but stopped. She had plenty of friends: casual acquaintances, workmates, running mates, people she saw a few times a week. They talked, they laughed, they shared snippets of their lives. But friends she could call on to do her shopping, or drive her to medical appointments? There was only Celia, and she wasn't always available. She shut her mouth again.

"I don't mean it in a bad way." Lizzie changed lanes to where the traffic moved quicker. "But you've only mentioned Celia. And she seems to be a busy person. Your parents aren't around. I'm wondering who's going to help you."

"Celia." She hoped her voice didn't hold the doubt she felt.

"Right. Is she close by?"

"Not too far."

"Are we talking the next suburb or halfway to Sydney?"

"Bentleigh. About forty minutes if the traffic's good." No need to mention Celia lived in the very furthest part of Bentleigh East, which added another fifteen minutes.

"I thought so." Lizzie changed gear as the traffic moved faster. "I've got a proposition for you. Hear me out before you say no."

Proposition. The word conjured up all sorts of things, most of them rather intriguing, and almost certainly not what Lizzie meant. She was probably going to suggest dropping by the supermarket on the way home.

"I live in Abbotsford in a single-storey terrace house. One step at the front, then flat all the way to the rear. I have a very comfortable guest bedroom which isn't used. I meant to advertise for a housemate after Sonia left, but I never got around to it. If you want it, the room's yours while you recover."

Shan opened her mouth to refuse. Sharing with Lizzie—a reminder of why she needed a single-storey house in the first place—would be difficult. Seeing the person every day who'd destroyed her life would just remind her of everything she'd lost. And why was Lizzie even offering? Shan had hardly been all sweetness and light—grumpy and difficult described her better right now. But then Dr Gupta's words floated through her mind: *If you live alone, you'll need to make arrangements.* And now an arrangement had fallen into her lap.

Shan worried her lower lip with her teeth. The offer was tempting. It would be amazing not to have to negotiate the steps to her apartment. And a house… Even if it didn't have much of a yard, she'd be able to get out onto the street, into the sunshine, see life pass by a lot closer than from her fourth-floor apartment. And Lizzie would be there, which would satisfy Dr Gupta's requirement that someone be with her. The snappy words of refusal died in her throat.

"Thank you. That's a kind offer," she said instead. For a moment, emotion overwhelmed her. *The kindness of a stranger.* She tried to imagine Celia making the same suggestion. No. If she asked, Celia would let her stay for a few days after surgery, but it would be difficult to get around from Celia's. She cleared her throat of the huskiness that might sound like tears clogging her voice. "But I can't accept it."

"Why not?" Lizzie flicked her a quick glance and then returned her gaze to the road.

"I don't want to impose."

"You won't be. I wouldn't have offered if I thought that. The room is vacant."

"I'm not the easiest person to live with." *And I still blame you for what happened.*

Lizzie's laughter pealed out into the small car. "You think I haven't worked that out already?"

"And I'm not sure I can look at you every day and not get angry. This is ruining so much of my life, Lizzie. That's not something I can just push to one side."

Lizzie sobered. "Look, I know you blame me for what happened. And yeah, I think you're partly right, and that's prompting my offer. That and the fact that this is something I can offer without too much difficulty. I understand you're not in a good headspace right now, and I'm not expecting us to be besties, but if you can avoid biting my head off *every* time I open my mouth, it will probably be okay. But"—her voice went hard, shiny like steel—"if you don't want to look at me, then you can forget it. I won't be ignored in my own home. I'm not your whipping boy."

Had she been that obnoxious to Lizzie? Shan tucked her chin into her chest. Yes, if she was honest, she probably had. But a little voice in her head argued that it was all Lizzie's fault she was going to miss the Commonwealth Games trials. What else would she miss?

What if I can't ever run competitively again?

No. Shan squashed that thought flat before it could grow wings. Dr Gupta was going to fix her up like new. She looked over at Lizzie. "Yeah, well, it's hard to be Ms Sunshine when your income and everything important in your life is ripped away."

"So you've said. Repeatedly. I'm trying to make amends." Lizzie hunched her shoulders. "And I'm about to retract the offer if this is how you're going to be, so think fast. If you do move in, I won't get in your way or give you restrictions. You could have friends around, come and go as you please." She slanted another quick sideways look. "Have someone stay over."

Shan carefully straightened her aching knee. "I think you're forgetting that I'm not working now. I can't afford to pay my rent and your room as well."

"I didn't mean for you to pay," Lizzie said. "It's only for a few weeks, right? Two weeks until surgery, a few weeks after. It's been nearly a year since Sonia moved out, and I've done stuff-all about renting the room in that time. I'm sure I can wait a bit longer."

"I don't want to cramp your space."

"You won't. No more than any other housemate."

Shan stared out at the slow-moving traffic as she weighed up the offer. Lizzie wouldn't be there all the time. Surely, she could cope with sharing the house with her.

"Look, if you don't want to, that's perfectly fine," Lizzie said. "You don't need to be polite; just tell me you'd rather not. After all, you hardly know me and my antisocial habits. I could play the trumpet. At midnight. In my underwear." She shot Shan a mischievous smile.

The knots in Shan's stomach unwound a little. It seemed Lizzie really was just being kind. And it would solve her immediate problem. "The trumpet? Well, that's okay. If it was the bagpipes, it would be a dealbreaker."

"That would be my neighbour. But he only does it on a full moon when there's an R in the month. So, March and April. You'll have to suck it up until May."

Shan grinned. "Maybe I'll howl back."

"You will? Does that mean you'll take up the offer?"

Shan considered. She'd meant her comment to be a throwaway line. But she was starting to come around to the idea. Then again, what if Lizzie was a night owl who had friends around until three in the morning? What if Dee and her tearaway son were constant visitors? What if Lizzie was a hoarder with a house full of junk?

"How about this," Lizzie said. "My house is on the way to your place. We'll stop off now and you can have a look, then go away and think about it and let me know. No pressure either way."

Warmth stole through Shan's belly like hot soup on a winter's day. Lizzie was just being friendly. She was right; they wouldn't have to live in each other's pockets. Shared houses operated the same way every time: first you were super-polite and kept to your own space, then you forced friendliness, then you either retreated to your rooms and lived completely separate lives, with the only communication being passive-aggressive notes about using the last of the milk and cleaning the toilet, or else you became inseparable best mates. It always seemed to be one or the other. And she wouldn't be with Lizzie long enough to get past the super-polite stage.

"Okay, I'll take a look."

"Great. And we're nearly there." Lizzie weaved through two lanes of traffic and took the right turn just as the lights turned yellow.

At least there were no Bentleys around.

Lizzie's house was in one of the narrow one-way roads off busy Hoddle Street. Shan looked around as Lizzie drove carefully through the narrow gap left between two rows of parked cars. Moving day would be a bitch here. A truck might not even get through.

"Start willing a parking spot into existence." Lizzie slowed as they came to a crossroads. "It often works for Dee."

Whether it was the karma of the universe or just luck, a laden truck pulled out in front of them as they approached. Lizzie reverse-parked and crept back and forth, getting a little closer to the kerb each time until she was satisfied.

"It's that one." Lizzie pointed to a tiny terrace house in a row of equally small Victorian-era houses. The door was bright yellow, which set off the mellow red brick. The veranda had a couple of comfortable-looking chairs and a low table.

The front door opened to a long hallway of polished floorboards.

"The first room's mine," Lizzie said.

Shan caught a glimpse of a bed strewn with clothes and laden with pillows and cushions. It seemed the sort of thing Lizzie would have—although she'd never seen the point. Surely, all the cushions ended up on the floor at night.

"This one's yours." Lizzie opened the second door. "At least, it's yours if you want it."

The room was small, with a queen bed, a built-in robe, and a bedside cabinet. A narrow window showed a view of a tiny glassed-in space filled with green plants. Shan pressed the mattress and gave a short nod. Good and firm, as she liked.

"I've got clutter in the wardrobe, but I can clear it out." Lizzie pulled open the door and a bundle of clothes, and what looked like craft supplies fell at her feet. "If you don't have queen bed linen, I have heaps."

"It's lovely." The room felt welcoming. Shan imagined curling up in the comfy bed with a book.

"Come and see the rest." Lizzie's lips quirked into a grin. "It will take you two minutes. These houses are teeny-tiny."

The miniscule bathroom had a shower and no bath, and the rest of the house was an open plan living and kitchen area. A laptop and what looked like work folders sat on the dining table. Lizzie hurried ahead and moved another pile of folders from the couch to the floor, where they toppled into an untidy heap. Most of the ledges contained collections of leafy green plants, and the kitchen bench was laden with appliances.

"Sorry about the mess. I promise I'll tidy if you come."

Shan hobbled over to look out the wide glass doors to the rear yard. The house was fine. And there weren't a hundred-and-eight stairs to navigate every time she wanted to breathe the outside air. Lizzie seemed untidy, sure, but she didn't appear a total slob. The house was clean, just cluttered. And it would save having to ask Celia.

But could she live with Lizzie? Shan considered. If Lizzie found she couldn't stand sharing with Shan, if her guilt ran out abruptly, then Shan would find herself back at her apartment—or maybe staying with Celia—and that would be difficult.

And was it fair to Lizzie? Shan examined her motives for wanting to stay. They were mainly selfish, she admitted. A nice house, no stairs, someone to keep her company and, importantly, satisfying the hospital's requirement that someone be with her.

"You can stop obsessing any time." Lizzie's voice sounded behind her. "I can see the cogs whirring in your brain. If you don't want to stay, just say so. Or if you do, just say that too. If it doesn't work out, it's no big deal."

Shan turned. Lizzie had come up behind her and was standing close. Close enough that Shan could see her huge, dark eyes and thick, black eyelashes. Lizzie's hair was caught in her swept-back office style, but a few strands fell around her face. Her skin appeared a darker golden in the overhead light.

Shan exhaled. Right there, standing in front of her, looking utterly sumptuous in her green-and-cream office wear and smelling sweetly of floral soap, was another problem. Lizzie was considerate and funny and easy-going. And gorgeous. More than gorgeous. The whole Lizzie-package was appealing in a way that Shan seldom found. Even her anger over Lizzie's part in her injury couldn't shut down that appeal. And Lizzie-shaped distractions couldn't possibly be a part of her life right now. Her priorities were set: surgery, rehab, regain her running form, build back her fitness, improve her times. Try to put aside the disappointment of missing the Commonwealth Games trials and maybe, just maybe, dare to dream bigger. To aim at the biggest, most prestigious goal of all.

If the surgery was successful; if she focused all her energy on it; if she was single-minded, laser-sharp; if she let nothing distract her…

Then maybe, just maybe, with a lot of hard work and pain, and a hefty dollop of luck, her goal might be within reach.

The Olympics.

Lizzie was a distraction she could not afford to have, and that distraction was staring at her, no doubt wondering why she hadn't replied.

"It's an incredibly tempting offer, but I don't know what you're hoping to get out of the arrangement. I'm not... I'm..." She shrugged; the words caught in her throat. How to explain the dedication and single-minded focus needed to reach her goal to someone who ran in a koala suit?

"Nothing. I thought I made that clear. You don't have to pay rent. Just chip in for food or buy your own."

"I don't just mean money." How could she get her point across without appearing totally up herself? "I'd be a lousy housemate. I'm not very social. I'll have to totally focus on my rehabilitation: exercises, physio, diet, mental health. I go to bed early, I—"

"I get it. You're an obsessive athlete, the highest echelon of runnerdom, and you don't want to hang out with me." An amused note had crept into Lizzie's voice. "I'm suggesting you move in as a temporary housemate, not that we get married. If you want to spend all your time in your room, that's fine." Lizzie spread her hands. "I get that runners can be selfish people—anyone who is at the top of their field like that has to be. I have no ulterior motive. I like to think I'm a nice person. Kind, even. And if I can make someone's life a little easier, if I have the answer to their problem, then yeah, why shouldn't I at least offer?" She turned away and picked up her bag. "It's okay, Shan. I'm not fussed if you want to be in your own space. Now, if you've made up your mind, let me drive you home. I need to get back to work at some point this afternoon."

Shan looked around once more. She was being an arse. A superior one at that. Lizzie's offer really did seem simply made from kindness. And it would make life a lot easier over the next few weeks. She turned to Lizzie. "I'm sorry; I'm being rude. If you're sure, then thanks, I accept your offer."

Lizzie flashed her a smile, and Shan's heart turned over in her chest. She could handle this. Oh yes, she could.

Chapter 8

Hey Presto

"SHE'S MOVING IN FOR A few weeks, that's all." Lizzie glared at Dee over the top of their monitors. "No need to go all legal on me. I'm sure a disclaimer isn't needed. Even if I knew how to write one."

"Has she said she's not going to sue you for tripping her?" Dee's eyebrows lowered and she pursed her lips.

"No. But what would she get if she did? A beat-up hatchback, and some old furniture."

"Maybe you'll be paying her a hundred dollars per week for the rest of your life."

Lizzie exhaled noisily. "She's not like that, Dee. I'm sure of it. Please stop assuming the worst of everyone."

"You're right." Dee opened a bag of crisps with a loud rip and offered them to Lizzie, who shook her head. "It's this job. Sometimes I think it sucks the joy out of life. Trying to shovel unsuitable people into positions. Or dealing with people who think they're too good for junior roles—despite having no experience." She stuffed a handful of crisps into her mouth and spoke through them. "I should have been a plumber." Crisp fragments sprayed over her desk.

"You'd have to stick your arm down other people's toilets," Lizzie said. "I'd rather organise data entry tests and check references."

"Yeah. When you put it like that, so would I." Dee brightened. "At least this job doesn't put me off my lunch. You fancy sushi?"

"Sure." Lizzie looked across at their manager, who was on the phone. She mimed eating lunch and received a thumbs up in response.

She stood, picked up her bag, and left with Dee. They wound their way through the knots of workers, tourists, and shoppers in Melbourne's city centre to the sushi place they liked. The shopfront opened onto the street, and a short line of people waited.

When they'd got their food, Dee snagged a table out front, sat, and rotated her shoulders. "I love this sunshine. Last night was freezing. Reece came into bed with me again. I don't mind that, but he tosses and kicks and steals all the covers and wraps himself in them like a sausage roll. No wonder I was cold. I need someone to keep me warm at night who isn't four years old. And not someone who's thirty-four and acts like they're four either. Did I tell you I got hit on by a client yesterday?"

"No." Lizzie opened her plastic tray of sushi and squirted soy sauce into the lid. "Which one?"

"Rather gorgeous-looking guy who applied for the receptionist role. A recent immigrant from Pakistan. He's an engineer, but is finding it hard to get that sort of work here, so he's applying for all sorts of jobs. I rather like him. If he wasn't a client, I'd be tempted."

"There's no reason you can't go out with him. I'd just have to handle his job-seeking instead of you."

"It might be awkward. I'm still thinking about it."

"Maybe he'll find engineering work and remember you."

"Maybe. Or else he thought he could flirt his way into the receptionist job." Dee squeezed wasabi onto her sushi. "Sometimes, it's hard to know. If you're not going to use your wasabi, can I have it?"

Lizzie handed over the packets. "You get all the flirts. I just get jobseekers behaving in a professional manner. Apart from yesterday." She snorted. "A woman came in for a typing test. When I graded it, she'd only managed nine words per minute. I said I was sorry, but we needed a faster speed than that. That's when she explained she couldn't leave her cat home alone or it would destroy the furniture.

She'd brought it in her bag, and it had started crying. Pacifying kitty wrecked her typing test. She let the cat out of the bag—literally. It escaped when she was showing it to me, and we spent the next few minutes coaxing it back. It's a work-from-home job, so she'd probably manage, cat and all, if her speed was better. I suggested she come back to retake the test when she has someone to mind kitty."

Dee's mouth hung open for a moment. "And I missed that! I'd have cuddled the cat while she did the test."

"You wouldn't. It scratched me when I tried to pet it." Lizzie extended her wrist to show the red marks.

"So when's Shan moving in?" Dee asked.

"I'm picking her up Sunday evening." Lizzie took a gulp from her water bottle. "It'll be strange having someone in the house with me. I've got used to being by myself since Sonia left. And sharing with someone, rather than being in a relationship. Being polite about bathroom time, kitchen time, and whose turn it is to put the bins out."

"Always your turn. She can't do that easily on crutches."

"I don't mind." Lizzie fiddled with her chopsticks. "Shan's a bit prickly—understandably so—but I think she'll loosen up. She's been almost friendly a few times."

"Uh-oh. I know that expression." Dee leaned forward. "You've got your meet-cute face on. Don't fall for her, Lizzie. Falling for housemates is as bad as—"

"Falling for hot clients." She sighed. "I know. And I won't. This should just be for a few weeks, then she'll be out of my life."

"You say that like you don't want it to happen."

"I don't know what I want, to be honest. Right now, I'm helping someone out."

"Right." Dee's expression turned knowing. "Let's see what the universe has in store for you."

"It has something sweet lined up for me. I fancy a vanilla slice, and it's your turn to buy."

"Yes!" Dee stood. "If we hurry, we've time for a coffee as well."

Celia threw herself onto Shan's couch, hooked up a knee, and regarded her. "You could have stayed at my place."

"Lizzie offered. She lives closer to the hospital too."

"You didn't ask me." Celia flicked a black curl away from her neck.

"I didn't want to intrude. Plus, your spare room is very busy."

"I'd have moved the treadmill and gym equipment," Celia said. She shot Shan a flirtatious glance from under lowered lashes. "And since when have we needed two beds?"

Shan bit her lip. "We agreed, Celia, that was...not a mistake, but something we shouldn't repeat. We need to concentrate on our running. The Commonwealth Games for you. A relationship between us would be difficult."

"*You* said we shouldn't have a relationship," Celia said. "I didn't. I don't live like a nun. Good sex gives me a natural high and I run faster. You should try it sometime."

Shan shifted on the bar stool, trying to get her knee into a comfortable position. "We've been friends for so long. I don't want to change that."

"You had no trouble changing that after the Albury meet. When you pipped me by two-tenths of a second, then we went back to our motel and fucked in the shower. Wow, Shan, that was off the charts."

"It was good." Shan shifted awkwardly. Celia's memory of their one time together seemed different to Shan's. Sure, the adrenaline high of the race had sent them tumbling into bed, but that had evaporated quickly. Shan remembered good sex overlaid by the discomfort that it should never have happened. She changed her position again. Her knee ached, a dull, deep pain that didn't ease, no matter how she positioned her knee. "But...to me, you're my friend and training partner. We've been through so much together with our running. I'm sorry, but don't think I can change our relationship in my head."

Ever since they were eight-year-olds at primary school, running helter-skelter around the playing field in what passed for "cross country", Shan had supported Celia through all the ups and downs with her foster parents, and had been there for her when they'd kicked her out at eighteen. Celia could be self-absorbed at times, but Shan had stuck with her. It was what you did with friends.

"Maybe you're right. Two runners together—we're both too selfish, too set in our ways, too goal driven." Celia wrapped her arms around her upraised knee. "I love you, Shan, in a bestie kind of way. We probably shouldn't try to change that. But holy guacamole, we were hot together. Remember when you made me come with—"

"I haven't forgotten." It wasn't that she was asexual. It was just that her running goals were so all-consuming that there was little room for relationships in her life. Or even hook-ups, such as Celia often enjoyed. "Lizzie's picking me up Sunday evening to take me to her place," she said, in the hope it would take Celia's mind off the past.

"What time? Maybe I should be here to check her out."

"Sixish, I think. There's nothing for you to check out." *Nothing except clear golden skin, lustrous black hair, an open face, and a warm personality. Nothing except a beautiful woman*—who was probably Celia's type, now that she thought of it. Something heavy weighed in Shan's chest at the thought of Celia and Lizzie together. Strange. It wasn't as if she wanted Lizzie for herself. She didn't want anyone, not in that way.

"How about I take you over instead?" Celia asked. "I'm working Sunday, and my last client's in Preston. It's not too far out of my way. We could have dinner together, and then go over."

Warmth shot through her at Celia's offer. That was what besties did, after all. "Sure. Can we eat here, though? It's somewhat awkward in busy places on crutches."

"No worries." Celia flashed her a full grin of white teeth. "I'll pick up something on my way over. Will your stuff fit in my car in one load?"

"It should do. It's only for a few weeks, after all."

"Great. I'll be over after six." Celia got off the couch and put her water glass in the sink. "I'll see you Sunday." She came over and bent to press a kiss to Shan's cheek, close to the edge of her lips.

Shan hugged her, pressing Celia's skinny body to her own for a moment. For a second, Lizzie jumped into her mind. Was she a hugger? Maybe. And as they would be sharing a house, she might find out.

Lizzie glanced at the clock. Nearly eight. Shan's text had said Celia would give her a lift over that evening, but she hadn't said when. Shan hadn't said if she would have had dinner either, and Lizzie hadn't wanted to ask and risk sounding like the matron of a boarding school. She'd made a huge bowl of salad, stuffed with protein and greens. If Shan had already eaten, it would do for weekday lunches.

She went over to the corner by the door where Presto sat anxiously on his rug. His ears drooped, and if she looked his way, he hid his face in his paws. She hadn't mentioned Presto to Shan, so hopefully she wouldn't mind. But when the shelter had called that morning and begged her to take a foster dog for a few weeks, she hadn't been able to resist. The kelpie had been rescued from a backyard where there was no food and very little water. His back was covered with scars from cigarette burns. Lizzie's heart twisted anew each time she thought of them.

The doorbell rang, just as she was contemplating having dinner without waiting for Shan.

"A new friend for you, Presto," she said. At least, she hoped so.

Shan leaned on her crutches on the step. Next to her was a slight Black woman dressed in the uniform of a personal carer. She was laden with three sports bags.

Lizzie swung the door wider. "Hi, Shan." She turned her smile on the other woman. "And hi, Celia. Come in." She led the way down the hallway, then pushed open the door to Shan's room. "You can put that in here. Is there more to come in?"

"A bit more." Celia dumped the bags on the bed and disappeared back up the hall.

Shan stood awkwardly in the doorway. "This is really nice of you. I hope you don't regret this in a couple of days."

"Don't worry about it. I won't be in your face all the time." She stood aside as Celia returned with the second load.

"Groceries," Celia said. "This way?" She nodded down the hall.

"Yeah. Except, I gained a new foster dog this morning. He's been abused, and he's still very scared and hasn't left his bed. It's best to give him some space and not try to pet him. I hope that's okay with you."

"It's fine. I like dogs. Maybe it will be helpful for him to have someone around in the day when you're at work."

"It probably will be." Relief swelled in Lizzie's chest. She hadn't wanted to decide whether to evict Shan, or Presto, if it had come to it.

"What's his name?" Celia asked.

"Presto. The shelter named him. When they went around to find him, they couldn't see him. One of volunteers went crawling under the house, and when they emerged, Presto, who'd been shivering on a pile of rags, appeared as if by magic. Hence, Hey Presto. It was as if he knew they were looking for him."

Presto was still on his bed when they entered the kitchen.

"Hey, Presto," Shan said in soft tones, but she made no attempt to approach him.

Celia's eyes widened at the sight of him. "The poor darling. What is he, a kelpie?"

"I think so. Or a cross. The shelter gets a lot of kelpies. People turn them in when they find out how much exercise they need."

Celia dumped the boxes on the counter. "Nice place you've got here, Lizzie. No wonder Shan chose to stay here rather than my place."

"Thanks." Lizzie offered a brief smile. "Have you both eaten? I have a big salad if you're hungry."

"We had dosas," Celia said. "But there wasn't much greenery in them." She wrinkled her nose at Lizzie, a twinkle in her eye.

Lizzie previously hadn't formed a good impression of Celia, but the woman in front of her was friendly and rather appealing with her crinkly mass of hair and smooth ebony skin. "I haven't eaten, and there's heaps if you'd like some."

Celia hitched her butt on one of the bar stools. "I never say no to food. Shan doesn't either; she's just being polite."

On cue, Lizzie's stomach gurgled like a drain. "Then let's eat." She pulled three of her mismatched plates and cutlery out and set them on the table, then followed them with an assortment of salad dressings. "I have some wine if you want it."

"Just water thanks," said Shan, and Celia nodded.

For a few minutes, there was silence as Shan and Celia dug into the salad. Lizzie ate more sparingly, amazed at how much the other two could put away. And this was their second dinner of the night! Runners needed their fuel—that she knew from her own efforts—but Shan wasn't active at the moment.

As if reading her mind, Shan finished her plate, hesitated, then set her cutlery down. "That was amazing. I could eat the same amount again, but I shouldn't right now."

"Does that mean I get your share?" Celia quirked an eyebrow and took a second, more modest portion.

When they'd finished eating, Celia helped Lizzie clear the table. "Shan, do you need any help unpacking before I go?"

"I'm fine. It'll give me something to do tomorrow."

Celia gestured to Presto, still on his blanket in the corner, his back to them. "You can make friends with this sweet doggo." Her eyes softened as she glanced at him again. "I don't understand how people can be cruel to animals."

Lizzie shook her head. "Me neither." She blinked away tears at the thought of the burns on Presto's back and shared a wobbly smile with Celia.

"Maybe the next time I come, he'll have settled in." Celia turned to Shan. "Kelpies make good running companions. Endless energy and stamina. Just sayin'."

"Slow down, Speedy," Shan said. "Presto and I both have a way to go before that happens. How long will you foster him for?" she asked Lizzie.

"It varies. Generally, I keep a foster dog until they're ready to go to the shelter to find their forever home. Some are ready for adoption in a couple of weeks. Others take months. I think Presto might be with me for a while."

"He's a lucky dog," Shan said.

Lizzie looked across. Shan was staring at her, rather than Presto. Their gazes collided and a jolt of energy lit in her belly. Shan's eyes crinkled and her look warmed Lizzie from chest to toes. She forced herself to look away.

Don't go there, Lizzie. She's a temporary housemate, a way to assuage your guilt trip, no more.

Lizzie swallowed hard. Suddenly, having Shan in her house seemed like a bad idea. A dangerous idea. Because how was she going to be around her for the next few weeks without making a total idiot of herself?

Chapter 9

A Polite Dance

SHIT! I'VE LEFT IT TOO late again! Lizzie dropped her phone on the bedside table and swung her legs out of bed. No matter how motivated she was to go for a run before work, every time it was easier to lie in cosy comfort under the quilt scrolling social media on her phone than it was to get up and go for a jog in the pre-dawn darkness. Even though she was working from home today, she still had to be logged on for work at exactly 8.30 a.m. There'd be no run for her today—again.

She scurried down the hallway in her pyjamas for a pee, to warm up the coffee machine, and to check on Presto. Hopefully, there were no accidents. She'd left him some puppy pee pads but had no idea if he was housetrained. The pee pads were unused, but there were no puddles that she could see, and the only sign of Presto was a humped shape underneath his blanket in the corner. Talking softly to him, Lizzie opened the rear door enough that he could get out to the yard if he wanted.

She glanced at the closed door of the guest room as she returned to her bedroom to get dressed. She had no idea what time Shan rose in the mornings; hopefully, she hadn't disturbed her.

Dressed in sweatpants, a flannel shirt, and thick socks, Lizzie returned to the kitchen. She flicked the heater on to take the morning chill from the air and poured herself a coffee. Out of the corner of her eye, she saw Presto in the backyard doing his business. She took her coffee to the couch that overlooked the yard and curled into the corner.

Presto was walking slowly around the yard sniffing her outdoor furniture and every centimetre of the fence. Then he returned through the open door, keeping as far away from her as possible.

"Hey, Presto," she said quietly. "This is your space now. You take your time learning it. I'm not going to hurt you."

Presto glanced her way, then his tail went between his legs, he slunk back to his blanket, burrowing underneath until only his nose and the tip of his red-brown tail showed.

Lizzie's heart splintered one more time. Every rescue dog did this to her, shaving off another piece of her heart and taking it with them. She'd cared for mistrustful dogs before, ones who were wary of children, of men, of traffic, but Presto was breaking her in two.

"I know you don't trust me now, Presto, but you're safe here. I'll love you, and then, later on, I promise I'll find you the best forever home I can."

There was no movement from the blanket.

Lizzie sighed. It would take time. A lot of time, a lot of kindness, and a lot of love. Luckily, she could give Presto all three. She rose and went to make a second coffee and set up her laptop for work.

The bed was firm and comfortable. Shan stretched out her good leg, flexing her toes under the covers. Even the sheets were softer than her own rather scratchy ones. Light filtered in from the window. It must be later than she normally woke. Her body clock was no longer on training time: awake at six, ready for morning stretches, a glass of water, then out for an hour's run. Her toes twitched. Maybe in a couple of months that would be possible again.

The house was quiet. Lizzie might be still in bed, or—more likely—already working. She'd pinned her working hours and work-from-home schedule to the fridge, and said she'd be working at home this week to give Presto some stability.

Shan sat up and eased her injured leg to the floor, then retrieved her crutches. Carefully, she rose and hopped to the door, wincing as her sore knee protested the change of position.

In the living area, Lizzie had her back to Shan as she set up her laptop. Shan slipped into the bathroom.

When she emerged, Lizzie was in the kitchen. "Morning." She held up a mug. "Coffee?"

"Yes, please." Shan offered a slight smile.

"Did you sleep well?" Lizzie spooned more ground coffee into the machine and pressed a button.

"I did. It's quieter than my flat."

"I guess you're used to strange beds." Lizzie turned from the machine to face her. "Oh!" A rosy blush crept up her cheeks. "I meant because you'd travel a lot. Running meets and so on. I'm not…that is, I didn't mean to imply… And it would be none of my business anyway." She shook her head. "Listen to me, blundering on."

Lizzie's confusion was rather endearing. Shan shook her head. "I get what you meant. Yes, there's a lot of hotel rooms—and dormitories at training camps. They're the worst. Other people muttering in their sleep and snoring. Once, a woman got into bed with me in the middle of the night. I thought I'd got lucky, but it turned out she was sleepwalking!"

Lizzie huffed a laugh. "What did you do?"

"She didn't wake, so I found her bed and slept in that. We confused a few people the next morning."

Lizzie set a mug of coffee on the bench and pushed across the milk.

Shan sat and picked up the mug. "Thanks for this."

Lizzie sat across from her and cradled her own coffee. "No worries." She gestured to the fridge. "I've got about twenty minutes before work. I was going to have fruit and yoghurt; would you like some?"

Clearly she'd been wrong about Lizzie being an unhealthy eater. "That would be great, if it's not too much trouble."

"It's not." Lizzie slid off the stool and picked fruit from the bowl. "We didn't discuss food last night—"

"You mean after Celia ate most of a bowl of salad that looked like it was meant to last you a week?"

"Maybe two days. And you made a fair dent in the salad too."

Heat crawled up Shan's neck. "I'm sorry. It was just so great. And Celia's a pig with food."

"Hey, I'm joking. I can clear you shelves in the pantry and the fridge if you prefer to do your own thing, or else we can share. I'm a reasonable cook—my traditional family, remember?—and I'm happy to do that if you want to chip in for the cost. But if you're on a strict nutrition plan, you might not want that."

"I'm not. Not now anyway." Shan's mouth fell at the corners. *Not for a while to come.* "How about I chip in? But I can prepare food too. It might not be to your standard though. Microwaved chicken is my staple."

"That's okay." Lizzie's lips twitched. "Occasionally, anyway. Just as I hope pizza is okay occasionally too."

"It is."

The blanket in the corner shifted, and Presto's head emerged slowly like a tortoise from a shell.

"Ignore him," Lizzie said quietly. "He might want to go back outside."

Shan watched out of the corner of her eye as Presto crept from under the blanket one cautious paw at a time. He slunk along casting anxious glances in their direction until he gained the yard.

"You better tell me what to do with him when you're not here," Shan said.

Presto was now walking a slow circuit of the yard, paying particular attention to the rear fence.

"Not much. Make sure he's got food and water, and when practical, access to the yard. When he's inside, I just talk to him, use his name a lot. I don't approach him or try to pet him, but I don't avoid his corner either. He'll gain enough confidence to come to me eventually."

Presto squatted to pee.

"That." Lizzie indicated him with a jerk of her head. "Most male dogs lift a leg. I think he's been mistreated since he was very young."

"Love and kindness," Shan murmured.

She glanced at Lizzie, who was watching Presto. Her shiny black hair was loose, and her baggy clothes hid her shapely figure. But her face wore a soft smile, and her eyes radiated warmth. For a second, she compared Lizzie's kindness to Celia's self-absorption. No. They were different people, with different goals and dreams. Although what dreams did Lizzie have? Maybe she'd find out over the next few weeks.

"Hi, Manda, this is Lizzie Carras from Best Foot Forward. I'm calling to see how Angie is working out for you in the admin assistant role." Lizzie pulled her notepad closer as she listened to Manda's reply.

When the call ended, she went back to the coffee machine. A door banged up the hallway, and a minute later Shan limped into the kitchen.

"Good timing. Want a coffee?"

Shan blew an upward breath that ruffled the spiky hair on her forehead. "Coffee won't fix me. I need a new knee." Her face was set in deep frown lines. Or maybe it was pain.

"I can't help with a new knee. Just coffee." Lizzie held up a mug.

"Fuck the coffee. I don't need to be more jittery than I already am. I just want my life back." Shan sat heavily on a bar stool, propped her crutches against the breakfast bar, and smashed the flat of her hand on the counter. One of her crutches fell to the floor with a crash. "I've been trying simple exercises—I can't even straighten my leg. Have you *any* idea how hard I've worked to get my fitness up? My times? My ranking? I'm the sixth best 10,000 metre runner in Australia. Or I was, anyway." Her voice turned bitter. "That's now out the fucking window."

Uh-oh. Lizzie turned away and busied herself at the machine, making a coffee for herself. She poured a glass of water for Shan and pushed it across to her, then picked up the fallen crutch. "Is there anything I can do to help?"

Shan's stony stare made her flinch.

"Invent a fucking time machine, go back to the race, and pay more attention to Dee's out-of-control kid."

"Anything practical?" Lizzie kept her voice steady. Right now, Shan was reminding her of some of her more belligerent clients. Calmness, not getting riled up or taking it personally, generally worked with them. But with Shan it *was* personal. *Different ball game.*

Shan stared for another few seconds, then buried her face in her hands.

Lizzie hovered, one hand in the air. Was she crying? If it were Dee in this state, she'd rub her shoulders, murmur soothing words, then hug her. But Shan was more likely to snarl at her. She withdrew her hand.

After a minute, Shan dropped her hands from her face and grabbed the glass of water, sculling it all at once.

"Want to tell me anything?"

"I can't do my physio exercises in my room. There's not enough floor space."

Is that all? Lizzie's lips twitched and she pressed them together so Shan didn't think she was laughing at her. "Why not do them here?" She indicated the living area.

Shan sucked her lower lip. "I didn't want to disturb your work."

"You won't. I work in a small office with Dee; I'm used to covering her F-bombs when I'm on the phone."

Shan flushed and turned her green-flecked eyes toward Lizzie. "Sorry about the swearing. I was just...just..."

"Frustrated?"

"Yeah, that. And angry. And feeling sorry for myself. I'd give anything right now for that time machine to be a real thing."

"And for me to have gone for coffee instead of donning my koala suit and going for a run?"

"That too. That most of all." She shook her head. "It keeps replaying in my head and I can't get rid of it."

"No wonder you're angry with me." Lizzie worried the teaspoon in her coffee. It was going to be a long few weeks if Shan remained this touchy.

Shan slid off the stool. "I'll go back to my room. You don't need me in your face like this."

"To do what? More exercises in too small a space? Don't be an idiot. Use the living area. Just try to keep the swearing down when I'm on the phone."

For long moments, Shan's stormy eyes bored into Lizzie's. Then her mouth twisted. "Okay. Thanks." The words were a subdued mutter. She retrieved her crutches and hobbled back to her room.

Lizzie turned away. The knife in her gut reminded her once again that Shan's predicament was all her fault. As if she could forget.

Shan was gone for long enough that Lizzie figured she'd decided to suck it up in her room. Then, she reappeared clutching a yoga mat.

"There might be a bit of grunting. If I'm making too much noise, just tell me to shut up. Or raise a hand."

"Like school."

"But hopefully without the kid behind aiming down my neck with his water bottle."

Shan's mesmerising eyes and almost-smile made Lizzie's stomach flutter as if a flight of sparrows was whirling around. And her consideration was an unexpected bonus. She turned to the coffee machine to hide her flushed cheeks.

When she turned back, Shan was spreading the yoga mat by the window away from Presto's corner.

"Dee's dropping around on her way home from work. Part work, part friend catch-up," Lizzie said.

Shan's mouth turned down at the corners as she came back to the counter. "She seems to think I'm about to shaft you for money or something."

"Don't mind her. She's unlucky in love at the moment and it colours her world." Lizzie sipped her coffee. "If you know a thirty-something, definitely single, not averse to a kid, financially responsible, monogamous person who lives in Melbourne, and has all their own teeth, then maybe you could introduce them to Dee."

"There's a couple of women in my running club who fit that."

Lizzie tilted her head. "And male. At least, Dee's never shown any inclination any other way."

"I'll give it some thought."

Her phone rang, and with a swift grin in Shan's direction, she answered the call. "Best Foot Forward, this is Lizzie. ...Hi, Lex. ... He didn't?... No, I haven't heard from him. I'll check with him and get back to you. If he arrives, you might let me know." She ended the call and blew a frustrated breath. "It drives me nuts when people don't show for work without any notification. Hopefully nothing's wrong, but half the time, someone's got a new job and hasn't bothered to tell us."

Shan finished her water and went over to the yoga mat, lowering herself carefully to the floor. "Bit rude. I always rang Daz if I couldn't work."

"Has he found someone for your job?" Lizzie's mind ticked back into work mode. Maybe they could help the café with a temp, so Shan's job would be there for her when she was fit again.

"Probably." Shan made a face. "Most of his workers are casuals—students and so on. Hopefully, he'll slot me back in when I'm able."

Lizzie nodded and scrolled through her contacts to find her worker's number. As she talked with him, her gaze kept fixing on Shan, now lying on the mat doing leg raises. *Good God, her legs are magnificent.* The running shorts she wore kept sliding up her thigh as she raised and lowered her injured leg. The muscles were taut, defined, and sculpted to perfection.

Lizzie let out a careful breath, hoping it didn't sound like longing. Still, maybe if she ran a hundred kilometres or more each week, she, too, would have legs like Shan's. Hah! Unlikely. It was probably as much genetics as fitness.

The rug in the corner twitched, and Presto's face burrowed out. His eyes followed Shan's leg movement as intently as if she had a beef treat strapped to her foot.

Lizzie grinned to herself; it seemed she wasn't the only one impressed with Shan's muscles. She ended the call and started an e-mail to the employer.

Shan was now doing sit-ups. As if her stomach wasn't rock-hard and flat enough already. Oh, this was cruel. How was she supposed to concentrate on work while the finest physical specimen of womanhood was dressed in brief clothing and on her floor doing exercises that kept Lizzie's mind on other physical pursuits that had nothing to do with knee strengthening? She angled her chair away so she wouldn't be tempted to stare.

Her phone rang. She reached for it with an inward sigh. It was going to be a very long day.

Chapter 10

Always Lock the Door

"WINE. I NEED WINE." DEE threw herself onto Lizzie's couch, and then bounced straight back up again. "Actually, I need to pee, then I need to tell you about Rohaan."

"Rohaan?" Lizzie frowned, trying to place the name.

"One minute." Dee rushed into the bathroom. When she reappeared, she said, "Sexy man with come-to-bed eyes who applied for the receptionist job and asked me out practically in the same breath."

"Right. *That* Rohaan." Lizzie nodded as if she'd known all along.

"He didn't get the job. They wanted a woman—how bloody sexist is that? As if it's beneath a man to answer the phone. Rohaan rang to thank me and tell me he's got an interview for an engineer's position through another agency. He asked if that meant I'd go out with him." Dee smiled a cat-got-the-cream smile.

"What did you say?"

"Wine first. Then I'll tell you."

Lizzie found two glasses and a bottle of red and poured. She waited until Dee was sitting at the counter and had taken a slurp. "Well?"

"I said if he got the job and therefore wouldn't be returning to Best Foot Forward, then I'd go out with him. Even if he was your client, how awkward would it be bumping into him in the office if you were counselling him after a failed interview and we'd just crawled out of bed a couple of hours before?"

"On a scale of one to ten, maybe a six or seven. Not that I've ever done it. And neither have you, unless you're holding out on me."

Dee hummed. "Not holding out. He has warm, kind eyes. He's probably sweet to puppies and carries spiders outside the house rather than smashing them with a shoe. I hope he gets the engineering job—then I'll be on that date."

Lizzie clinked her glass with Dee's. "I hope you are. Does he have a photo in the database? I'll take a peek."

"He does. But hands off; he's mine. Or I hope he will be. Although"—Dee lowered her voice—"what about you and the sexy runner you flattened? She has rather an appealing androgynous vibe, if I remember right."

"Ssh." Lizzie cast a glance at the hallway. "She's in her room."

"Her room, is it? What is it you lesbians do? Get a U-Haul on the second date? You haven't even made it that far."

"Please." Lizzie rolled her eyes. "She's my temporary housemate. And you know I'm not a lesbian. I'm—"

"Bisexual. Yeah, I know. Sorry. I shouldn't have got that wrong. All the same"—Dee took a slurp of wine—"she's no more sorta-off-limits than Rohaan is for me. You could lay the seeds."

"Dee, please. It's not like that." She hoped Shan wasn't in stealth mode down the hallway and overhearing this.

"Opportunity for fun. That's all I'm saying."

"I wish it were that simple. You know I'm not good at casual sex. I'm a nester, and after we've hit the sheets, I'm mentally reorganising the linen cupboard and dresser drawers to make room for them. So far, it hasn't worked out. Sonia came the closest."

Dee's expression softened. "I know—I shouldn't tease you. One day, you'll find your happy-ever-after."

A shuffle of feet in the doorway had Lizzie glancing that way. Shan stood there wearing her knee brace, her hand on the doorframe. "Hi. Am I interrupting? I was after a glass of water."

Shit. I hope she didn't overhear. "Of course not. You remember Dee?"

"I do. I may have been a bit spacey with pain when we last met, but I remember your close encounter with a Bentley, and I know not to accept any fruitcake from you." Shan's lips twitched into a smile.

"At least I'm unforgettable." Dee held up her glass. "Do you want a glass of Lizzie's wine?"

"Just water, thanks," Shan said. "I'm not sure about mixing wine with pain meds."

"Fair enough. How are you getting on with Lizzie? Have you burned her koala suit and confiscated her running shoes so she can't trip anyone else?"

"Not yet."

"I'm sitting right here," Lizzie grumbled. "Listening to you talk about me."

"Touchy." Dee looked around the room. "Let's talk about your new foster dog. Who is very absent."

"Nope. Presto's been here the whole time."

"That rug in the corner? I thought you were just messier than usual." Dee rose and took a pace toward him.

"Please don't," Lizzie and Shan said together.

Lizzie caught Shan's eye and they shared a smile. The embarrassing flush rose up Lizzie's neck again. Would she ever grow out of blushing like a fourteen-year-old in front of their first crush? It seemed not, at least not where Shan was concerned. Lizzie pushed that thought to one side to think about later.

"He's still very scared," Lizzie said. "I just want to cuddle him and tell him that no one will hurt him again, but I can't. Not yet anyway."

"Got it." Dee returned to her stool. "I want to do that with all the kids in the homeless charity ads. I know they're actors, but all the same, I want to scoop them up and take them home. Reece would be happy; he wants a baby brother."

"How is Australia's next greatest sprinter?" Shan asked.

"Still sprinting." Dee pulled a face. "I turned my back on him for two seconds in the supermarket yesterday and he disappeared. I found him in the cleaning products aisle building a tower out of dishwasher tablets. How he managed to get all the way over there, the box open, and construction started in under a minute, I have no idea. I could get him a job as a time and motion consultant."

Shan laughed. "At least he didn't get into a bag of lollies."

"I'd never have caught him then. All the sugar and preservatives. He'd have gone through the roof."

"My mate Celia eats red lollies before a race. Claims it's the only legal energy boost that works and red ones are best."

"Was she in the fun run too?" Dee asked.

"She came second." Shan's gaze settled in her lap and her hand massaged her injured knee.

Was Shan wondering how she'd have done if she'd finished the race? Lizzie gripped her wineglass.

"What were you aiming for before your wildlife encounter derailed you?" Dee asked.

"Top three."

Dee's eyebrows did a little dance. "Impressive."

As Dee and Shan began debating the merits of different energy drinks, Lizzie slid off the stool. "I'm cooking stir fry veggies. Dee, are you staying?"

"No, thanks. Got to pick up Reece before the childcare auctions him off." She stood, finished her wine in two gulps, and pecked Lizzie on the cheek. "See you next week when you're back in the office. I'll let myself out." With a wave to Shan, she disappeared up the hallway.

"It must be full-on working with her," Shan said. "I bet she can multi-task like a demon."

"She can answer the phone, type a file note, drink coffee, and play desk basketball all at once. But she can't stop Reece escaping when he puts his mind to it." Lizzie pulled down her wok. "Tofu or no?"

"Tofu. Can I help?"

Lizzie slid across a chopping board and knife, then dived into the fridge for the veggies. "You can do your worst on these. Pretend the veggies are a woman in a koala suit."

Shan's brows lowered and her lighter mood evaporated in a blink.

"Maybe not that then," Lizzie said. "I'd like to sleep easy without worrying you're coming to beat me up with your crutches. Pretend the veggies are Presto's last owners."

"Then the veggies have no chance." Shan's sombre smile hit Lizzie in the chest like a bolt of lightning.

Oh no. Please don't let me fall for her.

There were complications to navigate in any dance of attraction, but falling for Shan would be one of the biggest mistakes of all.

Shan woke early and for a moment lay in bed, enjoying the heavy weight of her limbs on the soft sheets. The first two days as housemates had gone reasonably well. Even though seeing Lizzie still had the power to tighten her muscles in memory, make her chest squeeze with the knowledge of how the accident could have been avoided, it was getting easier. Lizzie was relaxed company. Even Dee hadn't been as defensive as previously. Maybe Presto would come around in time too. The dog cracked her heart every time she saw him. Lizzie had told her about the cigarette burns on his back, but she had yet to get close enough to see them.

Her bladder twinged an early morning klaxon. Shan carefully got out of bed, and, grabbing the crutches, hobbled out of her room and up the hall, her bladder urging her to a faster shuffle than she normally managed. The house was quiet, and Lizzie's laptop wasn't yet set up on the dining table, but there was her usual disarray of discarded clothing, and a couple of manila folders on a chair. Shan's tidy-gene itched to straighten them.

Presto was huddled in his usual blanket in the corner. His nose stuck out one end and his tail out the other. The blanket twitched as she drew near, and she could have sworn his skinny tail thumped once.

"Hello, Presto, how are you this morning? Have you checked out the backyard yet? Maybe you're just back from a night out. Maybe you went for a beer at the Greyhound Tavern. I hear it's the in place for the canine about town."

Presto's tail definitely thumped that time.

Shan slid open the door of the bathroom and stopped abruptly. Lizzie stood in the steam-filled room, her back to Shan, towelling her body. Her naked body.

Heat exploded in Shan's chest and her nipples tightened. Lizzie was gorgeous. Stunning. Her golden skin had a sheen of moisture from her shower, and the ends of her long hair curled in ringlets on her back. Her spine curved down to a small waist and flared, womanly hips. Full buttocks begged to be cupped.

Oh hell. This is trouble.

"I'm sorry. Sorry. The door wasn't locked." Shan shuffled back, wincing as her knee twinged, her eyes still riveted to the glorious curve of Lizzie's bottom. She backed into the doorframe with a thump. "Shit." A half step to the side and her crutch caught the bottom of the stand that held spare towels and toiletries, which crashed to the ground.

Lizzie straightened and wrapped the towel around herself in an unhurried motion. She turned to face Shan, an amused expression on her face.

Shan's feet seemed rooted to the ground. She eyed the fallen jars of moisturiser and shampoo. There was no way she could easily pick them up. She shuffled another step backwards. Her elbow caught the doorframe. "Fuck."

Finally, she made it out of the door and slid it shut with a thump.

She was an idiot, blundering in. Luckily Lizzie hadn't seemed particularly perturbed by the intrusion. She limped over to the kettle and flicked the switch. At least she could offer a coffee in apology.

Shan pressed her hands to her flushed cheeks. One thing pushed its way to the front of her mind. She saw naked women all the time: in locker rooms, showers, and training camp dormitories. It was no big deal at all. Absolutely nothing to get embarrassed about, let alone make a total idiot of herself crashing into the walls like a drunk at closing time. But those naked women weren't Lizzie. Lizzie with the smoothest skin of gleaming gold; Lizzie of the hourglass shape that enticed Shan to run her hands over the indent of her waist, the curve of her hips. The women strutting around the locker room had never sent a burn of desire to her stomach, had never made her want to press her thighs together to dull the ache between.

But Lizzie had.

The bathroom door closed with a thump, and Lizzie blew out a breath. *Oh. My. Freaking. God. What just happened?* Shan had happened, that was what. Shan had burst in, obviously dying for a pee, and eyed Lizzie like she was chocolate cake. Or kale fritters. Her eyes hadn't just lingered on Lizzie's body, they had camped out for so long Lizzie should charge rent. And that was just the very modest areas of skin above and below the towel. Who knew what Shan had thought when she saw Lizzie's naked bottom?

Lizzie dropped the towel and reached for the body lotion then smoothed it over her skin. She was the one who should be embarrassed. Shan probably saw naked women all the time.

And her own reaction. Lizzie's lips twitched. The little curl of delight was because Shan had reacted in a way that made her attraction obvious. Lizzie did a little cha-cha-cha step in time with a hip shake.

This could change things between them. She stopped mid-dance step. It *could* change things, but that didn't mean it *should* change things. Shan was a temporary housemate, whose everyday life was far away from Lizzie's own. In a galaxy far, far away, if she was honest. And Shan didn't even seem to like her that much. Her prickliness made it clear she only tolerated Lizzie for what she was offering her. No. Lizzie shook her head. She'd take the ego boost of Shan's reaction and move on. Shan was only passing through. Falling for her would lead to heartbreak as surely as Dee would have to pay for the Bentley's damage.

As Dee said, falling for housemates was nearly as bad as falling for clients. Lizzie put extra lotion on her shins. She should stay away. Pretend Shan's fluster and clumsiness was because she needed to pee.

Shan was a temporary part of her life, and she needed to remember that.

Chapter 11

One Paw at a Time

"THE SURGERY WENT WELL." DR GUPTA peered at Shan over his half-moon glasses. "I'm confident the reconstruction was successful. We'll keep you in overnight, and all being well you can go home tomorrow."

Shan nodded and pushed her flattened hair from her forehead. It felt limp, just as she did.

"Remember, crutches or a knee brace for two weeks. The physio will see you before you leave and give you an exercise sheet. I'll review you in the second week to discuss your progress. Any questions?"

Shan shook her head. Her head spun, woozy with medication, and her knee throbbed a dull rhythm in time with her heartbeat. "Thank you."

Dr Gupta nodded and went to leave, then turned back. "By the way, your ACL had a pre-existing tear. Even if you hadn't taken that spill, you almost certainly would have ruptured it sooner rather than later." He nodded abruptly and left the cubicle, pulling the curtains closed behind him.

An existing tear? That was news. Sure, she'd had knee pain and slight swelling in the past, but she'd coped, and physio had always brought it under control. She touched her knee over the blanket, where it rested on pillows. So the joint had been on borrowed time even before Lizzie had tripped her. She blinked hard as her head swam from the after-effects of the anaesthetic. Even if that accident hadn't happened, something else may have derailed her running career.

Or not. Maybe she could have had months, even years, before it came to surgery. Time enough to get to the Commonwealth Games.

Or not.

How hard it was to second-guess medical conditions, accidents, fate. The karma of the universe, as Dee would say. But, maybe, Lizzie wasn't to blame as much as she'd thought.

Shan closed her eyes. That needed thinking about.

There was no turning back now. No debate about whether to let the knee heal naturally, whether she'd be able to run competitively again. She sighed and turned her face to one side, trying to find a cool spot on the pillow for her flushed cheek. She could only trust the medics. She didn't want to think about if they were wrong. A life without running, without the pounding of her feet on the track, of her muscles burning, her heart pounding so hard in her chest that it seemed it might break free. Of the exhilaration of the finish. Of winning. Of being a success. Of giving up so much for one goal.

The Olympics.

She squeezed her eyes tight, but still a tear trickled down her cheek. It would be all right. Exercises, pain meds, rehabilitation, training. That was her future now for the next few months. She clenched her fists so hard her nails dug into her palm. She'd worked hard; now she'd just have to work harder.

Tomorrow, she'd go home. No, not home, but to Lizzie's house. To the cosy bedroom with the most comfortable bed she'd ever slept in. To Presto, who even after a week would still only peer warily at her from the other side of the room. And to Lizzie and her sunny smile and kind nature and glorious body.

It could be worse.

"I made a welcome home dinner," Lizzie said as she helped Shan out of the car. "Lasagne—it just needs reheating—and salad. Dessert."

Shan paused for a minute as her head spun, still woozy from the meds. "It sounds like heaven after the sandwich I had at the hospital."

"I'm glad." Lizzie's smile peeped out.

Shan manoeuvred onto a stool at the counter, watching as Lizzie poured two glasses of water. Her head swam with fog, and every muscle in her body ached as if she'd run the Melbourne marathon instead of lying in a hospital bed. The thought of Lizzie's dinner was appealing, but the thought of the comfortable couch was more so.

For a moment, she pictured her apartment in Parkville. It was basic where Lizzie's house was cosy, spartan against comfortable. And it was up six flights of stairs which right now would be an impossibility. Dr Gupta's words about her knee tumbled through her mind. Lizzie wasn't really to blame. A twinge of remorse shafted through her chest. She hadn't been the nicest to Lizzie.

"Thank you." She said the words on a sigh. "For looking after me like this."

Lizzie's smile flashed. "It's really no trouble. And you gave me an excuse to cook lasagne."

"I'll have to think of some way to repay you."

"I don't want money, Shan."

"Some other way." She forced her gaze to remain on Lizzie's face, not allowing it to drop to the soft-looking skin of her throat where the pulse beat strongly underneath her infinity pendant.

"Really, you don't—" Her eyes widened. "Don't look around, don't move, but you're about to get a visit from Presto."

Shan froze on the stool and dropped her gaze enough that she could just about make out the reddish-brown fur of Presto's head and his ears at half-mast. He crept forward, one tiny step at a time until he was level with her leg.

"Don't look at him or address him directly," Lizzie said. "But say something to me in a soft voice. Anything. And hang your hand down by your side so he can sniff it if he wants."

"I wonder if it's rhubarb crumble for dessert. Midnight Oil is the greatest Australian band ever, and that blue T-shirt you're wearing looks good on you." She slowly dropped her hand.

"I made a coconut cake for dessert," Lizzie said in equally soft tones. "You're wrong about Midnight Oil. Give me Courtney Barnett every time. And this old T-shirt is one I wear for working in the yard, so you can save the flattery."

"I once saw Courtney in a coffee shop in Northcote. We were in line together, but I was too starstruck to say anything. What's Presto doing now? I daren't look."

"Standing there. Pondering."

A wet nose touched Shan's palm and sniffed up to her wrist and down the back of her hand. She fought not to react. Then, a furry body pressed against the calf of her uninjured leg. A human-sounding sigh wafted as Presto sat.

"What should I do?" Shan asked.

"Move your hand very slowly toward him from the side. See if he'll let you touch him on the shoulders or the base of the neck. If he flinches, draw back. And keep talking but use his name now."

"Hello, Presto. It's a good name for you. May I pet you? Gently. I'm not going to hurt you." Shan inched her fingers toward him, stopping when the tips brushed his shoulder. She paused, giving him time to move away, but he remained. She gently petted his shoulder and ruffled the short fur at the base of his neck.

"That's enough touching for now," Lizzie said. "Presto is the goodest boy, the bestest doggo. Are you comfortable if he wants to stay there?"

"Mm." The touch of his warm body against her leg was comforting. It was as if he knew she was injured—maybe he did. She glanced down at the cigarette burns on his back. Lizzie had said the hair wouldn't grow back.

"I think I want a glass of wine after that." Lizzie wiped the back of her hands across her eyes. "I'm a bit emotional. Do you realise that's the first time Presto's initiated contact since he's been here?"

Warmth spread through Shan's chest. It was for Presto, yes, with his big step forward, but it was also for Lizzie. She was the sun, the heat, and light around which they both revolved.

Lizzie splashed wine into her glass and topped up Shan's water. "*Yamas.*"

"Cheers."

They clinked glasses.

"Here's to Presto creeping out of his shell. And here's to you, on the first big step to recovery."

Shan heaved a breath. Suddenly, it all seemed possible. With Lizzie as her support, why, she could do anything.

Chapter 12

Free Beer Tomorrow

LIZZIE RUMMAGED IN THE WARDROBE, pulling out her running shorts and a long-sleeve wicking top. Where were her running shoes? On hands and knees, she pushed aside work shoes, slippers, and going-out shoes, until she found them pushed into a corner. She laced herself into them, found her running watch in the bedside drawer, pulled her hair into a ponytail, and crept out the front door.

It was still dark, but that was okay, it would cover what was going to be a pathetic attempt at a run. The last time she'd gone had been the fateful time when Shan had tumbled into her life. This wasn't going to be pretty, but she had to try.

Seeing Shan struggling so hard to get back on the track was a guilt trip in itself. Shan wanted so desperately to run again—but couldn't. Lizzie could run anytime she wanted—but wasn't motivated enough. It was too easy to curl into the couch with a book and a glass of red wine, too easy to stay in bed that extra thirty minutes after the alarm went off.

So here she was, shivering in the pre-dawn, ready for her first run in weeks.

She walked to the corner, swinging her arms and warming up her muscles, then turned left. She'd run the block to the next main intersection, do a circuit of the park, and then back home. Maybe two kilometres in total.

Easy, right?

The streetlights cast a yellow glow on the uneven pavement. A couple of early morning commuters let themselves out of their gates and headed for the train. A cat stared at her from atop a gatepost. Lizzie nodded to herself. She could do this.

At the corner, she sprang into a fast trot. Her feet slapped the pavement, arms swinging in time with her feet, breath coming in short, hard pants.

Too fast.

Her breath wheezed in her lungs. Half a block and she was dying. She'd never been a fast runner, more a steady pacer, and already she'd overdone it. She slowed her pace, determined to make the intersection at least.

She made it and dropped gratefully into a walk. The park circuit beckoned. She walked half of it, then ran again, but at her normal steady pace. She was no Shan.

Her legs ached, her ankles felt hot and swollen, and her heart rate was through the stratosphere, but she made it home without walking again. *Bloody hell.* Her throat burned and she wished hard for a glass of water.

Lizzie felt in the zip pocket of her running pants for the key. Nothing. She turned the pocket inside out. Still nothing, except a scrap of crumpled tissue. No doubt, the key was still on the kitchen counter. And of course, she'd never got around to hiding one, no matter how many times she thought she should.

The illuminated dial on her watch said just past seven, and she'd been out for twenty minutes. What to do now? She could sit on the step outside the dark house and shiver until Shan woke up, but that might be another hour, which would make her late for work. Or she could wake Shan. She managed a wry smile; what was the point of a housemate except to let her in when she'd forgotten her key?

Mind made up, Lizzie stepped up to the door and rang the bell. Nothing. No noise, no welcoming lights. She banged twice, cursing her lack of phone, which was no doubt on the counter with her key.

The hallway light came on, and the thump of crutches sounded, echoing on the wooden boards.

"Shan, it's me. I forgot my key."

A mumble came through the door, and then it swung open. Shan stood there, resting on her crutches, dressed in an old T-shirt and not much else. The T-shirt hung to her upper thighs. Was she wearing *anything* underneath? Lizzie averted her eyes, but not before a slow burn started low in her belly. Shan's legs were lean and paler than she remembered. A dressing covered her injured knee and yellow bruising spread above and below it.

"Sorry." Lizzie entered the hall as Shan stood aside. "I didn't mean to get you out of bed."

"S'okay." Shan yawned widely, covering her mouth with her hand. "I should be up anyway. Coffee. Pee. Not necessarily in that order." She did a double take as Lizzie entered the light of the hallway. "Have you been running?"

Lizzie grimaced. "That's being kind. I went for a jog. A lung-burn around the block. Two kilometres tops. And it took me twenty minutes. I need water." She headed for the kitchen.

Shan followed more slowly. "Hey, any attempt at a run is a good attempt." Her lips twisted like a stick of red liquorice. "I envy you."

Lizzie swivelled on her heel, a glass in her hand. "I'm sorry. I didn't mean to rub it in." She filled the glass and emptied it in five great gulps. "I just feel so pathetic. The last time I ran was when you and I met."

"Met? You make it sound like a Tinder date." Shan brushed a hand through her spiky hair and rested her butt on a stool.

Date. Lizzie's stomach gave a little leap that had nothing to do with cold water on an empty stomach. "When I sabotaged you, you mean."

"Better. Why haven't you been running since then? I was wondering."

Lizzie shrugged. "Too much work. Too many things to do. Like a couch that calls my name in the evenings, and a bed that holds me in a siren clasp in the mornings. Plus it's dark at 6.30 a.m. at this time of year."

"Wuss." Shan's eyes twinkled with the good-natured insult. "I used to run at that hour, year-round."

Lizzie went across to Presto's corner and picked up his water bowl. "Hey, Presto." A tail sticking out of the rug thumped once in reply. She opened the rear door and returned to the tap to fill his bowl. "I'd like to be that sort of runner, but I'm lacking in motivation. Not like you." She sighed as she took the bowl back to Presto's corner. "It should have been me, shouldn't it? The one with the busted knee."

"That's a defeatist thing to say." Shan tilted her head to one side. "And not relevant. It wasn't you."

"Mm. But I feel I should use my two sound legs more and shift my arse out the door in the mornings to go for a run. At least twice a week."

Shan slid off the stool and went over to the pad on the fridge. Flicking past the shopping list, she wrote a heading on the next clean page: *Lizzie's Running Plan.* With a quick smile at Lizzie, she added, *Starts Tomorrow.*

Lizzie peered over her shoulder. "That's no good. Like free beer tomorrow, that will never come." Shan's clean and spicy smell made her head spin. How come she smelled so good, having just got out of bed? She rested her hand on Shan's shoulder, feeling the warm hardness of muscle under her hand.

"True." Shan added, *Starts Tuesday, 3 April.*

"Better. Okay, so tomorrow, I'll get out of bed at six-thirty and shuffle around the block again. I can do that."

Shan slanted her a disapproving glance. *Week 1*, she wrote. *Tuesday, 10 minutes running, easy pace, 1 minute walking, 10 minutes running, easy pace.* She kept on writing, filling the lined pad with neat, upright writing.

"There." She laid the pad on the counter. "Your first two weeks. You're running three times a week, not two, but at the end of it, you'll be running four kilometres at a steady pace without stopping. After all, you planned to run five kilometres in a koala suit not so long ago. You can't be that unfit."

"Run and walk," Lizzie muttered.

Shan tapped the pad with the pen. "Still. You can do this. I expect a status report at least twice a week."

A movement in the corner made Lizzie glance across. Presto emerged slowly and shook himself from nose to tail. A cloud of dog hair lifted into the air. With a wary glance in their direction, he crept out the door.

"Kelpies are great running dogs," Shan said. "If Presto ever gains the confidence, he could be a fantastic training partner."

"Nothing like a dog with their heart in their eyes to get you out the door."

Presto returned through the door, but instead of retreating to his rug, he came across to them, one tentative paw at a time. He came up to Shan and pressed against her legs.

"Hey, Presto." She scratched the back of his neck.

Lizzie blinked hard. Presto was the timidest dog she'd ever cared for, but he seemed to be bonding with Shan. She pushed down the stab of envy it wasn't her. Dogs had their reasons and were seldom wrong. "Breakfast. Do you want scrambled eggs?"

Shan looked up, a soft smile painted on her face. "I'd like that. Thank you."

Lizzie grinned back, the warmth in her chest spreading out to tingle along her nerve pathways to her fingertips. Since the surgery, something had shifted with Shan. She still had her moments of introspection, but her prickliness had eased. She'd sheathed her claws. It was almost like they were becoming friends. She pulled the eggs from the fridge and a bowl from the cupboard.

Shan limped over to get the bread and slid four slices into the toaster, then grabbed the Vegemite from the cupboard. Old Shan had a cloud of gloom around her. New Shan seemed lighter.

"Something's changed about you." The words popped out of her mouth before she could second-guess them. "You seem more relaxed. Was it the surgery going well?"

Shan halted and turned to face Lizzie. "I didn't realise it was that obvious." Her mouth turned down and she tossed the Vegemite jar from hand to hand. "I'm relieved the surgery went well, but it was something more than that. And I should have told you before now."

Lizzie waited, but when Shan didn't say anything, she started cracking eggs into the bowl and found the whisk. Shan would talk when she was ready.

Shan cleared her throat. "I need to apologise to you. I know I've been difficult to live with." She hunched her shoulders. "I could have been nicer to you. Especially when you're doing so much for me."

Lizzie was quiet. It seemed there was more to come, and she didn't want to interrupt the flow of words.

"You know I blamed you for the accident, for ruining my career. But"—she heaved a breath—"the accident wasn't altogether your fault. You were with a section of runners who were going slow. It was reasonable to expect me to take more care. But more than that..." She moved around the breakfast bar so she was opposite Lizzie. "Dr Gupta told me I had a tear in the ligament already. That I was on borrowed time. I could have done any number of things and it would still have ruptured."

Lizzie stared into Shan's face. Sincerity shone from her eyes. A curl of relief coiled out in Lizzie's chest as Shan's words took root there. It wasn't all her fault. Shan likely would have ended up with the same injury eventually. And, importantly, Shan now acknowledged that fact. The guilt she'd been feeling unwound itself from her heart.

"Thank you for telling me. I'd been worried. Feeling terrible."

"I know. And it wasn't fair to let you keep believing you were mainly responsible. If this means, guilt absolved, and you want to throw me out of your house, I understand."

"Let me think about it for two seconds." Lizzie stared down at the eggs. "Maybe not. You're not much trouble. When you're not sniping at me, you're easy to get along with. Presto likes you." She peeped sideways. "I like you. And if you're now not going to be shitty with me, I'll like you more."

"You do? Despite me being a bitch at times?"

"Not those times. But generally, yeah. I'm not reneging the offer, Shan—and you still couldn't manage those stairs. Don't mention staying with Celia. We both know that's not going to happen."

"It could, if I actually asked her."

"Or you could continue staying with me. If you want to." Lizzie wrinkled her nose. She should be delighted Shan was offering to move out, to get her spare bedroom back. But it was true—she liked Shan. There was no reason for her to move out.

"Then thank you. I'd love to stay on."

Lizzie nodded and the heat in her chest exploded into a smile. "Good. Presto's glad as well." She glanced at Presto, sitting patiently facing them.

They could both get used to having Shan around.

Chapter 13

Doga

SHAN GRUNTED AS SHE WORKED through the exercises the physio had set. Challenge yourself, the woman had said as she'd massaged Shan's knee, easing the knots and kinks of the supporting muscles. Shan did. She wouldn't get back out in her running shoes if she took things too easy—Pieter had drilled that into her when she'd called with an update.

Presto lay on the ground near her head. "I've seen a dog on YouTube that does yoga," she said to him. "I think the least you could do is attempt my stretches along with me."

He blinked and inched closer to rest his damp nose on her neck.

The doorbell rang as she finished her final repetition. Carefully, she got to her feet and walked gingerly down the hall, Presto following a pace behind. Who needed a shadow when you had a dog?

The bell rang a second time as she reached it, and she yanked the door open.

Presto took an abrupt detour into Lizzie's room. His nose poked out from behind the open door.

Celia, dressed in her work clothes of dark pants and white tunic, held up a plastic bag with two takeaway containers inside. "Home delivery." She came inside and pressed a kiss to Shan's cheek. "I've taken a client to an occupational assessment in Clifton Hill, and I didn't have to stay. So I thought you might like lunch."

"Thank you. That's great. I hadn't got around to making anything yet."

Celia walked into the kitchen, where she started pulling bowls from the cupboard as if she, not Shan, had lived there for the past few weeks.

"Oh." She stopped, her hand in the cutlery drawer. "Is Lizzie here? I didn't think. I just brought two portions."

"She's in the office today."

Celia pulled out forks and returned to the cupboard, where she perused Lizzie's array of condiments, selecting two types of chilli sauce. She swung around to fix her gaze on Shan's face. "I haven't heard much from you."

"Nor me from you. Not since you called after my surgery nearly three weeks ago." Shan smiled to soften the comment. That was Celia all over. If a person didn't fit into her life, she tended to drift away.

"Sorry," Celia said. "Things have been crazy; you know how it is. You said then it went well. How's things since?"

"I'm healing well, according to the doctor. I've started physio, and I'm walking without crutches. Still have months of rehab, of course."

"That sucks. Will you keep your sports funding?"

"Yes, apparently so. It's enough to get by on—just. I have to be careful though, now that I don't have a job."

"I wish you could take on some of my job." Celia's mouth turned down at the corners. "That's what's kept me too busy to see you. And running, of course. The Commonwealth Games trials are this weekend."

"I know," Shan murmured. *As if I could forget that.* "How are you feeling about it?"

Celia drummed her fingers on the countertop. "Nervous. Wound up."

"That's a good way to be. Just hold on to that. When do you fly out?"

"Thursday. A day to rest up, then the trial is Saturday."

"Good luck." Shan opened the containers and started spooning chicken and rice into two bowls.

"I think I've a good chance of making the team. Now that you're out, it'll be between me and Lucy for the final place."

A grey mist settled in Shan's head. Yeah, she was out of contention and with an uphill battle ahead of her that resembled Frodo's climb to the Cracks of Doom if she wanted to have any chance of getting back to the top. Of making the Olympic trials, let alone selection. She swallowed hard against the lump in her throat. "Yeah, I'm out."

Celia dropped the cutlery to the counter with a clatter. Her face twisted, and she came around to Shan to envelop her in a hug. "I'm sorry, that was tactless. I wish you were going to be there too."

Her embrace radiated comfort and warmth. Shan sighed and rested her cheek against Celia's shoulder, slipping her arms around her lean waist. "There's no point thinking of what could have been." Her words were muffled by Celia's body. "I just have to move on."

Move on. She had to, and that included from Celia's open wish for a relationship between them. Even now, her hand was trailing down Shan's back, comfort becoming a caress. It would be too easy to take what Celia offered—but it was not the right thing for her, and it would be unfair to Celia. But for a moment, as Celia stroked gentle paths across her clothing, she was tempted.

Shan moved out of Celia's embrace. "We should eat the food before it gets cold."

Celia's mouth formed an O of surprise. "That's why microwaves were invented. Or we could go to your room. I'm leaping out of my skin with energy. I'd make it good for you."

She would. A flash of memory surfaced of their one and only time. Of coming hard against Celia's mouth. Pre-race sex energised Celia, and she was a generous lover. For a second, Shan hesitated. The image of a kiss rose in her mind. But it wasn't Celia's wild hair she imagined stroking, nor was it Celia's mobile lips that enticed her. Lizzie's shiny hair would slip through her fingers like strong silk; her full lips that curved upward so often were the ones Shan was imagining in the kiss.

Celia stared at her, an eyebrow lifted in question.

Lizzie. It must be the proximity of living so closely with her. Lizzie wasn't her type…was she? Shan forced a smile. "I'm sorry, but it's still a no."

For a second, she thought Celia was going to argue, but instead she nodded. "You can't blame a girl for trying."

"I don't." She reached for Celia's hand, squeezed, and released it. "Now let's eat. I'm starving." Relief shuffled through her chest at Celia's casual acceptance of the refusal, and she pushed the mental image of Lizzie aside.

"So how's it going with Lizzie?" Celia picked up her fork.

"Well. She's very easy-going. Pleasant to live with—she respects my space—and she's been driving me to the physio." Her mouth turned down. "I don't get out of the house much, apart from that, but it's lovely to sit in the backyard in the sun."

"Mm. This is a great place to live. I'm quite envious. All those bars and nightclubs for women around here. It's one of the gayest parts of Melbourne!"

"So Lizzie says."

"Isn't she straight?" Celia's gaze turned assessing.

"Bi."

"Oh-ho." Celia lifted an eyebrow. "I might have to visit more often."

Celia would eat Lizzie alive. A sour taste flooded her mouth at the thought. She hunted for a distraction, anything to get Celia's mind away from Lizzie. "Remember Presto, the rescue dog? Oh! I forgot him. He's probably still hiding in her room. Stay there while I go and check."

"I do remember him." Celia's gaze softened. "He's a darling. Go find him, then come and tell me how he's going."

Shan limped up the hallway. Lizzie's door was closed. She frowned. Maybe it had swung shut, or Presto had knocked it.

"Presto," she called softly. "Are you okay?"

A tiny whine answered her.

Slowly, Shan pushed the door open and entered. A toppling mountain of pillows threatened to overflow the bed, and various clothes were draped over the foot of it, as if Lizzie hadn't been able to decide what to wear that morning. Her running shoes cosied up to a pair of high heels in the corner. Presto was not to be seen.

"Presto?"

Another whine answered her.

She walked around the bed and Presto belly-wiggled to greet her. Careful of her injured knee, Shan sat on the edge of the bed and held her hand out to him. He came and pushed against her legs. "I think you should come with me, fella. Celia won't hurt you. Gotta be better than being shut in here."

She caressed the back of his neck and shoulders as he liked, then stood and walked slowly to the door.

Presto followed her, keeping close, down the hall and into the living area.

"Don't talk loudly," she warned Celia.

Celia held a hand out low. "Hello, Presto, you sweetheart, would you like to say hello to me?"

Slowly, the dog advanced until his nose touched Celia's hand.

"Good boy," she crooned, and her fingers inched over to stroke his chest.

Shan smiled. She and Presto were both healing in their own time, in their own ways.

Chapter 14

Accurate 9,000

LIZZIE BENT DOUBLE, TRYING TO catch her breath. Air rasped in and out of her lungs, and her thigh muscles burned, but not enough to quench the glow of achievement.

She let herself into the house. Music played faintly from the living area. Lizzie bounced down the hallway and burst into the room.

"I did it!" Even her sweaty face and tired limbs didn't matter in the euphoria of success.

Shan sat up from the floor where she'd been doing her exercises. Presto rose to his haunches from where he'd been lying next to her. Both eyed her expectantly.

"You're looking at a woman who just ran four kilometres with no walk break. Ta dah!" Lizzie flung her arms out. Her feet bounced a tattoo on the wooden floor in a little happy dance.

"Well done!" Shan's face split into a grin. "How do you feel?"

"Like the gold medal is within my grasp. Or at least a start with the runners not the walkers in the next fun run."

"When is it?"

Lizzie shrugged. "No idea. I haven't entered for anything. But when I do, it would be nice to run the five kilometres in under thirty minutes. Know anyone who can help me do that?"

They shared a grin.

"I know just the person," Shan said. "We'll make a training plan. If we increase the distance you run, the speed will come."

"Okay." Lizzie went to the sink to pour a glass of water. "You're the expert. But right now, I'm going for a short walk to cool down. Want to come? Just to the end of the street and back."

"Absolutely. Let's go."

Lizzie opened the front door and stepped out, then turned to see where Shan was.

Presto stood next to her, eyeing the front gate. When Shan came out, he followed.

Lizzie tilted her head. "Maybe Presto will come too. Let me grab a leash for him."

When the three of them stepped onto the road, Presto stayed so close Lizzie almost tripped over him. His ears flattened on his head, but he didn't hesitate.

Rehab 101. This walk will be good for all of us.

They kept a slow pace to accommodate Shan. Lizzie kept her gaze on Presto as he gradually relaxed until his ears were bouncing with each pace. Every so often, he'd turn and look up at both of them as if to reassure himself they were still there.

"Look at him," she said to Shan. "He's already so much happier." She peeped sideways. "You helped him with that. Being there in the day for him, talking to him. I heard you encouraging him to mimic your stretches. He loves the company."

"Still haven't got him to do yoga," Shan said. "The viral TikTok money-making scheme is so far not a success."

"I've told the shelter he still needs to remain with us...er, me...for a while longer. He's still too nervous for a potential adoption." Lizzie bit her lip, hoping Shan hadn't noticed her slip. It was becoming all too easy to think of her and Shan in the same sentence. Living with someone did that. It was the proximity, Lizzie told herself. Just because they were becoming friends didn't mean more would follow. She rammed her thoughts in another direction—one in which they didn't want to go.

There was a silence as they reached the end of the street then turned around.

"Have you got weekend plans?" Shan asked.

"Dee and I are going to Everyone's Choir tonight." She slanted a glance at Shan. "Want to come? Last I heard, there's still tickets. If we go early, we'll be able to get a seat for you." That was safe, something that friends did.

"Everyone's Choir?" Shan frowned. "I'm not sure I know what that is."

"You dedicated people miss out on so much," Lizzie teased. "Everyone's Choir is great, and you don't have to be Beyoncé to take part—it's just one song. They divide the room into the various parts, you have a few practices, a few drinks, and then we all sing the song together. It's fantastic fun and really uplifting in a way. Being with a bunch of people joining together to make a better outcome. One time we did 'Zombie' by the Cranberries. It was amazing." She focussed on Presto pacing between them. "It's up to you."

"Is it expensive?" Shan looked across at her.

Lizzie bit her lip. She should have mentioned that up front. With Shan not working, she must be watching her dollars. Sometimes, it was like tiptoeing through a minefield, the things she had to avoid. "It's ten bucks to get in, and then you buy any drinks you want."

"Sounds like fun. I'm in."

Shan's sudden smile started a slow burn in Lizzie's chest. She was gorgeous when she cracked a grin like that, her usually serious face lighting up. A flash of memory lit her mind: Shan's gaze scorching a path over her skin when she'd walked in on her in the bathroom. Sometimes, that intensity still flared in Shan's gaze. Lizzie's skin popped into goosebumps.

"Great. I'll let Dee know." Did her voice sound normal? She hoped so.

They reached the house and went inside.

"Want me to make breakfast while you shower?" Shan asked. "In the spirit of our new accord and all that?"

"Is that a polite way of saying I smell sweaty?"

"You do, but that doesn't bother me. Locker rooms are full of worse sweat than yours. No, I just thought you'd appreciate the hot shower now, rather than later. And I'm starving!"

"That would be great. Thank you."

Lizzie went into her room and stripped off her shorts and T-shirt. Wrapped in a towel, she headed back to the bathroom. Shan had her head in the fridge. Eggs and mushrooms already sat on the counter.

The hot shower was delicious on her tired muscles. Lizzie shampooed her hair, turning her face up to the spray. The water was like a caress. She sighed. Shan's face leaped into her mind, wearing a smile, not her serious expression. What would Shan be like as a lover?

Lizzie shook her head to clear the water from her ears. She was losing it, thinking about her housemate like that. But as she stroked shower gel down her legs, her mind spun to Shan's legs—leaner, more muscular, tougher than hers—and her breath caught in her throat. She would love to feel that strength under her fingertips. But Shan's focus was on greater things, and Lizzie had already mentally listed the reasons why she needed to stop thinking about Shan that way. She should write out the list and stick it on the bedroom mirror so she'd see it every morning.

When she exited the bathroom, Shan had her back to her, and something was sizzling on the stove. Lizzie went to get dressed.

She was pulling on her socks and snuggly sheepskin boots when her phone rang. She glanced at the screen. *Oh.* Her spirits dived, taking up residence in her boots. Her mother.

Familiar guilt pulsed in her throat, but Lizzie pushed it down. She'd made peace with her decision to move to Melbourne a long time ago, and for the most part she could live with that. But the echoes of that guilt sounded in Mumma's ringtone.

She accepted the call. "Hi, Mumma."

"Elisabet, I know you are a busy working woman"—her mother always made it sound like a shameful thing—"but your *baba*, he misses you. He misses your smile, and your caring nature."

"I miss you both too."

"When will you come and visit? You haven't come for nearly two months now."

Lizzie closed her eyes as the suppressed feelings threatened to swamp her once again. When would she visit? As if Sydney was the next suburb, not a seven-hour drive, or a flight.

"I'll see when I can get time off work."

"Maybe next month?"

"I hope so. I'll try."

A movement at the door of her room caught her eye, then Presto's nose and soulful eyes came into view around the door. He blinked at her then retreated. Gone to tell Shan she was on the phone? Lizzie's lips twitched at the thought.

"Independence is all very well, but you must put your family first. We need you."

Lizzie closed her eyes. If she let it, this conversation would continue for an hour or more, around and around in circles of blame and shame, never moving on. Often, she let Mumma talk, as if the time on the phone could replace her absence from Sydney. But not today. "I'm happy you called, Mumma, but I can't talk now. My housemate has cooked breakfast, and it's getting cold. I'll call you soon."

"Housemate?" Mumma's voice sharpened like steel. "A man or a woman?"

"Woman. She's staying with me for a few weeks only. I must go. Love you." She ended the call before Mumma could question her more about her sudden housemate. She threw the phone on the bed and went down to the kitchen.

Shan flashed her a smile. "Sit and eat. I've kept it warm."

Lizzie pressed the button for coffee, and as the machine went through its familiar grinding and whirring, she sat at the table.

Shan placed a warm plate in front of her and returned for her own.

"This looks amazing." Lizzie's mouth watered at the enticing smell of bacon.

"The eggs are a little tough from the oven."

"I don't care. It's wonderful having someone cook for me."

Shan ducked her head. "It's nothing. After all you've done for me." She went to retrieve Lizzie's coffee.

Lizzie blinked. Since the surgery—and what she'd shared about her knee injury—Shan had been a lot more relaxed. She tried a mouthful of eggs. "This is delicious."

For a few moments, they both tucked into their breakfasts in silence.

Lizzie took a sip of coffee. "That was Mumma on the phone. She always manages to call at bad times, and I can't just get rid of her."

"Family. Never there when you want them, always in your ear when you don't."

"They want me to come home and visit." She slipped a piece of bacon under the table to Presto. "I like to see them, but they make it hard to leave. I'll go later in the year—if I can resist the pressure that long."

"Are you out to them?" Shan tilted her head.

"No. That's one thing I'm not prepared to unload on them—yet. I will, when the time is right. I couldn't bring myself to tell them about Sonia, and that made things difficult between us. Her parents were lovely and accepted me as Sonia's partner. To my parents, she was a housemate they never met." Lizzie met Shan's eyes. "I've sworn not to do that again. If I have anyone special in my life, I'll introduce them as my partner. But until then…I'm keeping the peace."

"You have to wait until the time is right for you." Shan nodded. "So no temptation to move back?"

"None. My life is here now. But Mumma pours on the guilt, and it gets to me. I haven't even worked out how to keep the guilt for things like pinching Dee's stapler at work." She peeped sideways at Shan. "And for flattening elite athletes."

Shan laughed. "I think you've worked off the debt for that one. Dee and the stapler though… You're on your own." She crunched a piece of bacon.

"Dee thinks I hammer the top too hard which is why mine keep breaking. She's probably right, but it's so *satisfying*, thwacking the top with a fist." The tightness in Lizzie's chest eased with the change of subject.

Shan mimed zipping her lips. "Your guilty secret is safe with me. What time are we leaving tonight?"

"That depends. Dee suggested we eat on the way. There's an Italian place that does amazing gnocchi. It's up to you. We can eat at home if you prefer."

Shan bit her lip. "Would you mind if we ate here first? I don't mean to be a cheapskate, but with no job, I'm really watching what I spend."

"Sure. We can do that. Dee can come here." Lizzie tilted her head. "You know, where I work, we don't just hire for office jobs. Many jobs are work-from-home."

Shan propped her chin on her hand. "Like what?" Her intense hazel eyes, alight with interest, bored into Lizzie.

Lizzie suppressed a shiver. Shan's absolute focus sent a twist of warmth down her spine. "I'm always looking for medical transcribers. You need to pass a medical terminology test and have an accurate eighty words per minute."

Shan shook her head. "I don't know a humerus from a funny person. I certainly don't know how to spell it."

"Then there's various cold-calling sales jobs. No prior experience necessary, but it's base plus commission and it's hard to make a reasonable wage, especially at first. And I'm still looking for a data entry person. Accuracy rates higher than speed, and it's mainly numeric, entering figures into a database."

"What sort of speeds are you looking for?"

"Nine thousand keystrokes per hour. That's fairly low for numeric data, but they're after ninety-seven per cent accuracy." She ate the last mushroom and pushed her plate to one side.

"When I was at uni, I worked in various departments to help pay my way. I did data entry in the sports department, entering race times and so on. I got to be really accurate. It was a few years ago, of course, so I'm rusty, but I think I could come close to what you're after."

"Really? How about you practice this weekend and do the tests on Monday or Tuesday? You can do them from home. You're supposed to have a face-to-face interview in the office, but I reckon I can waive that. Does your laptop have a numeric keypad?"

Shan nodded. "It would be fantastic if I could get the job. Is the pay okay?"

Lizzie gave the rate and watched Shan's eyes light up. She was kicking herself. It had never occurred to her to ask if she could help Shan with work. She'd made the stupid assumption that Shan could run and make a decent mochaccino and nothing else.

"That's more than I earned in the coffee shop. Lizzie, you're amazing!"

Shan's smile sent a frisson of heat down to Lizzie's toes. Her eyes sparkled, and faint laughter lines bracketed her mouth. She fondled Presto's ears, and the dog looked up at her adoringly.

How had Lizzie ever thought her standoffish or prickly?

"You haven't passed the tests yet."

"I'll pass them. I'll find some practice tests online. Guess that's what I'm doing this weekend—well, apart from Everyone's Choir."

"Don't bail on me for that!"

"I won't." Shan reached across the table and clasped Lizzie's fingers. "I'm looking forward to it." Her thumb made a quick one-two pass over Lizzie's palm.

The slight friction, Shan's expression, the touch of her skin—Lizzie suppressed a shiver. "I can..." She cleared her throat. "I can point you to some good practice tests."

"Thank you. Again. I wish...I wish I could do half as much for you as you're doing for me."

"I'll think of something." Lizzie was drowning in Shan's clear eyes. An image shot into her mind of Shan kissing her. She shook her head trying to dislodge it, but it remained: Shan's lips welded to hers, their tongues moving together in a sensual dance.

Shan removed her hands and stood. "Would you mind showing me now?"

Showing her now? Showing what? Kisses? Lizzie stared, her mind a fizzing blank sheet of white.

"The tests," Shan prompted.

"The tests. Right." *Of course. What else could she be possibly be talking about?* "Sure. Grab your laptop while I clear up here."

Shan disappeared to her room, and Lizzie cleared the breakfast debris away to make room on the table, her mind humming on overdrive.

Chapter 15

No Swinging from the Chandelier

"I hope we get something loud and happy." Dee squinted at the line in front of them as they shuffled toward the entrance of the Overlander Hotel. "That Leonard Cohen song last time nearly put me in a coma."

"Anything is good with me," Shan said. "Seeing as I have nothing to compare it to." She balanced on her crutches and hopped another pace closer to the door. After mostly being without them at home lately, the crutches felt strange and cumbersome in her armpits.

"Are you okay?" Lizzie took her arm.

"Yeah. You know I don't really need them."

"The Leonard Cohen song made Lizzie cry," Dee said. "All those hallelujahs. I think she's a closet evangelical."

"Am not. My parents would kill me. Greek Orthodox or nothing."

"The nothing suits you well." Dee nudged her side. "Now, let's get some benefit out of Shan's situation. I didn't tell you to bring your crutches for nothing." With a wink at the others, she headed along the line to where the door people were checking tickets. A minute later, she returned. "Follow me. Because of gimpy here, they're letting us jump the line. You can thank me later with a drink."

Once inside the large music venue, Dee made a beeline for a table alongside the wall. Plonking her butt on a stool, and her bag on the table, she sent them a beaming smile that could have rivalled the stage spotlights. "Mine's a pint of cider."

Lizzie dumped her bag on the table and pulled out her wallet. "Shan?"

Shan considered. The pleasure of a glass of wine warred with her dwindling bank balance. But if she got the data entry job... No. That wasn't a guarantee. "I'll sit out your shouts if you don't mind. I'll just have a mineral water."

"I'll get your water." Lizzie disappeared in the direction of the bar.

Shan watched her retreat, enjoying the view of her curvy backside encased in tight, black jeans. Her gorgeous hair swung loose and reached nearly to her waist.

Dee nudged her arm and held out a tissue.

"What's that for?" With an effort, Shan dragged her gaze back to Dee.

Dee blew upwards so her fringe bounced on her forehead. "Please. Give me some credit for having eyes. It's to wipe the drool off the table as you stare at Lizzie's arse."

"Oh." The slow burn of embarrassment crept up Shan's chest. "Um...yeah. I guess I was looking."

"S'ok. I'd wonder if you didn't, you being of the female-attracted persuasion and all. Lizzie is gorgeous. Objectively speaking, that is. I like a partner with a stick-outie bit."

Shan flicked another glance toward the bar. No sign of Lizzie. She redirected her gaze back to Dee. "Guess I won't try to hook you up with any of my running friends then."

"No, thanks. Not if their stick-outie bits are on their chests. Although, I once had a boyfriend who had a fine pair of A cups."

"Are you on the hunt?"

Dee's expression turned inwards. "Hopefully not. There's a gorgeous engineer, who, if he got the job he went for, will be off our books and free for me to grab with both hands. He had a third interview. He should hear any day."

"Good luck."

"Now, you and Lizzie." Dee pinned Shan with a laser gaze. "Are you tempted?"

Shan massaged her bad knee while she thought. How to answer that? Anything she said would doubtless get relayed to Lizzie, and that could be all kinds of awkward. "Lizzie's lovely," she said when the silence stretched too long. "But we're just friends."

Dee made a rude noise. "Don't buy it. Your eyes were glued to her arse."

"I'm not looking for a relationship. Once my rehab is over, my training will intensify. I need to get back to the level I was at."

"If you say so." Dee sat back in her chair. "About time!" She directed her raised voice to Lizzie returning with drinks. "I'm about to die of dehydration."

Lizzie set the plastic glasses on the small table. "People were three-deep at the bar. And if you're dehydrated, you should drink water."

"I'll start with cider." Dee grabbed it and took a mouthful.

Lizzie pushed the mineral water over to Shan and picked up the remaining plastic cup. "*Yamas*."

"Gotta lubricate the vocal cords." Dee set the glass down. "And lose some inhibitions. The point of Everyone's Choir is to let go and sing, not worry if you're in tune. Lizzie will need at least another couple of vinos."

Shan sipped her water. Already she was regretting not choosing wine, finances be damned.

"We may have filled the data entry position," Lizzie said to Dee. She nodded at Shan. "Guess who was holding out on me. Shan tested at 8,600 keystrokes this afternoon, with good accuracy. Some more practice, and she'll ace the test."

"Really?" Dee turned glowing eyes at Shan. "Fantastic! The previous person lasted three days."

Shan wiggled on her stool. She'd make damn sure she did better than that. The job, if she got it, was a lifesaver. She picked up her water. Someone jogged her arm and the liquid splashed on her pants. She grinned at Dee. "I'll take that tissue now."

Dee winked and handed it over.

"It's filled quickly. We must be starting soon." Lizzie glanced around at the crowded room and the low-lit stage.

"There's probably a couple hundred people here." Shan, too, looked around. Teenagers jostled elbows with pensioners, and there was every age in between.

The background music lowered, and the stage lights rose. The band took their places on stage, and the drummer slid into place. A drag queen wearing an off-the-shoulder sequined ball gown that sparkled in the lights stepped in front of the microphone and flung her arms wide.

"Welcome one and all to Everyone's Choir. I'm Lotta Brests, your hostess with the mostest. And tonight we will make merry, make friends, and sing our little hearts out." Her scarlet lips pouted. "And what song will we be singing?"

"As long as it's not John Farnham, I don't care," Lizzie muttered.

Above Lotta's head, the screen lit up. "Ladies, gentlemen, nonbinary persons, and those who prefer not to identify. Tonight we will be singing 'Chandelier' by the golden-voiced queen of mystery, Sia."

"Fantastic!" Dee bounced off her stool. "I'm going to the bar before everyone else has the same idea. Shan, what do you want?"

"I'm fine thanks." She caught Lizzie's knowing look and shrugged. "You know my reasons."

"I do." Lizzie grinned and waggled her eyebrows at Dee, who headed for the bar. "We pay weekly. Hopefully, next time we go out you'll have one reason less."

On the stage, Lotta was dividing the room. "Sopranos to the left, bass to the right, everyone else in the middle."

"Lucky we're in the squeaky-voice section," Lizzie said. "I don't think I could manage a deep voice. Not that it really matters. People move around and sing the part they want to."

"But there's only one vocal part."

"You'll be amazed what they have us sing. All the la, la, las, and humming, and even some of the instrumental parts. When we did AC/DC we even did the bagpipes. It was amazing."

"There's some high parts in 'Chandelier'." Shan nodded at a group of blokes making their way across to the soprano section. "They could struggle."

"That's part of the fun."

Dee pushed her way through the crowd, a drink in each hand. "Here. I only spilled a little. I got you a large one, Lizzie, in case you want to share with anyone." She winked at Shan.

Lizzie peeped at Shan from under her thick lashes. "Now, who would I share with?"

Shan's pulse picked up. Lizzie's eyes tilted up in the most alluring, flirtatious way. Had Dee said anything? Impossible; she hadn't been alone with Lizzie this evening. Lizzie must be tipsy. Or... Shan's mind unravelled to the time she'd accidentally walked in on Lizzie in the shower. Her golden glow, the impossibly smooth skin on her back, the dimple at the base of her spine. "I don't know. Maybe you have a friend who'd like a mouthful."

Lizzie choked on her drink. "A mouthful. Of what?" Her eyes flashed sparks in Shan's direction.

Heat crawled up Shan's neck once more. "Of wine. Not anything else. What did you think I meant?"

Lizzie set down her drink and pushed it across to Shan. "Never mind. You're such fun to tease."

Teasing, was it? Shan picked up the drink and turned it so that she could set her lips to the part of the rim where Lizzie had drunk. She flicked the rim with her tongue, then took a dainty sip. Two could play at that game.

Lizzie's eyes darkened and her gaze never left Shan's lips as she took another sip then set the drink down.

"They're starting." Dee, who luckily hadn't been paying attention, nudged Shan.

She sat back and dragged a deep breath. Lizzie and her lowered gaze that then swept boldly upwards was doing strange things to her insides.

For the next hour, Lotta Brests and her team took them through their parts. When they were deemed as good as they would get, for the first time the parts came together to sing the complete song. As Shan attempted one of Sia's glass-shattering high notes, she glanced across at Lizzie, who was singing lustily but surreptitiously wiping the back of her hand over her eyes. Was she crying?

The song ended in a cacophony of cheers, stamping feet, and applause. Dee pulled both of them into a hug, sending the empty plastic cups flying and one of the stools crashing into the wall. "That was bloody magnificent. Best Everyone's Choir ever!"

"Top one out of one for me," Shan said. "What about you, Lizzie?"

Lizzie sniffed. "Fantastic." She wiped her eyes again.

Shan moved closer. "Are you okay?" Her hand found Lizzie's free one and she squeezed.

"Yeah. Everyone's Choir always gets me emotional. Like finishing fun runs. I sob at both. I think it's the shared achievement."

Shan nodded. That was a thing. She'd bawled like an abandoned toddler the first time she'd run at a state track meet. She tugged Lizzie's hand until she stood in front of her.

Lizzie's lips quivered. Her hand settled on Shan's waist.

Carefully, Shan wiped a gentle thumb under Lizzie's eyes, first one, then the other, collecting the moisture that had gathered there. "It's a good thing to cry. It shows you have empathy. Although I would have known that about you even without you sobbing along with Sia." She dropped her hand to Lizzie's shoulder and moved her thumb in slow circles above the neck of her shirt, then traced the leather cord that held her infinity pendant.

Lizzie's throat worked as she swallowed, and her gaze flew to Shan's face. For a moment, they stared at each other.

Shan's heart pounded. How had it come to this? To two people and a delicate connection stringing between them. To the caress of her thumb on Lizzie's skin—for it was a caress, however much she might disguise it to herself as comfort. To Lizzie's huge, dark eyes, still damp with tears, sending warmth and longing to Shan's own. To a fine thread connecting them, ethereal, but *there*, almost tangible enough for Shan to see it. Her thumb pulsed against Lizzie's neck. Lizzie's hand on her waist, even through clothes, sent a trickle of longing down her spine.

Dee cleared her throat, and the sound jumped Shan back to their surroundings.

"Are you going to devour each other here, or are you going home first?" Dee asked. "I'm sharing an Uber with you, remember?"

Lizzie's lips twitched. "We haven't forgotten, Dee. Do you want another drink, or shall we go?"

"It better be the Uber." Dee whipped out her phone and clicked a few times. "Ordered and on its way. ETA, ten minutes. Think you can hold out that long?"

Lizzie stepped back from Shan's not-quite embrace. "Of course."

Shan's thumb tingled from the lost touch. Lizzie's eyes still held hers, filled with warmth, humour, and something else. A promise? "We're grown women, Dee."

Dee sighed. "Don't mind me. I'm just jealous. The last time I thought someone was looking at me like that, it turned out Margot Robbie was standing behind me." She started heading toward the exit.

Shan retrieved her crutches and followed, using Dee to clear a path. Lizzie walked behind. They came to a halt as the crowd backed up by the exit.

Something soft pushed into Shan's back. She looked over her shoulder. Lizzie was jammed up behind her, full breasts pushed into Shan's shoulder blades. The trickle of heat down her spine became a torrent, threatening to sweep her away.

"Sorry," Lizzie said, breath hot against her ear. "I'm being shoved from behind." One of her hands crept onto Shan's waist and gripped her shirt.

"Anytime." Shan allowed herself a small smile. If this wasn't foreplay, the start of something more, then it had been too long, and she'd forgotten what foreplay was. What would happen when they got home? Her nipples hardened, pushing against her bra. She knew what she'd like to happen. Her heart pounded so hard in her chest she thought it might break out and fly free.

The crowd eased, and slowly they gained the street.

"The Uber's one minute away," Dee said.

When it arrived, Dee jumped into the front seat and gave Lizzie's address.

In the darkness in the back, Shan reached out a hand and found Lizzie's fingers, entwining them with her own.

The drive was only a few minutes, but to Shan it was an eternity before they pulled up outside Lizzie's house.

Lizzie pushed ten dollars to Dee. "Thanks, mate. That's toward the fare. I'll see you Monday." She leaned over the back of the seat to entwine her arms around Dee's neck and press a kiss to her cheek.

Dee whispered something in her ear, and Lizzie laughed and swatted her arm.

They reached the darkened porch, and Lizzie fumbled for her key. The door swung open, and Lizzie turned on the hall light.

"Presto will need to go out." For a few seconds, Lizzie remained, her gaze locked with Shan's. Then, she turned and walked to the rear of the house. Her voice drifted back, talking to Presto, then the rumble of the sliding door opening.

What now? Shan licked her suddenly dry lips. Should she remain in the hall waiting for Lizzie to return? Should she go to bed and leave the door open, for Lizzie to decide what she wanted to do? The seconds stretched to a couple of minutes, and still she hovered indecisively.

Lizzie returned. "Presto's taken care of." She tilted her head and studied Shan. "Did that kill the mood?"

The flare of desire returned to Shan's chest. She propped the crutches against the wall and took Lizzie's hand again. The heat between then jumped up another notch.

"Do you want coffee or anything?" Lizzie asked.

Shan shook her head. She was dying of thirst, but to get water might break the spell again. Instead, she tugged, pulling Lizzie a step closer. One hand settled on Lizzie's waist, the other traced up her arm and around the back of her neck. "I love your hair. It's so thick and healthy. I'd love to feel it on my skin."

Lizzie's eyes darkened. "Maybe you will." She took another tiny step forward and closed the gap between them. The points of her breasts pushed against Shan's own, and her breath puffed on Shan's cheek.

Shan leaned in so she could fit her lips to Lizzie's.

Oh! Sparks flew the second their lips touched. No, they didn't fly, they leaped and twirled and circled in the air above them. Lizzie's lips curved against her own as she flicked at first the upper, then the lower lip with her tongue, tracking their full shape. Then her lips parted, enough that Shan's tongue could trace their inner surface as well.

Lizzie wrapped both arms around Shan's waist and a finger traced the line of bare skin above her jeans in a sizzling pathway.

Shan shivered as a shaft of heat arrowed down between her legs. *Wow.* Maybe it was because it had been months since she'd last kissed anyone, or maybe it was because it was Lizzie, but this was one kiss, one gentle kiss, and she was feeling it down to her toes.

With a soft sigh, Lizzie opened her mouth more and her tongue darted out to trace Shan's lips then delve inside her mouth. Their tongues danced. Lizzie's touch was so scorching it must surely be leaving a mark. With her last gasp of sanity, Shan pushed Lizzie against the wall so she could press their bodies closer. Tighter. Full breasts flattened under her smaller ones. Her hand left the back of Lizzie's neck and traced around the line of her collar, trailing over the impossibly soft skin of Lizzie's neck.

The kiss grew hotter, more urgent, more desirous, until Shan thought her knees would no longer support her. *What now?*

For the first time in a long time, she wanted a hot and satisfying end to the evening. All the reasons she wouldn't normally pursue someone were blown to smithereens. Her running. What running? She didn't have that excuse anymore. For a second, Celia's offer of a no-strings relationship pushed into her head. She hadn't wanted that with Celia. But now, with Lizzie, it was all she could think about. Would Lizzie want the same? They were, after all, housemates, and this would be a layer of complication between them.

She drew back, enough to end the kiss. "What...where do you want to take this?"

Lizzie's breath left her body in a shallow exhale. "What I want, and what I think we should do are different. I want you, Shan. But I think we need to calm this for now. It's not like we'll kiss goodbye in the morning and never see each other again. I don't know if we want the same thing."

Tension pulled Shan's shoulder blades back. Lizzie wanted to talk? Now? What had happened to the kisses heating the air between them and seeing where things went?

She kissed the corner of Lizzie's mouth, her tongue flicking out to taste once more. "Do we have to decide now?"

Lizzie huffed a breath. "I want to push you down on my bed and fuck you. Very much. And very hard. But"—she closed her eyes for a second—"I'm trying to be sensible. We're living together. I don't want things to be awkward."

The air between their bodies now seemed like a chasm. But Lizzie was right. Shan wasn't looking for a relationship, and while she didn't know what Lizzie wanted, it wasn't right to take this further...now. Sanity and clarity. What sensible and thought-out words they were. But they were what was needed.

"I know what I want right now, but... okay." Her skin tingled where Lizzie had touched it, and she wanted nothing more than to say it didn't matter, nothing mattered, other than following Lizzie to her bed.

"That was a spectacular kiss. Mind-blowing. Amazing." Lizzie touched her lips with a finger that trembled. "I want more, Shan, don't think I don't. But this isn't something I can rush into. I don't want to feel uncomfortable in my own home."

"Only if we make it so." The white buzz of arousal still throbbed in Shan's belly, but with every breath she took, it eased. This was Lizzie's space; she was just sharing it for a short time.

"Yes, of course. But it's not just that." She blew out a breath. "I guess what I'm really saying is, I'm not ready for this. Can you give me some time?"

A deep breath. Another. The arousal was now a muted buzz of desire. Not gone. Just banked, like a fire ready to flare. "Of course. You don't have to ask, Lizzie. If we're not both totally into this, then it doesn't happen."

For a long moment, Lizzie remained, indecision flashing in her eyes. Then with a tremulous smile, she leaned in and pressed a kiss to the corner of Shan's mouth. "Thank you for being you. And for being so damn hot." The kiss moved briefly over Shan's lips once more, a quick flash of tongue and a gentle tug on her lower lip, then she stepped back again. "I think I better go to bed. I really enjoyed this evening. Especially the last part." A cheeky grin, and then Lizzie retreated into her bedroom and shut the door.

Alone in the hallway, Shan touched a finger to her lips. Swinging from the chandelier with Sia seemed like a viable option right now. *Lizzie.* She'd known kissing Lizzie would be pleasurable; she hadn't expected for it to be so spectacular. Her skin still prickled, and heat still buzzed in her belly.

How was she supposed to sleep now?

Chapter 16

Selective Memory

Two days later, Shan walked steadily down the street, Presto on his leash pacing beside her. Presto pulled on the leash while walking with Lizzie, but with her, he hung close, as if he knew she was still recovering and couldn't be messed with.

Her knee ached, but the physio exercises were doing their job and it seemed to be getting stronger all the time. She was still strictly barred from doing anything more than walking for a while yet.

Her mobile rang in her pocket, and she fished it out and glanced at the screen. "Hi, Lizzie."

"I've got good news for you. You aced your data entry test this morning and you've got the position. I'll need you to fill out some paperwork, but once that's done, and you've installed the software on your laptop, you can start immediately. Dee will be your point of contact with Best Foot Forward from here on in."

Shan gave a little leap, then stopped herself. *Nothing more than walking.* "That's great! Thank you so much. You got this happening."

"You made the effort with the tests. You'd be surprised at how many people don't bother. I'll bring the paperwork home with me tonight."

Shan's mind buzzed. "How about I cook a celebratory dinner?"

"Microwaved chicken and salad?" Lizzie's voice hummed in amusement.

"Not quite. I have two things I cook when friends come around. I'll do one of them."

"I never pass up on people cooking for me." Shan heard voices in the background. "Oops. Gotta go. I'll see you later."

The call ended, and Shan slipped the phone back into her pocket. "I've got good news, Presto. Shall we walk another block to celebrate?"

Presto cocked his head, watching her steadily.

"I'll have money again. Maybe I'll buy you bacon treats. You'd like that, wouldn't you?"

Presto gave a short woof. No doubt he was agreeing.

A job. Her body felt light, airy, as a load slid from her shoulders. She'd never had much money in the past, but with even less coming in, she hadn't realised how much it was weighing her down—until Lizzie had swooped in and saved her once again.

Lizzie. Her heart skipped a little beat. They hadn't really talked about their kiss. A kiss that had melted the cage around Shan's defences, until all the reasons why it wasn't a good idea for them to... to do what? Romance? Just sex? Friends with benefits? Shan wasn't sure what label to slap on it, but all the reasons why she didn't get involved with anyone because of her running were melting like ice cream in hot coffee.

She reached the corner and turned toward the busier Johnston Street. If she was to cook a decent meal tonight, she'd need ingredients. But Presto would be anxious tied up outside a supermarket. She retraced her steps. She'd come out later by herself.

Back home, she let Presto out into the back yard to enjoy the sunshine and went to sit outside with him. Turning her face to the sun, she drifted back to that kiss. Or That Kiss. It deserved the capitals. Lizzie, so warm, so responsive, so totally in the moment with her. Her toes curled in her shoes. Hopefully, one day soon, they could continue. More kisses. More *more*.

She went back inside. She should practice her data entry. And there were physio exercises to do. Ingredients to buy for dinner.

An insistent ringing from the front of the house made her cock her head. The doorbell rang again as she walked carefully up the hall.

"So you are home." Celia pushed her hands into her pockets. "I was beginning to wonder."

"I was in the back yard. Come in. Want tea?"

"Sure." Celia sat on the stool at the counter. "I thought you'd call me."

Call her? Because... The pieces fell into place with a clunk. *How could I have forgotten?* Guilt slashed through her. "The Commonwealth Games trials! Well...tell me." She flicked the switch on the kettle and dropped teabags into two mugs.

"You can't have cared that much." Celia gave a haughty sniff. "I've been home for a day."

"I'm asking now."

"You probably read it online."

"I've been busy. I honestly haven't looked. Tell me, Celia, what happened?" The kettle boiled and she made the tea.

"What could you possibly have been busy with?" Celia arched an eyebrow. "It's not like you've anywhere to go, anything to do."

The dismissal stung, but Shan acknowledged the truth in it. In normal times, she would have been refreshing the website for updates. And she'd just...forgotten. It had been blown out of her head by Everyone's Choir and data entry tests. And the big one: Lizzie's kiss. But still, they were ordinary things, not things that really mattered as running did. Her stomach turned an uncomfortable circle. What did it mean that she'd *forgotten*?

"I'll tell you later. What happened at the trials?"

Celia's face cracked into a grin, her grumpiness evaporating in an instant. "I made the team. Me *and* Lucy. Ezzy's Achille's tendon issues flared again and she's out. She needs surgery."

"Oh, poor Ezzy." To be so close and so far. "But congratulations to you! That's fantastic." Shan threw her arms around Celia and hugged her close. "I'm really happy for you. Like, really, really happy." She released Celia before the hug could become anything more. "If I can't go to the games, then I'm really glad *you're* going."

The sparkle had returned to Celia's eyes. "Thanks. To be honest, if Ezzy hadn't done her Achilles, I would have missed out. Lucy was that bit faster than me when it mattered."

"She was that day. You've beaten Lucy heaps of times."

"I can't believe it really." Celia hugged her own waist. "I'm going to the Commonwealth Games!"

"And who knows after that."

"The Olympics. I know. Maybe. Now I believe it could possibly happen." Celia slid off the stool and came around behind Shan, wrapping her arms around her shoulders. "You have to get that knee good and strong. Imagine if we both get picked for the next Olympic Games!"

"I'm working on it." On cue, her knee started throbbing, reminding her she needed to do her next set of exercises. A noise in the hallway made her glance around. Must be Presto.

"You'll make it," Celia said. "With this cushy set-up you've got here, and Lizzie to look after your every whim, all you have to do is concentrate on getting well and fit. Watch her though, Shan. She seems the needy sort. I don't think she'll keep running around after you without wanting something in exchange. I think she's after you."

What the hell was Celia thinking? Shan's mouth hung open for a moment. "It's not—"

"Excuse me." Lizzie's voice came from the hall door. It could have snap-frozen the ocean. "I didn't realise I was interrupting."

Shan ducked out from under Celia's arms. "You're not." Her gaze sought Lizzie's. Exactly what had she heard?

Lizzie refused to meet her eyes. "I came to drop off the paperwork for your job so you can start tomorrow. Lucky for you, I was available to run around after your every whim." She threw some papers on the counter and swivelled to face Celia. "I'm glad you set me straight. I'll keep out of Shan's way more often. In case, you know, she thinks I'm *needy.*" Her words held the cutting edge of a razor. She turned on her heel and marched up the hall.

"Lizzie!" Shan hurried toward the hallway. Her heart plummeted to the bottom of her thick socks.

Lizzie stood at the front door. For a second their gazes collided, then Lizzie wrenched open the door and stomped through. The door snapped shut behind her with a bang.

Shan stared at the door for a moment, a chill turning to ice in her stomach. She returned to the kitchen where Celia still stood at the counter.

"Whew." Celia came up behind Shan, rubbing her back in small circles.

Shan moved away. "That was bloody tactless, Celia. And rude. I'm in Lizzie's house and she's been the epitome of kindness. Now she'll think I was the one throwing it back in her face."

Celia shrugged. "It was unfortunate she heard, yeah, but she'll get over it. I'm sure you'll be able to sweet-talk her this evening."

"Did you actually mean what you said?" Shan screwed up her forehead. "Do you think people are just there to dance attendance on the likes of you and me?"

Celia's stare slid away and fixed on the glass doors to the rear yard. "No, of course not."

"At least try to sound like you mean it."

Celia returned to the counter and picked up her bag. "I need to get back to work. Lizzie will be fine; she's only miffed."

Shan gritted her teeth. Being an elite athlete didn't make her or Celia better than anyone else. "You're not a mind reader."

Celia shrugged. "It's training tonight. You should come along sometime to watch. The girls miss you."

"Maybe sometime. Not tonight though." Tonight she had dinner to cook and bridges to rebuild. If she could. An icy trickle of worry slid down her spine.

She walked with Celia to the front door. "Thanks for coming around. And I mean it; I'm delighted for you making the team."

"Thanks." Celia brushed her cheek with a kiss. "I'll call you, okay?"

"Sure."

Shan returned to the kitchen. Celia's untouched tea sat on the counter. She emptied it into the sink. Celia hadn't got around to asking why Shan had been busy, or even how her rehab was going. Were all professional athletes so self-centred? Shan didn't think she was. She hoped not, anyway. She grabbed her mug of tea and went to sit on the couch by the window.

Presto came over and rested his head on her leg, and she caressed his ears.

She stared out at the back yard, at the bright pots filled with colourful plants and the round table and chairs under the shade sail. Disquiet weighted her chest like a stone. Had Lizzie believed Shan agreed with Celia? Surely not after the friendship they were building. After That Kiss. She must have known it was Celia talking... Didn't she?

It was all very well for Celia to say that Lizzie would get over it. You got over someone cutting in the coffee line, or a rude comment from a stranger. Getting over entitled personal comments like that, well, that was different. Lizzie hadn't seemed angry. Sure, she'd been cold, steely, and hard, but Shan was sure it wasn't anger.

It was hurt.

She sighed and took a sip of her own untouched mug of tea. It was nearly cold.

Celia's words had reinforced something though. Anyone hoping to get to the top in anything that required the sort of dedication and focus athletics did, had to make sacrifices in their life. They had to put in ridiculous hours training. They fell into bed at a time most ten-year-olds were arguing to stay up longer. They were up at sparrow's fart. And relationships? Either, like Celia, they enjoyed brief encounters and casual partners, or they had an angel who looked after their every need and never complained they hadn't picked up the kids from school or bought milk on the way home.

Or, as Shan did, they simply avoided the tangle of expectations and demands on their time and stayed clear. After Tanya, it was an easy decision to make.

Presto nudged her thigh with his nose, and she stroked the back of his neck. No, she'd never worried about being selfish, as she'd only ever had herself to look out for.

Until now. Until Lizzie. And that was part of the uneasiness that roiled in her stomach and made her pulse jump in her throat. She'd forgotten all about the Commonwealth Games trials—because she'd been so caught up in her life with Lizzie. And that was the danger: Lizzie made her forget who she was.

Chapter 17

A Cut Snake

"I have to call Sarah Cunningham." Dee dropped her head to her desk and groaned. "Now. At 4.55 p.m. When I swore black and blue to Reece's childcare that I wouldn't be late picking him up. It's impossible to get off the phone from Sarah in under twenty minutes. I'm doomed."

Lizzie held out her hand for the message slip. "I'll call her."

Dee lifted her head. "Really? Don't you have to get home for a celebratory dinner with the hot athlete? One *she's* cooking?"

Did her smile look as tremulous as it felt? "That's okay. You go get your kid. I don't mind being a bit late."

"I'm not going to ask twice." Dee swished up from the chair and grabbed her jacket from the back of it in one movement. "You're a darling, and I owe you. Although you owe me for my tact at Everyone's Choir, so maybe we're quits. You know I prefer to sit in the back of an Uber ever since that skanky driver grabbed my leg."

"Go," Lizzie said again. "Before I change my mind."

"And you still owe me the story of what happened with Shan after Everyone's Choir. I saw you devouring each other with your eyes. You can't fob me off again tomorrow. Say, 'I promise I'll tell you, Dee.'"

"I promise I'll tell you, Dee." Lizzie managed a weak grin.

She waited until Dee had fled the office then pushed her chair back with a sigh. She'd call Sarah Cunningham. Even take longer than needed with the call. And then maybe she'd walk the five kilometres home rather than taking the train. Anything to avoid getting home, appearing keen and eager to see Shan. She was a bloody idiot. A naïve, too trusting, too damn *kind* person who had been taken advantage of. Not for the first time. *Yes, Baba and Mumma, I'm looking at you.*

At least with Shan, she'd heard it spelled out. "…Lizzie to look after your every whim," Celia had said. As well as, "Watch her. She's the needy sort." That had hurt. More than hurt. A knifepoint of anger still twisted inside her at the memory.

She picked up the phone and pressed Sarah's number. At least she could make Dee happy by making this call. "Hello, Sarah? It's Lizzie from Best Foot Forward. I understand you urgently need a temp for the rest of the week."

Shan glanced at the kitchen clock. After seven. Lizzie was usually home well before six. Shan had made the trip to the supermarket after Celia had left, and the ingredients for her signature pasta dish were ready on the counter. A decent bottle of red wine stood next to them, and a salad was in the fridge. She'd even gone to the Greek bakery she knew Lizzie liked and bought a selection of small cakes dripping with honey and gorgeousness.

It didn't take a detective to figure out the reason for Lizzie's lateness. Maybe she was out with Dee or hitting the after-work happy hours. Maybe she wouldn't even come home. Lizzie's words hammered in her mind: "I'll keep out of Shan's way more often."

Obviously, Lizzie had meant it.

Damn Celia and her big mouth. Shan picked up her phone and her finger hovered over the contacts. Should she call? Text? It was what friends did if the other person was late, to make sure they were okay.

Presto raised his head from his rug in the corner and then paced to the front of the house. A key scraped in the lock.

Oh, thank God.

Shan remained at the counter, phone in hand, and listened for Lizzie's slow footsteps down the hall.

Lizzie entered and set her bag down on the counter. "Hello."

"Hi." Shan's glance flicked over her face. Lizzie seemed as serene and relaxed as ever, except for her hands which were jammed into the pockets of her jacket. "How are you?"

"I want to say something." Lizzie's chin lifted, and finally she met Shan's eyes. "I offered you a room to help you out. Because, for all their faults, my parents raised me to be kind. I didn't enjoy hearing you and Celia talk today. This is still my home, and somehow you've taken a part of it from me." She glanced down at Presto, who was sitting next to Shan. His ears were flat, and he pressed close to her legs. "I just ask that you don't throw my good nature back in my face." She turned away. "I need a glass of wine. Or a run. I'm not sure which."

Shan rose and nudged the bottle of wine closer. "I can open this. Or if you want that run, dinner can wait." She tried a tentative smile. "I know how important running is."

Lizzie's face slammed shut like the front door had earlier. "Yes. You do, don't you."

Shit. Shan closed her eyes in mortification. "This isn't about me. I meant running is a great way to clear your head. Get rid of stress. Enjoy—"

Lizzie smashed her hand down on the counter. "For fuck's sake, Shan, stop being so bloody condescending. You caused the turmoil in my head; you and Celia, when you talked about exactly how you see me. As some lesser mortal whose place on earth is to run around after the gods and be grateful you let me do it."

"Celia said that. Not me."

"No, not you," Lizzie said. Her words held the menace of a coiled red-belly black snake ready to strike. "But I didn't hear you leap to my defence. I thought we were friends. Maybe becoming more. In my world, friends look after friends. They don't stand by and let them be eviscerated."

"I started to say it wasn't like that. You interrupted before I could finish." The heat against her leg lifted as Presto crept away to his corner.

A flicker of hesitation flashed on Lizzie's face. "Yes. You started to say something. But it wasn't heartfelt or loud enough to override Celia. Did she even hear what you said? Did she apologise to you? She certainly didn't to me."

Shan bit her lip. "I said she was out of order. She acknowledged it." *But Celia blew Lizzie's upset off as unimportant.*

"I'm hurt, Shan. Mad as a cut snake, too, but mainly upset. It's not pleasant to hear yourself dismissed as unimportant."

"I didn't—"

"Maybe not," Lizzie agreed. "But you were there. Listening. You didn't tell Celia she was an arrogant bitch, so I could only assume you agreed with her—and that's what hurts the most." She slid onto a stool at the counter. "I'm obviously not going to go for a run. The least you could do is pour me a glass of wine. A big one."

Shan poured a large glass and a small one. Lizzie might want to get shit-faced, but she sensed she'd need her wits for this conversation.

Lizzie took a big gulp, then looked up. "So, I've ranted. Now it's your turn."

What should she say? Excuses? Apologies? A defence of Celia—although, really, there wasn't one. Just the truth. "Celia's view isn't mine. I told her that. I tried to catch you, but you were already at the door. Celia is...very self-centred. She'd just told me she'd made the Commonwealth Games team, so she was a little more self-absorbed than usual."

"The team you were going to try out for? Until..." Lizzie gestured to Shan's knee.

"Yeah. But I've moved on from that. I'm happy for Celia. She's worked hard for this."

"How many people ran around at her beck and call to help her get there?" The edge of bitterness crept back into Lizzie's voice.

"Celia's very independent. She works a tough job. I think her comment was part envy—not that it's an excuse."

"And what do you think?"

"I've gained a lot from your kindness, and it's not something I take for granted. You didn't have to even take me to the hospital in the first place, let alone everything that came after." She gestured to the living area. "Let me into your home. Drive me to appointments. Cooking. Getting me a job."

"I'm glad you didn't add kissing you to that list."

Was that the tiniest thaw in Lizzie's voice? Shan stole a look. Lizzie's eyes were less stony, and she didn't now grip the stem of the wineglass hard enough to snap it.

"Kissing you was because I wanted to. Because we'd had a great evening, because I'd enjoyed your company, your pleasure, the sparkle in the eyes, and how utterly gorgeous you looked. And you kissed me back."

"I did. Because I wanted to. Because I'd enjoyed your company, your determination, and because I love your body, so lean, so wiry."

Shan's stomach tingled in anticipation. Lizzie's words sounded like an invitation. She took a step toward her.

Lizzie got off the stool and moved away, around the counter. "That wasn't an offer to take up where we left off on Saturday night."

Shan closed her eyes in mortification. Of course it wasn't. Lizzie was no pushover. "Do you want dinner? I have it all prepared; I just have the pasta to cook."

"Dinner sounds good." Lizzie tucked a strand of hair that had escaped from her formal office hairstyle behind her ear. "I'm not going to be a bitch about this. I'm just trying to understand where you're coming from, and then we can see where we are."

Relief made Shan's muscles go limp. "I'm glad." She gestured to the corner where a nose stuck out from under the rug. "I think you scared Presto."

"Oh!" Lizzie's hands flew to her cheeks. "Oh *no*. I forgot about him. How could I?" Talking softly, she approached his corner, and waited until he crept out from under the blanket.

Shan turned away, flicked the switch on the kettle, and picked up the fettuccine. Lizzie wasn't going to freeze her out—that had to be good. The wounded, silent treatment always made her stomach knot up and her mind spin into overdrive. At least Lizzie was prepared to talk like adults. She pulled out the frying pan and heated oil to brown the beef strips.

"Thank you for the wine," Lizzie said, making her startle. "It's delicious. Better, I think, than I normally buy."

Shan turned and saw Lizzie back at the counter, Presto beside her, tongue hanging out and staring at the frying pan.

"Well, I'm an employed person now, thanks to you. So I splashed out." She pulled a couple of raw beef strips from the plate and held them out to Presto.

He took them gently, staring up at her with soft brown eyes. Her heart melted.

"No wonder he loves you more than me."

Shan rinsed her fingers and added the rest of the strips to the pan. "I'm home more often than you. It's just proximity." The kettle boiled and she filled a large pot and added the pasta.

"Maybe. But dogs are good judges of people's souls and intentions. Presto loves you."

"I'm glad of that," she murmured. A tendril of pleasure curled around her chest. "It's mutual."

"But dogs don't see the subtleties that people do. Presto doesn't wonder if your love is conditional on him doing things for you. But I wonder that."

Love? Surely, she's not saying… Shan couldn't finish the thought, even in her own head.

Lizzie must have seen her startled look, as she said, "You can stop wondering if I'm going to whip out a ring and get down on one knee. It's an expression. The only love around here is for Presto."

She should be relieved, shouldn't she? Friends was great. Friends with benefits was potentially even better. But love? That was a giant leap too far. So why was there a sinking feeling in her stomach? Shan pushed it away and focussed on Lizzie's words.

"I can ask Celia not to come around again." She concentrated on stirring the pan.

"She's your friend. And right now, you live here. Don't stop her coming. Although, she can sing for her supper. I won't be cooking."

"Fair enough." Shan added mushrooms to the pan. "And...us? Where do we go?"

Lizzie's lips twitched. "On Saturday, after our kiss, I might have given you a different answer. But I need to back off. You're going to get better, and return to your normal life, with no time for anyone who's not a part of that elite set. You'll leave me behind. I suppose I should thank Celia for making that clear."

Shan opened her mouth and closed it again. What could she say to that? Nothing that would persuade Lizzie otherwise, because that was exactly what she'd been thinking too. Disappointment weighted her stomach. How strange. Earlier, she'd decided she and Lizzie couldn't have anything more than friendship between them. Now her chest was heavy with the knowledge that Lizzie didn't want more either. Her mind sparkled briefly with the thought of kisses and more. That possibility was now buried deeper than Presto under his blanket.

"I haven't had a relationship for years. Running... It's been my life."

"I understand that. You've never hidden it, and Celia brought it up again just when I was in danger of forgetting." Lizzie's lips compressed briefly. "I loved kissing you, Shan. But not enough to do it again, not if it means I could get trampled on. I nearly forgot that on Saturday." She heaved a sigh. "I'm going to be truthful, even though I think I might freak you out. But I've never been good at casual sex—my heart always gets involved." Her shoulders hunched. "You've made it clear that's all it can be. And I don't want another heartbreak."

"Is that what happened with Sonia?"

"No. She and I just drifted apart. It's the people before Sonia. The people I thought I had a connection with, and so I read more into their words and actions than was there. I need to toughen up, I know that. And it's best if I start now."

Shan stirred the mushrooms harder. "Can we go back to being friends?"

"Friends. Yes. But nothing more." Lizzie's glance flicked to Shan's lips, and then away again.

Shan caught her breath. For all her words, clearly Lizzie wasn't immune to her. But they both wanted to be friends, so that was what they would be. Right? She sipped her wine, hoping it would wash away the turmoil in her head.

"So, what are you cooking?" Lizzie's voice held a bright gaiety that had been missing before. "Anything I can do to help?"

"Nothing. It's all ready and will only be a couple minutes more. I've fed Presto, so don't believe him when he tells you otherwise." Shan turned down the heat and stirred in sour cream, paprika, and Parmesan. "You can grab the salad from the fridge though."

Lizzie did so, then sat at the table. She fiddled with the cutlery. "You didn't send back your job paperwork today."

Shan drained the pasta and divided it between two bowls. "It seemed wrong to do it, after what Celia said."

"I'll scan it to Dee tomorrow. She'll arrange for you to start the next day."

"Thank you." She spooned over the beef and sauce and carried the bowls to the table.

"This looks amazing!" Lizzie glanced sideways at her. "I thought you couldn't cook?"

Shan hunched her shoulders. "The next time I cook for you will be the end of my repertoire."

Lizzie took a forkful and ate it, closing her eyes in pleasure. "You can do this anytime."

For a moment, they ate in silence.

"How's Dee?" Shan asked.

"Over the moon. She got a call today from Rohaan, the bloke she's got the hots for. He got the engineering position, so he's off our books. Then he turned up at the office with a bunch of yellow roses and asked her out to lunch. She blew me off without a backward glance. They're going out again this weekend."

"That's great."

"Yeah. Dee hasn't had the best luck in love. She falls for bastards who are unfaithful, or who eventually just ghost her."

"What about Reece's father?"

"He left in a cloud of dust when Dee told him she was pregnant. She has no idea where he is. No child support, of course."

"I hope Rohaan is a keeper."

"Mm. He seems very nice so far, and he's obviously smitten with Dee."

There was a brief silence. Shan sipped her wine, nerves still jangling from before.

"I'm working at home tomorrow, so I can take you to your physio appointment." Lizzie gestured to the fridge where the list of appointments was held on by a Sydney Opera House fridge magnet.

"You don't need to—"

"I'm not going to abandon you to the tram system."

"I'm walking a lot more now. I'll be okay."

"I'll take you tomorrow. It's at eleven, right? We can have lunch on the way home. There's a café by the river that does a great burger."

Did Lizzie mean it? Shan didn't think she was a martyr type, but all the same...

"It's what friends do. Have lunch together." Lizzie set down her fork and reached a hand across the table. "Right?"

"Right." A zing of electricity trailed along her nerves from Lizzie's touch. Friends. She could do this... Couldn't she?

Chapter 18

Burning Carbs

LIZZIE PUSHED OPEN THE DOOR and entered the house as quietly as she could. Her morning runs were now a regular thing. How had she not done this before? Running had been a chore, something she did to eat doughnuts without guilt, and to participate in the fun runs. But now... Lizzie checked her running watch. Nearly seven kilometres in just under forty-five minutes. And she felt *great*. Sure, she wouldn't be taking Celia's place on the Commonwealth Games team anytime soon, but this was fun. Challenging. Enjoyable. The river path had been quiet; she'd only passed two other runners and a few dog walkers. Her feet had crunched on the gravel path, and the gleam of sunrise painting the sky orange had put a sparkle in her heart. The nods of solidarity with the other runners had made her feel seen. As if she was a real runner.

The light was on in the living area. She walked down the hall to find Shan stretched out on the floor doing her exercises, physio bands stretched between her legs.

Lizzie waited until she finished her repetitions. "Nearly seven Ks! That's the longest I've ever gone."

"Well done. What were your splits?" Shan got to her feet.

Lizzie handed over her watch.

Shan pushed buttons, looking at the points Lizzie had marked. "You're doing very well. You were only five seconds slower on the return leg. How did you feel when you finished?"

"I could have kept going." Lizzie grinned. Her blood pounded and she bounced on her toes.

"I think you're a natural distance runner." Shan's hazel eyes crinkled enticingly at the corners, making them sparkle.

No, don't look there. Don't tease yourself. "I wonder if I could run ten kilometres?"

"You could do it now, I think. But it would be better to take it more gradually. Is that your goal?"

"One goal at a time. Dee and I entered another fun run next month. We're going to raise money for the LGBTQ+ drop-in centre around the corner in Gaylord Street. I'm aiming for five kilometres in under thirty minutes." She started her cool-down stretches. "I've already told Dee I'm not going to stick with her during the run. She and Reece can raise chaos by themselves."

"You'll do it. I'll come to cheer you on."

"Will you? I'd love that. I've never had anyone cheering me before."

"Look out for me near the finish."

"Actually, the drop-in centre is looking for volunteers at their water station. You hand out bottles and cheer the runners." She rolled her eyes. "Listen to me telling you something you know all too well."

"I'll do that. I'll make sure I hand you your bottle. Also, tell me where to sign up to sponsor you."

"I will—everyone I know gets hit with that. Well, except my parents. There's no point. They're not champions of LGBTQ+ rights." She blew out a breath. "If I finish in under thirty minutes, you can buy another bottle of that fantastic red we had to celebrate when you got the data entry job. Now that you're a working woman again."

"It's a deal."

Lizzie met Shan's eyes. She wore a half-smile, and her gaze dropped briefly to Lizzie's chest in the close-fitting T-shirt, before jerking back up again. In her exercise wear of sports bra and yoga pants, Shan looked mouth-wateringly attractive. The weeks of little exercise had maybe softened her outline a fraction, but she was still lean and fit-looking. *Don't look.* Lizzie swallowed and glanced away. The veneer of "just friends" was crumbling already. She didn't need to reignite her attraction to Shan.

"I have my second specialist appointment today. One month after surgery." Shan picked up one of the blue exercise bands and stretched and released it.

"Today? I must have missed it." Lizzie glanced at the fridge where the chart hung. Red for physio. Blue for massage therapy. Green for the specialist appointments. "I'm in the office today, but I can ask Dee if she'll cover—"

"No." Shan reached out and touched Lizzie's hand. "That's not why I mentioned it. I'll take the tram."

"Are you sure?" It was hard to think with Shan's fingers resting on her hand. When she moved them slightly, the gentle friction made her melt.

"Perfectly. Thank you for offering, but I can do this now. In fact..." Shan's gaze dropped to their hands. "I'm going to see if Dr Gupta thinks I can manage the stairs to my flat. I've been here six weeks. It's time I went home."

Lizzie bit her lip. A shaft of disappointment shot through her. *Oh no.* "You don't have to go. I'm happy for you to stay longer, if it's better for you."

"I don't want to outstay my welcome. That saying about guests and fish both stinking after three days? On that scale I'm past the maggoty stage and should be dead and buried."

Lizzie huffed a laugh. "I don't think that holds true for housemates."

"This housemate doesn't pay rent." She squeezed Lizzie's hand and released it.

Her skin tingled from Shan's touch. *No, no, no. We agreed attraction was not an option.*

"I should free up the room so you can find a paying housemate. And I should get back to my own flat. Although it's been lovely here. Much nicer. Your guest bed is better than my own bed."

"Still. Six flights of stairs. It's not like you can be dropped in by helicopter if you can't manage them."

"That's why I'll take Dr Gupta's advice."

"Of course." Lizzie turned away and picked her running top away from her skin. "I should shower and get to work."

"Have you time for breakfast?" Shan gave her puppy eyes. "I'll make it. Coffee. Peanut butter and tomato on toast. It'll keep you going until lunchtime."

"That sounds weird, but strangely delicious," Lizzie said over her shoulder. "Thank you. I won't be long in the shower."

She kicked off her running shoes and socks and went into the bathroom, closing the door behind her.

For a moment, she sat on the closed lid of the toilet. Shan was moving home. Surely, that was for the best. After all, this had been a temporary arrangement, one that had gone on longer than she'd first thought. She should be pleased to get her space back all to herself. Maybe find herself a housemate to help with rent. But all the same... She stood and turned on the shower, stripping off her clothes and throwing them in a heap in the corner before getting in and letting the hot water stream over her head.

No more coming home to music playing, Shan in the living area doing her exercises. No more coming home to a tidier house. No more watching Shan concentrating as she did the data entry work. Acing it too. She was already in the top ten per cent of their operators. No more coming into the living area to be greeted by Shan's smile, Presto at her side, his ears lifting as he ran across to greet her.

Presto. He would miss Shan terribly. He'd bonded with her, more than he had with Lizzie. Which was fine. As a foster carer, she was used to dogs coming and going. She loved them all, but couldn't keep them.

Shan was like that, too: Lizzie liked having her around, but she couldn't keep her.

Shower finished, she wrapped herself in the biggest towel, with a second one around her hair, gathered up her dirty clothes, and left the bathroom.

As the door opened, Shan turned from the counter. "Perfect timing. This won't be...long." The final word was on a breath as her gaze licked over the skin of Lizzie's chest above the towel then dropped to her thighs below the hem. Heat scorched Lizzie's skin, as if she'd stepped too close to a fire. Maybe that's what it was. The fire and heat and crackling energy that was Shan.

Their gazes locked. Lizzie could no more look away than she could run a marathon. Until, with an exclamation, Shan dived for the toaster which was emitting a stream of smoke.

She freed the stuck toast, and the moment was gone.

Lizzie was more covered by the towel than she had been by her running clothes, but in the moments before the toast started smoking, Lizzie had felt more exposed, more naked than she ever did, even the time when Shan had barged in on her in the bathroom. Shan's gaze had not only stripped the towel from her body, but flayed the skin from her bones, leaving her nerves exposed and pulsating, emotions bare for her to pick apart.

Lizzie fled up the hall to the sanctuary of her room.

Shan was likely leaving. And this...longing, was a bad, bad thing.

But Lizzie would miss her.

Chapter 19

Leaving Home

SHAN REACHED THE BOTTOM OF the column of figures and sighed in relief. She was getting faster and more accurate at data entry, but it wasn't stimulating work. It wasn't stretching her muscles and bursting her lungs on the track, or even chatting with a customer as she made their coffee. But, right now, it was her income. She blew out a breath. If she couldn't return to competitive running, would this be her future?

No. That was negative thinking, and she would focus on the positives. The sunny, shiny, bright positives sparkling in her life right now. Things like Dr Gupta being pleased with her progress—even if he'd said it would be best to wait another week before returning to her apartment.

Shan stood and shook out her arms and rolled her shoulders. Hopefully, Lizzie would be okay with her staying. A curl of pleasure unfurled in her chest at the thought. Another week of Lizzie's company. Too easy. Too sweet.

Later, after dinner, she and Lizzie were sitting at opposite ends of the couch channel surfing for something they both wanted to watch.

Lizzie flung down the remote. "It's all crap. Maybe I should get Netflix or something. But it seems a waste when I hardly watch TV. Do you have it?"

"I have a different service to get the sporting channels." Shan lifted her feet onto the couch, smiling as Lizzie did the same. Her feet nestled up to Lizzie's thigh, and she raised her leg so Shan could push her toes underneath.

Lizzie's toes nudged into Shan's hip, and she lifted Lizzie's foot onto her lap, settling it so the heel didn't jab her. She rubbed Lizzie's socked foot, using her thumbs to work deeply on the sole.

"Dr Gupta was encouraging today." She kept her eyes on Lizzie's foot, holding tighter when Lizzie flinched at a tender spot. "My knee is becoming stronger. I can walk further now, but no running for another eight weeks."

"That's great it's healing well. Let me guess though: you asked if *just a little run* would be okay." Lizzie grinned as she mimicked Shan's precise voice.

"You must have been hiding in his office!" Shan lifted her eyebrows in pretend horror. "Those may or may not have been my exact words."

"Ah, my friend, I know you well. Did you beg?"

"Only a tiny bit." Shan grinned, and her hands slid up Lizzie's shin to the top of her sock. She traced a path on the skin with a finger. Even there, Lizzie's skin was soft, silky. Touchable. Shan's finger stilled.

Lizzie stiffened and raised her foot from Shan's lap. "The pressure point massage was good."

Shan dropped her hands. "Sorry." She waited until Lizzie's foot settled back in her lap. So that was the line and she'd crossed it. Not just the top-of-Lizzie's-sock line, but the friendship/romance line again. She resumed her massage, hoping the pressure would erase the need to stray onto Lizzie's skin once more. "I asked Dr Gupta about moving back home."

"What did he say?" Lizzie laid her head back on the couch and closed her eyes.

Did she not care? Was she hiding her reaction? Shan didn't know. "He said I should wait another week. That six flights of stairs are too much. I'm to find some steps and walk up and down them a few times a day, just one repetition."

"There's a flight of steps down to the river."

"That would work." Shan tapped Lizzie's foot. "But what about me staying with you for another week? I don't want to presume it's okay."

"That's fine. Honestly." Lizzie's eyes sprang open. "Take as long as you need." Her intense gaze pinned Shan to the back of the couch.

"If you're sure." The relief that spread through Shan's bones wasn't simply that she didn't want to tackle the stairs to her apartment. Living with Lizzie had become the norm, and relaxing times like this were pleasures at the end of the day that she looked forward to.

It would be hard to leave.

"I'm moving back home on Saturday." Shan set the phone on speaker and rested it beside the laptop. She flicked over the page and continued entering figures.

"Away from Luscious Lizzie the Lezzie?" The sharp edge to Celia's voice reverberated down the line. "No more home-cooked meals or chauffeur service? No more jobs handed to you?"

"It's not like that. I wish you'd be kinder in your word choices. You upset Lizzie that time. She's become a friend, Celia, and I don't like to hurt my friends."

Celia was silent for a moment. "You're right. I was a bitch. I'm a little bit jealous, to be honest."

"What, of Lizzie?"

A long sigh gusted down the line. "Not of Lizzie, exactly, but of what she offers you. She's just so *nice*. I guess I'd like someone to treat me like Lizzie treats you—even though she doesn't have to."

"I hope you don't have to fall flat over a giant marsupial to find someone."

Celia laughed. "I hope not either. Especially not before the Commonwealth Games."

"What's your training schedule like this weekend?"

"Why, are you wanting muscles for your move?"

"I don't have more stuff than what I moved in with. Even I can shift that myself. I thought it would be nice to catch up. And if that catch up includes you driving me home, then I'll shout you lunch along the way."

"Now that you're a working woman again?"

"Exactly. But if you've got something on that's okay. Lizzie may take me, or I'll take an Uber."

"I can come, if it's after ten."

"Perfect for lunch. Thanks, Celia. It'll be nice to hear how your training's going." A wave of jealousy surged in her throat, but Shan suppressed it. She was happy for Celia, really, she was.

"No worries. I'll see you then. You can think about where you're going to take me for lunch."

"Will do." Shan ended the call. So much for doing data entry during that conversation; she'd lost her place. She resumed, her mind whirring even as her fingers ticked away on automatic.

She was going home. Strangely, she wasn't looking forward to it. She should be. Her own space. Her big windows overlooking the park. Her plain white plates rather than Lizzie's mismatched bright crockery. No more piles of clothes and files strewn around and Lizzie's cluttered countertops. Her own bed. And the gravel track around the park that had been her training run for years. Silence. Quiet. No Lizzie blundering out the door in the morning for her run thinking she was quiet as a mouse. No loud phone calls between her and Dee that were supposed to be about work but seldom were.

No Lizzie cooking or offering her a glass of wine that she really should refuse, but now more often accepted.

She was going home, and that was a good, good thing. She just had to convince herself she meant that.

"Saturday?" Lizzie cocked her head and ate another forkful of pasta, then balanced it with two mouthfuls of salad. Since she'd upped her running, she couldn't seem to stop eating. "I can drive you. If you want, that is."

"Celia's offered. There's no need for you to."

"No worries, if that's what you want. What time's she coming?"

"Ten-thirtyish. We're going to shift my things then go to lunch. Do you want to come too?"

Lunch with Celia? She snorted quietly. "Thanks, but I'll pass. Celia and I are better off in separate spaces."

Shan's lips pressed together, and she looked uneasy. Was she worrying what Celia would do this time? Maybe snap her fingers and tell Lizzie to carry Shan's things to the car. Lizzie tightened her lips. Wouldn't happen. For a second, she considered going for a run, meeting a friend for coffee, or doing her grocery shopping rather than be home when Celia appeared, but no. To hell with Celia; this was her home, and she wouldn't be driven out of it.

"It'll be strange not being here." Shan said when the silence grew too long.

"I'm sure you'll settle right back in."

"I'm going to miss a lot." Shan's gaze dropped to where Presto sat between them in the ever-hopeful quest for table scraps. "Him for starters. Your coffee machine. The fantastic bed. The river path."

"Don't I rate the list? I'm a little miffed I come behind a dog and a coffee machine."

Shan's fork clattered to the table, and she reached across and took Lizzie's hand. "I'll miss you most of all. We've had our rocky times, but you've been a great friend."

Warmth spiralled through her at the touch. Friend. Yes, that's what she was, but why did the word seem so inadequate? Lizzie pushed down the thought. She was the one who'd called a halt to their foray into something more.

"What's with the past tense? Parkville is only up the road. We can still hang out. And you're coming to my fun run in a few weeks, remember? You're my cheer squad of one."

"I haven't forgotten. I'll call the drop-in centre this week to volunteer at the water station."

Lizzie shovelled another mouthful of pasta. Really, it was good. Shan was wrong when she said she couldn't cook. Pasta *and* beans in the same dish? It was the sort of food a runner would cook, a big bowl of carbs. And it was delicious. "I'm not running tomorrow, but I planned a walk along the river. Want to come? You can turn back whenever you've gone far enough. Presto can come too."

"I'd like that. Early tomorrow?"

"Of course."

They left the house at seven the next morning, and by the time they reached the river path, there were pink streaks of dawn in the sky. Shan set the pace, and they ambled along, Presto pulling on his leash ahead of Lizzie.

She looked out over the Yarra River. River red gums and bottlebrush spread a green canopy over the sluggish brown waters. A couple of ducks sailed serenely across to a clump of reeds on the far side. It was a calm, inner-city oasis, despite the buzz of traffic rattling over the Johnston Street bridge. It would be a lovely place to run. Still, it would be good to return to the park loop and running track near her apartment. Maybe Lizzie would come and visit. Go for a run. Share a meal.

"I was thinking I'd see if Presto wants to start running with me." Lizzie moved to let a cyclist ride between them. "My normal plod might suit him."

"He'd probably love it. Kelpies have so much energy."

"Exactly. I'll take him on a slow run tomorrow and see how he likes it." Lizzie moved back closer to Shan once the cyclist had passed. Their shoulders bumped, then hands.

Lizzie switched Presto's leash to the other side and took Shan's hand, linking their fingers together.

Shan stole a sideways glance. Lizzie seemed serene. She meandered along, her gaze on the river, as if it was the most usual thing in the world to hold hands with a friend. Maybe it was. Maybe Lizzie was remembering their kiss. More likely, she didn't want another cyclist to pass between them and run into Presto.

Whatever the reason, it felt good to walk like this. Shan relaxed her shoulders and let her hand remain where it was.

"Right now"—Lizzie slanted a sideways glance—"I'm thinking about breakfast."

"I'm thinking about the coffee stand at Dights Falls."

"I like how you think." Lizzie let Presto tug her along faster.

They sat with their coffees overlooking the river. Lizzie bought a puppuccino for Presto and after a few cautious sniffs, his long tongue cleaned the paper cup over and over.

Shan watched him press against Lizzie's side. She would miss him. But not as much as she'd miss Lizzie.

Shan took a last look around the room that had been hers for the past few weeks. It was tidier than when she'd arrived, the cupboard bare and ready for Lizzie to shovel her junk back into. She'd miss this room with its cosy feel and amazing bed. Hell, who was she kidding? Being home, away from Lizzie was going to be strange. And lonely. She'd miss the morning coffees, the shared dinners, the occasional glass of wine on the front veranda.

Lizzie had so very nearly been more than a friend. Shan sighed. One kiss, that's all it was. One steaming, arousing, toe-curling kiss. It shouldn't be this hard to forget. But it was.

Most likely, it was because she hadn't had a relationship for so long, not even a one-night stand. There had been Celia, and a woman she'd met on a flight to Canberra when she was going to the Australian Institute of Sport. An hour of pleasant conversation had led to a single date, and a single night together. Those were the only two drought-breakers in at least a couple of years. Her only serious relationship had been Tanya, ten years ago.

It would have been good to have a fling with Lizzie, when she had no training plan to follow, no immersive running plan. It was probably her only chance for the next couple of years when she could have done this. A few nights after That Kiss, maybe even the remaining weeks until she moved out—but that wasn't what Lizzie wanted. And Shan couldn't offer more than that.

Her bags rested on the bed. Presto stood in the doorway, ears down, tail tucked between his legs. Shan's heart twisted. He'd obviously figured out what was going on and realised one of the only two people he loved was leaving him. If only she could take him too. But even if Lizzie would let her adopt him, and even if her landlord would let her have a dog, an apartment wasn't the best place for a kelpie.

Carefully, she lowered herself to the floor and held out her arms. Presto came in for a hug, and she buried her face in soft fur at the back of his neck.

The doorbell rang, and Shan got to her feet to answer it.

"Hi," Celia bounced into the hall as if she had springs in her shoes. "Ready?"

"Yeah. I just need to thank Lizzie. You can wait here. You're not her favourite person."

Celia's mouth turned down. "I'll come, actually."

Shan raised an eyebrow. "Only if you're not going to be an insensitive bitch again."

"Trust me." Without waiting for Shan, Celia walked down the hallway.

Shan hurried after her. If Celia was going to insult Lizzie again, she needed to be there. To protect Lizzie? Somehow, she didn't think Lizzie needed—or wanted—that, but she wouldn't just stand by and let Celia get away with it.

Lizzie was at the dining room table, her laptop in front of her.

Celia sat in the chair opposite.

Lizzie gave her a quick glance and returned her gaze to the screen.

"I'm sorry," Celia said. She waited until Lizzie looked up. "I shouldn't have implied your purpose was purely to run around after Shan."

"You didn't imply. You said it."

Celia fiddled with the power cord, but her gaze remained on Lizzie's face. "I was rude."

Lizzie pushed back her chair and folded her arms. "You were. And hurtful. Being kind to someone doesn't mean I'm a pushover. If it had been you who fell over me, I'd probably have offered the same help. Although Shan appreciates what I do for her. You, though..." Lizzie shrugged.

"I've said I'm sorry."

Shan winced at the defensive tone of Celia's voice. *How not to apologise.*

"I'm not sure you mean it though." With a long look, Lizzie returned to her typing.

Shan blew out a slow breath. *Way to go, Celia. Make things worse.*

"I mean it." Celia's voice reverberated in the quiet room. "And I'm truly sorry. I was unforgivably rude to you—in your home as well. Shan's already chewed me out over it. I was jealous—Shan falling on her feet as she did—and it surfaced in what you heard. I'm sorry I said it, sorrier still you overheard. I didn't mean to upset you."

Lizzie stared, her face stony and immobile. "You haven't convinced me, Celia. You were jealous Shan had someone to run around after her. And your only discomfort is that I overhead exactly what you thought of me. Have I got that right?"

"No. Yes. No." Celia lifted her face to the ceiling and appeared to think. "I'm not making excuses. I realise I was a bitch. And no, I don't take people's kindness for granted—and I don't expect people to run around after me, despite what I said. Shan's lucky she found someone like you to care for her when she was unable to look after herself. And yeah, I should have been louder in my offer to help." She spread out her hands. "I don't know what I can say to convince you I'm sorry."

Lizzie stared at her with an assessing gaze. Then a glimmer of a smile appeared. "Shan fell on her side when she tripped over me in the fun run. So maybe it's time she landed right side up."

For a second longer, the two stared at each other.

Lizzie broke the look and stood. "Would you like a coffee before you go?"

Shan's feet were glued to the floor as tightly as Presto was stuck to her leg. Not even the thought of her high-ceilinged flat with its huge windows could make the idea of leaving here appealing.

"I'd love one," Celia said.

"I'll make it." Shan urged her heavy legs into movement and into the kitchen. As she spooned ground coffee into the machine, she listened to Lizzie and Celia chatting.

Lizzie's laugh pealed out like a bell, and the sound knifed into Shan's gut. It seemed Lizzie had got over her anger at Celia. She gripped the coffee spoon. Of course she had, that was Lizzie all over. She stabbed the button on the machine with more force than necessary.

When the coffee was ready, she brought three mugs across to where Lizzie and Celia stood by the window watching Presto pounce on his own shadow in the yard.

"You'll miss that dog." Celia took one of the mugs. "Maybe that's not all you'll miss."

Shan forced a smile. "There are a few things."

"Hey," Lizzie came closer to take her mug. "I'm not a thing!"

The bubble of longing in her chest moved into her throat. Shan set down her mug and took Lizzie's from her hand and set that down as well. Then she caught her and held her close enough that she could hear Lizzie's uneven breathing, smell the woodsy scent that was so uniquely hers. Lizzie's hair hung soft against Shan's face.

"Thanks. For everything over the past few weeks, but mostly, thank you for your friendship."

Lizzie returned the hug, her hands resting on Shan's waist. "You'll still be my friend when you're back in Parkville."

"You're welcome any time. You and Presto can come to the track in the park." She eased out of Lizzie's hug.

"We will." Lizzie pushed her hair behind her ears.

Shan didn't answer, just picked up her coffee again. Lizzie did the same, and for a moment, they stared at each other over the rims of their mugs.

A ripple of longing rolled from Shan's chest down through her belly to her toes. It would be good to be home. It really would. If only she didn't have the feeling she was leaving someone important behind.

Chapter 20

To the Stars

SHAN LAY IN BED IN her apartment and stared out the window at the treetops in the park opposite. European deciduous trees blended with native Australian evergreens. Now, in autumn, they were a mix of bare branches and patterned green. She shifted in bed. Her mattress was board-like in places, sagging in others. What it wasn't was Lizzie's super-comfortable guest bed. She picked up her phone and sent a text.

STILL can't get used to my bed after yours. I'm ruined for life. No more cheap mattresses for me.

It was fifteen minutes before Lizzie replied.

Sorry, was out for a run. 8km. Feeling GREAT! Presto says you can share his bed anytime. BYO blanket and chew toy.

Warmth spread in her chest. Presto's bed wasn't the one she fantasised about. Before she could talk herself out of it, she wrote:

I don't dream about sharing Presto's bed. Sometimes, I wish we'd been less sensible.

Heart beating fast, she set down the phone. Lizzie probably wouldn't reply. Or maybe she was already in the shower. And if Lizzie did respond, what could she possibly say? What could Shan respond? Their decision had been practical, with an eye to the future. She got out of bed and went over to the window. A couple of runners passed along the track. Only another seven weeks and that would be her again, and the single-mindedness and focus on her career would resume in earnest. It was better that Lizzie hadn't replied.

Her phone pinged and she turned abruptly to retrieve it. Her pulse sped up when she saw the text was from Lizzie.

Me too.

She stared at the words until the screen went dark. There was nothing she could say in response. Nothing sensible, nothing that could be anything other than a short-term fling. And Lizzie didn't want that.

Lizzie eyed her finish line, the drooping sheoak that was nearly opposite Shan's apartment. She pushed harder in a final burst.

Shan stood under the tree, stopwatch in hand. She'd insisted on timing Lizzie herself, rather than relying on Lizzie's haphazard button-pushing on her running watch.

Lizzie sucked air and sprinted the final few metres. She passed the tree and dropped to a walk, circling back to Shan. Although she'd only been walking, Shan wore running shorts and a crop top. *Wow.* The bright top was practical and necessary, but on Shan it looked incredibly hot. And sexy. Shan's legs stretched long and gorgeous below the brief shorts, gaining a slight tan now from her time outside. Her belly peeped out below the crop top. Lizzie sighed. Shan's belly was the definition of six-pack. Touchable.

"I can't believe how well you've come on in only two weeks." Shan's shape was edged by the golden lines of evening sunlight.

"I'm glad you think so. I'm still dying here. How did I do?"

"Guess." Shan's smile peeped out.

"Oh, maybe thirty-two minutes for the five kilometres?"

In answer Shan showed her the stopwatch.

"Oh my God!" Lizzie looked up at Shan. "I can't believe it. I smashed it! Five kilometres in 29:02. I did it!" She spun around, feet sliding into a quick salsa and hip shake. "I'm a runner! I really did it."

Shan grasped her hands. "I knew you could. And, even better, you looked really comfortable."

"I felt it—at least until the last hundred metres or so." Lizzie bounced on her toes. "And it's all your doing. Your running plan." Euphoria bubbled up and she went with it. A fist-pump, a grin at Shan, another shimmy.

Shan gazed back, her lips twitching in amusement.

Lizzie halted, even though the energy of achievement still fizzed in her veins. "Two months ago, if you'd told me I'd be euphoric simply from having run five kilometres in my personal best time, I'd have laughed at you and snuggled further into the couch. This is incredible!" She fist-pumped again and spun in a circle. "And if you'd told me even one month ago that my idea of a great Friday evening was running until everything hurt, I'd have howled and said you were thinking of another Lizzie."

"I think you've got the running bug." Shan's eyes crinkled at the corners, and she pushed a hand through her tufty hair. "You're going to ace that fun run."

Lizzie spun again, twirling so fast the trees blurred in her vision and the sheoak that was her personal finish line tilted. "Oops." Her foot caught as her world swam dizzily, and she staggered to the left and rested her hand on the tree's rough bark. "Thanks, Sheila-the-sheoak."

"Hey." Shan gripped her arm. "Steady on."

Lizzie stilled and let the world level itself out again. Shan's grip on her arm burned warm against her skin. Her senses must be supercharged after her euphoria, as every one of Shan's fingers was a separate point of feeling on her skin. Lizzie stood still, unwilling to move away. Somewhere, in a land far, far away, birds were singing their little hearts out, a woman called to a child to leave the poor dog alone, and traffic drove steadily along Park Street. They all registered, and all were unimportant.

Lizzie took a tiny step closer, enough that she could clearly see the green flecks in Shan's hazel eyes. Her heart pounded. *It's the run.* But as Shan's face became questioning and she grasped Lizzie's arm, her heart rate picked up even more.

No, not the run. It's Shan.

Lizzie swallowed. Memories of how Shan's lips had felt in their one and only kiss spun in her mind. Their one and only *magnificent* kiss.

Shan's grip loosened on Lizzie's forearm, and her fingers inched up and down. It could be a soothing motion, or an acknowledgment of Lizzie's joy. Or it could be a caress. An invitation.

Lizzie took another small shuffle forward. Maybe not even a step, maybe she'd just leaned forward in invitation.

Shan's gaze flicked from Lizzie's face, to where her hand rested on her forearm, and back again. "Lizzie? Are you…? Do you…?"

She shouldn't. A tiny flicker of sanity flared in Lizzie's mind, all the reasons why this was a terrible idea, but she pushed it aside. *Why the hell not?* Her world focussed on Shan's lips and how much she wanted to feel them on her own. Her breath hitched in her throat, and she closed the gap between them, sliding a hand around Shan's waist, curving the other around her neck. Their mouths came together in an urgent press of lips.

Lizzie closed her eyes and absorbed the sensations. Lips touching. Hand on skin. The tang of Shan's fresh scent in her nose.

Shan's fingers pushed underneath Lizzie's top and rested lightly on her skin. Her world had narrowed to Shan and her kiss. Her tongue teased at Lizzie's lips, and she opened her mouth to allow entry. The wet, hot glide of her tongue made Lizzie's knees buckle, and she gripped Shan harder.

The kiss exploded, cartwheels of light circled behind her eyes, and despite the cooling sweat on her skin, she was incandescent with heat. The burn of lust swept down into her belly like a bushfire. She pulled Shan even closer and let their tongues dance together. Where would this kiss end? It seemed obvious.

A wolf-whistle and a shouted, "Keep going, girls. Can we watch?" dragged her back to reality.

She opened her eyes and saw two grinning teenagers astride pushbikes who had stopped to watch. She was too happy with the world to flip them the bird. "I hope one day someone will kiss you like that."

The teens smirked, and one gave her a thumbs up, then they continued around the path.

Shan's hand still rested on her waist. Lizzie let her own hands drift down to grasp Shan's hips. "Do you...? That is..." She hesitated. What she wanted to suggest blew the idea of "just friends" into the stratosphere. And sent her own careful ways with romance on a drop kick into the sun.

Shan smoothed a thumb over Lizzie's lips.

Lizzie's heart boomed almost painfully, as if it were too big for her chest.

"Do I want to go back to my place?" Shan asked. "Where it's private?"

Lizzie could only nod. Flutters of anxiety tickled in the forefront of her mind. What if Shan said no?

What if she says yes?

Shan pressed another kiss to the corner of her mouth. "I want to," she whispered. "But... You know very little has changed. We may not be housemates anymore, but my life isn't simple. I have to concentrate on my fitness, and in a few weeks, my running. And I have to work. That's easier now, thanks to you, but there's still not much time left over." Her hazel eyes searched Lizzie's face. "I'm not good at relationships, Lizzie. I've only ever had one long-term one in my life. And while I don't know if we'd get that far, well, I like you too much to let you get hurt. And if that means you walk away now, I'll be sorry, but it's your choice to make."

Lizzie heaved a breath over the pounding in her chest. She should cut and run with a light-hearted wave and smile, say she'd rather remain in the friend zone. Heartbreak, her inability to keep it light—all reasons she should walk away.

But she couldn't. Not now, not with the thrum of achievement, the euphoria of Shan's company, buzzing in her blood. Not with a flat and a bed so close.

Shan was right. It seemed premature to call the boundaries of a relationship that hadn't even started.

And there was how she was feeling right now—so lit from within with the need to take this further, she was sure she'd burn up. She wanted Shan, now. And Shan, it seemed, wanted her. Why was she waiting? There was no predicting the future. It may be just for now, or for now-and-a-little-time. Or it may be more. But right now, she couldn't turn down an immediate happiness.

She took a small step away, enough that their bodies separated. Shan's face still filled her vision: hopeful, her pupils wide and dark in her striking eyes. "Let's go to yours."

A brief nod, then Shan took her hand, and they walked across the median and ducked through the traffic on the busy road.

The shared hallway was cool and dim. "One hundred-and-eight steps," Shan said. "Sure you've got enough energy?"

In answer, Lizzie tugged her hand free and ran the first two flights.

"Not fair," Shan called up to her. "I'm still not able to do that." She walked more sedately to the first landing.

Lizzie threw her a grin and took the next two flights two steps at a time. Her breath tossed in her lungs as if there wasn't enough air in the stairwell. It wasn't her fitness, not anymore. It was anticipation tightening her chest, trickling fiery pathways down into her belly, urging her on, up, faster. Get to Shan's flat, open the door, rush inside, and then…

Shan caught up with her in the hallway outside her apartment. She pulled the key from the zipped pocket of her shorts and, leaving her shoes on the mat, led the way inside.

Lizzie bit her lip, the urgency slipping away. Suddenly, it all seemed so *calculated*. They'd kissed, and now they were going to have sex. It seemed like something she should have put in her diary, like a work Zoom meeting.

"Hey." Shan stepped in front of her and picked up a long strand of Lizzie's hair that had worked loose from her ponytail. She wrapped it around her finger. "We can have coffee, if you want." The unspoken "instead'" hung in the air unspoken.

Lizzie took a deep breath. She wanted this—it was just nerves. After all, she hadn't slept with anyone since Sonia. The first time with a new person was always jittery and tense—at least for her. She leaned in and dropped a kiss on Shan's left cheek, then her right cheek. Drawing back, she gazed at Shan's face with its chiselled cheekbones and warm eyes, then moved in again to bring their lips together.

Shan's mouth softened under hers, but she remained passive. Letting her take the lead, Lizzie realised, and a rush of warmth surged in her chest at the thought. She rested her hands on Shan's waist once more, over the damp top. Softly, she traced Shan's upper lip with the tip of her tongue, then the fuller lower one. Shan tasted of salt, sweat from her walk. Lizzie had never thought of sweat as an aphrodisiac, but lapped from Shan's skin, it certainly was.

The arousal she'd thought muted surged through her again like a tidal wave. Lizzie's stomach muscles tightened, her skin tingled as if brushed by flame, and all she wanted to do was tug Shan by the hand and lead her to the bedroom. She kissed her again, allowing all her pent-up desire to flow through her lips to Shan's. Surely there could be no mistake about what she wanted?

For long moments, they traded kisses. With every sweep of Shan's tongue, every touch of her lips, Lizzie burned hotter. When the feel of her clothes against her skin was too much, she broke the kiss and took Shan's hand.

Instead of leading her to the bedroom, Shan took her to the small bathroom. "Would you like a shower?" Shan's lips curved upward "We can share it."

Lizzie flashed a look at the shower. It was a modern, open one, with only a sheet of glass dividing it from the room. Plenty of room for two. Rather than answer, she pulled her top over her head.

Shan's gaze licked over her exposed skin, and she reached out with a finger and traced a line around the upper edge of Lizzie's sports bra.

Lizzie's nipples hardened from the light touch. The bra was a barrier she didn't want. Holding Shan's gaze with her own, she removed the chunky sports bra and dropped it at her feet. The cool air of the bathroom caressed her nipples.

Although the bathroom was cool, the heat in Shan's stare could have raised it a couple of degrees. She took a step forward.

Lizzie took a tiny step back. "Let me undress completely." She tilted her head, confidence soaring at the appreciation in Shan's stare. Shan saw toned, beautiful bodies often, but she was staring at Lizzie with naked lust in her face.

Quickly, she pushed down her shorts and undies in the same motion. The damp material bunched around the tops of her thighs, and she tugged until they rolled into thick sausages and down her legs, so that she could kick them away.

"May I touch you now?" Shan asked, her voice smoky and low.

"Is that what you want?" Lizzie reached out to caress the front of Shan's top. "Here's me, shivering, you're still dressed, and the shower's not on."

Shan's mouth covered hers, and kissed her, a deep, slow kiss that made Lizzie's knees tremble.

"I'm not shivering with cold." Lizzie held out a hand to show the slight tremor. "I want you, Shan."

"I can take a hint."

Lizzie swallowed hard as Shan crossed her arms and pulled her top over her head. The flat, six-pack abdomen was such a contrast to her own curvy one. The contrast made her long to see them pressed together.

A pale-green sports bra joined the running top on the floor. Shan straightened and flashed her a smile that was cocky and confident.

Shan was sure of her own body; of course she was comfortable in her own skin, unabashed in nudity. Shan wore her skin like the finest of ball gowns. Then, once more, her gaze travelled leisurely over Lizzie's body, lingering on her breasts, her stomach, the curve of her hips. Between her legs. Lower.

"You're gorgeous." Shan's voice held a huskiness that had been absent a moment before. "You are everything that is beautiful in a woman."

Lizzie flushed, heat rising from her chest up her neck. "I'm glad you think so."

"You are." Shan reached out and placed her hand in the indent of Lizzie's waist. "You have shape. I'm just up and down like a stick."

Lizzie's pulse jumped and she reached out to touch Shan's breast. "No stick has these." Shan's breasts were small, but shaped like elegant teardrops, sitting proud on her chest. Rose-pink nipples topped the gentle swell. Mouth-sized breasts.

"Shower." Shan made no move to turn it on. "I think my feet are glued to the floor. Or maybe that's my sweaty socks."

"I can help you." Lizzie hooked her thumbs into the waistband of Shan's shorts and pulled them down, along with her undies.

They slid to her feet, and she shuffled trying to kick them aside, failed, and had to bend and remove them along with her socks. Naked, she straightened.

Lizzie's mouth went dry, and she rested her hand on Shan's waist. The contrast in skin tones—her golden warmth and Shan's milky coolness—added another layer of arousal to her already hazy mind. Shan's hipbones jutted slightly, giving a concave appearance to her stomach. Below, a fuzz of blonde hair covered her mound. Lizzie traced the line where the hem of her shorts usually came, the dividing line between pale and gold from the sun, lingering on Shan's inner thighs where the skin was softest.

Sunlight diffused by the frosted glass of the window painted Shan's skin, dappling it in the faintest of shadows. Lizzie gripped her shoulders and leaned in to kiss her once more. The kiss burned sweet and hot.

Shan walked her back into the shower and turned it on.

Lizzie gasped as a blast of cold water hit her overheated skin. Instant goosebumps popped as the water ran in streams over her head, her breasts, and down her back. "A cold shower isn't going to make me want you less."

"I hope not." Shan joined her under the spray, which was already becoming warm. She kissed her again, a deep, bone-melting kiss that ended in tiny pecks along her lips.

Oh, how Shan could kiss! The desire that had been trickling down Lizzie's spine increased in intensity until she thought she might fly apart into a million glowing stars.

"Shampoo." Shan pumped some into her hand and pushed it into Lizzie's hair, rubbing gently over her scalp. "Showers are for getting clean, after all."

It was never like this at the hairdressers. Lizzie suppressed a giggle. Her hairdresser, the very gorgeous and very gay André, never made her melt at his feet, despite taking equal care with her hair. She reached for the shampoo.

"Not yet." Shan nudged her hand away. "You have ten times the amount of hair that I do. I need the extra time." Her hands continued their sensuous caress, working the shampoo down to the ends. She piled the hair on top of Lizzie's head.

"Your 1950s beehive, ma'am." She leaned forward for another kiss, and the beehive toppled down over Lizzie's face. Shan chuckled. "Not the effect I was hoping for."

Lizzie pushed the mass of wet hair from her face. "Your hairdressing skills need work."

The knot of nervous tension in her stomach was muting and turning back into a buzz of lust. She pumped some body wash into her palm and lathered it over Shan's shoulders, caressing in sweeps down her arms. Shan's fingers got careful treatment, each one stroked and massaged in the soap foam. Lizzie took a second pump of body wash and focussed her attention on Shan's breasts. She circled each one, concentrating on the skin of her ribs, her side, and her breastbone above the slight swell. She'd never been one for caring about breast size—a woman was a whole package, after all—but she'd never seen anything as beautiful as Shan's small, perfectly shaped breasts. Her fingers spiralled to circle around the large, pink areolas. She dragged a finger across one of Shan's nipples and watched as her shoulders tightened in a convulsive shudder.

Shan raised her head and looked Lizzie in the face. "You have no idea how good that feels."

"Maybe I do." Lizzie circled Shan's other nipple, then moved to lather her back.

Shan adjusted the shower spray so it slicked the water back from Lizzie's face. She pushed her hands into Lizzie's hair, massaging her scalp, and coaxing the shampoo from the silky strands. When the water ran clear, she added conditioner, and ran her fingers through to the ends, detangling with her fingers.

Lizzie sighed and closed her eyes. This gentle care was a sensuous dream. When her hair hung straight and smooth down her back, Shan reached for the shampoo again, massaging it into her own hair with quick, economical movements.

Of course. Shan washed her hair every day. Lizzie had seen her, hair damp and spiky, after the shower. A quick rinse, a shake of the head, and Shan opened her eyes. Her eyelashes seemed longer, darker with water. Rivulets ran down her chest and abdomen.

Lizzie traced the line of drops with her gaze as it ran around Shan's belly button, then back up at Shan's eyes, which darkened to the richest gold. This was water torture of the finest kind. She put more body wash on her palm and rubbed long, slow strokes along

Shan's sides, over her hips, her fingers spreading toward the apex of her thighs. Nearer and nearer with every slide of her palm until her fingertips brushed the top of Shan's soaked pubic hair.

Even sodden with water, it was fine and soft. A warmth spread across Lizzie's chest that had nothing to do with the hot shower. Shan was gorgeous, with her lean lines, hard planes, and angles. A tough, fit body in a beautiful package. Desperate to feel more, Lizzie pressed her hand between Shan's thighs.

Shan gasped and widened her legs. Her hands settled on Lizzie's waist.

Her fingers twitched with the need to slide between Shan's folds and explore further, deeper, up to where she was sure would be wet from more than the shower. She resisted. This shower had a purpose beyond foreplay, and a bed would be a more comfortable place for exploration.

She drew back. "I think I want out of here."

Shan quirked an eyebrow in question.

"Tiles are hard on backs and knees." She wiggled her eyebrows and grinned as Shan's eyes darkened in comprehension.

They finished soaping their own bodies in silence and took it in turns to rinse off under the spray.

Torture. It was pure torture to take her usual time rinsing conditioner from her hair, but Lizzie did it anyway. Her pulse skipped and thumped, and her skin prickled in anticipation of what was to come.

Shan stepped from the shower and grabbed a towel from the rack. A swift dry of her body and hair left the latter standing up in damp spikes. She left the bathroom and returned with a second towel.

Lizzie stepped out of the shower and Shan enveloped her in the towel she held. She gently rubbed the moisture from Lizzie's skin.

"You're on a losing wicket." Lizzie twisted her hair away from where it was dripping on her already dried skin and wrapped it in the towel. "I don't suppose you have a hairdryer? Otherwise, I'm going to drip all over you."

Shan pulled out a dryer from a drawer. "For when you're ready."

Lizzie towelled her hair and then borrowed a wide-toothed comb. Not for the first time, she cursed her long, thick hair. If she had hair like Shan's, they'd already be in bed, rather than her standing naked and dripping in the bathroom. But then Shan picked up the hairdryer and started plying it over Lizzie's hair, fluffing it as thoroughly as any hairdresser. Her nimble fingers teased and primped and worked out the remaining tangles until Lizzie's hair was only damp.

Shan set the dryer down and rested her hands on Lizzie's hip, stroking one finger to and fro over her skin.

Warmth like melted chocolate drizzled down Lizzie's spine and she leaned in to kiss Shan, sweeping her tongue into her mouth and sucking gently on her lower lip.

When she broke the kiss, they were both gasping.

"Bed?" Shan asked.

Lizzie could only nod as her throat tightened in anticipation. She followed Shan the few steps to the bedroom. The curtains that covered the tall windows were pulled back, leaving the room open to the evening. Lizzie hung back. The fourth-floor window looked out to the park. "Can anyone see in?"

"No. No one overlooks us, and if we keep the light off, no one will be able to see anything even if they do look up to the window." Shan held out a hand. "Come and see."

Lizzie took a deep breath to quell her jitters. She joined Shan at the window.

Outside, cars passed in a steady stream. Across the road, the park was lit only by sporadic streetlights. A couple walked a dog. Behind them, the trees were shadowy mysterious shapes. Lizzie picked out Sheila, her finish-line tree. Apart from Sheila, there was no one to see what they did.

The streetlights cast muted yellow light into the room and across Shan's bed. Lizzie looked at it for the first time. Queen size, with a patterned quilt. She walked back to the bed and pulled down the cover, exposing white sheets, and climbed on. She held out a hand. "Come here."

Shan seemed sombre in the yellow light, her face turned into planes of light and shadow, her eyes dark and inscrutable. She joined Lizzie on the bed and turned on her side, facing her. "It's been a while since I've done this. I want you to know that."

Lizzie bunched the sheet in her hand. Why was Shan telling her this? "We'll do this together." Shan's face blurred as Lizzie moved in to kiss her.

The kiss was gentle at first, lips moving softly, fingertips drifting across dips and hollows, curves and planes. Lizzie's tongue danced with Shan's as the kiss deepened, grew more intense. She rested her hand on Shan's arm, until the long, slow burn lit in her belly as blazingly sudden as a bushfire.

Shan raised up and urged Lizzie onto her back. She hummed as she kissed her way down Lizzie's neck, hot breath leaving a moist trail along her skin.

Lizzie pressed her legs together. Already, the delightful buzz between her legs was expanding.

When Shan's lips jumped from the upper curve of Lizzie's breast to her nipple, her breath caught in her throat. She arched up into the caress as Shan took a nipple in her mouth, swirling her tongue around and around in warm, damp circles. Sparks skittered over Lizzie's skin, glowing pinpricks of pleasure that coalesced between her legs. She pressed her thighs more tightly together to intensify the feeling, then relaxed them. What if Shan thought she was nervous about being touched there. Lizzie suppressed a smile. Oh no. That was *not* the intent.

Shan's lips trailed their way to Lizzie's other breast. The sparks came together in a simmering line as Shan's lips tugged at Lizzie's nipple and her tongue swirled around the peak.

Lizzie relaxed her fingers on the bedsheets and brought her hands to Shan's head, stroking over the damp hedgehog hair and down her shoulders, over the soft, pale skin.

"Your breasts are beautiful." Shan raised her head to look Lizzie in the face. Her fingers replaced her tongue as if she couldn't bear to leave Lizzie's breasts alone, and she traced the curve.

She turned on her side facing Shan, and let her own fingers drift down to Shan's breast. She traced the underside and then up and over Shan's nipple. "Thank you. I love your perfect curves."

Slowly, with serious concentration, Shan's fingers drifted lower. They moved across Lizzie's belly in sweeping lines, tracing the small appendectomy scar, until they brushed the top of her pubic hair.

With a wicked smile, Lizzie mirrored her movements, trailing a switchback across Shan's ribcage, then dipping into the concave area beneath and over her flat belly. Her pubic hair was fine and so fair it was almost invisible. Lizzie dragged a finger downwards to the top of the secret cleft below.

When Shan mirrored her movement, Lizzie sucked a deep breath. Her sex pulsated with need and her nipples tingled as if Shan was still touching them. She raised her thigh.

"Muscles." The smile reverberated in Shan's voice. "You have magnificent runner's legs. I can see good definition of your quads—"

Lizzie snorted a laugh and leaned to kiss Shan, swallowing her words. When they broke apart, she said, "Hold the anatomy lesson."

Shan's eyes twinkled with amusement. "The only anatomy I'm interested in right now is yours, and your quads are not my area of interest. Although they are amazing." She swept her hand between Lizzie's thighs. Her eyes darkened. "You are so wet."

The words sent a shower of sparks into Lizzie's belly. There was so much want and need in Shan's tone that her legs turned to jelly, and she lowered her thigh, trapping Shan's hand between her legs. Wetness slicked her upper thighs, and she swallowed hard as the pulse of desire threatened to overwhelm her. And Shan had simply touched her. Nothing more. Oh, dear God, what would happen when she did more?

Shan's fingers wiggled between Lizzie's thighs. She rolled onto her back again and let her legs fall apart.

"Better."

There was magic happening between her legs. Lizzie closed her eyes and absorbed the sensations radiating out from her core. Her senses were supercharged: warm air in the room caressing her skin, Shan's clean scent of freshly washed hair and coconut body wash, and the cool, slightly scratchy sheet under her back. And Shan's fingers. They stroked a long motion from bottom to top, then a slow slip down the middle. The breath was stolen from her body, and the room spun behind her closed eyelids. The gentle touch, so at odds with Shan's energetic and direct personality, made her stomach melt.

"Look at me." Shan's words seemed to come from a world away. "I want to see your eyes when I fuck you."

A thrill ran through Lizzie at the blunt word, and her arousal ramped up another notch. How much more aroused could she become without imploding in a fiery cloud of lust? She opened her eyes to find Shan's glittering ones focussed intently on her.

Shan held her gaze as she moved down between Lizzie's parted thighs. Her palms ran up the inside of both legs. "I love your soft skin and strong thighs. You have a beautiful body, Lizzie." Her fingertips reached the junction of Lizzie's legs and halted. One finger brushed back and forth across Lizzie's lips.

She shuddered, her breath coming in tortured little gasps. *Please, Shan, don't make me wait.*

Shan raised an eyebrow and smiled.

Had she said that out loud? "Please," she said. "Just do it."

Still Shan teased, stroking through Lizzie's wetness, circling in spirals, close to but never quite touching her clit. She grasped at empty air. She wanted to close her eyes to better absorb the feelings, but Shan's gaze focussed on her face kept them open.

"Tease," she said, her voice a breathless wheeze. "What about your promise to fuck me?"

"Patience is a virtue," Shan said in a sing-song tone. Her tongue touched her upper lip.

Lizzie focussed on that tongue, on the pink tip touching down so lightly on Shan's bow-beautiful lip.

Shan ducked her head.

A gasp escaped Lizzie as something warm and moist touched her clit. Shan's tongue circled once, and then her lips closed around it and she sucked.

How could she ever have gone so long without this? Without sharing sex, without the joy and pleasure it brought?

Shan's tongue stroked up one side of her clit, another slow circle, then down the other side.

Lizzie bit her lip. This was incredible, amazing, explosive—and she didn't know how much more of it she could take without shooting like a rocket to the stars.

And then Shan flicked her gaze up to Lizzie's face, and as she circled her clit one more time, she pushed her fingers inside.

The world tilted on its axis, the moon and stars spun down from the heavens and landed behind Lizzie's closed eyelids. How many fingers? She didn't know and it didn't matter; she was so wet, so aching and needy, Shan could have slipped her entire hand inside and Lizzie would have been able to take it. Her belly clenched and the fullness inside held an intensity she'd seldom felt. She clenched around Shan's fingers and the ripples started, growing in intensity with every flick of Shan's tongue.

One more slow slide of her tongue, one in and out with her fingers. Stars wheeled and danced behind her eyes and Lizzie's body exploded from tautness to shudders of release. When the aftershocks had died down, she lay on the bed, her body boneless and limp from the ferocity of her orgasm.

She reached down to caress Shan's hair, sliding down to her face. "That was incredible. You were incredible." Her nipples tingled with tiny pinpoints of pleasure, as if the energy of her climax was reluctant to leave her body.

Shan moved up alongside her and kissed Lizzie with sticky lips. "You were the incredible one." She pressed another kiss to Lizzie's shoulder.

Lizzie sucked a deep breath, then another. Her heart rate still pounded as if she'd sprinted five kilometres. She was wrong earlier when she'd wondered how she could have gone without sex for so long; it wasn't just any sex, it was good sex. Like this. And it wasn't over yet.

She sat up on the bed and swung her legs from the edge. Holding out a hand for Shan, she urged her to stand in front of her.

"Another shower?" Shan's eyes crinkled at the corners.

"Not yet. You're not dirty enough."

She reached out to cup Shan's breasts. How firm and sweet they were, how touchable. How perfect. She gathered Shan to her, reaching down to cup her buttocks and inserting a leg between Shan's. Her wetness slicked Lizzie's thigh, and she urged Shan closer, so she rubbed back and forth on Lizzie's thigh.

A delicate pink flush crept up Shan's chest and she gripped Lizzie's waist. "I could come doing this alone."

"Slow down." Lizzie bent to kiss her once more. The slickness of her mouth mirrored the slickness of her sex. "This isn't the Olympics." For a second, she wondered if she'd gone too far, if Shan would be offended.

Shan's lips twitched. "If it were, you've just got the gold medal."

"We're not at the finish line yet." She removed her thigh from between Shan's and shuffled back to sit on the bed, then tugged Shan closer once more. Her heart thundered as she took in Shan's flushed face, her engorged, puffy lower lips. "Come closer."

Shan's eyes widened as she caught Lizzie's intent.

Would this work? First times weren't the best time to try out new things, but the scenario beat in Lizzie's head. She grasped Shan once more and encouraged her forward so that her sex was in front of her mouth. Her enticing woman-smell coiled out to meet Lizzie, so thick and beautiful she could almost taste it on her tongue. *In just a moment...* She ducked her head and pressed a kiss to Shan's blonde mound, then lower, her tongue darting out for a quick taste. *Just as delicious as she smells*. Lizzie's heart pounded faster, and her own sex pulsed in response. Another touch. She thrilled as Shan groaned, pushed her hips closer, and grasped Lizzie's shoulders in a grip like steel.

She pressed her mouth to Shan's sex once more, using her fingers to part her folds and then running her tongue over her lips, circling around and then finally over her clit.

Shan gasped and her grip tightened on Lizzie's shoulder. "That feels... Oh!" Her hips thrust forward again. "Please...faster."

Warmth coalesced in Lizzie's chest. How could she not do what Shan wanted? That wasn't even an option. She was surrounded by her: skin, taste, the piercing glitter of her eyes, her hips thrusting forward. When Shan tensed and then came with a shout, a thrill ran through Lizzie, as intense as if she'd come again herself. It had been too long since she'd been with anyone, but this...this was worth the wait.

Shan collapsed on the bed next to her, reaching out an arm to pull Lizzie down by her side. "Tell me why we didn't do that when I was living in your house?"

"Too difficult. Too many layers." She hesitated. Now was not the time to reiterate the reasons for her hesitation, or that Shan didn't want the commitment. Now was the time for enjoying what they'd just shared...and maybe doing it again.

"Mm." Shan nodded against her shoulder. "It was the wrong time then; maybe now it will be okay."

For how long? A night, a week, a month? Longer? Lizzie took a deep breath and drained the tension out of her shoulders along with the breath from her lungs. She stared out the window, at the branches waving against the streetlight. "It's like being in the treetops here. You must have missed that, staying with me."

"Not really." She lifted a strand of Lizzie's hair from her cheek and wound it around her finger. "Your place is lovely. I still miss Presto."

Presto. How could she have forgotten? Lizzie bit her lip. She'd been ready to snuggle in for the evening. Order takeaway, maybe dress enough to sit on the couch, drink a glass of wine, talk about running, and where they might go for dinner the next time. Go back to bed for another earth-shaking orgasm. After-sex sex was the best. Though their first time would be hard to beat.

For a second, she considered calling her neighbour and asking him to look in on Presto. But no. Presto would be anxious enough when she didn't come home; she couldn't sic a stranger on him as well. "I have to get back to him." She shifted restlessly. "I can't leave him alone all—" She bit her tongue. "He's never been left."

"I wish you could stay." Shan leaned in to kiss her, lips soft and enticing.

Words hovered on the tip of her tongue: *Come with me.* Lizzie swallowed them. That was a fair way up the neediness chain. "I wish I could stay, too."

She stood and looked around for her clothes. Her damp, sweaty running clothes were scattered on the bathroom floor. She picked them up and started to dress, suppressing a shudder at the feel of the clammy clothes against her superheated skin. After Shan's arousing touch, the damp clothes were like diving into a swamp. *Way to come back to earth.*

When Lizzie was dressed, Shan wrapped herself in a large towel. "Do you mind if I don't come down to your car?"

Lizzie shook her head. "Of course not. You don't want to scare the neighbours." She hesitated. "So what happens now?"

Shan swallowed. "Your race is next week?" At Lizzie's nod, she continued, "Do you want to train here in the week? A slow, gentle run so that you're well rested."

Did Shan really think she was asking about running? Lizzie's mouth hung open for a second. "I meant about this." She waved at the rumpled bed. "I'm already hoping we can do it again soon." Her smile quivered on her face, and she stretched her mouth wider to stop the tremor.

Shan touched her face, fingertips grazing her cheek and then brushing the corner of her mouth. "You have a race next week."

The race? Lizzie's head spun. "I'm a fun runner. Some pre-race sex won't put me off my game. And if it does, well, that would be okay too."

Shan's face shuttered. "I have to concentrate on my fitness too."

"So that's a no then." Rejection gripped her heart. Shan had mentioned her priorities; she was the foolish one thinking one evening of spontaneous sex changed things. That she meant something. "No worries." She lifted her chin. *Let me out of here before I make a bigger idiot of myself.* "I'll see you around."

"How about a slow run on, say Thursday evening? Here? You could bring Presto for that."

Was that an invitation for more after their workout? Lizzie stared at Shan's face, trying to figure out what she really meant. But Shan's expression gave nothing away. "Sure. We can make it earlier, if you want. I'll be working from home that day." And maybe there would be time for bedroom games after the run.

"Sure." Shan tucked the ends of the towel between her breasts. "Is six too early for you?"

"I'll see you then." Lizzie hesitated. After what they'd shared, it seemed wrong to just walk out as if she'd made an appointment at the dentist. She came closer, placed her hands on Shan's waist, and leaned in to kiss her. "Tonight was spectacular. Thank you." She kissed her slowly, using lips, tongue, all the gentle, dancing tricks in her book.

When they broke apart, they were both breathing heavily.

"I wish you could stay tonight." Shan pecked her on the lips.

"Maybe another time?"

A soft smile was Shan's only answer.

"I'll see myself out." Lizzie pressed a final kiss to Shan's cheek, gathered her keys, and let herself out the door.

She sat in her car staring out at the pathway around the park. The drooping branches of Sheila-the-sheoak mocked her. So, she was a running partner, a friend, and maybe now an occasional sexual partner. And it seemed there would be nothing more. Could she live with that?

Chapter 21

Who's Getting Lucky?

SHAN SLUMPED ONTO HER COUCH, rested her arm along the back, and stared out the window. The evening light was fading fast, but it was enough to see the drooping tree that marked Lizzie's finish line. She'd even given it a name. Seriously, who named a tree?

She pulled her legs up and reached for her water glass. It was five days since they'd seen each other. Lizzie had sent a text the day after they'd slept together, a chatty, breezy text saying how much she'd enjoyed the evening and that she hoped they could get together soon. Shan hadn't responded.

She rested her head against the back of the couch. What could she say? Indeed, she didn't know how to respond. The evening—not even a night—with Lizzie had been spectacular. The sex had been mind-blowing, but past that, there'd been a warmth to it that had been missing when she'd slept with Celia. The last time she'd had sex.

What should she do? Shan closed her eyes. She should never have slept with Lizzie; it was as simple as that. She'd said, over and over to herself, to Celia, and recently to Lizzie that she couldn't allow herself a relationship, didn't have time for one. Running was everything, and any sort of semi-regular relationship would blow that commitment out of the water. It wasn't just the physical; for her, sex was a whole body–whole mind experience that sapped her energy and turned her mind to mush. How could she perform at her best after that? She couldn't. She knew that from bitter experience.

Shan sighed. The last time she'd been infatuated with someone, running had suddenly become not as important. Thoughts of Tanya had chased through her head at all times, like a primary school tag team. She'd find herself training and thinking not about her own body and race times, her performance and effort, but instead, how Tanya looked when she came. Sleek tanned skin, mass of curly hair, the way her nose wrinkled when she smiled. And she'd been completely unable to drive Tanya from her head and concentrate on running.

She'd been dropped from the team. The first and last time that had happened—apart from injury. And so she'd dropped Tanya from her life and worked until she'd regained her place.

No, that...obsession...couldn't happen again with Lizzie. She wouldn't let it.

Suddenly restless, Shan sprang from the couch and paced to the kitchen. Food. Dinner. A picture of Lizzie's cooking flashed into her head, so vivid she could almost smell the herbs, taste the fragrant chicken, the crunchy salad. Images flashed through her mind like a deck of cards being shuffled: Lizzie cooking, Lizzie smiling, Lizzie playing with Presto. Wrapped in a towel from the shower, laughing with Dee, happy at Everyone's Choir. Lizzie naked. The metal deck of cards halted their shuffle. Lizzie *naked*. Her big, dark eyes, her glorious mane of hair, her full breasts, her smooth, olive skin highlighted by the infinity pendant she always wore. The way her eyes flicked a wicked glance as she moved between Shan's thighs. The way she cried out when she came.

Shan yanked open the fridge with such force the door flew out of her hand, hit the wall, and bounced back to close with a bang. She pulled it open again and took out chicken breast.

How dull. Exactly as her life seemed without Lizzie in it.

Lizzie checked her texts for the millionth time. Nothing. She threw the phone on the couch with a sigh.

Presto padded over and rested his head on her knee. Big sorrowful eyes stared at her as he raised first one eyebrow then the other, giving him a comical look.

She petted his head. "You miss her too, don't you, Presto?"

The first eyebrow lifted again.

"She was your floor exercise buddy. She even shared her yoga mat with you...and then, *poof!* She's gone."

Presto's ears drooped and his tail fell to half-mast.

"I thought we had something." Lizzie picked up Presto's ears and encouraged them to stand up. "We were friends before we had some of the hottest sex known to womankind. And now we have nothing. She doesn't even text me to go running." She let go of Presto's ears and they drooped once more.

Lizzie's phone pinged, and she grabbed it, heart thumping.

It was a spam text telling her to log in and update her bank details. She rolled her eyes and threw the phone back on the couch. One million and one times now she'd checked her phone.

Shan had suggested a run on Thursday. Tomorrow. Surely, she could send a chirpy text reminding her of that. Before she could talk herself out of it, she picked up the phone again. It took three tries to get the text to sound as light-hearted as she wanted.

Presto and I are ready to run our paws off with you tomorrow evening. Still on for that?

She pressed Send, then heaved a sigh. She would not wait around any longer. "Fancy a walk along the river, Presto?"

He barked once, and his tail did gyrocopter circles at the magic word.

A walk was exactly what was needed. A few kilometres' stroll along the Yarra. Maybe she'd see a kingfisher, or maybe she'd meet the person of her dreams walking a rescue greyhound. And she'd leave her phone right there on the couch.

Shan stared at Lizzie's text. It was friendly, light, nothing heavy at all. No demands on Shan's time other than for running. Wasn't that what she wanted? She was being an arse. Ghosting Lizzie of all people was rude and made her little better than Celia with her suggestion that the world revolved around her simply because she was an elite athlete. She bit her lip. Lizzie wanted to see her. She wanted to see Lizzie. Was that so terrible? She'd just have to make sure they kept to the friend zone. If they did, then surely this yearning would fade away in the demands of fitness and physio and getting her body back to its peak. She picked up the phone.

Of course! Still on for 6?

It was nearly an hour before Lizzie replied with a thumbs up, by which time Shan's anxiety that she'd blown their friendship was at stratospheric levels. Her breath whooshed in relief and a frisson of energy twirled in her chest. Suddenly, she couldn't wait to see Lizzie again.

"Rohaan and I had our third date last night." Dee shrugged out of her jacket and threw it over the back of her chair. "Know what he did? He took me to St Kilda, and we went out to the end of the pier and had a picnic on one of the benches there."

"It must have been bloody freezing," Lizzie said.

"We had a rug and snuggled underneath. He's a cuddler, Lizzie. And he's sweet and generous and kind and likes kids. He wants to meet Reece."

"Are you going to let him?"

Dee wiggled her mouse and thumped it hard when it didn't respond. "It's too early for that. I almost think he's too good to be true. I'm half-expecting him to tell me he's got a wife and triplets in Karachi."

"His employment form with us would say if he's married." Lizzie opened her e-mail program, grimacing at the volume of messages.

"We don't check those details. He could have a wife on every continent for all we know."

"He wouldn't see the one in Antarctica very often. You can only go down about twice a year."

Dee rolled her eyes. "You know what I mean. Anyway, I'm seeing him again tonight. I might see if Mum can keep Reece overnight." She wiggled her eyebrows. "I might be getting lucky."

"Shall I put in your personal leave day for tomorrow now?"

"Maybe not. I don't want to jinx myself." Dee opened her own e-mail. "Oh *great*. Sarah Cunningham wants me to call her urgently first thing. She needs another last-minute temp." Dee reached for her coffee mug. "We're early. She can wait a little longer. Can we have coffee here this morning? I'm saving my money to take Rohaan out for dinner. He's treated me every time so far."

"Sure." When they were settled at the break room bench, Lizzie said, "I got lucky too. At least I did for a bit."

"What! When?" Dee pushed over the choc-chip cookies. "And you didn't tell me. Have a biccie to give you strength then I want the details. *All* the details. It's Shan, isn't it?"

"Yeah." Lizzie picked two cookies from the packet, then added a third. "Last Friday, after our run. We just had this crazy moment of euphoria after I smashed my personal best for five kilometres. We fell into bed." She crunched into a biscuit.

"And?"

"And what? We had sex. It was amazing."

"How amazing? Top ten best-ever? Top five? *The* best-ever?"

"I can't even complete a top ten. You know that. It was…definitely top three. Maybe number one."

"You're going to check those stats again, aren't you? This weekend? Tonight?"

"I don't know, Dee." Lizzie fiddled with the biscuit packet. "She went quiet, and I've only had a text about running since. She thinks that sex and relationships mess with her running."

Dee's brow crinkled. "But she's not running much now. She's injured."

"But she's working hard on her fitness and regaining strength in her knee. She has big goals. I'm not sure I fit in there with them."

"But you could give it a try?"

"I'm not sure she wants to. And even if we did, I'm not sure it would work."

"It doesn't have to be happy ever after. It could be happy for now. Or happy for tonight. What's wrong with that?"

"Absolutely nothing—for most people. Happy for tonight doesn't work well for me—you already know that. I ignored my own rule when I slept with her the other night. I should have protected my heart and walked away."

"Maybe this time will be different." Dee crunched loudly. "This time, the sex will be so amazing you won't want anything more."

"Maybe. Or not. But I don't want to find in a couple of months that we've drifted into a casual relationship where her needs come first all the time, and I have to work around her. I'm a giver, Dee, and I don't want to be taken advantage of in that way." She sighed. "I'm getting ahead of myself, aren't I? First, we have to have a second… whatever the first one was."

"You are a bit." Dee rested her elbows on the bench and leaned in. "Lennie's headed this way to tell us about last night's episode of whatever boring TV he's hooked on at the moment. So before he gets here, you just need to figure out what you want from her, and then see if your stars align. You're no pushover Lizzie. You don't have to dance to her tune." Dee straightened and winked as Lennie ambled in. "So, who died in last night's episode, Len?"

Lizzie rested her hands against Sheila-the-sheoak and pushed back, stretching her calves. Beside her, Presto panted, his head swivelling between her and Shan.

"I really enjoyed that." Lizzie looked across at Shan, who was completing a Pilates routine on her mat on the grass. "There's something so meditative about running like that. Footfalls, fresh air, using my body. I can't believe now that running used to be a chore."

"You're a convert." Shan glanced across. "And so is Presto. He's one happy dog now. Very different from when he first came to you."

"I know. He's nearly ready for adoption. Even the scars on his back are less obvious now that he's filled out and his coat is thicker."

"I'll miss him." Shan abandoned her Pilates and encouraged Presto over.

He pressed against her, covering her face with kisses.

"He'll miss you. It's a pity you don't want a dog. You could apply to adopt him." Lizzie's heart twinged. Shan was not the only one who'd miss Presto.

"I can't have pets in my apartment. And even if I could, it wouldn't be fair on him. When I get back to competing, I'll be away too often."

Presto gazed up at Shan with adoring eyes.

It was a pity. If ever there was a doggo match made in heaven, it was Shan and Presto. They seemed to understand each other.

"So, are you still coming to my run on Sunday?" Lizzie's heart sped up. If Shan said no, well, she'd try not to be too disappointed. Shan had got her to the point she was at now. She'd like to share the moment with her.

"Of course." Shan stood and shook out her shoulders. "I contacted that LGBTQ+ drop-in centre you mentioned—it's called Number 94. I'm going to be handing out water bottles with them during the race."

"Great!" Lizzie finished her stretches and picked up Presto's leash. "I'll shun all others so you can give me my bottle."

"You shouldn't need it for only five kilometres."

"Still. I *want* you to give me one." Lizzie gave Sheila a final pat and turned toward Shan's apartment where she'd left her car. "You started me on this journey. I want to share it with you."

"You will." Shan came closer, enough that the green flecks in her eyes were visible. "I'll try to get to the finish line as well, but I might not be able to get away from water duty." She took Lizzie's hand, linking their fingers together.

"Would you...?" Lizzie's stomach quivered in nervous anticipation. "Would you like to go out to dinner afterwards? We could go back to my place for a shower after the run, and then maybe find somewhere in Brunswick Street." The words *and you could stay over* hovered on the tip of her tongue. Should she say them?

Shan crouched to retie her shoelace.

The silence stretched and Lizzie counted her heartbeats. When she got to twenty, she said, "No pressure. You probably have other things to do."

"It's not that." Shan stood again and rested a hand on Lizzie's waist. "I want to spend time with you. We're still friends, right?" Her intense gaze scanned Lizzie's face.

"Friends. Is that what we are?" The nerves coiled into a tight knot in Lizzie's stomach. "With benefits, or just friends?"

"I don't know." Shan gripped harder. "I don't know if I can do the with benefits part when I'm training intensely."

"You're not doing that now. You're still doing strength and fitness conditioning." She kept her tone deliberately light. Non-judgemental—or so she hoped. She took a deep breath. *Say it, Lizzie.* "I was hoping you'd stay over, too, on Sunday. If you bring your laptop, you could do your data entry from my house so you don't have to rush away on Monday. Presto would love the company." *Ooh, nice one, Lizzie. Use Presto for emotional blackmail.*

Shan hesitated, then her shoulders relaxed and her eyes crinkled. "That would be good, if you don't mind."

They reached Lizzie's car, and she opened the boot to get Presto's water bowl. She poured him some water, which he lapped up quickly.

"I know, Presto," Lizzie said. "Shan's only coming to spend time with you." She winked at Shan.

"No." Shan touched Lizzie's hand. "Don't joke about that. I'm coming to be with you. I don't know… I hope I can do this. Be with you in this way. But only a couple of days ago, I decided we'd have to stay in the friend zone. I'm not good with distractions, which is why I haven't been in a relationship for so long. The last person I slept with was Celia. I've been deflecting her ever since."

Celia? Oh. Something heavy settled in Lizzie's chest. Celia, Shan's perfect match. On the surface at least. And if Celia couldn't sustain anything with Shan, not even friends with benefits, then what hope did she have? A big, fat zero.

"But, I'd like to try with you. My decision to stay away lasted less than a week." Her thumb made a slow back and forth on Lizzie's hand. "I can't stop thinking about you."

Warmth drizzled down Lizzie's spine like melted chocolate, and just as sweet. "I'm glad." She took a half step closer and pressed her lips to Shan's. Softly at first, but in a burst of energy, the kiss escalated and grew fiercer.

Their lips melded, tongues seeking entry. A split second to change position, slant their mouths the other way, and then the kiss started once more.

"You could come in," Shan said. Her fingers traced the line of skin above Lizzie's shorts.

Butterflies circled in Lizzie's stomach like an aerial acrobatics team. She nodded. "If Presto can come. I don't want to leave him in the car."

"Of course."

They walked in silence up the stairs to Shan's apartment. When the door was open, Shan found a bowl and filled it with water for Presto, stroked his head, and murmured softly to him.

Lizzie watched, the tide of desire settling deep in her bones, but not wanting to disturb the moment.

When Presto was settled on a blanket in the corner, Shan took Lizzie's hand and led her to the bedroom.

The door closed with a thud and Shan was all over her—hands, mouth, lips, tongue. Their clothes vanished in a blur of motion, and then Lizzie was on the bed with no coherent idea how she'd got there. Shan lay next to her, kissed her, laved her nipples with her tongue, and then when she was panting, writhing under her touch, Shan moved down the bed, pushed Lizzie's thighs apart, and pushed her fingers inside.

Lizzie groaned as Shan's fingers curled to press her G spot, gasped as her thumb strummed her clit. She came in an avalanche of sensation, clenching around Shan's fingers. Once the aftershocks had eased, she rose onto her knees and crouched between Shan's legs, her tongue circling her clit, fingers tracing her entrance. When Shan had come, she turned her attention to her breasts, and the taste of her skin, the slow slide of fingers, until Shan came a second time with a hitch of breath.

For long moments, they lay side by side.

Shan linked their hands together. "And that is why I can't leave you alone."

"The sex?" Lizzie's heavy-lidded eyes flew open. *Just sex?* There was no real reason why that should make her feel sad, but it did. There was nothing wrong with just sex.

"That's part of it. But it feels right being with you. You're easy company."

Well, that redeemed it somewhat. Lizzie tightened her grip on Shan's hand. "Thank you. Maybe we're just easy together."

"That must be it. Will you stay for dinner? It's only chicken and rice and sauce from a jar. Presto could have some chicken."

"I'd like that—if I can have a quick shower first and borrow some clothes."

"Of course." Shan kissed her then got off the bed to rummage in the wardrobe.

Once Lizzie had showered and was dressed in one of Shan's T-shirts and her sarong, they ate at the small table by the window, catching up on their few days apart.

Would Shan ask her to stay? Lizzie sighed. She couldn't, not tonight. "I have to get home. I'm working from the office tomorrow, and Presto needs a better dinner than those bits of chicken. Can I borrow your clothes?"

"Of course."

Lizzie returned to the bedroom. Her sports clothes were scattered over the floor. She gathered them up.

"I'll see you at the race on Sunday." Shan said.

Lizzie nodded. "I'll look out for you cheering me on."

She heaved a breath, trying to subdue the sinking feeling in her stomach. It felt incomplete, leaving like this. She didn't need everlasting love, but this made her feel like she'd taken a sideways step from her own skin.

"I'll be there." Shan kissed her again, her lips moving softly over Lizzie's own.

Lizzie found Presto's leash and clipped it on. "I'll see you then."

With a smile that didn't quite match what she was feeling inside, she left.

Chapter 22

What Runs Faster?

It seemed strange to attend a race—even a fun run—without participating. Shan's fleece hoodie and leggings kept out the morning chill, and her feet snugged comfortably into an old pair of running shoes.

As arranged, she found the meeting point for the crew from the drop-in centre. A dozen or so people wearing bright yellow sweatshirts with *Number 94 LGBTQ+ Centre* written on them milled around.

The organiser, Jorgie, handed her a sweatshirt. "Can you wear this? You can keep it afterwards if you want."

"Thanks." Shan pulled off her hoodie and shrugged into the sweatshirt.

"We're working in groups of three," Jorgie said. "Two to hand out bottles, one to keep the other two supplied. Do you have anyone in the race you're supporting?"

"Yeah, my…friend, Lizzie."

Jorgie's eyes twinkled at Shan's hesitation. "Then you'll want to be one of those handing out the bottles, so you don't miss her. I'm doing the same; my girlfriend and best mate are running. I'll put you with Cilla and Coral." She waved toward two women wearing matching yellow sweatshirts. The older of the two wore a pair of purple high heels with slacks. How on earth was she going to manage in those?

Jorgie led her across and introduced her. "I'll leave you to it to sort out who does what, but if you three could take the middle station, that would be great. Good luck." She turned away to talk to the next group.

"Nice to meet you, Shan. I'm Cilla, and this is Coral. Thanks for helping out."

"This morning is as cold as a witch's tit," Coral grumbled. She reached into a bag at her feet. "But I have coffee to keep us fired up." She produced some tin mugs and a thermos and poured each of them a cup.

Shan took a sip and coughed. The black coffee had a burn to it like fire. "What's in it?"

Coral blinked through heavily mascaraed eyelashes. "Is it too strong? I got a bit distracted when I was adding the whiskey. Still, it will rev us up nicely. Pity we can't give that to the runners instead of water."

"Which of us is going to do what?" Shan asked.

"I can't scamper about in these shoes," Coral said, "So Cilla's going to do the bottle supply. You and I have to hold them out so that people can grab them as they go past. And we're the cheer squad for Leo and Marta—Leo's the director of the centre, and Marta's Jorgie's girlfriend."

Shan nodded.

"So who are you supporting?" Coral asked. "Wife, girlfriend, significant other, cute kid in a koala suit?"

Shan laughed. "Don't talk to me about koala suits. I'll tell you the story sometime." She smiled at Coral's assumption that she was gay. "My friend, Lizzie."

"We'll cheer her on as well," Cilla said in a soft voice. "Don't mind Coral. She's totally devoid of the tact gene."

"Am not." Coral took a mouthful of coffee. "Didn't I—?"

The starting pistol cracked, and Cilla picked up four water bottles and thrust them at Shan. "Here you go. It won't be long until they come past." She handed another four to Coral.

For the next while, the three of them were kept busy pushing bottles into outstretched hands. Shan scanned the runners for Lizzie. Where was she? Maybe she'd missed the start or got trapped behind a line of walkers. But then Shan saw her, running strongly in her red shirt and dark shorts, black plait swinging.

"Here's Lizzie," she said to Coral and Cilla. She stepped out a pace and waited until Lizzie came close before holding out the bottle. "You're doing fantastically!"

Behind her, Coral and Cilla started a can-can. "Liz-zie, Liz-zie, rah, rah, rah!"

Lizzie flashed her a quick smile. Sweat beaded her flushed face, but she seemed comfortable.

Shan watched as she overtook a pair of teenagers and a flagging older runner. Her even stride looked good, her back upright. And her legs in those shorts… Shan let her gaze dwell on them until Lizzie was swallowed up by the crowd.

"Hey," Coral nudged her. "Put your eyes back in your head. If she's just a friend, you can slap my arse and call me Shirley. You make sure you celebrate with her properly this evening."

"Sorry about Coral," Cilla said as she handed Shan more bottles. "She's always like this, but we love her anyway."

A heavily muscled blond man ran up to them, accompanied by a slight white woman. "Leo!" Coral shouted. "My vibrator runs faster than you. You're holding Marta back."

Leo flashed a grin of white teeth, then pulled up his yellow T-shirt and beat his muscled chest. From behind them, a brown-skinned man ran out to Leo and forced him to stop for a kiss. Leo swept him into a deep backward swoop over his bent knee like a black-and-white movie hero.

Cilla and Coral wolf-whistled and applauded. Laughing, Shan joined in.

Next to Leo, Marta sucked deep breaths, her hands on her hips. Maybe Leo's gesture was as much to give her time to recover as to kiss his boyfriend. It seemed likely; Shan was fast learning the Number 94 crowd was a close friendship group.

The rest of the race passed in a blur of motion and noise. The three of them passed out water bottles until the last of the walkers and charity runners had passed. Shan handed a bottle to a man dressed in a tree costume, his branches waving as he shuffled along. How he would manage to drink it, she had no idea.

When the tree had passed, Shan turned to Coral and Cilla. "I'm off to find Lizzie. Thanks for letting me help. I hope Leo and Marta made it to the finish line."

"I'm sure they did—eventually," Coral said.

"Thanks for coming," Cilla said. "You're welcome any time at Number 94. Drop in and say hi sometime. There are normally some of us there."

"I will." With a wave, Shan turned and walked fast to where the finish line flags waved in the breeze.

Her phone beeped with a text.

27:28!!! You owe me a bottle of that great wine. Meet you at the sports drink stand.

Wow. Lizzie had excelled. A flash of images flickered through her mind of the last time Lizzie had beaten her personal best. Would they do that again? Against a tree in a crowded park was not the place to have sex—although Coral might disagree—but later, at home, when they went to bed.

As Shan arrived at the drink stand, Lizzie was talking with Dee, who hung on to Reece's hand with what looked like a grip of steel.

"Hi." Lizzie's smile could have melted the glaciers. "Did you see my time? And I didn't feel like I was pushing myself. I never thought I could do this." She flung her arms around Shan and kissed her cheek, close to her mouth.

Shan hugged her back, smelling the scent of fresh sweat, and underlying that, the sharp, clean scent that was Lizzie. "You did brilliantly."

Dee pulled Reece closer when he tried to tug free. "She did. Lizzie's the sporting superstar of our office."

"How did you and Reece go?" Shan asked.

Dee rolled her eyes. "Well, we made it to the end. Both of us together, but I reckon I ran twice as far as everyone else as I had to keep darting off to foil his escape plans."

Reece tugged at her hand. "Choccy milk."

"Later," she told him. "Maybe I should start running with Lightning here so that I can be as fast and look as good."

"Anytime," Lizzie said.

They said their goodbyes to Dee and Reece and headed off across the park to Lizzie's car.

"Thanks for the water," Lizzie said. "I was rather focussed on running, but you looked like you were having fun."

"I was. The Number 94 crowd are a hoot. I'll help them out again if they sponsor another race."

They reached the car, and Lizzie paused. "Do you mind if we walk a little further? Once around the park or something? I'm still buzzing from the race. I feel like I could run around Australia right now. Maybe we could get a coffee from the stand on the far side of the park and then head back."

"That sounds good. I had a mouthful of whiskey with a drop of coffee in it that Coral gave me." Shan shuddered. "I don't know how she drank it and remained standing."

Lizzie grabbed a sweatshirt and pants from the car, and then they headed for the coffee stand.

"I'm already thinking of next time." Lizzie glanced across at Shan. "Is that crazy? I'm wondering what to try next."

"What do you like the most: trying to get faster or run longer?"

"Longer," Lizzie said without hesitation. "I love pushing myself, but it's the longer, slower runs that I truly enjoy. It's almost meditative.

Each time, I say I'll use the time to solve a work problem or figure out the best way to deal with my parents, but each time, I just run with an empty head. It's wonderful."

"Maybe you're a marathoner."

"I don't think I'm that committed." Lizzie gave a little hop and skip. "But a half-marathon—twenty-one kilometres. Maybe I could do that. I'd like to try."

"I'll draw you up a training plan, if you'd like."

"I would."

They reached the coffee stand and ordered, then took their coffees to a bench overlooking the sweep of parkland leading down to the city. Overhead, the slate-grey sky showed through the bare branches of trees, and a cool wind whipped across the park.

Shan looked across at Lizzie. She had her head tipped forward, studying her coffee as if the secrets of life were hidden in the curls of steam. Stands of her inky hair hung loose, pulled free of her plait, and she had a soft half-smile on her face.

Shan's heart turned over once in her chest with a thump. Lizzie was the complete package: a kind and generous person, warm and loving, attractive, with a shared passion for fitness and eating well. And dynamite in bed. There was no reason Shan shouldn't enjoy the time with her while she could. After all, it couldn't be a long-term thing, not when her knee recovered. In one month, she'd be able to start running again. The next appointment with Dr Gupta should be the last. A thrill of anticipation zagged through Shan's belly. Oh, how she'd missed that. And today had brought it home. As great as it was to assist the Number 94 mob and support Lizzie, she missed being out there. Striding along near the head of the pack. Pushing herself to do her best, knowing that her absolute best was good enough to win a Commonwealth Games medal if she was lucky.

She'd missed out on that goal, but there was another, more glittering prize in two years' time: the Olympics.

Nothing could get in the way of that.

Nothing.

"The training camp was great." Celia shifted down a gear and accelerated through the lights. "A week wasn't long enough though. The team is really coming together. There's also a chance I might get a place in the 5,000 metres as well. Selena's having personal issues and can't pull it together at the moment. She's seeing the sports psychologist, but apparently it's not going well."

"Poor Selena," Shan murmured, gripping the door handle as Celia took a left turn too fast. She hoped she didn't drive like this with clients in the car.

"How soon until you can start running again?" Celia braked and slammed a hand on the horn. "Bloody idiot. Learn to drive!"

"If I get out of this car alive, hopefully in about four weeks."

"You've done everything right for recovery. And for most of that time, you had Lizzie to look after you. You still seeing her?" Celia shot her a quick sideways glance.

"Mm, yes. We go out to eat and catch up maybe once or twice a week." No need to mention the sex. "And of course, she now takes her running seriously. She's planning to enter a half-marathon. Maybe the Bendigo one."

"Tourist marathon," Celia said dismissively.

"So? The scenery will make the experience great. She's not out to break records."

"Obviously."

Shan was silent. She'd thought Celia's animosity toward Lizzie had faded, but it seemed not. She stared out the window, at the traffic on St Kilda Road as they headed south toward the beach.

"Are you sleeping with her?" The question fell abruptly into the quiet car.

Shan startled. What should she say? Lying wasn't her thing, but the truth would likely upset Celia. And it wasn't her business anyway. She bit her lip, pondering her choices.

"You don't have to answer that—your silence tells me it's a yes. She must be good if she could get you out of your self-imposed celibacy. Or are you just taking advantage of the break from training, and you'll dump her once you start running again?"

"It's not like that." Shan's voice scratched in her throat. "We were friends first. The other…well, it just happened."

Celia pressed the accelerator and the car surged forward. She cut into the outside lane, earning a blast of the horn from the truck behind. "Is it serious?"

Shan searched for the meaning behind Celia's question. Was she jealous? Was it just pique? "Why do you want to know?"

Celia sighed and slowed just before the speed camera. "Truth? I'm miffed. What's she got that I haven't? Other than wider hips. But that's okay, I'll get over it. If it's what you want, then I'm truly happy for you." She reached out a hand and took Shan's.

"I don't honestly know what I want. Lizzie and I… I really like her. But I can't see where this will go. I'll be training fully again soon, and I can't… I just can't afford the distraction."

"We're a pair of relationship losers, that's what we are," Celia said. "Neither of us have a great track record…no pun intended. Maybe we'll end up together after all, in about twenty years when we can barely dodder once around the track."

Shan laughed. "Maybe." She might not be with Lizzie, but she already knew that she and Celia would never be more than friends.

Chapter 23

Dead in the Desert

SHAN WAITED ON THE PORCH as Lizzie shuffled out into the cool morning, her face split by a yawn. She dropped her key, picked it up, closed the door, and jabbed at the lock before turning to Shan.

"Ready?"

"Ready." A bubble of excitement simmered in Shan's chest. As expected, Dr Gupta had given her the go ahead. And now, she was about to *run*. Sure, it would be more of a jog than a race, but she would have both feet off the ground at the same time. The road underneath her feet. The cool air in her lungs.

"We better stay on the road," Lizzie said. "It's smoother."

Shan nodded and led the way out of the gate.

"To the river!" Lizzie stuck out an arm, pretending to be dragged along by it. "You set the pace."

Shan swallowed hard. Was her knee up to this? Was it a mistake? Tentatively, she broke into a slow jog. Her feet found their rhythm on the pavement, her arms and breathing fell into sync. The muscle memory in her legs kicked in and she increased the pace. Her mouth stretched into a grin so wide it felt like it would swallow her face. She was *running!* Sure, it was slow and steady and wouldn't set any records, but she was *running*.

They reached the path that led steeply down to the river and Shan slowed. "I better walk this stretch."

Lizzie nodded. Her breath came in fast pants.

Once they reached the flat path alongside the Yarra, Shan broke into a run again. She glanced at her running watch. Just under five minutes per kilometre. Easy as anything. She could go forever at this pace, even after months of couch-potatoing.

Shan glanced over at Lizzie. Sweat beaded her forehead and her breath rasped. But her face radiated determination and she ran on doggedly, only half a pace behind Shan.

Shan's watch beeped. Ten minutes. She slowed to a jog and then to a walk.

"Thank...the fuck...for that." Lizzie halted and bent over. Her breath wheezed through her mouth. "You nearly killed me. I was about to keel over on the path like one of those weirdos who run for days across the desert. You could have kicked me into the river, and I'd have sunk like a rock." She sank to her haunches.

Exhilaration hummed in Shan's blood, but after a glance at Lizzie's red face, she reined it in. "Are you okay?"

"Not now, but I will be. To think I thought I could run with you on your first run in bloody months. I must have been dreaming." Lizzie stood again. "But all the same. I've run with an elite athlete. Once. Probably never again."

Shan glanced across. Lizzie's breathing was already returning to normal. "Don't knock yourself. You did great."

"Compared to what? My grandmother who barely leaves the house? Not great compared to you."

"With respect, we're very different when it comes to running."

"Yeah. And I've just realised how much. But"—she turned to Shan and her face shone with the smile spreading across it—"that was fantastic! I never knew I could run so fast. For so long. I loved it. Even if I thought I was going to puke at the end."

Run until you puke yet love it anyway. Shan smothered a small smile. She'd done that. And only a true runner knew how truly satisfying it was. Knowing you'd given your all, put in 110 per cent effort, whether it was an elite 400 metres or a ten-minute run along the river path.

She shot a smile at Lizzie. "I'm serious. You did great. Want to come again with me next time?"

"Yeah…no…yeah…no. Who am I kidding?" Lizzie spread her arms wide. "Hell, yeah, I'm coming, if you'll have me. That was amazing! Imagine what I could do if I ran with you more often! But enough about me. How's your knee feeling after that?"

How was it? Lizzie's joy in the run had wiped thoughts of her own injury from her head. Shan delved into her body. Was there pain? Did she feel strong? There was a tiny ache in the knee, but no weakness, no sharp pain, no feeling of instability. "Good. It feels great!"

"I'm so glad." Lizzie turned and started walking back. "Your first step back to greatness."

Was it? Shan squeezed her arms against her sides in anticipation. Maybe.

"Dee wants to know if you're coming to Everyone's Choir this weekend." Lizzie put the phone on speaker and laid it on the bench so she could open Presto's dogfood.

He sat expectantly, ears pricked, waiting for his dinner.

"I don't think I can," Shan said. "I have training at six in the morning on Sunday."

"Choir will be over by nine." Lizzie spooned the food into his bowl and set it on the floor. "It's in Richmond. If you stay with me, we'll be in bed by nine thirty."

"That's half the problem. In bed doesn't mean asleep when you're in it."

"I didn't hear you arguing last time. You did a lot of moaning, but it wasn't the complaining sort."

In the last month, she and Shan had fallen into the habit of going out a couple of times a week. Each time, they ended in Lizzie's bed. So far, Shan's running didn't seem to be suffering, at least not that Lizzie could see. And the sex was still amazing. Still off the charts.

"Sunday is important. The first training session with my club since my injury. I can't afford to be tired or distracted. I'll have to pass on Everyone's Choir. I'm sorry."

"Do you want to stay here anyway? You can let yourself in and be tucked up asleep when I come home." Lizzie held her breath. Was that too much of an intrusion into Shan's carefully constructed routine? "I promise not to jump your bones if that's what's bothering you." She kept her tone light-hearted.

Shan was silent for a moment. "I still think it's better that I stay home. I'm not sure I could resist seducing you. Maybe we could catch up the next day after training? Have lunch somewhere? Maybe go to the St Kilda markets?"

"Sure. That would be good. I can tell you what you missed at choir. Dee's convinced we're going to be doing that 'Grace Kelly' song from several years ago. She's been practicing the high notes."

"Is she hitting them?"

"Not any better than when we did the Sia song. She's now banned from singing in the office."

Shan's sigh wafted over the line. "I'm sorry, Lizzie. I know you'd like me to stay over, but I can't. Not this time."

Lizzie bit her lip. "This is difficult for me, Shan. You're here, you're not here. You're with me, you're not. We have sex. Or not. I feel like I'm in little pieces and sometimes a couple of them come together for a short while before they break apart again. The dinner and sex pieces, say. Then some days later, maybe the running and coffee pieces. But never the whole picture."

"What are you saying?" Shan sounded cautious.

"I don't know what I'm saying, to be honest. Just that I love seeing you in all those ways, but…" Lizzie blew a frustrated breath and was silent.

Shan's breathing over the phone sounded loud in the pause.

"Forget I said anything. I'm trying not to be needy and demanding—you've made it clear what you can offer me. I'm not asking for anything you can't give. I guess I'm just thinking aloud. I'll cope."

"I'm sorry, Lizzie." Her voice was low, steady. "I warned you that I would be like this. I love what we have together, but if it's not what you want..."

Was it? Lizzie's stomach clenched at Shan's words, and the slither of ice down her spine made her pause. She wanted Shan in her life—in whatever way she was prepared to offer. And for now, it was okay.

Just.

"We're feeling our way into each other's lives. There's not an instruction book. Me and Presto might have to snuggle up together instead." She forced an upbeat lilt to her voice.

"As long as he doesn't drop hairs on my side of the bed."

"I'll bring him to lunch. He's missed you."

"I've missed him too. Are we good, Lizzie?"

Her breath released in a shudder. "We're good." What else could she say without shattering everything?

"I'll call you after training and we can figure out where to go. Bye."

The call ended. Lizzie stared at the phone and threw it on the couch. Shan was a frustrating person to be in a relationship with—if she could even call it that. It was the little things she missed. Like lounging on the couch together, reading in bed, cooking. Sometimes, it seemed when Shan had been her housemate, they'd had more of a couple relationship than they did now.

Dee had I-told-you-so commiserated and suggested maybe it was time to move on. But even though when Dee said it, it made a lot of sense, the next time she saw Shan it was the absolute last thing she wanted.

Even their running was now something they did together-but-not-together. They'd meet at the track near Shan's apartment and then follow their own plans. Sometimes, as Lizzie was jogging around the park at her steady pace, she'd see Shan circling the track at a speed that, to her, seemed impossibly fast. But that was another difference between them: Shan was an athlete; Lizzie was a fun runner.

"What shall we do, Presto?"

He cocked his head and regarded her. "Do I have a girlfriend or not?"

He barked once.

"Not very helpful. I don't know if that's yes or no. At least I have you." And that was a whole other issue. Presto was turning into a lovely dog. He'd lost most of his earlier nervousness and was ready to find his forever home. Foster carers weren't supposed to get too attached the dogs. *Too late for that.* She should call the charity and let them know Presto was ready to be adopted.

Her heart weighed heavy in her chest. She didn't know if she could hand him over. Would it be so bad if she kept him? It would be the end of her fostering; she couldn't have more than one dog in a tiny house like this.

It was something to think about another day.

Like Shan.

Chapter 24

Jasmine Queen

SHAN MATCHED CELIA STRIDE FOR stride as they rounded the final corner. Next to her, Celia's face was a rigid mask of concentration. In the final hundred metres, Celia pulled away as Shan knew she would and crossed the finish line a couple of metres ahead.

Shan put her hands on her hips and bent over, sucking deep breaths into her tortured lungs. Her first time-trial since injury and she hadn't done too badly at all. She suspected Pieter had asked Celia to push her to see how she did. She looked at her running watch. Yes, the finish time was slower than would be normal for Celia.

"Good, good." Pieter approached with his stopwatch. "Shan, you're not back to where you were before injury, but you're getting there. You've lost stamina. Work on that. But all the same, it's enough that I'll send you to the week-long training camp at the Australian Institute of Sport next month. I'll e-mail the details. Good to see you back." Pieter swung around and marched back to the group warming up.

"Well done." Celia put her hands on her hips. "You're back!"

Excitement fizzed in Shan's blood that had nothing to do with the adrenaline of the run. This was the start. The next time she and Celia went head-to-head like this, Shan swore it would be a more even match. "You're going to the camp too?"

"Of course," Celia said. "Don't blow this, Shan. It's important."

"Yeah." Shan's grin felt like it might crack her face. "I'm not going to stuff up."

"As long as you don't blow your knee, you'll be all right." Celia fist bumped with Shan. "Let's walk to cool down. I have news for you."

"Oh?" Shan fell into step with Celia. "You've finally bought a new car to replace that bomb of yours? You're dating Sam Kerr?"

"Ha! I wish," Celia said. "She's got a girlfriend. Neither of those. Wait until we're away from everyone."

They walked to the centre of the track and stopped to stretch.

"I heard Pieter talking to someone in the locker room about you the other day." Celia concentrated on her hamstring stretch. "He said it was a pity you blew your knee, as otherwise you would have been a shoo-in for the Commonwealth team. He said you had the best work ethic and gained the most from training."

"Oh!" Heat stole up Shan's neck. "Thanks for sharing that. Hopefully it means I'll be in with a chance for the next race squad."

"More than that," Celia said. "He ranks you as one of our best Olympic prospects, after Yusra and Jamila. Says if you put in the hard yards, regain your lost fitness, and manage to avoid further injury, then in eighteen months you should be peaking—at just the right time."

"Really?" Shan's heart pounded faster. "Pieter said that?"

"Yeah, of course. I wouldn't bullshit you." She looked down. "You were the only person he talked about."

"Wow." Shan's mind spun. "I never expected that. I'm just slogging on, you know, just trying my best."

"Maybe your approach is the best way." Celia switched to stretch the other hamstring. "The monastic stay-at-home life. Few nights out, a good diet." She sighed. "No sex. Maybe I should try it."

"It might not work that way for you," Shan said diplomatically. "You've always done well with your approach."

"True. But how much better could I be if I didn't waste energy on seduction and nights out?"

"There's one way to find out if you're serious about it. Try it for a few weeks."

"I might do that. You know, this run we've just had… Pieter asked me to stick with you but push you faster than you seemed comfortable with. I thought it would be an easy cruise for me. It wasn't. I had to work to stay ahead of you."

That was unexpected. Shan concentrated on her quad stretch. Maybe, just maybe, her dream was still in reach. But what would that mean for her and Lizzie?

∞

Rather than call ahead, Shan went around to Lizzie's. She'd brought a bottle of what had become their celebration wine, and some bacon treats for Presto. The day was warm for winter, and Lizzie's front door stood open.

Shan called out a hello and walked down the hallway.

Lizzie was in the living area, her phone pressed to her ear. She wiggled her eyebrows at Shan. "I have to go, Mumma," she said into the phone. "My friend is here and we're going out for lunch. Love you." She ended the call and went over to greet Shan, pressing a kiss to the corner of her mouth. "Hi. You're early."

"Training was cut short. I thought about doing a couple of hours of data entry but that thought lasted less than a minute. And here I am."

"I was wondering about that," Lizzie said. "Now that you're fit again, are you going to return to your barista job?"

Shan set down the wine and treats on the counter and bent to pat Presto. "Actually, Daz called yesterday, asking if I was fit. Seems a couple of his staff have moved on. I told him I wasn't coming back. The data entry might not be the most exciting job in the world—"

"I thought it was," Lizzie said, deadpan.

"—but it pays better and has more flexibility. So I'll stick with it. Unless you're about to tell me I'm being replaced."

"No way! You're one of our better ones. I saw the wine you brought and wondered if we were celebrating you getting your old job back."

"No, that's for this evening. I thought we could order takeaway from Royal Thai."

Lizzie's eyebrows shot up. "You must be celebrating something good. Royal Thai is nearly twice the price of our usual place."

"Mm." A tiny part of Shan's mind wondered when she and Lizzie had gained a 'usual place'. Couples had usual places, just like they had in-jokes, and an equal division of chores. Friends with benefits didn't have those things.

"Let me close down my computer, then I'm all yours. I have some news too." Lizzie started shutting down her laptop. "I can't shut this thing down any faster. Will I like your news?"

"I hope so." For a second, a shard of doubt flew through Shan's mind. Would Lizzie be excited? The camp was only for a week. It wasn't that, though; it was everything else the camp stood for. Increased training, a higher level of commitment, stricter diet, a more rigid routine. She looked at the wine on the counter. No more wine. And a lesser amount of time to spend with Lizzie.

Celia's words about Shan's previous monastic life flashed through her mind. Maybe she shouldn't even be trying to keep something— anything—going with Lizzie. Maybe now was the time to call it a day.

She spun around to the counter.

Lizzie was crouched, her head in one of the kitchen cupboards. "This sounds serious enough to find the good crystal and open the wine now." She stood, two wine glasses in her hands.

Shan swallowed hard. But she couldn't back out of telling her the news now. Lizzie would be pleased for her. Pleased and hopefully proud. She watched as Lizzie opened the wine and poured two glasses.

"Shall we sit in the back yard?"

Shan nodded and followed Lizzie outside to the small table and chairs. Presto followed them out and settled at Shan's feet with a long sigh.

Lizzie went to the trailing jasmine bush that hung over the fence from the neighbour's yard and pulled off long strands of flowers. She sat at the table and started winding them together into a circlet. "What's your news?" Deftly, she worked the vines around and over each other, forming a crown of scented white blossom.

Anticipation bubbled in Shan's throat, the words threatening to spill out. But it would make it sweeter to go second. "You first."

"Mine's not that exciting," Lizzie said. "I sent off my entry for the Bendigo half-marathon. I really hope you'll come along and support me."

"Remind me when is it?"

"Three months' time—in September. I hoped we could make a weekend of it, stay somewhere nice the nights before and after."

She nodded. "I can do that."

"I'm looking forward to it. I'd never have dreamed I'd be excited about running thirteen miles without stopping. Six months ago, I'd rather have gouged out my kidneys with a fork." Lizzie leaned forward. "Now tell me your news."

"I was at training today."

Lizzie nodded. "How did it go?"

"Good. Great." She took a deep breath. "I've been invited to a training camp next month in Canberra at the Australian Institute of Sport. It's one of the regular camps for the top-flight athletes, and I'm lucky to sneak in. Apparently, too"—she leaned forward, pushing her hands under her thighs to subdue their excited flutter—"it's a camp so they can get a preliminary look at those who might, just maybe, be thought of as Olympic hopefuls."

"The Olympics?" Lizzie's eyes grew wide, and her fingers stilled on the circlet. "Oh my God, Shan, that's *huge*. Bigger than the Commonwealth Games! To think I'm sitting here with a future gold medallist!"

Shan chuckled. "You are such an optimist. This is just the first baby step on a very long ladder. Bodies will fly off it in all directions. But they're looking at the potential they've got for the games in eighteen months' time." She raised her glass. "Cheers!"

"*Yamas*." They clinked glasses. "I'm so very happy for you. It's a huge step toward your dream. Just think… you'll be on the podium, a gold medal around your neck as they play the Australian national anthem!"

"You are so far ahead. I'm just looking at Canberra next month."

"Tell me when it is, and I'll get Dee to approve your leave request."

"I hadn't even thought of that," Shan admitted. Leave. Data entry. It was all so mundane compared to the glittering promise that now lay in front of her. "This first one's only a week. I've been on similar things before. After the last one, I came home and slept for two days straight."

"Wow." Lizzie spun the jasmine circlet on her finger. "My friend the Olympian." She leaned forward and placed the circlet on Shan's head. "I crown you Queen of the Olympics. We should definitely order from Royal Thai this evening."

The sweet smell of jasmine was overpowering. Shan took Lizzie's hand. "My treat."

The buzzing, jumping whirl of excitement in her stomach meant she might not manage to eat much. She'd make the most of it though. Thai food most likely wouldn't be on her diet sheet for the next few weeks. There were many things that wouldn't be part of her life. Like wine. She swirled the liquid in her glass, watching as its ruby colour clung to the side. She shot a glance at Lizzie, her delight at the news still evident on her face. And Lizzie. She would not be a part of her life soon. At least the sex part.

Shan swallowed. It would be hard, very hard to move back to the friend zone, but she'd have to try. Falling for Lizzie wasn't part of the plan, but it seemed to have happened anyway. But now she had to be strong, to subdue her feelings, her desire for Lizzie, and keep things platonic. They'd been friends before, and they could do it again. She'd had her time out for pleasure, now it was back to the grind of being an elite athlete. And for her, that meant no distractions. And Lizzie was one major distraction.

So friend zone it would have to be. If she couldn't do that... Shan shut down her thoughts. She didn't want to think on that.

But they still had now. The camp wasn't until next month. She could have another few days with Lizzie, another few nights in her bed, just as she could enjoy the bottle of wine and rich Thai food later. Then, in a week, she'd go back to the monastic life that Celia was trying. She had to give this camp her best shot. She may not get a second chance.

Chapter 25

Doggo Date

"Lizzie? It's Helena from the shelter. I'm calling about Presto."

Lizzie gripped the phone and shot a glance at Presto, who was on his rug slobbering over a strip of rawhide. "He's doing well. He's back to a healthy weight and has become less timid. He's still afraid of new people though, especially loud ones."

"You've fostered him for more than four months now. How do you think he'll go if we transfer him to the main shelter and offer him for adoption?"

Lizzie hesitated. "Honestly? I'm not sure he'll do well in that environment. He could stay with me, and potential adopters can meet him here." Her heart clenched. Of all the dogs she'd cared for, Presto was special. She would miss him more than most. Also, he was inextricably tied in her heart with Shan.

"How about you bring him to the shelter for a visit, so we can see how he reacts?"

Lizzie closed her eyes. This seemed like a bad, bad thing for Presto…but maybe it was the way forward. Shelter dogs were adopted quicker than ones seen in a foster environment. For Presto's sake, she would do this. Even if it was wrong for him in the short term, he would hopefully get a loving forever home from it.

"Sure. But can you give me another couple of weeks to socialise him more?"

"No worries," Helena said in brisk tones. "Thanks, Lizzie. I'll see you and Presto soon."

She ended the call and stared at her dog. *Her dog.* That was how she thought of him now. Hers and Shan's. Poor Presto. He would need a lot of care and love from his new family to help him get over losing the two people he loved.

She stood and went to change into her running clothes. She'd go for a run. "Want to come?" she said to Presto.

His ears shot up and he bounded from the rug and over to her, wagging his tail. When did he not want to come? Presto had lucked out being fostered by someone who gave him so much exercise. Any new home for him would have to do the same.

She clipped on his leash and let herself out of the house. A slow run along the Yarra would be perfect for both of them.

Lizzie sat at her kitchen counter. Saturday afternoon and evening stretched in front of her. Despite a fifteen-kilometre run earlier, she was still full of energy. Maybe Shan would like to go to Federation Square where a hip-hop band was playing. Maybe they could eat in Chinatown after, or go to one of the small, hidden bars in the Melbourne laneways. She frowned. They usually had plans for the weekend: something to do with running, or they'd drive out of Melbourne go to bushwalking in the Yarra Ranges or visit a market. Saturday nights usually ended in Lizzie's bed.

Lizzie shrugged. She'd been busy, and Shan must have been busy too. That was doubtless why she hadn't heard from her. Her skin tingled in anticipation of time with Shan. Were they girlfriends now? Neither of them had ever said, but there was the assumption they would spend the weekends together, and a couple of evenings in the week.

For all Shan's protestations that she couldn't have a relationship alongside her athletic career, the two of them had fallen into something that seemed exactly like a relationship to Lizzie. Dinner, bed, and breakfast. Weekend plans. Sex. Shared interests. Occasional evenings in front of the TV. Sure, Shan had only met Dee of Lizzie's friends, and she'd only met Celia, but they were the main players in the friend's arena—the ones that counted.

She sent a quick text asking if Shan wanted to go to the free music in the city.

Her phone pinged a minute or so later.

I'm sorry, I'll have to pass. Really tired. Fierce day of training. Need to rest.

Rest? Well, she could do that too.

Want me & Presto to come around & rest with you? We can bring dinner.

This time, the time between texts stretched longer. Presto was curled up on his rug in the corner, blissfully unaware his fate may be decided soon. She should mention that to Shan, just in case she was, after all, interested in adopting him. She tapped the phone, wondering whether to send a message about that, when her phone pinged again.

Honestly? I'm that tired I'm nearly asleep now. Toasted cheese sanger & tomato soup then bed. Training tomorrow, plus I have extra data entry to make up.

Was this real or a brush off? A cold feeling slithered down Lizzie's neck. Shan had always managed something before now. Even when she was tired, one of them had gone to the other's and they'd eaten dinner, watched TV. Lizzie had massaged Shan's legs. Shan had cuddled up to her. Even if they hadn't had sex, there'd been the warmth and pleasure of having a warm body in bed with her.

No worries. I'll see you next week sometime. Time for us is special—let's make sure we fit it in.

What else could she say without being the demanding, clingy girlfriend who didn't understand the stressful life of an elite athlete?

There was no point texting Dee; she was out with Rohaan and would be lucky to make it into work on Monday, let alone answer Lizzie's text. At least someone was having a great relationship.

There wasn't really anyone else she could call on short notice. Most of her other friends were in relationships, doing couple things on the weekend. With a snort, Lizzie picked up the TV remote. "Looks like it's you and me tonight, Presto."

He came over and rested his head on her leg.

She encouraged him up on to the couch where he usually wasn't allowed. But who else would she cuddle with on this Saturday night?

Guilt and regret twined in Shan's chest. She wasn't so tired that she couldn't have gone to Lizzie's. She had last week, and the week before. Maybe they'd have gone to the music, left early, and curled up together in Lizzie's bed. Maybe Lizzie would have rubbed her legs as she had last week. There would be sex, long, slow, and caring, with no hurry in the world, no rush to completion, just a gradual path to satisfaction that was all the more intense because of the familiarity and comfort to it.

But no. Celia's words had rattled around Shan's head, and she'd turned down Lizzie for no reason other than she felt she should. Her feeling that she ran better, was more focussed, if she didn't have Lizzie around. If she took the long, lonely path.

Even Celia seemed to have adopted that approach. She hadn't been out with anyone for a couple of weeks. At least, that's what she'd said.

Shan's fingers twitched. It was all very well saying that, but the reality was, she didn't know if it was having an effect or not. Maybe it wasn't; maybe her running would be gradually improving, Lizzie or no Lizzie. In which case, all this self-denial would be for nothing. After all, thinking about Lizzie when she wasn't with her was as bad as being in a relationship. It was Tanya all over again: the yearning, the craving for Lizzie's company. The inability to shift the other person from her mind. Shan groaned and massaged her temples.

She rested her head back against the couch and picked up the TV remote. Next week she was going to Canberra. She'd see how she went at the camp.

Nerves fluttered in her stomach. If this camp went well, she'd be back on the circuit, back in contention, back on the upward road to her peak. That was what it was all about, wasn't it?

Wasn't it?

Chapter 26

Circling

MARIETTA GLANCED AT HER HANDS loosely clasped on the pad in her lap, then back at up Shan. "It has taken a lot of dedication to recover from injury the way you have and return to the sport as good as you were before you left it. How do you think you managed that?"

Shan sucked in her cheeks and considered her answer. She knew Marietta wouldn't rush her. This was her second sports psychology session of the week, and Marietta would wait with a slight smile and unwavering focus until Shan was ready to answer.

"I think, no, I *know* that running is the most important thing in my life. To have it taken away made me feel...less of a person. Less of what makes me *me*. And I wanted that back. So I kept my fitness up as best I could and followed the doctors' advice to the minutest detail."

Marietta's clear, grey eyes sharpened. "And that's all it took? Following advice?"

"No, of course not. I had to prioritise things: I found work I could do that brought in money to get by. I kept a routine. I researched exercises and treatments."

"And you did all that alone?"

"Of course." Shan frowned. "No one else can do those things for me."

"So you had no partner, no family, no friends to assist? What about home care services?" Marietta's focus didn't waver, but if anything, her gaze became more intense.

Shan shifted restlessly in the chair. What was Marietta getting at? Why did it matter how she'd recovered? The important thing was she *had* got better—stronger, fitter, and more determined than she was prior to her injury.

She pushed aside her irritation at the seemingly irrelevant question and focused on her answer. "I had some practical help. I live in a fourth-floor apartment. My friend Lizzie let me stay in her house, so I didn't have to deal with the stairs. She also helped me get my job. She was great, too, with driving me to appointments, and taking on the heavier chores I couldn't do."

Marietta nodded, "She sounds like a very close friend to do all that for you."

"She's a good person. Kind."

"Tell me about your relationship."

Shan squirmed inside. How could she define her relationship with Lizzie to someone else when she'd avoided labelling it to herself? "I guess…friends with benefits. Although I'm pulling back from the with benefits part. I need us to be just friends."

"Why is that?"

A spurt of irritation lodged in Shan's chest. Marietta should know the answer. She was an ex-athlete, now psychologist for the AIS. She must know how it was. "I can't let a relationship distract me from my athletic goals."

"If you didn't have those goals, would you ideally like a partner or partners by your side? Or would you still prefer to be alone?"

Why was she asking these questions? Distance running was a solo sport, and you could only rely on yourself. A relationship would blur that focus.

"It's obvious."

"Tell me anyway." At Shan's silence, she added, "Work with me, Shan. I'm not questioning your dedication or focus."

"You're asking me a hypothetical. I *do* have those goals, and so there's no point in asking what I'd do if I didn't have them."

Marietta blinked, and her lips twitched. "Fair enough." She jotted a couple of words on the pad. "Let me ask you something else, then. Do you ever get lonely?"

Shan closed her eyes briefly as the hollowness the question brought swamped her. "Of course. Doesn't everyone? It's human nature to want to be around others, at least some of the time."

"So who are you around? You've previously told me your family are loving, but not nearby. That most of your friends are other runners. Running is a lonely sport, Shan, but it doesn't have to be that way in your life as well. Try not to shut others out."

"I talk with my mother on the phone." She pushed aside the fact she hadn't done that for a while. "My best friend Celia is my training partner. And..."

Marietta inclined her head and waited.

"And Lizzie. We haven't been friends for long, but I hope we'll continue to see each other."

"She sounds like a good friend."

"She is. The best." Shan licked her dry lips as thoughts of Lizzie pulsed through her mind. "If I weren't an athlete, if I didn't have these goals, then I'd hope for more with Lizzie." One part of her mind registered she'd just answered Marietta's earlier question, but not to acknowledge Lizzie in this way felt...wrong.

"More?"

"A relationship. If I was able to have one, then she would be perfect. She is perfect."

"I'd like to hear why you feel you're not able to have one now. Many athletes do."

Shan swallowed her irritation. Had Marietta not listened to her reasons? "When I was younger, I had a fairly long-term relationship, and it didn't work out. When I was with Tanya, my running fell into a slump. I couldn't focus. All I could think about was her. My times suffered, then I was dropped from the team." Her shoulders tensed and she gripped her knees and leaned forward. "I can't let that happen again. Not now. Not with the Olympics coming soon."

"How many years ago was that?"

"Most of ten."

"So you were seventeen? Eighteen?" Marietta's voice remained neutral, but she quirked an eyebrow.

Shan nodded.

"And since then?"

"Nothing much. A few one-night stands." Shan clenched her toes inside her running shoes and resisted the urge to shuffle her feet. "And Lizzie."

Marietta remained silent and simply crossed one tracksuit-clad leg over the other, regarding Shan.

"Many athletes avoid relationships. The time apart, the demands of training, the extra burdens put on a partner." Shan cringed internally at the defensive tone of her voice. She shouldn't have to justify her choice.

"Yet Lizzie, your friend with benefits, took your care on willingly."

"For a short time. It wouldn't be fair to her to ask for more."

Marietta nodded. "I'm glad you're considerate of her. But have you asked how she feels about this?"

Shan sat back. How Lizzie feels? The session wasn't about Lizzie. She frowned as Marietta's words settled in her mind. Lizzie had made the reason for her initial offer of help clear. But now… Shan *hadn't* asked her. "A relationship is different from caring for someone who's hurt. Many athletes have found their performance takes a dive when they enter a long-term relationship. Not just track and field athletes. Tennis players, swimmers—"

"Paula Radcliffe might not agree. But yes, there are some. However, most find a balance. One that benefits both partners."

"I'm not sure what you're getting at."

"Lizzie is a friend who let you stay with her, who is caring for you in a lot of ways. Whom you sleep with sometimes. Are you happy with that?"

"It's not that simple." Shan brushed a hand through her hair and tried to keep the frustration from showing in her voice. "I'm not sure what you're trying to do. Do you think I would be better in a relationship with Lizzie?"

Marietta made another note on the pad. "My job isn't to push you anywhere, just to give you clarity about your choices. However, I'm concerned you're too one-sided, Shan. You've told me you have few outside friends, and you haven't mentioned any outside interests."

"I have other interests!" At Marietta's tilted head, she said, "I enjoy Everyone's Choir. And I'm involved with fostering a rescue dog."

"That's great. How did you get involved with those things?"

The knot in Shan's chest grew bigger, tighter. "Through Lizzie."

"Lizzie again. I'm not pushing you in any direction, Shan, but everyone needs balance in their lives. Even you. And there is a middle path between needing no one and being subsumed into a relationship. You were very young when you were overwhelmed by your relationship with Tanya. Maybe you need to ask yourself if a choice you made when you were a teenager is still the right option for you now."

Shan stared, unable to get the words out. She swallowed away the lump in her throat.

At her silence, Marietta said, "Your incredible comeback from injury has come about when you were with Lizzie. I'm not saying you wouldn't have managed it anyway or that Lizzie should play a greater part in your life; I'm just giving you something to think about."

"I..." She gripped the sides of the chair. "I don't know..."

Marietta glanced at the clock on the wall. "That's the end of our session. You don't have another formal one with me this week, but if you'd like to see me again, my door is open to you." She smiled. "I know I've given you a lot to think about."

"Thank you." She stood and Marietta ushered her to the door.

Once outside, Shan dragged deep breaths. Marietta's words tumbled through her head. She hadn't been wrong in her approach all these years...had she? She couldn't be. Even Celia had converted to her more rigid way. But Marietta's words wouldn't go away.

Shan turned toward where a path wound between the buildings. A circuit of the campus would give her some thinking time. About what? Her career? The best way forward? Lizzie?

Or maybe, they were all intertwined in a way she hadn't been able to see before now.

Shan stared out the window as the plane circled at Tullamarine Airport. Melbourne spread out as far as she could see, rows and rows of houses, arterial roads radiating out from the city skyscrapers. She smiled at the flight attendant as he did the final pre-landing check. Hell, she'd smile at anyone right now.

Celia shifted in the middle seat next to her. "At least you don't have far to go from the airport. It's most of an hour for me."

"You don't have to work tomorrow. Happy weekend, training partner."

"Yeah." Celia's smile flicked up the corners of her mouth. "I'll sleep in until, oh, at least seven. Then I'll have breakfast that isn't muesli and fruit and stare at my phone for an hour. Maybe then, I'll call Sienna."

"Sienna?" Shan searched her mind. A friend? A client?

Celia nudged her. "Come on, you can't have been that blind last week. The high jumper." At Shan's blank look, she added, "The field athletics training camp that was happening the same time as ours. Sienna. Reddish-brown hair, blue eyes, pale skin. Legs up to your nose. If she was double-jointed, they'd have wrapped twice around me."

"Honestly, I didn't notice. I was too wrecked after the fitness sessions to do more than eat and sleep. And then the psychological sessions too. How can talking make you so tired?" It was the soul-searching after her second session that had exhausted her, but she wasn't going to tell Celia that. And Sienna couldn't possibly compete with Lizzie for space in her head. Sienna, whoever she was, could have walked through the dining hall naked and Shan wouldn't have noticed.

"Those psychs don't just make you talk, do they? They dive into your head and scoop your brains out with a spoon." Celia grinned. "Luckily, they didn't divine what Sienna and I were up to in quiet locker room showers."

"You had sex in the shower? In the Australian Institute of Sport? You can be excommunicated for that!"

"I doubt it." Celia shrugged. "From what I heard, we weren't the only ones. Adrenaline is such a turn on."

Shan scrunched her nose. "What happened to the monastic way of life?"

"Oh, that." Celia glanced to her right. The businessman in the aisle seat was still engrossed in his *Time* magazine and wasn't paying them any attention. "I did say that, didn't I? It may work for you, but it's not for me. I lasted a week, then I met up with a nurse I'd been out with a couple of times."

"Did it have any effect on your running?" Shan shuffled the new information in her mind. Celia had been running well the past week. Somewhere, in the spaces in her head not occupied by training and Lizzie, Shan had thought Celia's new focus had something to do with her embracing the quiet life. Obviously not.

"I think it got better. I've always said that. Sex gives me a natural high. My head is clearer. Olympic villages are just one big hook-up joint. Kes was in Rio; she said the longer the games went on, the hornier it got. She had three different women in one night after she won her bronze."

The businessman shot them a quick glance. He hadn't turned a page in the last few minutes. Not so engrossed then.

"Sienna lives in St Kilda," Celia continued. "I'll give her a call."

Shan raised her eyebrows. "What about the nurse?"

"She's lovely, but Sienna is something else. It's her I want to see."

Wow. For Celia, this was akin to a marriage proposal. "That's great. Maybe I'll get to meet her."

"You already did. She ate at our table a couple of nights last week, but you were rather zoned out at the time."

"I must have been."

"Maybe we could both come along to that Everyone's Choir you talked about. It sounded like fun. If you and Lizzie don't mind us there."

"Sure. I'll let you know when it is." Shan's mind raced. So Celia was back to her old ways and it obviously wasn't doing her any harm. On the contrary.

But everyone's different, her mind argued. *I can't do that; have a relationship* and *be a top-class athlete. I tried it with Tanya. It didn't end well.*

"I was only eighteen," she murmured to herself.

"What?" Celia tilted her head.

"Nothing." Shan angled her body again to stare out the window. The seatbelt light came on and the pressure in her ears told her the plane was descending. She gazed down at the lights of the city then further out to the curve of lights of suburbs around Port Phillip Bay and thought back to when she'd decided she couldn't manage an athletic career and a relationship. Constantly thinking about Tanya, pining for her, jealously wondering what she was doing while Shan was circling the track as repetitiously as a seagull around the Art's Centre spire. It was mental; she knew that.

But she was older now, more mature, no longer the insecure eighteen-year-old she'd been when she and Tanya were together. First love. Wasn't that always full of angst and heartbreak?

She shifted restlessly in her seat and shot a glance to her right. Celia had her earphones in. The businessman—now that the juicy confessions had finished—had returned to *Time*.

Maybe she was wrong in her thinking—and Marietta was right. This was Lizzie, not some faceless potential partner. This was about whether Shan could have it all with her: an athletic career *and* a partner she cared about. She'd backed off from Lizzie before going to Canberra, but that hadn't stopped the thoughts of her. It had taken a great deal of fierce concentration and repetition of her mantra, of counting breaths and clearing her head to get Lizzie to stop living there, at least most of the time. But she'd done it, and her running had been good. Better than good. Great.

What if she hadn't backed off from Lizzie? What if Lizzie had been in the back part of her mind, peacefully occupying space, a warm and fuzzy background for her thoughts? What if Lizzie's support had been the bedrock of her training rather than something to be flung away so she could concentrate?

Would it be so terrible to take what Lizzie offered, return that caring equally, and use it as the springboard for more? Both in her career and their personal life together. What if she woke every morning with Lizzie, to the warmth and stability that would bring? Shan closed her eyes as the plane descended. The landing gear lowered with a grinding sound, the ground rushed up, and they landed with a thump.

What if Lizzie was her ground? Shan's thoughts whirled in a confused and chaotic pattern. Marietta wouldn't have raised Shan's lack of a personal life if she didn't think it was important. The goals of the AIS psychology sessions were to strengthen an athlete's ability, give them the mental skills to excel. And Marietta had focussed on Shan's personal life.

She opened her eyes as they rushed past the warehouses and planes waiting for clearance to take off. She had just reset her life in the time it took a 737 to circle and land. Was that a world record of sorts? Maybe.

The plane shuddered to a slower speed and began the taxi to the terminal. Somewhere in the background, the flight attendant was telling people they had landed in Melbourne, the temperature was nine degrees, and they were to remain seated until the plane was stationary at the terminal.

Shan blocked the rest of the announcement from her head. What if she could forge an actual relationship with Lizzie, a give and take where they shared their lives and supported each other? Maybe they would live together. Maybe they would adopt Presto. Her mind spun into a happy place: Lizzie at the finish line of Shan's races, cheering her on. Shan cooking dinner so Lizzie could finish her day's work. Time together, relaxing. Time in bed together, doing anything but relaxing.

She dragged a shuddering breath. Lizzie was in her life, whether she wanted it or not. Maybe, just maybe, it was time to embrace that.

The plane halted, and Celia leaped to her feet to grab their bags, leaning practically in the businessman's lap as he folded his magazine and stuffed it in the seat pocket.

She passed the bags to Shan. "How are you getting home?"

"Uber." Lizzie hadn't suggested picking her up, and Shan hadn't liked to ask.

"Are you going to Lizzie's or your place?"

"Mine, I guess." She chewed a thumbnail. It wasn't late. Maybe she could go to Lizzie's. Her new-found knowledge beat in her chest like a caged bird. If she set the words free, if Lizzie felt the same... "I'll text Lizzie though. See what she's up to."

"Right." Celia winked.

Shan turned on her phone, waited impatiently for it to find a signal, and fumbled out a text, something about having landed and wondering if Lizzie was home.

The reply came a few minutes later, as the line of passengers was shuffling toward the exit.

I'm home. Didn't expect to hear from you so soon. Come around if you want.

There was a coolness in the lines on the screen. Her new-found optimism nosedived. None of Lizzie's warmth flowed through in the text. But it was an invitation, nonetheless.

She sent a quick reply saying she'd be there hopefully within the hour, then tapped Celia on the arm. "I'm going to Lizzie's. Want to share the same Uber that far?"

"Sure." Celia shot her a wink over her shoulder.

Chapter 27

Talk the Talk

WHAT DID SHAN WANT? LIZZIE frowned at the text. On the TV, two men in suits were arguing whether the body had been moved after the time of death. She turned it off.

Presto curled into a tighter circle at the other end of the couch, his nose tucked under his tail.

"You might have to move," she told him. "You shouldn't be on the couch in the first place." But it had been comforting to have him by her side, his head on her leg.

There'd been a couple of e-mails and a text from Shan while she was in Canberra. Short, chatty e-mails, about her training, and how it was going in the camp. How she was pleased with her progress. Nothing personal.

Lizzie had replied in a similar fashion, adding kisses from her and Presto at the end of each. Nerves fluttered in her stomach. Maybe Shan was coming to say she wanted to end their relationship. That she had to focus on that Olympic pinnacle. The last couple of weeks, Shan had backed away from her faster than a politician from a campaign promise. Lizzie got up from the couch and went to the kitchen to pour herself a glass of water.

For a second, her thoughts spun to the bedroom. She hadn't changed the sheets, and there were probably clothes and shoes strewn around the room in her usual untidy fashion. She shrugged. If Shan wanted to stay, if Lizzie agreed to that, then Shan would just have to take her as she came.

She was fighting a losing battle with herself about changing into something more alluring than sweatpants and a T-shirt from a grunge band she couldn't remember ever seeing when the doorbell rang.

Presto leaped from the couch as if on springs and ran, barking, to the door. His tail twirled in circles, and he leaped at the door and whined. Clearly, he knew who was on the other side.

Lizzie smoothed her suddenly damp palms down the sweatpants and went to answer the door.

Shan stood there, dressed in a dark-blue tracksuit. A bulging sports bag was between her feet. Her short hair stood up in its usual spikes. Even standing still on the porch, she seemed bursting with energy. Lizzie's gaze raked her from head to toe. Her mouth watered. Shan looked totally edible.

"Hi, come in." Lizzie stood aside.

A car outside the gate hooted, and Celia leaned out the window to wave as it pulled away.

"You're back." Lizzie rolled her eyes at herself. "I mean, obviously. Do you want me to say something else as stupid as that?"

"I'm just off the plane." Shan came in and dropped the bag in the hallway. Then she walked Lizzie backwards to the closed front door and leaned in to kiss her.

Lizzie sighed into Shan's mouth. The nervous tension, the doubts, the uncertainty of why Shan was here evaporated into the hot, sweet dampness of Shan's mouth. Their tongues slid together, gently at first, then more urgently, and her fingers burrowed into the space between top and bottom at Shan's waist, to touch her soft skin.

Shan broke the kiss. "I missed you." Her eyes glittered gold in the hallway light before she reclaimed Lizzie's mouth in another searing kiss.

"Is this what you missed? Kisses? Sex?"

"I missed *you*. Kisses are part of what you are to me, but not all." Shan touched Lizzie's face with a shaky hand.

The tightness in Lizzie's chest loosened like a knot giving way. What were they to each other? What could they ever be? "I missed you too. So did Presto."

At his name, Presto came forward and leaned against Shan's legs. She bent to pet him. "I'm not here with any expectations. I just wanted to see you. Can we sit for a moment?"

"Sure." Lizzie led the way to the living area. "I was going to have a peppermint tea. Would you like one?"

"That sounds nice…but soothing. I'm not sure I want soothing." Shan picked up Lizzie's hand. She encased it with hers, holding it close.

Lizzie flicked the switch on the kettle. "No tea then. What would you like instead?"

"Just water, thanks."

When they were settled on the couch, Presto at their feet, Lizzie asked, "How was the training camp?"

"Amazing." Shan took a gulp of water. "We were up at six, and I was usually asleep by nine. The coaches are really good—they should be, they're involved with the Olympic squad. In fact, this camp was mostly the team who are going to the Commonwealth Games, plus a few other people."

"Like you."

"Like me." Shan hooked a knee up and faced Lizzie.

"Wow!" Lizzie, too, pulled up her legs and tucked her toes underneath Shan's thigh. "That's fantastic!"

Shan's face split into a grin. "It's happening, Lizzie. This was a huge career step for me."

"I'm really happy for you." Lizzie picked up Shan's hand and held it between her own. A kernel of disquiet lodged in her chest. This was fantastic for Shan—but what would it mean for them? She pushed it down. She wouldn't be churlish enough to spoil Shan's moment with questions.

"There's one thing though." Shan gripped Lizzie's hands. "This last week made me sort through some baggage I've been carrying for a long, long time. Most of ten years in fact. We had sessions with a sports psychologist. One thing that came up for me was that it's not enough to just be an athlete. You have to make time to be a person as well. To spend time with friends and family rather than shutting them out. And that the best athletes aren't the focussed loners as we're led to believe. They're ones who have lives away from the track. And then Celia…"

The hard shell around Lizzie's heart tightened a little. Was Shan going to say that Celia was her best friend, her surrogate family, and now they wanted to be lovers again? Surely not, not the way that Shan was so obviously pleased to see her, was gripping her hands as if she never wanted to let go. Although Celia had eased her suspicion, had apologised even, Lizzie didn't think they'd ever lose the edge of distrust between them.

"Celia and I have always had opposite approaches to relationships. She's footloose and fancy free and loves nothing more than a hook-up. I've mostly stayed away from them. They're a distraction. Then you came along, and I wondered…I thought…"

The coldness slithered lower. So this was it then. She was being dumped for the ethereal chance of being picked for the Olympics in eighteen months' time. Lizzie resisted the urge to pull her hands away, wanting nothing more than to break the contact, but Shan gripped tighter.

"You're different, Lizzie. And I hoped I could have both: an athletic career and a relationship with you. Before I went to Canberra, I'd decided it wasn't possible. That I couldn't have both, and that I had to choose athletics."

Lizzie's fingers twitched in Shan's grasp. Something in her voice, a nervous edge, a hopeful tinge, told her there was more to come. And, maybe, it wouldn't be bad.

"The psychologist made me see I could be wrong. She gave me a lot to think about. And then Celia… She tried my way of staying out of hook-ups and relationships, but it didn't work for her. She's actually fallen for someone she met at camp. A high jumper. She's thinking it could be more than a casual thing."

Relief drizzled down Lizzie's spine. "I'm happy for her."

"I want it all," Shan said in a rush. "I want a career, and I want to be with you. If you'll have me, if you want the same. I couldn't stop thinking about you when I was away, and thinking you might still be there for me made it different from other times. Knowing I had your support meant I could still focus on what I had to do. I care a lot for you. And I think you care for me?"

The tilt on her words, the uncertainty in her voice made Lizzie shiver. This wasn't a declaration of love, but it was a commitment they'd never put into words before. But something still wasn't right— for her. She rewound Shan's words in her head. She was now saying she could make the commitment...but did she mean it?

"I do care for you. And I'd like to be a part of your life. But..." Lizzie heaved a breath. "I can't take you blowing hot and cold. Not anymore. If things don't work out, well, that's the way life goes sometimes. But if that's what either of us are thinking, I'd like us to talk about it rather than you just withdraw from me. Can you do that?"

Shan stared solemnly back. "I'll try. I'm not good at talking things through. It's been easier just to act." She nodded. "But we can do this."

"We can," Lizzie echoed. Such a small, simple promise, but it felt right. The knot of anxiety in her chest loosened, enough that warmth wiggled in and eased the tightness even more.

"Your life too." Shan freed a hand and touched Lizzie's cheek. "It's not just about me."

There was so much tenderness in the touch that her heart swelled. She leaned into Shan's palm.

For long moments, as they sat together, Lizzie unwound the covering around her heart. Shan's words touched a chord, and she didn't doubt her genuine intent. "So, does this mean I have an official girlfriend?"

"If that's what you want. I do. But it won't be sweet all the time." Shan's voice gained a serious tone. "I'm not the easiest person in the world."

"You're not?" Lizzie clutched imaginary pearls. "You don't say."

"Early starts. Asleep by nine. Weird diets."

Lizzie gestured to the kitchen. "Have you looked in my fridge lately? And I have my own routines too: working from home, a demanding dog. Half-marathon training."

"We're both no-hopers in the relationship stakes then. Maybe we can make it work?"

"Maybe." Lizzie settled back on the couch and opened her arms.

Shan moved into them, resting her head on Lizzie's chest. "I could fall asleep like this. Except...there's something I want to do before that."

"Oh?" Lizzie's cheeks ached from smiling. "You're going for a run? Or maybe you're going to meet your new friends from Number 94 in the pub? Or give Presto a bath. He needs one."

"None of that. I was hoping to see you naked. You know, see if you're as gorgeous as I remember. Maybe you're not. Maybe I imagined it all."

"Now I'm worried. Maybe I can't live up to the hype." Lizzie ran a palm over Shan's spiky hair. "But then again, maybe your tongue isn't as devilishly talented as I remember. Maybe I imagined that."

Shan got up from the couch and held out a hand. "Let's go and find out."

Chapter 28

Hidden Melbourne

"I HAVE TO GO HOME and unpack," Shan said the next morning. "Do laundry, find clothes that aren't sportswear. See if my fingers remember how to do data entry."

"I need to do a few things around here, too. Housework." No need to mention she'd let it slip when she was agonising over Shan. "Then I'm meeting a friend for lunch. You can come too if you like."

"Thanks, but I need to catch up at home as well. Do you want to do something this evening? Something to make the day end well?" Shan bent to fondle Presto's ears.

"I'd like that. I can check to see what bands are playing if you fancy that?"

"How about you leave it to me? I have an idea. Can you and Presto can be ready by six? Wear comfy old clothes."

"Oh? That sounds intriguing. Presto too?" Lizzie stretched to kiss Shan's mouth. "We'll be ready for you."

Shan wheeled her bike in through Lizzie's gate, removed her helmet, and hung it on the handlebars. The bike panniers bulged. Not for the first time, she hoped the bike she'd seen in Lizzie's backyard worked, that there was air in the tyres and the chain didn't hang in loops. Really, she should have checked.

She propped her bike against the wall and rang the doorbell. Two barks, the thundering of paws, and then a little whine greeted her.

"Hey, Presto," she said softly. "Ready for your evening out?"

Footsteps echoed down the hallway, then the door opened, and Lizzie stood there. Her hair hung in a thick plait over one shoulder, and she wore faded jeans that clung to her hips and thighs, and a plaid shirt. She had running shoes on her feet.

Shan drank in the sight, then leaned in to kiss her, her lips moving softly over Lizzie's. "Ready?"

"I am." Lizzie wrapped her arm around Shan's waist. "Although for what, I don't know."

"Does your pushbike in the back yard work?" Shan mentally crossed her fingers. If it didn't, her romantic plan would need some modification.

"It does. I cycle to work occasionally—and I last used it just a few days ago."

"Then grab it, your helmet, and Presto's longest leash, and we'll get going."

"Do I need water for him?"

"I have that." Shan gestured to the laden panniers. "I just need you."

"Are you telling me where we're going?"

"Soon. Although maybe you'll figure it out." Shan waited until Lizzie joined her with Presto and her bike, then she pushed off and cycled slowly down the street toward the river.

Lizzie followed. It took her a few tries to sort out with Presto which side he wanted to be on and to encourage him to keep his distance from the bike, but eventually they managed it.

Once they reached the bike path along the river, Shan turned in the direction of the city.

"We're going to one of the riverside bars in Richmond," Lizzie said. "Good move. It won't take long to get home."

"Wrong." Shan pushed over a slight rise.

"Further? We're going to the city? I'm not sure how Presto will go in crowds."

"No city, no crowds."

"Is there an open-air event on that I don't know about? The shelter did a Bring Your Own Dog pub crawl some months ago. Is it something like that?"

"Wrong again. This is a private event for three people—one of whom must have a tail."

They took the path that led up to the boulevard which ran high above the river. The city stretched out in front of them, hazy in the early evening sunlight.

"I don't come here very often," Lizzie said. "I should. It's gorgeous. Especially now."

Shan slowed, looking at the slope down from the road. It would spoil the mood if she missed the narrow path and had to backtrack to look for it. There! A trodden path around one of the safety barriers at the edge of the pavement. She halted and dismounted from the bike, then pushed it around the barrier and a short distance down the faint path until she was hidden from the road. She unbuckled the panniers and hefted one in each hand, then looked back.

Lizzie was following, Presto on a tight leash, pushing through the long grass at her side. "Mysteriouser and mysteriouser. I'd worry you're going to push me down the slope, but it would be easier to shove me under the number 48 tram."

"No pushing. But I hope you've got a head for heights." She rounded an outcrop of rock, and the path narrowed to follow the edge of a steep drop. She looked back to where Lizzie was encouraging Presto to go ahead of her. "Nearly there."

Another few steps and the path ended on a small rock platform underneath a rocky overhang. Shan looked around; it still seemed as scarcely used as before. Every time she came here, she was amazed her secret spot still hadn't made some Hidden Melbourne tourist guide.

"Welcome to the best picnic spot in inner Melbourne." She flung an arm out as if she'd conjured the expansive view for Lizzie alone.

"I can't believe this." Lizzie took a step back from the edge and looked around with wide, sparkling eyes. "It's like a secret grotto, just for us. Are we supposed to be here?" She touched the edge of the overhang. "I wonder what stories this rock could tell?"

Her delight was infectious, and an answering bubble of joy surged in Shan's chest. She'd never taken anyone here before and now she was glad. Her special place was shared with Lizzie alone. She came to stand next to her, entwining their fingers together as they stared out at the city. "It's public land, so I don't see why not. Luckily, few people know about it. Right now, it's ours."

Lizzie turned to Shan and took the half step to press their bodies together and kiss her. "I know what story I'd like to make here." Her hand drifted down Shan's neck and along her arm to squeeze her hand.

A slow burn started in Shan's belly. "I'd like that too. But"—she flung out an arm to the view—"the sunset awaits. And we have wine and food."

"Later, then." Lizzie kissed her again. "I won't let you forget."

The air around them seemed to shimmer with promise. Shan's breath hitched. How could she have considered pulling back from Lizzie? Her sparkle added so much to Shan's life. Her toes curled with the perfection of the moment.

For a moment, they stared into each other's eyes, and Shan was sure that Lizzie's wide smile was echoed in the besotted grin on her own face.

Reluctantly, she turned away and set the panniers on the rock and unbuckled them, taking out a picnic rug and spreading it over the rock. Two small cushions followed.

Lizzie sat cross-legged on one of the cushions. "I can't wait to see what else is in your magic expanding bag."

Shan pulled out a collapsible dish and filled it with water from a bottle for Presto. He padded over and drank. Next, she extracted a bottle of red wine and two plastic glasses. "Maybe you can do the honours and open this." She handed the bottle to Lizzie.

Finally, Shan pulled out a thin plastic board and then added food: cheese, dolmades, cold meat, chutney, marinated octopus, falafels, veggie sticks, and two different types of crackers. "Dinner is served."

Lizzie's eyes widened. "This must have taken you ages to get ready. It's lovely. And the best view in Melbourne. I can't believe I didn't know this was here."

"A friend showed me a couple of years ago. I keep expecting it to be blocked off as unsafe. I'm glad it's not."

"Seems perfectly safe to me." Lizzie poured the wine and held out a glass to Shan, who took it. "Thank you. This is simply wonderful."

"I'm glad you like it." Shan watched as she sipped the wine, then rested back on her hands, her gaze taking in the hazy city. Her plait nearly grazed the ground, and the pose pushed her breasts forward. Shan let her gaze linger on them. Lizzie's breasts were magnificent covered in a loose shirt. Naked, they were glorious, perfectly curved, with large, dark nipples that Shan's mouth seemed made for. What would Lizzie do if she leaned forward, unbuttoned her shirt, unhooked her bra, and worshipped those breasts with her mouth?

Shan sighed. While this place was private, it wasn't unknown for people to visit, especially now, at sunset. She switched her thoughts to the city skyline and the huge glowing sun slipping toward the horizon. Beside her, Presto sighed and rested his head on her knee, and she stroked his ears.

Lizzie leaned forward, and Shan's gaze jumped to the shadowy vee between her breasts where the shirt dipped.

Before she could stop herself, she ran a finger around the metal infinity pendant, then flicked the next button open with a finger. "Better."

Or was it? Now she was even more tormented by the memory of Lizzie's breasts. She ran a finger around the edge of her bra and withdrew.

"Tease." Lizzie's eyes darkened and she flicked Shan a mischievous glance before returning her stare to the sunset.

Shan withdrew her finger. "You want me to stop?"

Lizzie sucked a breath and pushed her chest toward Shan's hand. "You're kidding me, right?"

How could she resist an invitation like that? She danced her fingers around the upper curve of Lizzie's breasts, then made a quick pass over her hardened nipples where they pushed out her bra. They peaked even more, sending a shaft of desire along Shan's nerve pathways. Suddenly, the picnic didn't seem such a good idea. Reluctantly, she lifted away and sat back.

"Presto's watching us."

Lizzie's smile crinkled her eyes. "And we can't guarantee he won't be the only one." She picked up Shan's hand and kissed her fingertips. "Hold on to what you want. We'll be home later."

"Mm." It was hard to think of crackers and cheese when Lizzie's kiss still tingled on her fingertips. "I went to the Victoria Market for this. It would be a shame to waste it."

"It would." Lizzie picked up her wine and swirled it. "Wine tastes different from plastic cups. It makes me think of fresh air, music festivals, picnics. Special places like this." Lizzie glanced down at her glass then back up to hold Shan's gaze with her own. "Special people like you."

Warmth trickled through her at Lizzie's words. "I'll drink to that."

The words hovered on her tongue. Lizzie had enriched her life, too, in ways that went far beyond her initial kindness. But they still had to navigate the start of a relationship. It was all very well them saying they wanted that, but actually making it work could be tricky. Rather than dwell on that, Shan picked a dolmade from the container and switched her gaze back to the view.

The city gleamed in the dying sunlight. Down there were millions of people living their lives, balancing jobs, relationships, family, leisure, and more. Many of them managed it. Surely, she and Lizzie could. She cut a slice of cheese to go with a cracker.

"Food is your distraction, isn't it?" Lizzie's dark eyes stared at the food in front of her. "Your brain is churning and so you're eating cheese." Her grin sparkled. "Good move. But save some for me."

"Am I that obvious?" Shan cut a second slice, placed it on a cracker, and handed it to Lizzie. "It's better than being distracted by bad TV or social media clickbait."

"And you won't believe what happened next!" Lizzie rolled her eyes. "Usually, it's exactly what you think, and totally underwhelming. I stopped looking at social media in bed."

"I should hope so! Especially if I'm in the same bed." Shan feigned outrage.

"If you're in it, there are plenty of other things to do." Lizzie slanted her a wicked look. "Reading, embroidery, yoga."

"Yoga? Is that what they're calling it now?" She wiggled her eyebrows.

"Keeps you flexible for...other things."

Shan laughed. "That's not your problem."

Lizzie popped a piece of octopus into her mouth. "Thank you. The yoga must be working. I told Dee that, so given her relationship with Rohaan is now at the bedroom level, she thought she'd give it a go. But every time she lies on the floor, the cat sits on her stomach, and Reece uses her as a hurdle to practice his jumping skills. Which, surprisingly, aren't very good. Dee lasted two sessions."

For the next hour, they chatted, and ate, and watched the Melbourne skyline light up the growing darkness.

"Do you have plans for tomorrow?" Shan played with Lizzie's fingers.

Lizzie's mouth turned down at the corners. "I'm taking Presto for a visit to the shelter. They want to check in on him. See if he's ready for adoption. I'm to take his rug and toys in case he's ready to stay." She looked at Presto asleep on his back. His paws were in the air, jerking as if he was dreaming about chasing rabbits. "I'm not looking forward to it. This is always the hardest part of fostering dogs: giving them back. And I'll miss Presto more than any of the others."

"Me too. Maybe he's not ready for adoption?"

Presto jerked awake, rolled onto his stomach, and belly-crawled toward them for a pat.

"Maybe not. But that will make it harder when he does go."

"Do you want me to come too?" Shan asked hesitantly. If it would be easier for Lizzie to go alone, she wouldn't butt in. But maybe she'd like the company. Her heart turned over at the thought of Presto leaving. He'd been with them all the way, moving into Lizzie's house the same time that she did.

"I'd like that." Lizzie ruffled the fur at the nape of Presto's neck. "But if he does stay, it won't be easy. I'll understand if you'd rather not come."

Presto sighed and shifted so he could rest his head on her thigh. Shan's fingers tangled with Lizzie's in his fur.

"I'll come. For you and for him." If only she could adopt him, but it was impossible. And if Lizzie wanted to keep him, she surely would have made it official already.

They were silent, fingers brushing as they both petted the oblivious dog between them. Presto couldn't know he was only with them temporarily. He probably thought he'd already found his forever home. She'd miss him so much.

Lizzie stretched. "My bum is getting numb from the rock. And I have terrible night vision. Would you mind if we head back? I don't want to end up at the bottom of the cliff."

"That's a good plan." Shan started putting the lids back on the food containers. "Plus my bike doesn't have lights, which I should have thought of when I came up with this idea."

"Naughty. We'll put you on the inside. Lucky most of the way home is bike path, not roads."

"No street lights. It'll be the blind leading the blind."

"We'll manage." Lizzie stood and started putting the food back into the panniers. "Presto can lead the way."

The journey to Lizzie's place was slow. It was a moonless night, so they cycled carefully. And they stopped to kiss on every corner, at the start of the bridge over the Yarra, and before, during, and after the climb up from the river.

Lizzie kissed like a dream, soft, lazy kisses that sought and invited, rather than demanded and thrust. They were an echo of the woman herself, caring and gentle, but capable of ramping up to incendiary levels. Shan wished hard they were home, and in Lizzie's bed. The perfect end to date night.

Eventually, they wheeled their bikes through Lizzie's house to the backyard. Noise came from next door: music, loud conversation, laughter.

"They're having a party." Lizzie indicated her neighbour's house with a tilt of her head. "They invited me. We can go if you'd like."

Shan came closer and wrapped her arms around Lizzie's waist. "Is it antisocial to say no? I'd rather stay here. Have an early night."

"I was hoping you'd say that." Lizzie pushed her fingers into Shan's hair, combing until the short strands stood up in a fluffy halo. "We can have a party for two in my bedroom."

The drizzle of lust that had been swirling through Shan's body since their picnic flared anew. "That sounds perfect."

∽

The shelter was a short drive from Lizzie's house. She glanced at Presto in the back seat, safely clipped in his harness. He was good in the car, his ears pricked as he tried to squeeze his nose out of the partially open window to bark at other dogs. As she returned her eyes to the road, Lizzie caught Shan's gaze. She, too, had been looking at Presto.

She parked a short distance from the shelter, so they could walk the last part. Presto's rugs stayed in the boot—surely he'd be coming home with them.

"C'mon, Presto. Time to make some new friends."

He licked her hand then Shan's and then bounded out to full-stretch of his leash.

The shelter was tucked into a corner of parkland so the noise wouldn't disturb nearby residents. A cacophony of barks greeted them as they entered reception.

Shan winced and bit her lip. Lizzie could guess what she was thinking—the first time she'd come, her heart had split so badly she'd thought it might never be whole again. Shan was no doubt wondering how Presto would fare here. But the truth was, the shelter was his best chance of a good adoption.

"Hey, Lizzie. Long time, no see." Gina, one of the volunteers, looked up from the desk. "You here to see Helena?"

Lizzie nodded.

Presto pressed close between her and Shan and looked around, eyes large and anxious. His tail tucked between his legs. Lizzie's heart cracked a little. Most of the dogs she fostered were like this when they were returned to the shelter for adoption, but Presto's trembling made her want to turn around and take him home. Even though the shelter had rescued him from his tortured situation, and he'd only been there for a couple of nights, he must associate it with bad times.

"Hi, Lizzie." Helena, dressed in jeans and a T-shirt with the shelter logo, came to greet her.

Lizzie introduced Shan. "She's been as involved as me with Presto."

"Thank you." Helena offered Shan a warm smile. "Presto looks like a different dog to the one that you took home a few months ago, Lizzie." She crouched by his side and held out a hand for him to sniff, talking softly all the while.

Presto cowered and his shaking increased.

After a minute, Helena stood. "Let's go outside. Maybe he'll be more comfortable there."

They strolled along the street.

"I think he's ready for adoption," Helena said after a while. "He wasn't happy in the shelter, but look at him now." She nodded to where Presto padded along in front of them, ears bouncing with every stride. "There's a family who are interested in him. Two teenagers. Presto would get a lot of exercise."

"Teenagers? I'm not sure that would be the best home for him. He's been used to a quieter life. He can still be nervy and timid a lot of the time."

"He's relaxed now, and he doesn't know me." Helena looked thoughtfully at Presto.

"But..." Lizzie closed her mouth. What could she say? Foster dogs found homes. And she'd done the best she could with him, all so he would hopefully find a forever home with people who would love him. That was what it was all about. Every foster dog she'd owned had taken a tiny piece of her heart away with them. Presto should be no different—even if he took a great big chunk.

She opened her mouth to say she wanted to keep him herself—but closed it again with a snap. Fostering was perfect. It fit with her life, and she was bringing hope to many dogs. If she kept Presto, she couldn't foster anymore. Her house was too small, her landlord wouldn't allow more dogs. But all the same... She pressed her lips together to stop the words spilling out.

"How about I take him back to the shelter now?" Helena said. "You can drop his toys and rugs off in a few minutes."

Shan gasped. "So soon? Can we bring him back tomorrow? Have one last evening with him to say goodbye?"

"Dogs are sensitive. They know when someone's about to leave them. I know it's harder for you, but it's better for him." Helena cocked her head. "Lizzie?" She held her hand out for his leash and her expression softened. "You know it's better this way. You'll only worry him with goodbye hugs. If you could drop his things off on your way home?"

Helena was right. This was how she'd handed over every other foster dog. She should do the same for Presto. Tears blurred her vision, and she nodded and handed the leash to Helena.

Shan stepped close and put an arm around her shoulders, pulling her into a sideways hug.

Presto stopped and turned around, looking up into their faces.

"Please find him the best home ever. He's so very special." Lizzie's voice cracked.

Helena's gaze softened. "I will, Lizzie. I promise. When he goes, I'll let you know what his new family are like."

Lizzie nodded and turned away into Shan's embrace, the tears she'd suppressed instantly dampening her cheeks.

Presto whined and it took every ounce of strength she had not to turn around, rip his leash from Helena's hand, and run off with him.

"He's gone." Shan's voice sounded thick, as if tears were clogging her throat. "I will miss him so much. It's like he was part of us, part of you and me."

"He was." Lizzie could hardly get the words out through the tears. She hiccupped. "But while he'll be unhappy in the shelter, hopefully he will find his forever home soon."

"Let's go home." Shan pressed a kiss to the top of Lizzie's head.

"Home," she echoed. But it wouldn't feel like home without Presto.

Chapter 29

Reverse Settled

"My race number for the half-marathon has arrived." Lizzie walked down the hall clutching a large envelope. "Now all I have to do is show up in Bendigo and run 13.1 miles without stopping."

"21.1 kilometres." Shan looked up from where she was curled on the couch.

"I know. It just sounds less in miles."

"You'll be fine. Didn't you run nineteen kilometres last week?" Shan swung her legs to the floor.

"Yeah." A bubble of excitement pulsed in Lizzie's throat. "I now almost believe I can do it!"

Shan rose, came over to where Lizzie stood at the counter, and peered over her shoulder. "Three weeks' time. Have you booked that hotel?"

"You still want to come?" Lizzie craned her head around and regarded Shan. "I wasn't sure."

"I want to." Shan wrapped her arms around Lizzie's shoulders. "I'm an excellent cheerleader."

"You are." Lizzie kissed the tip of Shan's chin.

Even the silly little kiss started a buzz of heat that made Lizzie's toes curl in delight. Quiet days and evenings with Shan, both of them relaxing, working, or reading, were simple joys that she was starting to treasure. Shan seldom went back to her own apartment now, and there were more clothes at Lizzie's than at her own place.

"There's a winery that has cottages on their estate. If we can get a booking, we could splash out and stay there."

"Idlewild Estate?" Lizzie arched an eyebrow. "You are feeling fancy, Ms Metz. I'll have to check if I have suitable clothes."

"Check the availability." Shan kissed the back of Lizzie's neck. "Let's lash out. We're worth it. You're worth it."

Lizzie went over to her laptop and found Idlewild Estate's website. "There's a cottage with a vineyard view available for… Ouch." She pursed her lips. "Maybe we better stay at a chain motel."

"My treat." Shan's words rang with conviction. "I'm doing well with the data entry. Let me shout us for two nights."

"Are you sure?" Lizzie glanced at the website again. Yup, still more than her week's rent for the two nights. "I don't want to send you to the poor house." At Shan's nod, she said, "How about I buy dinner both nights then?"

"We have a plan. Now all we have to do is execute it. Visualise yourself powering down to the finish line. The crowd is clapping. There'll be at least one person yelling 'C'mon, Lizzie!'"

"You." Lizzie's smile stretched her face. Having someone who supported her like this, who *cared*, made her all warm and fuzzy inside. Sure, her friends and family were supportive, too, but not in this way.

"Yes, me. But if you write your name on your number, people will cheer you by name."

"Sold." Lizzie clicked the *Book Now* button. "But there'd better be cheering or I'll want my money back."

"Cheering and streamers. I promise."

"No streamers. They're unenvironmental. I want you in a cheerleader's outfit with pom poms."

"Don't hold your breath." Shan sat opposite. "I'll do my training runs for the day between points of course so I can cheer you on at a few places. The course is a circle, isn't it? So I can cut across the middle with my pom poms. But no skirt. I'll be in my usual shorts."

"Your shorts make my heart race every time." Lizzie reached under the table to stroke Shan's leg. "Your muscles are a thing of beauty."

"Flatterer."

"Now that the administration part of the day is completed, fancy going for a walk?"

"Sure. In fact, if you don't mind driving, let's go down to the beach. Maybe we can swim. It's warm enough today."

Lizzie stood. "That sounds great. Lucky, too, that you've got your bathers here. Along with most of your other clothes."

"Lucky indeed."

Lizzie went into the bedroom to gather her things. Shan's clothes were draped over a chair, and she now had nearly half of the wardrobe and drawer space. Her books were on 'her' side of the bed, and a litter of running shoes were piled by the front door. It felt right.

For a moment, Lizzie drifted into a fantasy of being together every night, not just the four or five that they managed currently.

She changed into a pair of cotton shorts and a T-shirt and slipped into her sandals. Shan, no doubt, would go exactly as she was, in cargo pants and a polo-shirt. Then again, if she looked like Shan, all lean and sleek and butchy with her hair sticking up, she wouldn't change clothes either.

Thoughts of Presto leaped into her head. He'd have liked the beach. He'd have raced along, the breeze ruffling his fur. Would he have swum with them, or would he have hovered at the edge of the wavelets? A twist of sadness spiked her chest. She'd never know how Presto would enjoy the beach. Helena had called to say the family with the teenagers had adopted him, and sent photos of him chasing a ball, and curled up on a very posh-looking dog bed. There had been no sign of his old rug or toys.

She sighed. He'd looked happy. It was for the best.

"Would you mind if I took next Monday and Tuesday off?" Dee asked as they ambled down to the coffee shop for their morning fix. "I know they're bad days. I want to check you're okay with it at short notice before I put in the request."

"Sure," Lizzie said. Her mind spun away. Maybe she, too, could ask for the Monday and Tuesday off after the Bendigo half-marathon and she and Shan could road trip for a couple of extra days. "Are you going somewhere?"

"Rohaan's hardly been out of Melbourne. I want to show him the Great Ocean Road. Mum's going to take Reece for the weekend. No doubt she'll give him back bouncing off the walls from too many lollies, and with no respect for bedtime, but that's part of the deal. We thought we'd hire a campervan. I'm thinking long evenings parked in a secluded spot, the rear door open, making love to the mournful cry of seagulls and the crashing of the waves."

"More like locked in the van in the heat avoiding mossies and other tourists."

"Don't burst my bubble, and I won't burst yours. I'm not the only one in love these days."

Love. Is that what it was? Lizzie's feet slowed and her gaze fixed on the middle distance. Love. *Love*? Sure, she cared for Shan, enjoyed being with her, cherished their time together...but love?

Maybe.

"—Reece in a campervan. I love my son, but that's a nightmare waiting to happen. We're not telling him what we're doing."

Lizzie shook the static out of her mind and refocussed on Dee's words. Something about Reece. A campervan. Whatever it was, it couldn't compete with the new knowledge settling like sand through water in her mind.

Love.

Maybe.

Chapter 30

Runner's High

"Lizzie!" Shan's shout came from the living area. "It's starting."

"I have to go," Lizzie said into the phone. "A friend is running in the Commonwealth Games. The race is about to start."

"A man?"

"No, a woman."

Her mother's disapproval pulsed down the line. "How will she get a husband if she is muscular like a horse?"

Really? Her mother's gender stereotyping was reaching extreme levels. "She doesn't want a husband. Lots of women don't. I have to go. The race is starting. Love you, Mumma."

"Lizzie! They're on the track! Hurry!"

She ended the call and stifled a nervous laugh. She picked now, when Celia's big race was starting in seconds, to challenge her mother for the first time on her hurtful views. Better now than never. She hurried to the living area.

Shan was on the couch, eyes glued to the TV. On the screen, the runners for the 10,000 metres final were lining up at the start. "Celia's in lane three."

Lizzie perched on the couch next to Shan. "The race you hoped to do," she murmured. Her hand found Shan's and linked them together.

"Yeah." Shan glanced away from the screen and sought Lizzie's gaze. "It was." She squeezed her fingers.

The pistol cracked, and the runners sprang away. From the overhead camera, they could see Celia, seemingly comfortable, running freely. As they rounded the first bend, the pack settled into place. A Nigerian runner took the lead, a metre or so ahead.

"Pace is slow," Shan said, without taking her eyes from the screen.

Lizzie watched the runners with their free-flowing strides keeping a pace she could never manage. Tears pricked the back of her eyes; this was true beauty. These strong, fierce women using their bodies in such an elemental way. It was glorious. She shot a glance at Shan who still stared at the TV. How was she feeling now, watching the race she had hoped to do?

The pace stayed constant for the first twenty minutes, then the leader kicked up a notch.

"Watch Celia now," Shan murmured. "If she sticks to her race plan, she'll make a move soon."

Gradually, Celia's dark hair and green-and-gold colours worked their way to the outside edge of the pack and edged forward.

Lizzie gripped Shan's hand tightly, and her breath seemed clogged in her lungs. What would it be like, running at this level, with everything to go for? Glory, medals, personal achievement.

"Now, Celia. Now," Shan's grip on Lizzie's hand increased to the point where it felt like her bones were rubbing together.

The bell rang for the final lap.

A runner wearing the colours of Uganda surged from behind Celia, striding out powerfully. Celia and a Canadian runner followed. The Ugandan woman drew level with the leader and then past her, followed by Celia and the Canadian.

"Stay with her, Celia," Shan muttered.

To Lizzie's eye, the woman who had led all the way was gone. She dropped back as the rest of the pack swarmed around her. The three in front had increased the gap between them and the rest of the field. Celia clung to second place. The camera closed in on the three of them. Celia's face was etched with concentration, her black eyes fixed on the final goal. Sweat sheened her shoulders, and for a second, she grimaced, just before she lengthened her stride a fraction.

But the gap between the leader and Celia lengthened, and the leader exploded into the home straight and across the line.

Shan surged to her feet. "C'mon Celia!"

For a second, the Canadian was level with Celia, then with a kick she was past. Celia came in third.

"She got bronze!" Shan turned to Lizzie with an exultant look on her face. "That's incredible!"

Lizzie swiped at her damp eyes. The joy of watching the women run choked her. "Celia did great," she said when she could speak.

On screen, Celia was bent over, hands on her knees, sucking air. Then she straightened and went to congratulate the gold and silver medallists.

Lizzie swallowed away the thickness in her throat. Shan often used to beat Celia, she remembered that. Was Shan wishing for what might have been? She was generous in her excitement for Celia's success, but surely there was a curl of sadness that it could have been her. Lizzie reached out and took Shan's hand again. "Next time, that will be you."

Shan sent her a rueful look. "I hope so."

Lizzie bit her lip. She wanted to ask if Shan was thinking of what could have been—that it could have been her on the podium, a medal around her neck. Maybe a silver or gold, even. But to revisit that now seemed a backward step. They'd made their peace with how they'd met. "It *will* be you next time," she said instead. "And I'll be there, cheering you on."

She pressed a kiss to Shan's lips, then another, tiny, gentle kisses until Shan's lips softened under hers and the curl of a smile started in earnest.

"I can't think of anyone I'd rather have at the finish line," Shan murmured against her lips.

Lizzie's breath hitched at the words. There was a promise in there, the suggestion of a commitment. She pressed her lips more firmly against Shan's, rejoicing in the warmth of her mouth as her tongue swept inside. She drifted her hand down Shan's side to cup her butt.

"Is there another finish line you want to reach sooner?" She pressed her hips into Shan's.

"Maybe."

Lizzie drew her hand back up along Shan's side, delving underneath her top and angling her body away so she could cup her breast. Shan's nipple peaked against her palm.

"Definitely."

Shan's wide, dark eyes shot sparks into Lizzie's soul. Little explosions of desire spread ripples in her belly. Lizzie walked them back until Shan's back contacted the wall beside the couch. Maybe it was the joy of watching the women race, but there was a pulse in her blood as if she had run herself. She hooked her thumb into the waistband of Shan's shorts and dragged them down along with her undies. Shan's wispy pubic hair brushed softly against Lizzie's fingers.

Lizzie grabbed a cushion and dropped to her knees in front of Shan. "Put your foot on the arm of the couch."

Shan's eyes darkened even more as she obeyed.

Was there anything better than giving pleasure like this? If there was, Lizzie didn't know what. Shan's position opened her to Lizzie's gaze and seeking fingers. She ran one finger from her mound, down over those pale furred lips to the bottom, and then back up, then leaned in and trailed her tongue over the path her fingers had just taken.

Shan pushed her hips forward in mute appeal.

Lizzie flicked a glance up, along Shan's body, naked from the waist down, and so utterly gorgeous. She pushed one finger inside, amazed at how wet Shan was already, as if she'd been ready for Lizzie for a long time. "Watching running makes you wet?"

"*You* make me wet. Instantly, immediately, absolutely soaking."

The flip-flopping feeling in Lizzie's stomach intensified. How much harder could she fall for Shan? Every day, it seemed they grew closer, more of a couple. Lizzie pushed her hair out of the way and focussed on Shan. Fingers, tongue, every move she knew Shan loved, every swipe and slide of her tongue, every circle and stroke—she didn't stop until Shan convulsed around her fingers, her body a taut-strung sheet of muscle.

Lizzie sat back on her heels. "Enough?"

"Enough." Shan's hazel eyes gleamed gold. "I don't think I can even lift a finger for a while. I'll just go and lie down like a diva and think how unbelievably lucky I am to have met you. Koala suit and all."

Lizzie's heart melted like marshmallows on a campfire. "Me too." She pressed a kiss to Shan's belly. "Me too."

Chapter 31

Celebration Red

SHAN GOT UP FROM HER laptop to get a glass of water, and then stood at the rear window looking out over the yard to the empty spot where Presto used to lie in the sunshine.

She'd run her first competitive race since the injury and been cautiously pleased when she'd come in third. Celia, still on a high from her Commonwealth Games medal, had won easily. Sienna had been there at the finish line along with Lizzie, and both of them had cheered her and Celia as they'd crossed the line.

The ping of an incoming e-mail made her return to her laptop. The name of the sender leaped out at her: The Australian Institute of Sport. Her heart rate sped up until it was thumping almost painfully in her chest. Various scenarios as to why they'd be contacting her paraded through her mind, but her funding wasn't due yet, she wouldn't have failed a drug test, and her credentials were up to date. That left one likely reason. She opened the e-mail.

Dear Ms Metz,

We are holding a week-long training camp commencing Saturday, 26 September. You have been identified as a top-tier Olympic hopeful and were first reserve for the camp. Due to a last-minute withdrawal, we are delighted to offer you a place. The camp is an opportunity for top-level coaching, physical and fitness assessments, access to physiotherapy, sports psychologists, and other therapies. Due to the short notice, if you are able to attend, please reply to this e-mail within 24 hours to secure your place.

The words jumped out in crazy flashes before her eyes. *Training Camp. The Olympics.* She heaved a shuddering breath. *The Olympics.* Her fingers shook and she made typo after typo as she replied with her acceptance. Eventually the e-mail was error free, and she hit Send.

She leaped to her feet and paced the room. There was no way she could do any more data entry today, not with her brain in overdrive picturing the camp and all it stood for. A mental picture of her blitzing the pre-selection. Arriving in the Olympic village. Winning her heat. The finals, her standing at the start with the cream of the world's distance runners, shaking her legs one after the other, over and over, to keep them warm. The starter's pistol, and then her striding out in glorious free-running motion. Strong, fast, running like the wind, like a panther, passing other runners until finally she crested the line. Gold medal.

Shan's heart pounded as if she'd just run the race of her dreams.

She went to the bedroom and changed into her running clothes. With dreams in her head and exaltation in her heart, she went out for a run.

Lizzie's key in the door signalled she was home.

Shan got up and nudged the glasses on the counter to a better angle next to their celebration red wine. By the time Lizzie entered the kitchen, the bubbling excitement in Shan's stomach was threatening to explode. She greeted Lizzie with a kiss, wrapping her arms around Lizzie's shoulders and tugging her close, so that the kiss deepened to a song of desire that fizzed in Shan's blood. She broke the kiss. "Welcome home."

Lizzie rested her palm on Shan's cheek. "Thank you. I could get used to this sort of welcome." Her glance moved to the counter. "Especially if it involves this particular wine. What's the occasion?"

Surely her face would split from the grin she couldn't contain. "I got an e-mail today from the Australian Institute of Sport. I've been offered a place in a training camp for the top tier of Olympic hopefuls!"

Lizzie's eyes widened. "The Olympics? Oh my God, Shan, that's incredible! All your hard work is paying off. You're going to the Olympics!"

"Maybe." Shan flung her arms around Lizzie once more, hugging her tight. "It's very, very early stages, so there's still a heap of hoops to jump through. But I've made another tiny step. They said I was first reserve, so someone must have dropped out, but I don't care. Today, first reserve, eighteen months, gold medallist."

Lizzie kissed her, her lips moving urgently over Shan's own, her tongue pressing against her mouth until it gained entry.

The kiss was hot, and damp, and as arousing as hell. Sparks travelled along Shan's nerve pathways, meeting in a heated knot between her legs. For a moment, she considered leaving the wine and dragging Lizzie off to bed to celebrate another way.

Lizzie stepped back. "Let's open this." She picked up the bottle and handed it to Shan, watching as she twisted the top and poured two glasses. "To Shannon Metz. Future Olympian and gold-medal girlfriend." Her lashes lowered flirtatiously as she peeped at Shan over the rim.

Shan raised her glass. The warmth of being wanted, of being supported trickled through her body. Who better to share this with than Lizzie? No one, was the answer. Her mother and stepfather would be pleased, Celia would consider it as commonplace. But Lizzie—her delight wrapped Shan like a heated blanket.

"Details," Lizzie said. "When is it, how long is it for? Is Celia going too?"

"I don't know about Celia, but I think she would be. It's a week in Canberra. And it starts next Saturday."

"The twenty-sixth?" Lizzie set her glass down carefully, as if it might shatter.

"Yeah. We have to arrive by ten in the morning. There are briefings, a shake-out-the-knots trackwork session, assessment by a physical therapist, and a sports psychologist."

"The twenty-sixth," Lizzie repeated. Her face had taken on a closed-in look, her smile wiped. She stared at the counter.

"What's the matter?" Shan frowned. What had happened to make Lizzie go from excited to the point where she wouldn't meet Shan's eye?

Lizzie looked up. "My half-marathon's that day. It starts at seven in the morning, and I won't finish much before ten."

Shan's stomach flip-flopped. *Oh no. How could I have not remembered?* She spread her hands. "That's terrible timing. Oh, Lizzie, I'm so sorry. I was really looking forward to seeing you run. Cheering you on at the finish. Celebrating with you afterwards—" She halted as she remembered she'd booked a romantic—and expensive—place for them to stay. She looked at Lizzie. Her face was immobile, different from her usually open expression. Surely Lizzie couldn't expect her to give up the camp to cheer her in an amateur race? She closed her eyes. This was why she'd shied away from relationships. This was why she couldn't let herself fall for someone. But Lizzie's shuttered face still floated behind her eyes. She opened them. "Lizzie, I'm so very sorry. But I can't...I mustn't turn down the offer of the training camp."

"Stop." Lizzie's smile flickered briefly. "I understand. Trust me, I do. And I'm not asking you to miss the camp. It's not just important to you—it's your dream, your career. It's okay, Shan."

Lizzie understood. Relief throbbed along her veins. "I'll make it up to you."

"You don't have to. I get that plans are difficult for you. I understand your dreams, Shan. I know you won't let anything stand in their way. I just..." She shook her head. "Don't worry. I'm disappointed, but I'll get over it. Maybe Dee would like a fancy weekend in exchange for some pom poms at the finish line." Her smile was a little wider, but it still trembled.

Shan's heart squeezed. What else could she do? She couldn't turn down this camp—she may never get another chance. And she'd lost one great chance already thanks to her knee injury. She couldn't—*wouldn't*—lose another one.

If that destroyed her relationship with Lizzie... Shan's mind skittered away from the thought and her skin went cold. She couldn't let that stop her going.

But the thought of losing Lizzie stabbed her in the chest.

Chapter 32

Presto's Wisdom

LIZZIE LAY IN BED ALONE; the other side yawned empty and cold. Shan had gone home, pleading the need to run at the track in the park in the morning. Lizzie sighed. Was this what life was like with an elite athlete? With Shan? It seemed so.

Memories of Shan saying early on she couldn't commit now haunted her. Why hadn't she listened? Smiled and waved goodbye once her knee healed? Or taken the no-strings sex and kept her heart locked away.

Lizzie turned over restlessly. She wasn't able to do that. Her heart had a habit of stealing into any relationship, however casual. It was only living up to its reputation.

There was no one she could really talk to. Dee was on her romantic weekend away with Rohaan, but all the same, she would answer Lizzie's call, sympathise, and very nicely tell her she'd always had reservations about Shan. Certainly not her parents. Even Presto wasn't here anymore to talk to.

Lizzie bit her lip and eyed the book on her nightstand. The romance with its undoubtedly happy ending wasn't what she needed right now. She turned on her side and looked at the rug on the floor, where Presto used to lie the few times she'd let him into the bedroom. Her gaze fell on a stuffed dog that Shan had bought for her, saying it reminded her of Presto with its brown fur and half-cocked ears. Presto was still lodged in her heart. The shelter had asked her to take another foster dog. A poodle mix, nothing like Presto, but she'd refused. It was too early to care for another dog.

She put the stuffed dog on the rug and addressed it. "I've got two choices, Presto, and both of them will break my heart. One will break it instantly; the second will take longer. I can break it off with Shan now, or I can hang on and let her slip away until one day, I'll wake and realise we've just faded out of each other's lives. Or else she'll break it off as, despite her saying she wanted to try, she'll find she can't, after all, deal with the demands of athletics and a relationship. Which, to be fair, is what she's always said—until recently."

The glassy eyes of the stuffed dog stared back at her. "I wish you were the real Presto. I wish you could give me advice." She fondled its ears. "See, Presto, I'm trying very hard not to be clingy and possessive and passive-aggressive about Shan not being able to come and watch me run. I understand why she can't this time, and that's okay. The problem is what it means in the wider relationship." She stared at the stuffed animal. "I'm talking like a HR manager, aren't I?"

The real Presto would wag his tail in agreement about now.

"I'll assume that's a yes. Basically, Presto, if Shan and I want to be together, I'll have to get used to coming second at times. To not having her there to support me all the times I ask her. It's just that"—her breath hitched—"I feel I'm the one doing most of the giving in this relationship. Am I selfish to wish it was a bit more even? Given there's no way it can be, not while she's an elite athlete. But I have to decide if I can accept that in a relationship. I always hoped I'd find someone who would be a real partner. That we would be there for each other, sharing and supporting."

She sighed. "Why am I talking to a stuffed dog? I must be losing it."

She picked up the dog and cuddled it anyway. For a moment, she thought of asking Helena where the real Presto was living so she could maybe go and visit him. She squeezed her eyes shut against the sudden hot tears. No Presto, maybe no Shan. Presto had moved on to his

forever home and it wasn't fair to disturb him by visiting. And Shan…
Her heart squeezed.

Lizzie pulled the quilt up to her chin. There was no decision she
could make right now. None that she wanted to make. Tucking the
stuffed Presto under her arm, she closed her eyes and tried to sleep.

Shan slumped on the couch in her apartment and stared out the
window. The light poured in, traffic rumbled past, and over the road
she could see the drooping grey-green leaves of Sheila-the-sheoak. It
had been two days since the e-mail had arrived from the Institute of
Sport, nearly that long since she'd seen Lizzie. Shan had mumbled
something about needing to get home, and that she'd see Lizzie soon.

"Soon" was now nearly two days, and she was doing exactly what
she'd promised Lizzie she wouldn't do—run away without talking first.

She should be on top of the world, setting out a training plan,
calling Pieter, evaluating her diet. She should be leaping out of her
skin with excitement. Instead, her butt was superglued to the couch
and a grey mist wove around the problems in her mind.

What else could she do? It all came back to that. Nothing. She
couldn't turn down the opportunity. She twisted her hands together.
There was no way in the known universe she would—and Lizzie had
said she didn't expect her to. So why did she feel wrong inside, like she'd
failed Lizzie? Why did she feel like the ground was shifting, like there
was no stability in her life? That was crazy—she'd only known Lizzie
a few months; she shouldn't be her rock. She'd always been her own
strength. Rely on yourself, as there's no one else who can do a better
job. That's what she'd always told herself. It had defined her decisions
to pursue a solitary sport, to live alone, to avoid relationships. At least
until now.

She got up from the couch, went into the bedroom, and picked
up the bag of dirty clothes she'd brought back from Lizzie's. She went
over to the washing machine off the kitchen and upended the bag,

stopping as one of Lizzie's shirts tumbled into the machine. She must have grabbed it along with her own. The shirt was mint-green with a dark stripe, one of her work shirts that she always wore with tailored pants. A shirt that made her look so fine, elegant, and professional, with her lustrous hair swept up. The shirt didn't even look dirty. She pressed it to her cheek for a second, the soft material caressing her skin. It smelled faintly of Lizzie, of soap and a hint of citrus. She put it in the machine with everything else and turned it on.

For a moment, she looked out the window. A young couple were kissing, the man's back against Sheila-the-sheoak. Was their life as complicated as hers? Shan sighed. Probably. Most everyone thought their lives won the gold medal for complicated.

She returned to the couch. Her head was telling her a break with Lizzie might be for the best. But her heart wasn't listening.

Shan walked down the hall to Lizzie's kitchen, her heart in her mouth.

Lizzie turned from the stove to greet her. "Hi." She pressed a kiss to the side of her lips and her gaze searched Shan's face.

Shan's face relaxed into a smile. "Hi yourself. I've missed you."

"It's only been two days."

"Yes." Shan sat at the counter and watched as Lizzie swept around the kitchen pulling some olives and air-dried ham from the fridge. "I felt like I needed to spend time at home. Water the plants, run my usual track. I missed being here with you, though."

"I ran too. It wasn't the same without you lapping me every few minutes." Lizzie shook back her hair.

"I'm glad you feel that way." She picked an olive from the plate and wrapped a slice of ham around it.

"What are you doing for the rest of the week?" Lizzie asked. She opened the pantry and pulled out some crackers. "I'm resting before my race now, but I can come and watch you train."

Shan was silent. The words she wanted to say pulsed inside her. Thoughts of previous nights together swirled around her mind. She knew what she wanted. The question was: was it fair to Lizzie? Would the demands of Shan's life eat away at Lizzie until she could no longer deal with it? Until their relationship deteriorated to one of shouted words and unanswered demands? But the alternative was worse: not to try at all.

"I'd love that," she said eventually. "But I've been thinking. Mainly if I'm being fair to you. I don't think I am. This is my life, Lizzie. It won't get any easier than this for us. But, despite all that, I want to be with you."

Her fingers stilled, the tidbit uneaten, as her words cleared something in her mind, a veil being drawn back. The real Lizzie was arranging crackers on the plate in front of her, but in her head a dozen Lizzies jostled for airtime. Lizzie with her big, generous heart making room for Shan in her life. It wasn't just the big things, like sharing her home, it was the everyday little pieces of Lizzie that took up space in Shan's mind. Her yawning in the mornings, fumbling around for a coffee mug, but always finding one for Shan as well. Linking their fingers together as they strolled along the river path, then raising their linked hands and pressing a kiss to Shan's knuckles. The silly growly voice she'd used with Presto when he wanted to play. Lizzie in her life.

And she'd missed this, these small things that cemented them together and made her feel she belonged.

Marietta was right; Shan finally fully accepted that. Marietta had seen—somehow, in her rummaging in Shan's head—that she needed that closeness with someone. She needed it with Lizzie, not that Marietta had known that, although she might have figured it out.

Words exploded in her head. *I love you*. But she bit them back. Now wasn't the time to say them. Maybe not ever. Because as much as they threatened to burst from her, the question was still out in the air for Lizzie to answer: Was their relationship fair to her?

Lizzie looked down and fiddled with the cracker box. "I know. I realise that. And I'm not asking you to give away your dreams for me.

That would be so very wrong of me, so very unfair. I've been trying to decide if I can live with what you're able to offer me without becoming swamped by your life."

Shan's breath swam slowly in her chest. She'd finally admitted her feelings to herself, but was Lizzie about to say she couldn't do this? A cold fist encircled her heart.

Lizzie looked her full in the face. "I have to try. That is, if you still want the same. Maybe you're here tonight to break up with me. I guess I wouldn't be surprised." Her lips twisted. "But life with you is magical in so many ways. I don't think we'll ever be one of those couples who are together twenty-four-seven, but I'll take what you can give me—as long as you can accept that sometimes, my dreams will clash with yours. Like my half-marathon."

A crack appeared in the ice chest around her heart. Shan's breath loosened. Lizzie wasn't breaking up with her. Her head swam with relief. "I still don't think I'm being fair to you. Relationships are give and take, and I think I'll be doing more of the taking than you will."

Lizzie's lips twitched. "Maybe. But bigger dreams need bigger sacrifices. I think I love—" A flush of red stole up her neck from the vee of her shirt. "Oh. I didn't mean to say that." She raised her chin. "But since I have, well, I think I love you enough to carry your dreams as well as my own."

Time froze. Shan's mind stuttered with the implications of Lizzie's words. She wasn't breaking up with her. Lizzie was there for her. She *loved* her.

"Now," Lizzie said briskly. "You don't have to say it back to me. I don't expect that." She nudged the olive plate closer. "You're not eating enough. Please don't embarrass me further. I've got chicken and—"

Shan slid off the stool. *Lizzie loves me.* Her heart expanded so much she wondered if it would burst out of her chest and fly free, up to the ceiling. She went around the counter and caught Lizzie around the waist. "Do you know how amazing you are? How honest, how kind, how desirable? How strong, how intelligent, how hard-working? Please don't ever apologise for being you." She hesitated, but she'd said too much now to stop. The words *I love you, too* curled in her chest, but she couldn't say them. Not yet. To say it now seemed like a response to Lizzie's declaration, something to offer her as a reward—and that seemed wrong. Soon. She would say it soon, when the words would stand alone and not as a knee-jerk response to Lizzie's declaration. "Thank you for telling me you love me. It's hard to say the words sometimes." She wrapped Lizzie tightly in her arms.

Lizzie returned the embrace, her hand running over Shan's back from shoulder to butt and back again. "Love. It's such a charged word, isn't it? I've fought it, as I didn't see how it could end happily for us, but my heart won't let me walk away. I thought about it, you know."

Shan closed her eyes as the image of Lizzie saying a final goodbye, turning away, closing the door, assailed her. "I'm glad you didn't."

"I couldn't." Lizzie leaned her forehead against Shan's. Their breath mingled in the space between them. "You've swept me off my feet."

The soft waft of Lizzie's breath caressed Shan's lips, the touch of Lizzie's hand against her skin. The warmth of her all-encompassing heart. "I don't think I deserve you."

"Maybe not." Lizzie's words were accompanied by a beaming smile and a wink. "But you've got me."

"And you have me." She caught Lizzie's lips in a kiss, nudging them apart with her own, sliding her tongue into her mouth, drinking in the soft sounds of pleasure, the sweet familiarity of it all.

Lizzie's soft breasts pressed against Shan's chest and a swell of desire pushed lower.

"Are you hungry?" Lizzie's words penetrated Shan's fogged brain.

Food. Right. Behind them, a saucepan on the stove bubbled away. Lizzie had doubtless prepared an amazing meal. It would be wrong to let it go to waste. Shan dragged her mind away from the bedroom. "I am, yes. That smells delicious."

Lizzie reached behind her to turn off the gas. "I didn't mean for food."

Her lips descended once more.

Chapter 33

Zen and the Art of Half-Marathons

"SHOES, SHORTS, SHIRT, SOCKS," LIZZIE said. "More socks. Running watch, water bottle, energy bars. Race number." She held up the paper with *Lizzie* in black marker above the number.

"You remember your plan?" Shan said. "If you average seven minutes per kilometre, you'll finish in your goal time of under two hours thirty minutes. You've been running 6:40 kilometres for nearly this distance. You can do this."

Lizzie nodded. Butterflies ricocheted around her stomach, and she rotated her tight shoulders.

"Don't panic if you find yourself getting passed by lots of others. Stick to your plan. It's easy to think you should be running faster at the start because everyone else seems to be. It's not about beating others; it's about beating yourself."

Lizzie nodded again. She pulled a second wicking shirt from the drawer and added it to the pile.

"The hardest part will be the final five kilometres," Shan said. "That's when if you go out too fast, you'll crash and burn. Hitting the wall, we call it. You need to save energy reserves for then."

Shan's advice rocketed around her head. She hoped she'd remember it all. She zipped the sports bag closed. "I'm ready. What about you?"

On the other side of the bed, Shan's bag was covered in running clothes, toiletries, a pile of underwear, and a couple of tracksuits. Her laptop was the only other thing. Lizzie eyed Shan's pile. "Sports bra! How could I forget that!" She darted to the drawer and drew out a couple of sturdy bras and crammed them in a corner of her bag.

"You can run in most things," Shan said. "But not without a supportive bra."

"True." Lizzie sighed. "I wish Dee had been able to come. It will be strange staying at a fancy hotel by myself. But she's introducing Rohaan to her parents this weekend. I hope it goes well."

"Rohaan's lovely. Even Reece loves him."

"Yeah, Dee got lucky." Lizzie came around the bed to kiss Shan. "As did I." She looked over Shan's pile of clothes again. "Don't you need real clothes? Jeans, T-shirts, shoes that aren't runners?"

"Please! These *are* the real clothes." Shan's eyes crinkled. "But no. This is what I'll be wearing for the next week. Tracksuits double as relaxation wear. Not that I'll be doing much of that."

"I'm already dying to know how you go." Lizzie took a last look around the bedroom. "I want a full blow-by-blow report when you return. What time's your flight tomorrow morning?"

"Eight-ish. I've booked an Uber."

"So you'll have landed in Canberra when I'm chugging up to the finish line. I hope, anyway."

"You hope I've landed, or you hope you're finishing?" Shan asked.

"Both." She leaned in to kiss Shan. "I'll be thinking of you." Lizzie put all that was in her heart into the kiss: joy, excitement, anticipation...and love.

"I'll miss you so much," Shan said. "I'll call Saturday to see how you went. It might be late, though. The psychology sessions don't finish until nine."

"I'll be waiting in the big bed, with a glass of wine." Lizzie's eyes softened. "I have to go." Her feet had welded themselves to the floor. Leaving Shan behind seemed wrong. She shook herself. This was what she'd signed up for. Instead of Shan at the finish line, she'd settle for what she hoped would be a happy phone call tomorrow night.

"It will be the best part of my day." Shan touched her palm to Lizzie's cheek.

With a sigh, Lizzie leaned onto Shan's hand. She closed her eyes and absorbed the warmth and love flowing through that gentle touch. Then, she picked up her bag and car keys and went out the front door, closing it quietly behind her. This was her life now. Heart-tugging farewells, and then hopefully, joyous reunions. She started the engine and nosed from the tight parking space, heading for Bendigo.

The other runners seemed much more confident than Lizzie. They were leaner, fitter, better dressed, more relaxed, hopping from foot to foot at the starting line as they chatted to their friends. Lizzie hunched her shoulders and moved down the groups until she found the one for her estimated finish time. Even the runners here oozed confidence. She took her place and, for the fourth time, retied her running shoes and tightened the elastic on the end of her plait.

It felt strange being alone in a crowd of runners, without Dee there to chat to. Lizzie lifted her chin and looked around. Her first half-marathon. She *would* enjoy this.

Her watch showed three minutes until the start. Despite the early hour, there was quite a crowd of spectators. People kissed their partners good luck, held up waving toddlers, and then disappeared toward the coffee stand. Lizzie sighed in envy. She'd only had one coffee.

Two minutes. Lizzie's stomach ramped up the full buzz of excitement. This was it. She'd worked hard for this, and now was the time to see what she could do. She turned to the man next to her. "Good luck."

The man nodded. "You too."

One minute. The chatter in the pack fell silent, the tension so sharp it could cut.

The starting pistol fired, and Lizzie's heart leaped and started pounding faster. After a few seconds, the pack began shuffling forward.

The constant ping as each runner's timing chip crossed the starting line and the background warble of magpies filled the air. She was off! The slap-slap of running shoes hitting the tarmac joined the magpie chorus.

"Don't waste time weaving in and out of the crowd." Shan's advice came back to her. "You'll burn energy doing that. Keep straight and people will space out."

The first part of the course went along Bendigo's main street, past the imposing art gallery, before heading out of town. At the one-kilometre mark, Lizzie checked her watch. 6:19. She was well under time. Shan's advice about slowing her pace crept into her head, but she ignored it. Her body felt good, her energy high, her breathing easy. She'd keep this pace a little longer.

As the runners wound their way out of town and into the national park, Lizzie relaxed into the run. Her mind floated away until all there was in her head was the slap of feet on the tarmac and the feel of her body. There were few runners around her, eyes distant as they inhabited their own worlds. Lizzie took a bottle of water at the five-kilometre mark. Nearly a quarter of the way already and only thirty-four minutes.

She ran on steadily, bathed in sunshine, surrounded by birdsong and the perfect Zen experience of the moment.

Chapter 34

The Tullamarine Blues

SHAN THANKED THE UBER DRIVER and hefted her bag over her shoulder outside Tullamarine Airport. For the hundredth time, she patted her pocket to check she had the e-ticket and her wallet. Yup, both there. She'd arranged to meet Celia at check-in, and Celia, always the nervous traveller, would almost certainly be there already, waiting impatiently.

Shan turned from the terminal to face the road. Cars and minivans swooped in and out, dropping off people and leaving again. Passengers slung bags over their shoulders, raised the handles of their wheely-cases and trundled them into the terminal. People hugged and kissed farewell. It was the normal airport bustle. She looked at her watch. 6.45 a.m. Lizzie would be near the starting line, maybe retying her shoes, making sure her chip was secure, having sips of water. Would she stick to the plan Shan had laid out for her?

A couple of men in hiking shorts and boots with bulky packs on their backs pushed past her with muttered apologies. She moved away from the terminal entrance, out to the kerb. The sky was a clear blue, the sun already warm. A dry heat, comfortable for running. Shan closed her eyes. Deliberately she railroaded her thoughts to the plane she had to catch in an hour's time to take her to Canberra, to the red tan track she knew so well. What would today's session be? A loose, easy run probably; not any great distance.

How would Lizzie go with the distance? A half-marathon wasn't an easy race for a novice. And Lizzie was running it alone, with no one to encourage her when fatigue struck. No one to cheer her on at points along the course. No one to fling their arms around her and hug her as she cried tears of exhaustion and happiness at the end.

No one.

Shan walked further away, out to the edge of the vehicle ramp up to the terminal. From here, Melbourne's suburbs spread out in front of her. Bendigo was to the north. She turned in that direction and stared at the blank walls of cargo warehouses. How far was it?

A cold wash of shame flooded her chest. Lizzie should have someone with her. If Shan wasn't there, well, she should have begged Dee, called some of Lizzie's other friends, even asked the crew from the Number 94 drop-in centre. Maybe a couple of them were running today. But she hadn't. She'd done nothing, just apologised, and continued with plans for Canberra. But what else could she have done? Begged off the first night of camp? They'd probably have given her place to someone else if she'd done that, someone more deserving, with no commitments, no other life, no partner.

She'd made the wrong decision.

The thought thumped into Shan's head. She loved Lizzie. What loving partner let her girlfriend take on such an achievement alone? *Shit, shit, shit.* She leaned on the railing and hung her head.

Her phone rang, startling her out of her introspection.

"Shan, where the hell are you?" Celia sounded harried. In the background, an announcement gave the last call for passengers for a flight to Darwin. "The plane goes in forty-five fucking minutes, and you haven't checked in."

"I'm outside the terminal." She should be picking up her bag and hurrying in, racing for the booth and the luggage drop, praying there wasn't a long line at security. Still she didn't move.

"Well get in here. The security line is short. If you hurry now, you'll make it."

Her throat closed over. The words "I'm nearly there" stuck in her chest.

"Shan?" Celia's voice sharpened. "I'll give you five minutes. Then I'll have to go through security without you. Get your arse in gear, woman." The line went dead.

She looked at her watch. A couple of minutes past seven. Lizzie would have started. She'd be revelling in those glorious first moments of potential at the start of a race, when emotion overflowed. Maybe she'd cry a little—Shan had done that in her first serious race. Lizzie would be—

Shan lifted her face to the sky. She knew what she had to do.

She had to call the Institute of Sport. Shan bit her lip. As difficult calls went, this one was right up there. She set down her bag, dragged their printed e-mail from the outside pocket, and unfolded it. There were two contact numbers at the bottom. She fiddled with her phone.

"Tell the truth or lie?"

She hadn't realised she'd spoken aloud until a man dragging a wheelie case shot her a glance. "If you're asking me, I'd say don't lie, but if it's tricky, don't tell the whole truth either. You can explain later, hopefully."

"Thank you." She gave him a thumbs up. Random advice from a stranger was as good as anything else.

"Good luck," he said and hurried on.

Before she could talk herself out of it, she entered the first contact number.

The call answered on the second ring. "Athletics. Miranda speaking."

"Hi Miranda, it's Shannon Metz here. I'm supposed to be joining a training camp that starts later this morning."

"Metz. Yes. What can I do for you?" Miranda's voice held a cool professional crispness.

"I have a family emergency, a last-minute one. I'm sorry, but I won't be able to arrive today. Can I join the camp early tomorrow? I'll get the first available flight."

There was a frosty silence on the line. Shan held her breath.

"It's most unfortunate," Miranda said. "There's no way you can get here today?"

"I'm afraid not. It's a serious situation involving another person. I'll ensure I'm on the first flight tomorrow."

Another longer silence. "In the circumstances, that should be acceptable. However, we cannot pay for the second airfare."

"That's fine." She swallowed bile at the thought of the cost. "I'll be there tomorrow. Thank you." She ended the call, relief drumming through her. Her place in the camp was secure, despite the undoubted wrath of those in high up places. And her decision was made.

She was going to Bendigo.

The dragging feeling lifted like the planes taking off from Tullamarine. She pulled up the mapping app on her phone. From here, it was one hour thirty minutes to Bendigo. If she could get an Uber soon, she'd be there by 8.45 a.m., and Lizzie would still have a few kilometres to run. She opened the app on her phone, but her eye caught a yellow sedan with the rideshare sign in the back window. Maybe the driver didn't have a fare after the airport drop off. She picked up her bag and ran to where the car had pulled in.

She was in luck. The driver had no other fare and was delighted at the idea of a cruisey drive to Bendigo. In a couple of minutes, Shan had booked it through the app, thrown her bag onto the back seat, and jumped in the front.

As the car pulled away, she imagined Celia's furious face pressed against the window of the terminal. She tapped Celia's number, but it went straight to voice-mail.

"Hi, Celia, I'm sorry, but I won't be making it to Canberra today. I hope I can get a flight tomorrow. I've had a last-minute emergency. I'll call you later."

The Uber idled down the ramp from the terminal in a line of traffic, then accelerated onto the highway toward Diggers Rest.

"You were supposed to be on a plane this morning?" the driver asked.

"Yeah. I was going to a training camp in Canberra. I'll need to book a flight for tomorrow."

"Call the airline. If your original flight hasn't already left, you might be able to rebook. Cheaper than booking fresh."

"Thank you…" She looked for a name but couldn't see one.

"Adrian."

"I'm Shan." She shot him a grateful glance, pulled out her ticket, and called the airline. There was a fifty-dollar change fee, and she was able to rebook for the same flight the next day. Relief coursed through her. The hard calls were done. Now all she had to do was get to Bendigo in time and find Lizzie on a twenty-one-kilometre course.

"What training camp are you supposed to be on?" Adrian asked.

"Running. It's a pre-Olympic training camp."

Adrian whistled. "Whatever the reason you're postponing, it better be worth it."

"She is. I just hope I haven't left it too late. My girlfriend's running her first half-marathon in Bendigo—I can't let her do it alone." She looked at her watch. "I hope to see her at the finish."

Adrian accelerated onto the Midland Highway and set the cruise control for five kilometres over the limit. "I left my last boyfriend when he kept putting work above our time together. It wasn't just once; it was every evening and most weekends. When he was over an hour late for my birthday dinner, the one he'd arranged as a make up for all the other times he'd worked late, I left him. I ordered French champagne and ate my way through the most expensive items on the menu, and then walked out, leaving him with the bill." He lifted a shoulder. "I found out later that 'working late' involved one-on-one meetings of the intimate kind with his muscular assistant."

"Are things better now?"

"Honey, you have no idea." Adrian shot her a wink. "I'm a popular boy-about-town these days."

"I'm glad." Shan stared out at the highway. While the circumstances were different, maybe Lizzie was thinking the same as Adrian—that she would be better off without Shan. Maybe Lizzie would brush past her at the finish line and embrace a fellow runner that she'd bonded with in the last couple of hours. Maybe Dee had changed her plans at the last minute and taken on the role of guard dog. Maybe—Shan shuddered—Dee would set Reece on her.

"Stop obsessing." Adrian tapped her arm. "She'll fall into your arms, all sweaty and gross after her run, and you'll have one of those finish-line kisses that makes the local news."

She hoped he was right.

Chapter 35

Runner's Low

EVERYTHING HURT.

Lizzie barely glanced at the eighteen-kilometre marker as she passed it. Her breath rasped painfully in her chest, her feet felt pulpy and swollen, and her thighs burned with weariness. Every fibre of her being screamed at her to stop this torture, to drop into a walk for a minute, for five minutes, before resuming. But if she did that, she would walk off the course into the bushland, lie down under a tree, and go to sleep. If she was asleep, nothing would hurt anymore. Not her feet, not her right hip, which was twanging like a badly tuned guitar, and certainly not her heart, which was booming painfully in her chest.

That booming would continue, she knew, long after the race had finished. Long after Shan returned from her camp. Maybe it would ache forever.

She pushed herself on, counting her steps. Another 500 steps and then she'd take a walk break. Tendrils of hair escaped her plait and stuck to her damp face. She longed for water, but there were no more water stations until the finish line.

If she got that far.

She reached 500 steps and grimly started counting again. 500 more. Then she *would* take a walk break, and hope she had the willpower to restart. She clutched her infinity pendant, willing some strength from the iron symbol. She'd run the last kilometre in eight minutes, the slowest she'd ever done since her fun run days with Dee.

Running steps came up behind her. A middle-aged man gained slowly on her, one plodding pace at a time. For a minute, they ran side by side in painful solidarity.

"This…is the worst…every time," he said between breaths. "Every time…I swear never again. And I stick by that…until the next time."

"My first time," Lizzie said.

A short nod. "Then you're…really feeling it now." He reached out a fist and Lizzie bumped it. "You can do this… When you reach the finish…all be worth it."

Would it be? There were no guarantees she'd even get that far.

The man pulled away slowly.

The nineteen-kilometre mark came into sight as the course headed back into town. Just over two kilometres to go. Lizzie stumbled and broke her plodding stride. Those two kilometres might as well be the thousand kilometres across the Nullarbor Plain. There was no way she could keep going. She was done, finished, spent. Her tank was empty. Moisture gathered in the corners of her eyes, not enough to form tears and fall. She'd failed. Not only at her running goal, but in her relationship. She should have been happier for Shan going to her camp. After all, if Shan was here now, what would she see except a woman who'd tried and failed.

Her steps slowed.

Adrian dropped Shan near the finish line. "Good luck. Go get your woman."

"Thanks." She gave him a thumbs up, then turned and scanned the crowd. Many runners had already finished, and she could hear the beeps as yet more crossed the line. She looked at her watch: 9.03 a.m. Lizzie would hopefully be close.

Shan put her wallet and phone in her pocket and stashed her sports bag under a tree before jogging toward the finish line. There was no sign of Lizzie in the crowd; she wasn't among the runners collecting water and finisher's medals. Shan grabbed a bottle of water from a sponsor's table and set out along the course in reverse. She passed a steady trickle of runners, weariness etched on their faces, as they ran, jogged, or walked toward the line. She gave a few high-fives of encouragement as she went. Where was Lizzie? She passed the twenty-kilometre mark. Still no sign of her. Maybe she'd hurt herself and dropped out. Maybe she'd been too tired to continue. Maybe—Shan gulped as the thought stole into her mind—she'd changed her mind before the start.

If she was still going, she'd need all the encouragement she could get. She was behind her estimated finish time. Shan increased her pace as she ran toward the outskirts of town. She scanned the road ahead, hoping to see Lizzie's dear familiar shape. Worry sat in her throat as she passed a dozen or so runners with no sign of Lizzie.

Then her gaze latched onto a runner ahead. There! Just at the nineteen-kilometre marker. Shan increased her pace again.

This was it. She was done. Each step was agony—her feet, her hip, her breath all screamed at her in a concerto of pain. No more. Lizzie slowed again until her feet were barely moving. One more minute. That was all.

"Lizzie!" The shout came from far away. It was different to the occasional spectator calling her name in encouragement. This shout was to get her attention.

"Lizzie!"

She shook her head and concentrated on her shoes, watching their one-two beat on the tarmac. The shout had sounded like Shan. She was now so tired she must be hallucinating. But when she looked up again, Shan was in front of her. Her feet stopped of their own accord.

Her mouth dropped open as she panted. "Shan? What are you…doing here?"

Shan smiled and her rather austere face softened, her hazel eyes gleaming warmly in the sunlight. "I came back for you."

"Your training camp… You can't miss that."

"It's okay. I'm going tomorrow morning. I told them there was an emergency. There is, Lizzie. I couldn't not be here for you. I'm sorry. I should have done this earlier." She touched her palm to Lizzie's face.

Lizzie melted. Maybe there was hope for her and Shan. She choked back a sob, and the tears that had been threatening started to fall.

Shan held her, one arm loosely around her waist, the other rubbing soothing circles on her shoulders.

Lizzie raised her damp face. "You came back for me? And here I am failing."

"You're not." Shan handed her the water bottle. "Drink some of this, and let's finish this race."

Lizzie drank deeply and handed the bottle back to Shan. "Thank you. I don't know if I can do this. But I'll try."

Shan's gaze was steady, her eyes radiating reassurance. "One step at a time. Let's get you across that line." She looked at her watch. "If you can run the last two kilometres at a pace of 7:10 per kilometre, you'll make your goal time of 2 hours 30 minutes. Can you do this?"

"Will you run with me?"

Shan nodded and held out her hand.

It was as if the pain, the agony, the torture of the run was drawn out of her by Shan's touch. Sparks flew through her body, giving her new hope. Not only that she could finish the race, but more, so much more. Yes, she could do this. With Shan at her side, she could do anything.

She set back her shoulders and turned to face the road again. The first few steps shot stabs of pain into her joints. Her muscles had cooled and stiffened, her ankles seemed to have lost their flexibility, and she could now tell there was a blister on one of her toes. But she would get through this.

Her breath rasped in her throat, but she concentrated on the woman by her side who matched her stride for stride keeping up a steady stream of words.

"I love you, Lizzie, and I believe in you. I know you can do this. You can do anything you set your mind to. Remember Presto. He loved you too, although not as much as I do. But you persevered with that sad, scared dog. And I know you'll persevere with this race too. You are so close. So very close.

"I was at the airport. Celia called me from the terminal, told me to get my arse inside and check in, but I couldn't. I kept thinking of you, and how I'd let you down. How your dreams are as important as mine, and how I couldn't bear to lose you. So I walked away and got an Uber here, hoping I could see you finish, hoping you'd see me."

Her words flowed over Lizzie like a soothing salve. She wrapped the red-hot pain from her blister in a compartment in her mind and ignored it. The tiredness in her body floated away. Shan believed in her. She could do this. She increased her pace, and Shan did as well so they were still in step.

Would they always be in step? Lizzie didn't know, but right here, right now, it was what was important.

The twenty-kilometre mark came far more quickly than Lizzie could have hoped. Shan found her hand and squeezed it. "You're so close. Just over one kilometre to go."

Lizzie managed a short nod. Her throat rasped, her eyes burned, and her left foot squished inside her shoe. Probably blood. But she could do this. She would finish strongly.

"I love you," she said. Then she turned her gaze on the road ahead, the straight road into the centre of Bendigo, and, setting her jaw, pushed herself to run faster.

The twenty-one-kilometre mark came and went in a blur. People lined both sides of the road, and their cheers lifted her even more.

"Go Lizzie!" and "You can do it, Lizzie!" She heard them, but it was Shan's silent support by her side that gave her feet their wings.

The finish line came into sight, bunting festooning the arch. The crowds were thicker and the shouts louder.

Tears of happiness sprang into Lizzie's eyes. She dashed them away and released Shan's hand. She would finish in style. Her heart expanded with the emotion of the moment and the pain and tiredness fell away. The impossible was now possible. Both the here and now of her personal running goal and the bigger goal, the one that made her heart sing. Shan. Her and Shan. Together.

She pushed faster, and as the exhilaration and strength flowed into her limbs, she wanted to keep running forever. She could keep running forever. Faster still, and the line was now only twenty or so metres away.

"You are going to smash this, Lizzie," Shan said by her side. "Finish now. I'll be there for you at the far side of the finish line."

"No!" Lizzie held out a hand but didn't drop her pace. "Finish with me... Together."

"Are you sure?" Hesitation crept into Shan's voice. "I don't want to steal your moment. You've worked for this. This is your time."

"No." Lizzie wiggled her hand. Her breath was gone. "Together."

Shan took her hand and Lizzie gripped it tightly. Ten metres to go. She pushed faster, the finish line blurring in front of her teary eyes. And then she crossed the line in a sprint, Shan at her side. She looked at her running watch. 2:29:54. Then she staggered and moved to the side to grip the barrier. The world tilted around her but that was okay. She would recover, and Shan was by her side, stroking her shoulders, pouring soothing words in her ear.

She barely remembered sucking down an entire water bottle, collecting her finisher's medal, and then sitting, taking off her shoes and seeing her bloody sock, or Shan going to the first aid tent for blister plasters. They must have collected Shan's bag from under the tree, and then she hobbled slowly and stiffly to her car.

Shan held out her hand wordlessly for the keys, and Lizzie handed them over with a sigh.

Shan drove them to Idlewild Estate, up the long driveway lined with vines, then swung the car around outside the door of Lizzie's cottage.

"I don't think I can move." Lizzie stiffly lifted one leg, then the other outside the car.

"An ice bath would help, but that's not possible here. A shower will have to do."

"I hope so." She handed Shan the cottage key.

"We'll have a walk later," Shan said. "Very necessary if you want to be able to move tomorrow."

The cottage was one large room with a king bed and wide glass doors opening to a veranda which overlooked the vines sweeping down from the cottage.

Shan looked around. "This is gorgeous. I should have been here with you last night."

"You're here now." Lizzie leaned in to kiss her.

Shan's lips moved softly under her own for a minute, until Shan broke the kiss. "Shower."

Lizzie opened the french doors, then moved to the bathroom, shedding her clothes as she went and releasing her hair from its plait. Shan was ahead of her, the water already turned to hot.

Lizzie stepped in and groaned in pleasure as the hot water cascaded over her muscles. "This is heaven."

She ducked her head under the spray and shampooed her hair. When she opened her eyes again, Shan was naked in the shower next to her, reaching for the body wash.

"This is like the first time we made love." Lizzie sighed as Shan's hands moved purposefully across her body, soaping her. She moved her legs apart and braced against the wall as Shan crouched to soap her legs and feet. Despite her exhaustion, her blood thrummed.

"It is." Shan stood again and kissed her. "But this time, I'm not going to seduce you in the shower. I'll wait until you've recovered."

Her hands soothed and aroused in equal measure, and the hot water kept pouring down, taking away the aches and pains. When

Lizzie was finished, she turned off the shower and reached for the towel. Shan was there already, and she dried her as carefully as if she was as breakable as spun glass and dreams.

Lizzie went back to the main room and flopped down on the bed, still naked. She yawned. Tiredness warred with arousal. What if she and Shan were to celebrate in another way that didn't involve sleep?

Shan lay next to her. "I know what you're thinking, but it can wait. Sleep now." She stroked Lizzie from shoulder to hip and shifted so Lizzie could turn on her side and rest her head on Shan's shoulder.

Chapter 36

Entwined Like Vines

SHAN WOKE SLOWLY. SUNLIGHT FLOODED the room through the open french doors, and a pair of rainbow lorikeets twittered away at the bird feeder on the veranda.

Slowly, so as not to wake Lizzie, she turned her head to find her phone and look at the time. Nearly noon—they'd slept for most of an hour. Her stomach rumbled, reminding her she'd planned on grabbing food at the airport. She looked back at Lizzie. She was lying on her side facing Shan, her fingers curled loosely on the pillow, her chest rising and falling in deep, even breaths. Shan's gaze traced the soft line of her cheek, her lustrous hair spread in a snarl on the pillow, still slightly damp, her light-gold skin darker on her shoulders and arms from the sun. Her full breasts invited Shan's touch.

There was a fridge in one corner of the room, near a kettle and microwave. Shan stole off the bed to investigate.

Lizzie rolled onto her back and stretched. She blinked. "Hello. Are you sneaking off?"

"Only as far as the fridge." On cue, her stomach rumbled.

"Right." Lizzie's lips twitched and she sat up, pulling the pillows behind her back. Her hair fell in a snarl over her breasts. "You runners and your food requirements." Her stomach growled too.

"*Us* runners." Naked, Shan went to the fridge and pulled open the door. "Someone's stocked this well. You?"

"I brought food with me, but the wine, strawberries, and cheese platter came from the winery."

Shan pulled the fruit and cheese from the fridge and set them on the bench. "Get up, lazybones. My stomach needs feeding."

Lizzie slid lower. "Call me when you've got the veranda table set."

Shan returned to the bed and sat to press a kiss to Lizzie's lips. Her stomach lurched with more than emptiness. Kissing Lizzie was nectar and champagne, warmth and love. She deepened the kiss, sliding her tongue into the warmth of Lizzie's mouth. Her head spun with the knowledge that this beautiful woman loved her. Not just a beautiful woman; Lizzie was the whole package, from her kind and giving soul to her gentle personality.

Lizzie returned the kiss then broke away. "I have to pee. I need food. I need you. Not necessarily in that order, although the first is non-negotiable." She got out of bed. "Ouch, ah...." She hobbled to the loo. "I might be somewhat stiff."

Shan dressed in shorts and a T-shirt and carried the food out to the veranda table along with a jug of water and two glasses. She found a baguette and crackers and put them out too. When Lizzie joined her, dressed similarly in fresh clothes, Shan had two mugs of coffee steaming on the table as well.

Lizzie sat and picked up her finisher's medal from where Shan had draped it across the table. "I know a couple of hundred people got one of these earlier, but it feels like such an accomplishment. A personal challenge, and I passed." She glanced at Shan. "Does that sound strange to you? My achievement is tiny compared to yours."

"No! Don't think that. Less than one per cent of the population manage what you did today."

"So I'm part of a super-fit minority?"

"Probably." Shan sliced the baguette and loaded it with cheese and quince paste. "Now, eat! Keep your energy up."

Lizzie snagged a cherry tomato and popped it in her mouth. "I will. I hope to need plenty of it...later." She waggled her eyebrows.

A wave of love and longing washed over Shan. Lizzie held her heart and soul in her tender, careful hands. But that love was a two-way street, and she was determined not to trample over Lizzie. Was now the time to say the words that buzzed in her chest like a swarm of bees? No, she had to let Lizzie refuel first.

When the bread was reduced to crumbs and most of the cheese and strawberries eaten, Lizzie sat back. "This place is gorgeous. I'm sorry you missed out last night. Are you able to stay tonight?"

Shan worried the knife. She simply hadn't thought of how she'd get to the airport. "My flight's at just before eight tomorrow morning. I'll have to leave just after five. I'll see if I can get an Uber."

"No need." Lizzie's smile was lit from within. "We'll go together. I'll ask for a breakfast basket and then I'll take you to the airport."

"Don't you want to enjoy your last day here?"

"After you upended your life for me? No. I'll drive you. Maybe we can return another time and stay a weekend."

"I'd like that." Shan reached across the table and took Lizzie's hand. Lizzie, it seemed, had none of Shan's doubts about making this work. "Thank you."

Words beat in her chest, and she knew she had to let them free. Sure, she'd told Lizzie exactly how much she loved her earlier, in the final kilometres of the half-marathon, but how much of that did Lizzie remember? Her focus would have been on getting to the finish line. Shan's words would have been just words. Maybe they'd washed over her, without her taking them in among the pain and concentration of the run.

"About what I said earlier during the race," Shan began.

Some of the light dimmed behind Lizzie's clear eyes. Her lips twisted. "Are you going to tell me you didn't mean it?"

"No! I wasn't sure if you remembered. I meant every word I said. Every single one. I love you."

Lizzie's expression relaxed. "Then that's all right. If they were true, then there's nothing we can't do together. I love you so much, Shan. Together we can work this out."

A deep breath as Lizzie's words soothed her churning mind. "What did I ever do to deserve you?"

"I think you'd say that to every woman in a koala suit who smashed up your life."

Shan laughed. "No, only you. Can we make this work, Lizzie? I know I'm not the easiest person to live with. There'll be other training camps, running meets, time away from you."

"Love shouldn't stifle dreams." Lizzie's thumb caressed the back of Shan's hand. "And yours are big dreams. I'll support you any way I can."

"And I'll be there for your dreams too. We just have to remember what's important: that we're two people who love each other and choose to be together. I think we can make this work."

"I think so too." Lizzie looked down at their joined hands. "Maybe we'll live together. Maybe we'll get married. Maybe not. Right now, none of that is important. I just want to be with you and love you."

The drama, the emotion, the love came together in a hard knot in Shan's chest. Her breath caught in her throat, choking any words she wanted to say. It seemed her new love and her biggest dream would work together. She *could* have it all. She rose and went to stand behind Lizzie, wrapping her arms around her shoulders, dropping her face to nuzzle her hair.

Lizzie put her hands on Shan's arms, and as they swayed together, the rightness of them together encompassed her.

After lunch, they went for a stroll up and down the vineyard paths to ease the stiffness in Lizzie's legs. Shan paused to touch a fresh curled leaf, then take in the view over the surrounding vineyards and bushland. When the scenery had been admired, she took Lizzie in her arms and kissed her thoroughly and passionately among the tangle of vines and new growth.

Their stroll ended at the winery restaurant, where Lizzie changed the dinner reservation to two people and arranged for the next day's early breakfast basket. They went to the tasting room and sampled the winery's range, then purchased a dozen reds to take home with them.

Lizzie's phone rang as they walked back to their cottage. She glanced at the screen. "It's Helena. From the shelter. She's probably going to ask me to take another foster dog." Her mouth turned down.

"Maybe it's about Presto."

"I doubt it." Lizzie answered the call and set the phone on speaker.

"Hi, Lizzie," Helena's cheerful voice came down the line. "I have news about Presto, and I thought I'd call you first."

"How is he?"

"He's back at the shelter. The family got a second dog—the pedigree puppy they *now* say they were hoping for all along—and the puppy and Presto aren't getting along, so they returned him. I've blacklisted them. They won't ever get one of our dogs again." There was an edge of anger in Helena's voice. "I was wondering—"

"I'll take him back."

Shan stared at the phone. Presto was coming home. Could anything be more perfect? Her gaze collided with Lizzie's.

"Thank you. I thought you would." Helena's sigh gusted down the line. "But I'm going to ask you to consider something else. Presto is miserable. He seemed happy in his adopted home—until the blasted puppy came along—and he doesn't understand why he's now back at the shelter. He's not eating, he's lying in his run and won't come out. Lizzie, I know you said you didn't want to give him a permanent home as it would mean the end of your fostering, but Presto bonded so well with you before. If he returns to you and then is adopted out again, well, I don't know how that will go."

Shan closed her eyes. She wanted to yell into the phone that yes, they'd adopt Presto, give him the forever home and all the love he deserved—but she wasn't the one Helena was asking, and it wasn't her decision to make. Anxiety bubbled in her chest. What if Lizzie refused? She'd break her heart along with Presto's—again.

"Can you wait one minute, Helena?" Lizzie said into the phone. "I just want to talk with my girlfriend."

"Sure," Helena said.

Lizzie put the call on hold and faced Shan. Her face held a softness, and a small smile lifted her lips. "I always said I didn't want a dog of my own because of the constant responsibility. Fostering allowed me the best of both worlds. But this is *Presto*—and he deserves the world and people to love him."

Shan waited, her heart beating hard. Surely Lizzie wasn't going to refuse?

"Will you share him with me? Can we make him *our* dog, not just mine? He loves you so much?"

"Yes. Of course. I was hoping you'd want that." Tears pricked at the back of Shan's eyes. Presto was coming home. They had a dog.

Lizzie placed her palm on Shan's cheek. "It's a lot of responsibility to share with me. Are you sure?"

"Positive. Just as I'm sure that I love you."

Lizzie's throat worked as she swallowed, and she took the call off hold. "Helena? We'll take him. Presto's really found his forever home this time. We're in Bendigo now, but I'll come and collect him first thing tomorrow morning."

Shan hardly heard Helena's effusive thanks or the relief in her voice. She only had eyes and ears for Lizzie as she ended the call and wrapped her arms around Shan's waist.

"This day can't get any more perfect. My race, Presto, and the big one—you came back for me. I still can't believe you did that. Thank you." She drew Shan's head toward hers for a long kiss.

Later, they changed for dinner. Shan had no clothes with her suitable for an upmarket restaurant, so she wore Lizzie's wraparound long skirt with a clean white T-shirt and her sandals. Lizzie wore an elegant deep-red dress that clung to her curves. The hem fell to just above the knee and showed off her toned legs. Her mid-height heels gave her legs an elegant length, and with her hair spread in a shining curtain over her shoulders, she looked beautiful, something that Shan told her repeatedly and then showed her with her kisses and caresses.

"Stop!" Lizzie said, when kisses started to lead to something more. "Our reservation's in ten minutes."

"I can work fast." Shan nipped lightly at the delicate skin between her neck and shoulder.

"You can, I know. And so efficiently too. But you also can work slowly, and I'm looking forward to that even more."

They had chosen to eat early, and they were shown to a table by the window, set with white linen and silverware. The waiter handed them the menu and lit the white candles. The view overlooked the ubiquitous vines and the long driveway in from the road.

Lizzie picked the wine—a rich, red vintage from grapes grown outside the door—and they selected their appetisers: scallops for Lizzie, a delicate vegetable flan for Shan. Shan chose chicken in a mustard sauce for her main course while Lizzie opted for the locally grown fillet steak, saying she needed the protein after the race.

They finished by sharing a slice of pavlova. Lizzie had a small glass of brandy; Shan abstained.

There were two women at the next table who were obviously partners. They only had eyes for each other, and when the appetiser dishes were cleared away, one slid a small box across the table to the other. The question must have been asked and answered, as both women stood, and a chair clattered to the floor in their haste to embrace.

One of the women apologised to the server who hurried to right the chair. "I'm sorry for that. Kaz has asked me to marry her, and I've said yes."

Lizzie and Shan exchanged smiles. The pair at the next table were seated again, holding hands across the table as if they would never let go.

Maybe one day, that will be us. The thought edged into Shan's mind. Maybe. But in the meantime, there were their lives to mesh more fully together and see where it led them.

As they left the restaurant, they stopped briefly to congratulate the newly engaged couple, who accepted with a smile and a nod of recognition at their joined hands.

The short walk to their cottage took them along a tarmac path through the vines. Shan's heart overflowed with the magic of the weekend, of where they were. She tugged Lizzie a couple of steps from the path and rested her hands on her waist. "You look beautiful. I wish we could stay here tomorrow and relax together. But there's our dog to collect."

Moonlight gilded Lizzie's cheekbones with silver. "There is. And the Institute of Sport might blacklist you forever if you failed to show. Not to mention Celia's wrath."

"Celia is possibly the scarier of the two." Shan slid her hand to the base of Lizzie's spine and urged her closer.

"We have this," Lizzie said. "And tomorrow, you'll take a step toward your dreams."

"I already have." Love and desire welled up like a spring tide in Shan's chest, so full she wondered how her heart could contain it all. "You're part of my dreams, Lizzie." She leaned in enough that Lizzie's dear face blurred in front of her. Tears? She hadn't realised they were falling until Lizzie wiped a careful thumb underneath her eye.

Lizzie kissed her, a long, deep kiss of love and longing and promises.

Shan's lips tingled when Lizzie ended the kiss. "Let's go to the cottage."

Inside, Lizzie drew the curtains, but left the high side-windows open so the moonlight could stream in. They undressed slowly, and when they were naked Shan took Lizzie's hand and drew their bodies together. She ran a hand along Lizzie's side, from her shoulder, over the edge of her breast, and down to the indent of her waist to her hip bone.

Lizzie shivered in the silver light and traced a similar path along Shan's body.

The light and shadows enticed Shan to explore, and she took one of Lizzie's peaked nipples in her mouth, running her tongue around the edge then sucking lazily.

Lizzie whimpered, and Shan smiled against her breast. She urged Lizzie to the edge of the bed and then down onto the soft sheets. When they lay together, they kissed as if they had all the time in the world for loving. Shan pushed her hands into Lizzie's hair and kissed her long and slow, then deep and urgent until her heart felt so full of love her chest couldn't contain it. She encouraged Lizzie onto her back and trailed her lips down Lizzie's body, pausing at her nipples, her belly button, then lower, down to where her dark triangle beckoned.

Lizzie shifted restlessly, her thighs falling apart invitingly.

Shan sat back on her heels and, ignoring the beckoning push of Lizzie's hips, smoothed her palms up the inside of Lizzie's legs, back to the apex of her thighs. Her mouth joined her fingers and she teased and tormented until Lizzie whimpered for completion. Then when Lizzie made her own explorations, stroking as she knew Shan liked best, she came as well, arching as Lizzie pushed fingers inside her.

They lay together, limbs entwined, whispering words that were both loving and nonsensical with tiredness, until when Lizzie took too long to respond, Shan raised up and looked down on her face, relaxed in sleep. She pushed Lizzie's hair to one side and pressed a kiss to her forehead.

Lizzie smiled but didn't wake.

"I love you," Shan whispered. "I'll always be here for you. I promise."

Epilogue

Eighteen Months Later

LIZZIE LOUNGED AGAINST THE PILLOWS and watched Shan riffle through the drawers. A half-packed suitcase sat open on the bed. Presto watched from the door, his tail dragging.

"I don't see the problem," Lizzie said. "You need running gear, your Australian team uniform for the opening ceremony, and comfy clothes for relaxing—all green and gold of course."

"It's not that simple." Shan pushed a hand through her short hair. "I have to take my lucky undies, newest sports bras, six pairs of running shoes, more socks than I could possibly need—nothing worse than sweaty, smelly socks—and somehow keep my Aussie team uniform smooth and flat."

"I'm sure they have irons in the Olympic village." Lizzie removed the shampoo from Shan's case. "They even give out free condoms, so I'm sure you'll be able to get shampoo. What if the bottle bursts all over your uniform?"

Shan's phone rang, and she glanced at the screen. "It's Celia. Will you answer it? She panics worse than me."

Lizzie picked up Shan's phone. "Hi, Celia. Yes, Shan's packing and she asked me to talk to you… Hang on, I'll ask her." To Shan she said, "Celia wants to know if you've got a spare universal power adapter. Apparently, Sienna borrowed hers and lost it."

"I don't think so; tell her she can buy one at the airport."

Lizzie relayed that. "Bye, Celia. Good luck. I'll see you over there." She ended the call. "Celia sounds in a worse tizz than you, and that's saying something."

"Don't know what you're talking about." Shan closed the lid of the case. "I'm done!"

A tiny whine sounded, and Lizzie's heart melted. "You may be done, but Presto's worry is at full throttle. The poor love." She got off the bed and went over to ruffle his fur. "Don't worry, darling. Your mummy will come back to you. And I'll be here for you still."

"Until you fly over as well. Then his Auntie Dee and Uncle Rohaan will look after him and his cousin Reece will wear him out playing." Shan joined Lizzie on the floor, much to Presto's delight. He climbed into her lap and covered her neck with kisses.

Lizzie leaned over Presto to kiss Shan on the lips, pushing Presto away when he wanted to join in. "I'll be there for the opening ceremony. Somewhere up in the nosebleed seats with thousands of others, but I'll see you walking out in the green and gold. I'll be the one crying her eyes out and beaming a ray of love in your direction."

"I'll feel that love. I always feel it coming from you. Love in everything we do together." Shan leaned in also and wrapped her arms around Lizzie's shoulders.

Presto squirmed in delight between them.

Tears pricked at the back of Lizzie's eyes. This was the finish line of Shan's journey. Her knee was strong, and she'd avoided further serious injury—and women in koala suits... She'd fought her way onto the Olympic team and was a serious contender for a medal for Australia. But even if she didn't gain a medal, her dream was secured.

And our dream is coming true too. Lizzie smiled through misty eyes at Shan. They'd navigated their lives together as a couple over the last eighteen months. There'd been small setbacks, of course, clashes of schedule, and occasional tensions. But they'd worked through it— together. Now, they lived in what had been Lizzie's house, but was now their house—and Presto's. Sometimes Lizzie thought he was the happiest of the three of them, and that said a lot.

Shan had stayed true to her word, and Lizzie's dreams and achievements were equal to Shan's in both of their eyes. Shan placed in the prestigious Stawell Gift, the highest paid race in Australia. Lizzie completed a marathon, running the last kilometre with tears of joy streaming from her eyes as she crossed the finish line into Shan's arms.

The small things, too, were shared and cherished: walks along the river with Presto, Everyone's Choir evenings with Dee and Rohaan, cosy evenings with takeaway and their favourite red wine.

When Shan's parents returned from their travels around Australia, they were frequent visitors. Shan and Lizzie had gone to Sydney together and visited Lizzie's parents. While Lizzie's introduction of Shan as her partner had initially sparked breast-beating and prayers for her salvation from Lizzie's mother, and a tight-lipped silence from her father, slowly, they were coming around. They had called Shan two nights ago to wish her luck at the Olympics.

Lizzie kissed Shan once more, a soft kiss that grew incandescent with the longing and love between them. She broke the kiss, rose to her feet, and held out her hand.

"You're all ready for your flight tomorrow?" At Shan's nod, she said, "Then come to bed and let me show you again how very much I love you."

Dedication and Acknowledgements

I never used to be a runner.

From time to time, during my twenties, I'd get the idea of going for a run. I'd go out the door, run as fast as I could to the corner, and then, out of breath and half-dead, I'd walk home. End of story.

Some years later, I related this sorry state of events to my sister, Leslie. My elite athlete sister, Leslie, who tried out for the Canadian Olympic team and ran the Boston Marathon at warp speed. For Leslie, running is as natural and life-affirming as breathing. She told me, very kindly, that my non-runner status was because I'd never gone about it the right way. She drew up a training plan, checked in on me often, answered my stupid questions, and encouraged me along the way. It took a lot of time, effort, and determination, and, if not for Leslie, I'd almost certainly have slunk away. But the day came when I could call myself a runner. A slow, plodding, ungainly sort of runner, but still. If the term fits...

And I loved it! I puffed my way up the Highlands of Scotland, got attacked by a Doberman in the laneways of Ireland, cruised along the beaches of Australia, and struggled at altitude in the Colorado Rockies. I ran longer and faster, and got to understand the joy of running until I puked. I never became anything other than slow and lumbering, but it didn't matter. I loved it.

I'm no longer able to run without constant chiropractic intervention, but I still dream about it sometimes. So I did the next best thing; I wrote a book where the characters, in their very different ways, are runners.

I dedicate this book to Leslie, the best runner I know and my equal favourite sister. Thank you for putting up with my stupid questions, and also for reading the draft and making sure the running parts were believable.

As always, I want to thank the folks at Ylva Publishing, particularly my editor, Alissa. Ylva's team of content editors, copy editors, proofreaders, formatters, graphic designers, layout queens, social media gurus, translators, and royalty payers is second to none.

I'm lucky, too, to have three fantastic beta readers on three different continents. Erin, Laure, and Sophie—thank you very much for your tough-love comments, eagle-eyes that can spot a typo at ten paces, and care. You're the best!

A huge thank you, as well, to Sandra, who helped me rework a scene involving a psychologist.

My great mate, Marg, is fantastic for a final read. Discussing the book with her was a good excuse for a brekky wrap by the beach at Alex Surf Club.

A special dedication, too, because I told her I would, goes to Tree 1565010, a drooping sheoak in Melbourne's Royal Park. Tree 1565010, who appears as Sheila-the-sheoak in this story, was kind enough to respond to my e-mail. Think I've lost the plot? You can directly e-mail individual trees in inner Melbourne. Try it! You might get a response, as I did.

Finally, For the Long Run is my tenth sapphic romance. The biggest thank you goes to everyone who buys my books, reads them, begs or borrows them, enjoys them, reviews and recommends them, and e-mails me about them. Thank you, one and all.

Cheyenne Blue
Queensland, Australia

Other Books from Ylva Publishing

www.ylva-publishing.com

The Number 94 Project
Cheyenne Blue

ISBN: 978-3-96324-567-1
Length: 288 pages (100,000 words)

Renovation takes a sexy turn in this light-hearted lesbian romance.
When Jorgie's uncle leaves her an old house in Melbourne, it's a dream come true. Sure, No. 94 is falling apart, and she has to deal with her uncle's eccentric friends. But she'll do it up, sell it, and move on.

What she hasn't counted on is falling for Marta, who's as embedded in Gaylord St as the concrete Jorgie's ripping up.

Puppy Love
L.T. Smith

ISBN: 978-3-96324-493-3
Length: 149 pages (40,000 words)

Ellie Anderson has given up on love. Her philosophy is "Why let someone in when all they do is leave?" So instead, she fills her life with work and dodges her sister's matchmaking. Then she meets Charlie—a gorgeous, brown-eyed Border Terrier. Charlie is in need of love and a home, prompting Ellie to open the doors to feeling once again. However, she isn't the only one who is falling for the pup…

Up on the Roof
A.L. Brooks

ISBN: 978-3-95533-988-3
Length: 245 pages (88,000 words)

When a storm wreaks havoc on bookish Lena's well-ordered world, her laid-back new neighbor, Megan, offers her a room. The trouble is they've been clashing since the day they met. How can they now live under the same roof? Making it worse is the inexplicable pull between them that seems hard to resist.

A fun, awkward, and sweet British romance about the power of opposites attracting.

Looking for Trouble
Jess Lea

ISBN: 978-3-96324-522-0
Length: 312 pages (109,000 words)

Nancy hates her housemates from hell, useless job, and always dating women who aren't that into her. She'd love to be a political writer and meet Ms. Right.

Instead, she meets George, a butch, cranky bus driver who's dodging a vengeful ex.

When the warring pair gets caught up in a crazy Melbourne election, they must trust each other and act fast to stay alive.

A quirky lesbian romantic mystery.

About Cheyenne Blue

Cheyenne Blue has been hanging around the lesbian erotica world since 1999 writing short lesbian erotica which has appeared in over 90 anthologies. Her stories got longer and longer and more and more romantic, so she went with the flow and switched to writing romance novels. As well as her romance novels available from Ylva Publishing, she's the editor of *Forbidden Fruit: stories of unwise lesbian desire*, a 2015 finalist for both the Lambda Literary Award and Golden Crown Literary Award, and of *First: Sensual Lesbian Stories of New Beginnings*.

Cheyenne loves writing big-hearted romance often set in rural Australia because that's where she lives. She has a small house on a hill with a big deck and bigger view—perfect for morning coffee, evening wine, and anytime writing.

CONNECT WITH CHEYENNE
Website: www.cheyenneblue.com
Facebook: www.facebook.com/CheyenneBlueAuthor
Instagram: www.instagram.com/cheyenneblueauthor
Twitter: twitter.com/iamcheyenneblue

For the Long Run
© 2022 by Cheyenne Blue

ISBN: 978-3-96324-728-6

Available in e-book and paperback formats.

Published by Ylva Publishing, legal entity of Ylva Verlag, e.Kfr.

Ylva Verlag, e.Kfr.
Owner: Astrid Ohletz
Am Kirschgarten 2
65830 Kriftel
Germany

www.ylva-publishing.com

First edition: 2022

Credits
Edited by Alissa McGowan and Sheena Billet
Cover Design and Print Layout by Streetlight Graphics